DEAD SHORE

A CORNISH CRIME THRILLER

BOOK 4

BERRICK FORD

HARVEY
BERRICK
PUBLISHING

CONTENTS

DEAD SHORE

A CORNISH CRIME THRILLER #4

Newquay, Cornwall: UK's surf mecca, and the Boardmasters competition where the reigning kings and queens are crowned.

Five days of surfing, partying and hanging ten with the top surfers in the world – until one of them is found dead.

With millions of pounds in sponsorship money, tourist visits and small businesses at stake, and the reputation of the Devon & Cornwall Police in tatters, Police Constable Tamsyn Poldhu goes undercover to find the truth: tragic accident ... or murder?

To Bats

Top cop

Couldn't have done it without you, my friend

CORNISH CRIME THRILLER SERIES

#0.5 *Dead Start*
#1 *Dead Water*
#2 *Dead Man's Dive*
#3 *Dead Reckoning*
#4 *Dead Shore*
#5 *Dead and Buried*

PROLOGUE

The cliffs above Newquay were filled with a chaotic wonderland of coloured lights, exotic food, fairground rides, music blasting from hidden speakers, and 58,000 people partying like it was 1999, even though most of them hadn't been born until well after the new millennium.

The sea below stretched blackly into the distance, the far horizon lost in the night sky, and stars competed with a thousand strings of fairy lights strung across the party ground.

Tamsyn was hot and sticky from a long day of crouching in a battered builder's van at the campground, buying 'second-hand' – a.k.a. stolen – surfboards, wetsuits, phones, cameras, GoPros, even an outboard motor and a jet ski, as well as vapes, cigarettes, and numerous counterfeit goods; too many hours of socialising with drug dealers and low-level criminals. All part of her job with Devon & Cornwall Police.

Every approach, every conversation and every deal was covertly filmed, with officers carefully logging faces associated with this high-volume, low-level crime, often perpetrated by a small but prolific crew. It was well known among the local surfer fraternity that wetsuits and surfboards were stolen from tops of vans and unlocked cars, then sold on quickly. The police operation was to build up evidence profiles, and then in the coming weeks and months, the perpetrators would be rounded up and taken off the streets.

Tamsyn was one of a team of younger officers aiming to look like someone who'd buy drugs or dodgy merchandise: a TPO, or test purchase officer. Normally, undercover officers were longer in service and specially trained, but for this operation, the younger officers blended in better with the festival-goers. When Tamsyn bought 'product', she'd also drop into the conversation that her 'friends' were always interested in 'good gear'.

It had been a dreary day that tarnished cherished memories of Boardmasters, her favourite annual music and surf festival. She'd always known that this grimier side existed, but in her pre-police days, she'd happily ignored it, maybe even tacitly accepted it.

And sharing a stuffy tent with three sweaty guys hadn't been on her to-do list either. After just one night, she was over the sounds and smells, the hilarity ensuing from her fellow officers as they lifted one arse-cheek to fart. So over it.

"I'm going for a surf," she announced, rising stiffly from the patch of parched grass where she'd been sitting.

"It's nighttime," said Jamie, yawning widely.

"Thank you, Captain Obvious," Tamsyn replied, more sharply than she'd meant.

"Yeah, alright! Keep your shirt on," he said, sounding annoyed.

"Let her go," Sully smirked. "She's probably on the rag. Maybe she won't be as uptight when she gets back."

Tamsyn stared at him.

"It's the truth," he laughed. "What?"

"Nothing. I'm just trying to imagine you with a personality," she shot back.

"Play nicely, children," Andy said quietly, his voice a low, authoritative rumble.

Andy was one of the older members from E-team at Penzance police station, a calming influence, and an officer whom Tamsyn liked and respected.

PC Jamie Smith had been Tamsyn's friend when she'd first started at Penzance police station, but then he'd made the mistake of dating a complete and utter bitch who'd had it in for Tamsyn from day one. That relationship had ended badly – very badly – and Jamie had not come out of it unscathed.

It wasn't that he blamed Tamsyn, but he was still cool towards her, which was unfair. She hoped that with time they could get back to being friends again. Although not if she kept lashing out at him like she just had.

She blamed her bad mood on the fourth wheel of their wonky surveillance wagon.

Freddie 'Sully' Sullivan had come down from Plymouth and seemed to think that because he was a city cop and they were from the more rural far west, that they had straw in their hair and 'yokel' for a surname.

Tamsyn had met him for the first time only a couple of weeks ago when they'd begun preparing for this op. He'd seemed immature then, even though he was 24 which made him two years older than her, but then an uglier truth finally emerged – Sully was a giant dickhead who'd made a pass at her and hadn't liked being turned down. His digs ever since, subtle and not so subtle, were irritating, as was his habit of talking over her.

But those were Tamsyn's problems, and it wasn't fair to drag Jamie and Andy into it.

Tamsyn drew in a deep breath.

"Yeah, sorry, Jamie. Long day."

"And four more to go," Andy pointed out mildly.

Tamsyn felt chastised but didn't say anything else – she'd already apologised.

"Sully, you're out of order," Andy said pointedly.

But Sully rolled his eyes and went back to scrolling on his phone. He didn't offer an apology.

Tamsyn slid a battered surfboard from the van's roof rack along with her shorty wetsuit. The sea was warm in August, up to 16°C, but you could cool down quickly on a night surf.

She stripped out of her sweaty t-shirt and shorts, pulling the wetsuit over her bikini up to her waist, and slid on a pair of flipflops.

Then she sheathed her work phone in a waterproof case and slung it around her neck. She was still on duty.

"Are you getting the shuttle bus to Fistral?" Andy asked, naming Newquay town's largest beach where the surfing competitions were held.

"No, I can't be bothered to go that far. I'll walk down to Watergate Bay. It's only ten minutes and it's a mellower wave."

"More like a 15- or 20-minute walk," Jamie muttered moodily, but Tamsyn ignored him.

"You definitely speak the lingo," Andy smiled, propping himself up on one elbow as he sprawled on the picnic blanket. "Enjoy your 'mellow wave'," and he hooked his fingers around air quotes.

"Always!"

Tamsyn was happy to leave the noise of the campsite behind her for a while, and she walked briskly, the moon illuminating the coast path.

Sound carried a long way in the still night air, but

gradually the campground's music sank beneath the rumble of waves breaking on the beach below.

The path became steeper and Tamsyn could see the lights of Watergate Bay Hotel. It was an upmarket place where several of the pro surfers were staying.

Flames flickered on the beach, throwing shadows across small groups of festival-goers who'd found a quieter place to drink, laugh, fight or fall in love.

Tamsyn kicked off her flipflops, making a note of where she'd left them, then dug her toes into the warm sand, a small sigh of pleasure escaping her.

A light breeze lifted her hair as she stared out into the blackness, listening intently as she counted the seconds between each wave to give her an idea of what the swell was like before it broke into white foam.

As she breathed in deeply, enjoying the salty air, she became aware of another figure standing a short distance away. The woman was tall, statuesque, with broad shoulders and flowing dark hair. She looked like an Amazon about to do battle, her surfboard a spear.

A shock of recognition went through Tamsyn. Erin Viljoen was a professional surfer from South Africa, tipped to win at Boardmasters. The woman had been in the news recently for other reasons too, the subject of speculation, conversation and controversy.

Her trademark sparkle-encrusted surfboard glittered in the moonlight, glitzy and glamorous, a board that shouted, *look at me!* It was just one of the things she was known for.

"Good luck in the opening round tomorrow," Tamsyn blurted out, just for something to say.

It was true. Kind of. Maybe. Tamsyn wasn't sure what she thought, whether she wanted Viljoen to win, but she knew that the woman hadn't had it easy either.

"Hey, thanks! I'm looking forward to ripping at Fistral – the waves should be awesome tomorrow and I've never surfed in the UK before." She nodded at Tamsyn's battered board. "Stealth mission?"

Translation: night time surf.

"Yeah, Watergate works on most tides, although the best waves are at mid- to high-tide and it's less busy than Fistral. It gets a lot of ground-swell, too..."

Tamsyn realised she was babbling and that Viljoen would already know all this; with a major competition on the World Surf League tour, she couldn't afford *not* to have done her research.

"Well, have a great surf," Tamsyn finished lamely.

"You, too," Viljoen replied politely. "See you out back."

She flashed a brief smile at Tamsyn then darted into the water, belly down on her board as she made long, clean strokes through the breakers.

You could tell that she was a pro surfer. Only someone who spent every day of their lives in the ocean had that ease in the water, an affinity with the element that made them seem born to it.

Tamsyn followed behind, a competent surfer, possibly even good, but nowhere near the level of the Amazon who was already charging down the face of a wave, fierce joy on her face.

Tamsyn understood, felt it as well, the cold water soothing something in her too-busy brain.

In the distance, a fishing boat bobbed on the water, its lights orange against the darkness as it slowly chugged southwest. She wondered where they were going and if the catch had been good.

She paddled out into the darkness, not seeing but able to feel the rise and fall of the water beneath her, duck diving through two small waves, then stroking up the face of a third as the telltale roar of a larger wave lifted her board up, up, up, then speeding down the other side.

As her board began to rise again, Tamsyn spun around quickly, facing the lights of the hotel, something to aim for in the darkness. The fourth wave in the set was even bigger, and she raced for the peak, pulling hard through the water, then leaping to her feet and soaring down the face of the wave, the salty spray on her lips and in her eyes, adrenaline pumping through her body.

There was nothing like it, nothing came close to this feeling.

She rode the wave until its energy began to dissipate, then turning her surfboard back out to sea, she caught wave after wave, her mind emptying as her body obeyed the ocean.

After nearly an hour in the water, she began to feel chilled and knew it was time to go back to the stifling tent – and try to ignore Sully's stupid jokes and Jamie's snoring. It wasn't a fun thought, but sharing the tent had to be done to build their credibility as lowlife crims on the make.

Her ears caught the sound of the next wave in the set and she knew that this was the one she'd catch to carry her back to the beach.

The wave rose up behind her and she popped up, both feet landing squarely on the board, making micro adjustments to her balance as she tore across the smooth face, crouching low, pumping the wave, working it hard.

But then one of her surfboard's fins caught on something below the waterline, and Tamsyn was tossed into the air, plunging down as the wave broke over her head.

The weight of the water pushed her down and tumbled her around as if she was inside a washing machine, but she didn't panic, she held her breath and waited until her natural buoyancy brought her to the surface.

She wondered what she'd hit. Had some discarded fishing-line snagged her fin? And it wasn't unheard of for seals or dolphins to join surfers, especially at night. Could she have run over one of the dogs of the sea?

Tamsyn yanked on her board's leash to bring it towards her, then she belly-boarded back to the beach. The shore shelved more steeply here, the tide tugging at her knees as she released the Velcro strap that leashed her board to her right ankle.

And then she saw what her board had collided with – a body floating face-down in the restless water, long hair fanning out around the head and shoulders.

Tamsyn tossed her surfboard towards the beach, shouting for help as she charged back into the sea.

"Call 999! Get an ambulance! I need help here!"

Tamsyn flipped the woman over, recognising Viljoen instantly. The woman's eyes were half-open, her limbs loose.

Grimacing, Tamsyn hooked her hands under the woman's armpits, dragging her through the water and heaving her as far up the beach as she could.

She was heavy, much heavier than Tamsyn, and she was still half in the sea, water swirling around her calves.

"I need help!" Tamsyn yelled again to whoever was nearby. "Call 999 and ask for an ambulance! Now!"

She felt for a pulse, trying to find any sign of life as Viljoen's skin cooled beneath her fingertips.

Nothing.

"Come on!" Tamsyn whispered hoarsely, her own breath roaring in her ears. "Come on!"

Still nothing: no pulse, no sign of life.

"Hey! What's going on? Are you serious?" a male voice shouted back. "What's happening?"

"Yes! Possible drowning, no pulse. I'm starting CPR now!"

And she began compressions, her arms shaking with the effort.

Even though she knew it was too late.

CHAPTER 1

Detective Inspector Robert Rego was enjoying a rare, and long-awaited date night with his wife when his phone rang.

It was their last evening together before she left to visit her mother. It was only for three nights, but he'd enjoyed having his family with him for the last few weeks after so long apart, and he'd miss them.

So, he'd gone to the trouble of reserving a table at an expensive restaurant and letting the kids stay home with a pizza from Dominos which, no doubt, would be shared with Bill, their Labrador puppy.

As he guiltily slid his phone from his pocket, his wife replaced her glass of wine on the restaurant's table, her face carefully neutral.

"Sorry, Cass," he said. "It's work."

"Of course it is."

She crossed her arms and looked away, disappointment shadowing her expression.

Rego knew he'd have some fences to mend later, but the

second he'd seen Detective Sergeant Tom Stevens' name on the caller ID, his brain had already moved into work mode.

"Tom, what's up?"

"Sorry to bother you on your evening off, boss," said Stevens, Rego's very able sergeant from Penzance police station, "but a body's just been found at Watergate Bay – unexplained death. The press are all over it, even the mayor's here – it's a bleddy circus."

"Any particular reason for the interest? Other than the fact it's happened at Boardmasters?"

Rego had been on the Devon & Cornwall Police planning committee for policing the event, and was well aware how much money the surfing and music festival brought into the county: somewhere in excess of £40 million. Although it had started a number of years ago as a small event for local surfers, the investment giant KKR had bought Boardmasters' parent company for a reported £1.1bn, and it was now the top surfing event in the UK, giving Cornwall a presence on the worldwide surfing circuit.

As well as the tickets selling for £100 per person per day, sponsorship for surf apparel, wetsuits and boards was in the six-figure region. Sales of alcohol and beverages added to the profits, and festival-goers had to stump up £5 for a hot shower, and if they wanted boiling water for their Pot Noodles, that was another £2 a pot.

In a county where tourism was the main breadwinner, Boardmasters was a shot in the arm for many businesses. It was in everyone's interests that negative publicity was kept to a minimum. Hence the year-long planning and large police presence from stations across Cornwall, and a number from Devon, too.

Rego wondered how much longer Devon & Cornwall Police would provide a police presence free of charge. In

London, the Metropolitan Police Commissioner, Sir Mark Rowley, was pushing for event organisers to pay for police attendance. The press interview that he'd given was primarily focused on policing football matches, but it seemed inevitable that in future, for-profit events like Boardmasters would be required to make a contribution toward policing costs.

Of course, Boardmasters also employed private security, but they didn't have anything like the same powers as the police.

Despite all the difficulties, the system was working fairly well. The previous year, there had been just 11 arrests: three people had been charged for drugs offences, four released on bail, two cautioned, and two released with no further police action.

It had been a good result, although everyone knew that many petty thefts went unreported. It was simpler for a member of the public to tell their insurance company that they'd 'lost' their phone than to report it stolen, because that then required a crime reference number before the insurers would pay out.

Even so, the top brass always wanted to improve the figures, especially since His Majesty's Inspectorate of Constabulary had published their recent PEEL assessment which had found D&C Police 'inadequate at investigating crime' – a finding that had made the national press. The fact that this referred mainly to lower-level crime hadn't been reported. And the truth was, a lot of thefts from vans and garden sheds hadn't been investigated and were simply written off. *This is what people pay their rates for'* screamed headlines in the local papers.

A considerable number of the crimes that D&C recorded were classified in the minds of many police officers as minor: high-volume/low-value crime, such as stolen bikes and, more and more frequently, electric bikes – property that wasn't easily traceable but the revenue was sufficient to buy a day's fix. Thefts from cars and vans were always a bit more lucrative, but again, the arrest and conviction rates were very low.

Rate payers demanded more from the police service than a call handler's voice – assuming that you could get through on the 101 number for non-emergency enquiries – or while you were waiting on hold, the automated voice helpfully suggesting that you use the online reporting facility. To the victim, a stolen mower or bike was very important; tools taken from a van were a tradesman's livelihood and loss of income.

It was an unsatisfactory state of affairs, and Neighbourhood Police officers who conducted surgeries in local areas were often met with, "What's the point of reporting it when you lot don't do anything?"

Victims of these crimes wanted an officer to turn up, reassure them, make them feel safe: just getting a crime number to claim for their insurance wasn't making the public feel safe or the police popular – but there simply weren't enough officers to do the work.

Murders, however, were investigated to death.

And given the importance of Boardmasters to the business community, a death at the event would definitely be getting the Chief Constable's attention – and probably giving him ulcers.

"I hate to tell you this, boss," said Stevens, "but the deceased has been identified as Erin Viljoen."

"The name rings a bell..."

"The transgender surfer from South Africa, here on a Dutch passport."

He paused but Rego didn't need him to say anything else.

He remembered exactly who Viljoen was and why the shit was about to hit the fan.

Transgender athletes had been a hot topic since before President Trump had threatened to withdraw funding from educational institutions in the US who allowed transgender men on female sports teams. The UK press was giving the story a good go, too, but seemed more aerated by the fact that Viljoen had been given a Dutch passport just days before Boardmasters, making her the top-seeded European female surfer and odds-on favourite to take the women's title, thus knocking Britain's previous number one female surfer off the top spot.

"Why aren't Major Crimes at Camborne on this?" Rego asked.

He had no aversion to taking on a difficult case, but he hated having to play politics while he did it.

"They are," Stevens said uncomfortably. "MCIT is on scene."

The Major Crimes Incident Team dealt with homicides, stranger rapes, abductions, kidnapping, serious and violent crime. MCIT was made up of a number of experienced officers, any one of them easily capable of taking this case, so why was Rego being called in? What the hell was going on?

"Had threats been made against Viljoen?" Rego asked.

"Yes. A lot of hate online, and the manager has some letters he thinks we should see."

That made sense, but it still didn't explain why was Rego being called in.

"And?"

"And, um, the Chief Constable asked for you, boss ... something about being 'media friendly'."

Rego's scowl deepened as his sergeant continued talking.

"DCI Finch says you'll be the Senior Investigating

Officer," Stevens finished awkwardly. "I was under the impression you'd already been told. Sorry, boss."

It was the second time Stevens had apologised to him, but now Rego got it.

When Rego had transferred down from Greater Manchester Police, he'd brought the grand total of Cornwall's black officers to thirteen; obviously his lucky number.

The dead athlete was transgender, already controversial before her death, so the powers-that-be must have decided to wheel out their only non-white Detective Inspector. Rego could only guess their thinking: the deceased was from a minority, so they wanted a minority officer to head up the investigation.

That pissed him off. And really, did anyone these days care about the colour of a cop's skin, trying to fool the general public that maybe there would be a more thorough investigation because of it? Rego thought it was typical of the police's media relations crap. Or the Chief Constable's obsession with 'optics'.

"Sorry, boss," Stevens said yet again, correctly reading Rego's silence.

"I'll be there in thirty... forty minutes," Rego sighed.

By the time he'd finished the call, Rego's wife had already paid the bill, put her coat on, and was waiting at the restaurant's door.

"You owe me, Ace Boy," she said with a long-suffering sigh.

"I'll make it up to you."

"Yeah, yeah. Just drop me off on the way."

"You look beautiful, Cass," he said.

She gave him a knowing look, but at least she was smiling.

After Rego had left his wife at the small former fisherman's cottage which they were currently renting – and which Rego had come to think of as home – he headed north up the coast to Newquay.

He'd planned that his first call as he drove north would be to his immediate boss, Detective Chief Inspector Finch, but it was the Boardmasters Gold Commander who called him first.

"Rob, this is Detective Chief Superintendent Richards. I take it you've been notified about this unexplained death – are you on your way?"

"Yes, sir. ETA 40 minutes."

"Traffic is a bugger – use your blue-lights."

"May I ask why someone from MCIT isn't the SIO on this case, sir?" Rego asked politely, despite knowing the answer, but feeling in the mood to poke the bear. "Is there anything suspicious about the body that I haven't been made aware of?"

"The Chief Constable asked for you," Richards said curtly.

Rego didn't bother to reply to that.

"Just get there, Rob," Richards barked. "All hell's breaking loose. The press are having a field day, by all accounts. Christ knows what crazy theories will be bandied about.' Rego could hear the irritation in the man's voice. "I'll get a press officer down to you, if I can find one that's not too pissed," he muttered. "The Chief will want an update asap, so call me back when you've got something ... something useful."

And on that encouraging note, DCS Richards ended the call.

When Boardmasters had begun in its present music/surf/skate format 20 years earlier, there had been 5,000 visitors to Fistral Beach and spread across the town. So, it hadn't mattered that the small, beach town of Newquay (population 23,342 at the last census) had one road in and one road out, with a limited number of parking spots; and it hadn't mattered that the campsite at Watergate Bay was on a farm, down a narrow track.

But the event had grown exponentially and the locals coped as best they could. It wasn't perfect, but the event organisers tried to learn from their mistakes, as did Devon & Cornwall Police. It was a shame that hundreds of people had missed flights from the nearby local airport the previous year due to sheer weight of traffic heading for the festival. The police had come in for a substantial share of the criticism.

This year, Chief Superintendent Nathan Richards was the Gold Commander for Boardmasters, and Rego had attended many meetings where the team had discussed contingency planning involving management of traffic and illegally parked cars – their removal if causing an obstruction, was just one topic. They discussed specific road restrictions and checkpoints for vehicles entering the area during the event. There was a 'hard closure' point beyond which only residents and businesses had access.

There were representatives from the Cornwall Fire and Rescue Service discussing the prevention of cliff falls, managing firework displays and fire assembly points; all working with a team from D&C's HQ who spent their days managing events, parades, and demonstrations, ensuring that the correct licences had been issued, and the correct level of policing was allocated given the expected number of people attending. Although those figures were always revised upwards for any demonstrations.

Then there were more meetings with the landowners and the festival organisers to discuss drug issues. Rego knew that there was a medical evacuation point in the event of an emergency, as well as a medical tent with staff on hand 24/7, but also drug amnesty points at the festival entrance – no questions asked. After that, anyone caught supplying was likely to be found by sniffer dogs and arrested.

The festival organisers had arranged a designated meeting point for revellers trying to find their friends but had also designed the Boardmasters App which could be used for visitors to find each other, and location-sharing apps were encouraged, as well as the popular app *Find My Tent*.

Rego had listened as they'd discussed where the tradespeople would park, the safety of the stage set-up (no re-runs of a stage collapse the previous year), car parking and shuttle buses for visitors, and on and on. He'd sat in on endless planning meetings where the policing logistics had been discussed – everything from the mundane (using drones to help drunken and lost campers back to their tents), to the serious – how they would cope with a terrorist attack.

Rego had been at the nightmarish aftermath of the suicide bombing at Manchester Arena in 2017. So, at this event with thousands of young people and families on the beach or at the Watergate Bay campground, a key part of his contribution was his expertise in planning for the possibility of another terrorist incident: it had to be considered. He wanted something more material than the advice, *run, hide, tell, #dontbeabystander*.

He was passionate about the 4Ps: prevent, protect, pursue, prepare – and these days, people listened.

But you couldn't prepare for everything; you couldn't prevent every act of violence. And right now, there was an unexplained death for him to attend.

Knowing what he did about the inevitable Boardmasters traffic jams on the narrow roads, even at this time of night, he took the long way round to avoid getting caught up. Even the blue lights wouldn't do him much good on roads that were barely fit for two bicycles to pass each other.

As he drove through the darkened lanes, the names of the villages were strange, foreign, with a musical quality: Zelah, Trevarren, Trekenning, St Mawgan. It reminded him again that he was a long way from Manchester, a long way from the city where he'd been born. But in the 15 months that he'd been in the far distant southwest county of Cornwall, he'd come to appreciate the wide-open spaces and golden beaches; maybe even love them.

From the road above Watergate Bay, he could see an array of lights illuminating the night sky. A uniformed officer stopped him at a checkpoint just beyond the hotel, then directed him to a parking area and the officer with the scene log who recorded the times of people attending or leaving the scene.

Members of the public were being kept away behind police tape, but being that many of them were residents at the hotel, it wasn't an easy job and Rego knew that he had to work as quickly as possible.

Rego recognised the solid form of his sergeant, Tom Stevens, his shiny bald head, glowing under the electric lights.

They shook hands, and Rego opened his car's boot to pull out a new forensic suit, tug it on over his clothes without tearing it, and tuck several pairs of nitrile gloves into his pocket.

Stevens filled him in as they walked down to the beach together, and even wearing the forensic paper booties, Rego could feel grains of sand filling his town shoes.

"What have you put in place, Tom?" he asked. "How big is your cordon?"

"Guests aren't allowed to leave or enter the hotel, and that's causing problems," he admitted.

"Noted: I'll speak to the manager in a moment," Rego acknowledged, knowing that even a dead body didn't stop members of the public griping because they couldn't get into their four-star hotel rooms. He was fairly sure he'd hear the words 'I know my rights' at least half-a-dozen times before the night was out.

"Do we have a photographer and Crime Scene Investigators on the way?"

"CSI are on scene and we're expecting the photographer in the next quarter of an hour, boss. Sooner, I hope."

Rego threw him a look.

"The tide's coming in," Stevens clarified.

Rego sighed. Of course. Because they really needed another challenge.

"Has the water been checked for any other bodies?"

"The Coastguard are out there now."

Rego nodded, not for the first time thanking his lucky stars that he had such an efficient sergeant.

"Has anything been found to explain this death?" Rego asked.

"No, boss. No obvious injuries. Well, one contusion that I can see on the deceased's back, but we know how that happened."

Rego threw him an inquiring look.

"Tamsyn Poldhu found the body, boss. Actually, she ran into the deceased with her surfboard. The impact threw her into the water."

"Tamsyn found the body?"

"While she was surfing – literally ran over the woman. Then she dragged the body up the beach and did CPR for at least 15 minutes before the ambulance arrived." Stevens paused. "The paramedics couldn't revive Viljoen either."

"Poor Tamsyn," Rego sighed.

"And she was one of the last people to talk to the deceased."

Rego pulled a face.

"What was Tamsyn doing out here?" he asked. "Attending the festival?"

"She's here working undercover as a TPO. This evening, she just fancied a surf. Bleddy bad luck."

That was one way of putting it. Police Constable Tamsyn Poldhu had an uncanny knack for stumbling across dead bodies. Last summer it had been a missing diver who'd turned out to be a murder victim; now she'd literally run over the highly controversial Dutch-South African transgender surfer.

"Can you find out who's managing the team that Tamsyn's on? We'll need to have a conversation about whether or not she stays on as a TPO after this."

It wasn't Rego's call, but if he was asked for his opinion, he'd want Tamsyn to stay on the job and keep her ear to the ground; people would want to meet the woman who'd found the body. It would give her a unique opportunity to talk to a lot of festival-goers without arousing suspicion. It could be incredibly useful if she was tasked to mingle, to find out who the deceased had been hanging around with.

"One bit of good news, boss," said Stevens, "the mayor decided to go home – said he'd make a statement to the press tomorrow."

"Thank God for that! Has anyone from our Media Office turned up yet?"

"Yes, Isla Forrester."

"I don't think I've met her. Is she any good?"

"Yes, you'll have no problems with the reporters while she's around. She's a civilian, but she knows what she's doing."

Rego was relieved: one less thing to worry about.

As they crossed the beach, Rego saw that a forensic tent had already been erected at the shoreline to preserve evidence from weather, contamination, unauthorised access, and of course, to hide the body from public view. But the sea was creeping closer each second, lapping at the far sides of the tent.

Rego pulled on a pair of forensic gloves and checked the booties covering his shoes before he stepped into the tent.

It was a myth that dead bodies looked as though they were sleeping: they didn't, they just looked dead. A complete absence of life, of *animus*, of the spirit or soul or whatever you wanted to call it.

Rego's first impression was that the woman had been strong, large-framed with powerful legs, bulging biceps and wide hands. Her long, dark hair was tangled around her face like seaweed, and she was wearing a shorty neoprene wetsuit which covered her torso and legs to the level of shorts, and t-shirt length on the arms.

The crime scene investigator nodded at him, "Boss, we're going to have to move the body soon – the tide's coming in."

"How long?"

"Maybe fifteen minutes. Probably less."

Rego grimaced as the man edged out of the small tent.

He needed more time. The Chief Constable had already conferred with the senior coroner and appointed a Home Office registered forensic pathologist, even though a suspicious death hadn't been confirmed, but that was the Chief hedging his bets.

Rego could have done with the forensic pathologist at the scene, but the incoming tide wouldn't allow enough time. Instead, he'd have to wait for the pathologist to view the body at the hospital's mortuary. Which wasn't an ideal start to an investigation.

Rego crouched down to look closer, his knees clicking audibly.

As Stevens had said, there was no obvious sign of an

injury, but Rego knew that didn't necessarily mean there wasn't one. His first case in Cornwall[1] had seemed like a drowning victim, but the post-mortem had shown otherwise.

His eyes took in everything, ticking off a list of mental images, constructing questions for witnesses and a to-do list for the investigating team.

He made a silent promise to the dead woman, then stood up stiffly and exited the tent.

"Do we have next of kin yet, Tom?"

"No, boss, but her manager is staying at the hotel with his wife: Phil and Julie Ford. South African passports."

"Was Viljoen staying there, too?"

"Yes. Checked in two days ago, a sea-view suite," Stevens raised his eyebrows. "Seven hundred quid a night plus."

Rego whistled.

"She wasn't a skint surfer sleeping on the beach in her board bag then," he said, matching Stevens' surprise.

"Apparently, Viljoen was big news, and not just for being transgender. She'd recently signed a multimillion-pound modelling and sponsorship deal."

"Did her manager tell you that?"

Stevens shook his head. "No, Google."

"Verified source?"

Stevens waggled his hands.

"Maybe yes, maybe no. I read it online at *The Guardian*'s website, but they were quoting her manager."

"See if you can confirm that independently, and I'll check it out with the manager, as well," said Rego.

They both turned when they heard raised voices. A uniformed officer was trying to stop an angry-looking man in a three-piece suit from interrupting them.

---

1. This event takes place in *Dead Water*

"Who's that?" Rego asked.

"The hotel manager: Martin Caterham. He's a bit anxious to get his hotel back."

"I'm sure he is."

"And he's South African, as well," said Stevens.

Rego paused and looked at his DS.

"Significant?"

"Couldn't say, boss. Maybe just a coincidence..."

Rego walked back up the beach, the paper booties slipping in the sand, making progress harder, and he could feel sweat breaking out on his body under the forensic suit.

The Watergate Bay's manager, however, had no such sartorial issues. Despite the lateness of the hour and the fact that he managed a laidback beach hotel, the man was smartly dressed, his trousers pressed with creases so sharp they could have sliced bread, and his shoes shone to perfection. No grain of sand would have dared to find its way inside his socks.

At the cordon, Rego stripped off the gloves, booties and forensic suit, dumping them all in a black bin bag positioned for that purpose. Then he walked purposefully towards the hotel manager who was pacing up and down the patio, glancing at his ostentatious watch every few seconds.

"Mr Caterham," he said, offering his hand. "Detective Inspector Rego."

Caterham frowned almost imperceptibly.

"I thought that other officer was the inspector?'

"I'm the Senior Investigating Officer," Rego answered. "I'm sure this has been a trying situation for you and you're under a lot of pressure; we'll get out of your way as quickly as possible."

"Thank you," said Caterham, the wind being swiftly taken from his sails.

"But I'm sure you can understand," Rego continued, "that

with an unexplained death on the property, we have to ensure that the scene is carefully examined first."

Caterham reignited immediately.

"Do you know how many guests I have staying at this hotel?" he snapped, his voice rising. "A hundred-and-fifty! Half of them are waiting outside!"

Stevens had already told Rego that fewer than 30 guests were affected.

"It's ridiculous!" Caterham stormed. "You have to allow them back to their rooms." He shook his head. "I knew this Dutchman would be trouble."

Rego was momentarily thrown by the comment.

"Do you mean Ms Viljoen?"

Caterham rolled his eyes.

"Yes, the Afrikaaner ... the dragzilla!" He snorted impatiently at Rego's expression. "The transgender surfer, Inspector!"

Rego remained polite, but his tone cooled by several degrees. He did not need this man up his backside, spouting his questionable opinions.

"Mr Caterham, right now you are taking me away from the job I'm trying to do. We'll stabilise the scene, photograph the body, and once our forensic officers have completed as much as they can before the tide comes in, then and only then, we'll open up this area, but the more you remonstrate with me, the longer it will take."

Caterham blinked several times then let out a long breath.

"Of course, Inspector. My apologies. It's been ... quite an evening. May I offer food and soft drinks to your officers?"

Rego gave a brief nod.

"Thank you. That would be appreciated. I'll let you coordinate that with my sergeant."

He left Stevens and Caterham talking together, and was

pleased to see the crime scene photographer's van enter the car park.

"Rego, hold up!"

Rego turned around to see someone walking across the beach. That annoyed him: firstly, because this was supposed to be a sterile area, and secondly because he recognised the man approaching him.

Late forties, thinning blond hair, eyes hard, and body as lean as a miser or a marathon runner.

"Rob," the man said stiffly. "I hear you've landed SIO. Congratulations – it's a big story already. It'll get you noticed."

Yes, Rego knew Detective Inspector Lance Lloyd from Camborne's Major Crimes Incident Team.

A brown-nosing wanker of the first order.

CHAPTER 2

Last Christmas, Tamsyn had killed a man.

She'd been defending her own life and that of Inspector Robert Rego, and the man she'd killed had murdered more than one person, including a friend and colleague, but still, she'd taken a life. She didn't know what to think about that; she didn't know *how* to think about it, how to feel about it. He'd been a bad man: a murderer, drug dealer and crime boss; a monster who'd hurt many people and ruined many lives. But it was a life, and she'd ended it.

An inquiry had exonerated her, but she wondered – did her colleagues look at her differently because she'd killed someone? Did her grandparents look at her differently, her friends? It felt like they did. But would it be worse if they *didn't* feel differently, if a man's blood on her hands changed nothing, meant nothing? She couldn't sort out her thoughts, didn't know how to approach dealing with them; they were too tangled, too complicated, too unknowable, and there wasn't anyone who could help her.

She was still seeing the police psychiatrist regularly, but she didn't think it helped. With each online session, she felt as though she was re-living the traumatic events leading up to the death of Besnik Domi. Her nightmares were always worse after a session – and that was a secret she wouldn't be sharing with anyone.

Tamsyn closed her eyes, but the scene played out behind her lids: the gun in Domi's hands pointing at her, Rego jumping from the quay on Bryher island to tackle Domi, missing and plunging into the freezing water; Tamsyn taking Domi's moment of distraction to wrap the anchor rope around his neck and push him over the side of the boat; the realisation that she couldn't see Inspector Rego, diving into the water and fighting the waves and the currents and the deadly cold to reach him; praying for help as the tide dragged them out to sea.[1]

Her thoughts shifted to Erin Viljoen – the woman with the bright smile, who loved surfing enough to go out alone at night, with no fanfare, no press, no fans; the body with cooling flesh, who'd been unresponsive as Tamsyn had desperately performed CPR.

She pressed her fingers against her eyelids as if she could massage the image away.

"Tamsyn?"

She opened her eyes, blinking to clear the tears as Inspector Rego crouched down next to her.

"How're you doing?" he asked, his warm brown eyes full of concern.

She shook her head, trying to find the words, but her thoughts scattered like dandelion seeds in the wind.

Rego glanced around to see if anyone was listening. The arc lights set up in the forensic tent cast a soft glow across the beach and no one appeared to be close enough to hear them.

---

1. These events take place in *Dead Reckoning*

Lloyd was engaged in questioning the CSI tech, but Rego didn't want to risk anyone overhearing his conversation with Tamsyn – especially as she was still officially undercover.

"Hold that thought," he said quietly before Tamsyn could reply, and she gave a jerky nod of understanding.

Rego helped her up then led her towards a pair of patio chairs, safely away from prying eyes and ears, away from anyone who might be filming the night's events on their phone.

"I understand that you're a TPO at Boardmasters. Start from when you left the campsite this evening," he said quietly.

Before she could answer, Rego saw Lloyd hurrying towards them, his pocketbook flipped open, his gaze assessing and impatient.

Rego swore inwardly.

"PC Poldhu," said Lloyd in a carrying voice. "I'm Detective Inspector Lloyd from Major Crimes. You were the last person to speak to the deceased, correct?"

Tamsyn blinked, glancing up at Rego and seeing the spark of irritation in his expression at the other senior officer's brusqueness.

"PC Poldhu is an undercover TPO," Rego said tersely. "Let's try and keep it that way."

Lloyd stiffened, his mouth tightening at the rebuke.

"Do you need a moment, Tamsyn?" Rego asked pointedly.

"No, I'm fine, thank you, sir." She turned to Lloyd. "I don't know if I was the last person to speak to her, but I did speak to her immediately before she went for a surf."

Tamsyn relayed the brief conversation to the two men, her gaze flicking between them uncertainly.

"And how long were you surfing before you came across the body?" Lloyd asked.

"About 45 minutes," she replied. "Maybe an hour."

Lloyd's pen was paused over his pocket book.

"You're not sure?"

"Nearly an hour," Tamsyn said more firmly, making an obvious attempt to pull herself together.

"That's a long time in the cold water at night," Lloyd said, frowning down at her as if trying to catch her in a mistake. Or a lie.

"Um, not really," said Tamsyn. "It was a really clean ride, three- to four-feet, with some small barrels."

Rego's lips lifted imperceptibly as he enjoyed Lloyd's confusion.

"So, the surf conditions were good," he clarified for Lloyd's benefit.

"Yes," Tamsyn nodded.

"Did you see any other surfers out there?" Rego asked.

Tamsyn closed her eyes, picturing the dark water, remembering how she'd listened to the sound of the waves approaching, being aware of Viljoen for only a few minutes until she lost herself in the moment, the freedom from thinking that surfing gave her.

"No," she said, at last. "I don't remember seeing any other surfers, but that doesn't mean to say there weren't any. I *do* remember seeing at least two bonfires on the beach. The one nearest to me had five, maybe six people sitting around it. I couldn't see how many people there were at the second bonfire but I heard at least two voices. I don't know who called the ambulance," she said, pausing to think. "But they were closer by, so probably from the first bonfire. A guy about my age," she said, more confidently.

Lloyd tapped his pen against his notebook.

"So, you didn't see anything, didn't hear anything, and don't know anything?" Lloyd summed up coldly.

Tamsyn was taken aback.

"I ... I ... she looked happy," Tamsyn said quietly. "She was looking forward to surfing Fistral tomorrow."

"Thank you, Tamsyn," said Rego. "You did well under very difficult circumstances. Very well indeed."

"I couldn't save her," she said bitterly.

"You did everything you could," Rego said firmly. "Now, I want to talk to you about something else. I understand you're here as a TPO."

"Yes, sir."

"Who are you reporting to?"

"PC Andy Millson from Penzance is our lead officer, and we're working with the Project Servator team from Exeter."

Rego nodded.

"Look, Tamsyn, after what you've been through tonight..."

He ignored Lloyd's impatient snort in the background.

"...after what you've been through, it would be completely reasonable for you to take some time off. But I'd be lying if I didn't say that I hope you'll stay on in role. The word will be out that a female surfer found the body – I'm sure your campfire buddy will see to that – but we can use it to our advantage. It'll be your 15 minutes of fame..."

Tamsyn wrinkled her nose.

"...and everyone will want to talk to the woman who found the body. It'll give you a chance to meet a lot of festival-goers without it seeming odd. I want to know who the deceased talked to, who she was hanging around with, what the other professional surfers thought about her."

"Do you think there's something suspicious about her death?" Tamsyn asked.

"Right now, it's an unexplained death," he said, then looked her in the eye. "But professional athletes don't drop dead for no reason, and professional surfers don't drown in clean, four-foot waves either."

Tamsyn nodded in understanding.

"The post-mortem will tell us more, but until then, keep your ear to the ground."

"Yes, sir."

He pressed his hand to her shoulder.

"Make sure you talk to Sergeant Stevens before you go back to the campsite, okay? Someone will be in touch with you in the morning to sort out a time and venue for you to make a full statement."

She nodded again then stood up slowly, shivering slightly in the night breeze, still wearing her damp wetsuit.

"Get yourself a hot drink at the hotel – something with plenty of sugar – it's good for shock."

Rego watched her go, then turned to DI Lloyd.

"Don't ever talk to one of my officers like that again."

"What?"

Lloyd looked annoyed and confused.

"*You didn't see anything, didn't hear anything, and don't know anything.*"

Rego repeated the words back to him.

"She's a young officer, young in service, who's had a traumatic experience. She needed support."

Lloyd rolled his eyes, his voice dismissive.

"Come on, Rego. ACC Gray sent me. I'm not treading on your toes. I just need to keep abreast of this case because it's so high profile. You know how it is."

Rego thought of several responses he could have made to that, including, *Yeah, well the organ grinder sent me, not the monkey, so sod off and let me do my job*, but he was too professional to say it. He definitely thought it, though.

"We can talk inside," Rego said glancing around him.

deliberately. "Fewer people contaminating a crime scene, as you know..."

"Lead the way, Rob," Lloyd said with forced cordiality.

My mates call me Rob. You're not my mate.

Rego didn't suffer fools and didn't trust people until he knew them.

Besides, there was something about Lloyd that rubbed him up the wrong way – even more so now he'd seen the way the man had treated Tamsyn.

Lloyd was ambitious, sniffing for promotion, and had a reputation for hogging the limelight and leaving out the achievements of his team to make himself look better in the press. Everyone knew he was frustrated by being stuck as a mere detective inspector – the same rank as Rego, but Lloyd was ten years older.

Rego had transferred in fairly recently but had already worked some big cases, coming to the attention of the powers-that-be. Some people didn't like that, and if Lloyd thought Rego was benefitting from positive discrimination because Rego was biracial, well, it wouldn't be the first time someone had suggested that behind his back, or even to his face.

Rego knew that gossip was rife at police stations and not always to be believed, but the fact that Assistant Chief Constable Gray had sent Lloyd didn't win him any points with Rego either. Gray was more politician than policeman, and just clever enough to be dangerous. He and Rego shared a mutual dislike.

"I'll bet you a fiver it's a suicide," Lloyd said, still trying to sound like he and Rego were on friendly terms. "Couldn't cope with the pressure, attacks in the press, and all that. Nah, make it a tenner."

Rego walked away, because if he didn't, he might say or do something that his career would regret.

The CSI photographer had arrived at the forensic tent and was taking pictures of the deceased surfer, with the coroner standing by to remove the body. The police press officer was waiting to get five minutes with Rego to prepare the press statement, the CSI team were on their way to process Viljoen's room, and he needed to speak to Viljoen's manager who was also staying at the hotel.

Rego had enough to do without starting a pissing contest with Lloyd, even if the guy was a tosser.

He nodded at the woman in the suit, guessing that she was the press officer. She'd waited patiently for his attention, and he appreciated her not interrupting him until he was ready.

"Isla Forrester from the Media Office," she said, striding forward and holding out her hand.

"Rob Rego. Good to meet you."

She gave a quick smile. "I've drafted a press statement – if you could give it a once-over, I'll crack on."

Rego read the statement, suggesting only one minor change before agreeing the wording.

"And remember, Isla," Lloyd said, annoyed at having been left out, "avoid all use of the word 'suicide' until we've confirmed it."

Rego shook his head. Lloyd really couldn't help acting like a knob.

"Of course," said Forrester, her voice frosty. "But the deceased's name is already out there and there's speculation online which is why we're hurrying to contain it by releasing the press statement."

"Then you'd better get on with it," said Lloyd.

Forrester's nostrils flared with annoyance but she didn't reply.

Lloyd clearly had a talent for making friends wherever he went.

"I'll make sure the statement is issued immediately, Inspector Rego," she said smoothly, ignoring Lloyd's presence. "I'm also liaising with the mayor's office to ensure that their wording aligns with ours."

Rego smiled, thinking how expertly she navigated the complex politics and personalities.

"And I'll set up the press conference," she continued.

"What time tomorrow morning?" Rego asked.

She raised her eyebrows.

"I'd like to do it tonight."

Seeing the look on Rego's face, Forrester hurried to explain.

"Reporters were on the story quickly because several of them are staying at this hotel. Viljoen was in the news even before tonight, as you know. I think we should get ahead of the story as much as we can." Her voice dropped. "ACC Gray says he wants to keep the press contained, but it's already online, and what people don't know, they're making up. Some are saying it's suicide because she was trolled, and others are saying that it was a transphobic attack." Forrester paused. "There were a lot of online threats against her."

"Anything credible?" Rego asked, knowing that in this case picking out the facts from speculation and gossip would be half the job.

Forrester shook her head.

"Unknown at this point."

"Okay, set it up."

Rego made a note to have one of his officers go through the online hate mail.

A CSI officer appeared from the forensic tent and nodded

at Rego. They all glanced to where the sea was creeping beneath the tent flaps: *time's up*.

Rego led Forrester and Lloyd further up the beach, then watched as the body was zipped into a body bag and carried to the coroner's van which was parked next to the forensic tent.

The team moved quickly to dismantle the forensic tent as water swirled around their feet.

Rego hoped that the coroner's van would be able to get off the sand. He was relieved to see that the team had put a set of bright yellow tyre traction grips under both sets of wheels.

"Inspector Rego," Forrester said, pulling his attention away from the coroner's van. "If I announce that the press conference will take place inside the hotel shortly, the journalists might miss getting shots of the coroner's van leaving."

Rego smiled grimly.

"Good thought, Isla," he said with a quick smile. "Let's do this."

He straightened his tie and brushed the sand from his clothes, mentally running through the words and key phrases that they'd agreed.

Isla hurried off to speak to the hotel manager and print off some press kits to hand out to the waiting reporters. Lloyd watched her go, then pulled out his phone, and Rego assumed it was to keep ACC Gray up to date. DCS Richards could wait a few more minutes for an update, Rego decided.

The next person needing Rego's attention was Sergeant Stevens who was waiting on the hotel's patio, accompanied by a tall, wiry man whose shaved head gleamed like polished wood. He wore a green and gold Springboks rugby shirt, jeans and flipflops.

"Boss, this is Phil Ford," said Stevens, introducing the man. "He's Ms Viljoen's manager."

"I'm Detective Inspector Rego, the Senior Investigating Officer," he said, as they shook hands. "My condolences."

"Detective Inspector Lloyd," interjected Rego's nemesis, thrusting his business card into Ford's face and whipping out his pocket book. "Had you known Ms Viljoen long?"

Ford hesitated for a couple of seconds, his puzzled gaze flickering between Rego and Lloyd as if he wasn't sure where to direct his answers.

"Yes, a couple of years. Nearly three."

Ford's South African accent was strong, the vowels altered, the words clipped.

"My wife is devastated..." he paused, drawing in a long, ragged breath. "Erin was like a daughter to Julie, to both of us. I can't believe this. I had no idea that Erin was so desperate. Why didn't she talk to us?"

A question that had no answer.

And another unspoken assumption that the deceased had killed herself. Rego wanted to have this conversation in the manager's hotel room, not here, not out in the open, and not with his protégé's body cooling in the coroner's van a short distance away.

"Are you in touch with Ms Viljoen's parents or other family members?" asked Rego.

Ford shook his head.

"No, she had no one. Maybe a distant cousin, but no one close."

"A partner?"

Ford shook his head again.

Lloyd opened his mouth to speak but Rego got there first.

"Okay, thank you, Mr Ford," said Rego, handing the man

his own business card. "I'll need to talk to you and your wife later." He nodded at Sergeant Stevens. "If you could take Mr Ford back to his room, I'll be along shortly."

"Yes, boss."

Rego's phone beeped with an incoming text – everything was ready for the press conference. He sent a quick update to DCS Richards, then headed inside.

Isla Forrester had done wonders in a short space of time: she'd commandeered a large room that was more usually used for weddings, set up a table at the front for Rego, and placed press packs on all the seats.

Rego was impressed.

She'd also opened the doors so a cool breeze wafted through the doors, dispelling the stuffiness. Behind the table, the sea was a glossy backdrop, the sound of the waves soothing.

"I've checked the WiFi connection," she said, "and the Media Office team have given us a dedicated phone number and email address for any information from the public pertaining to the deceased. There's a sign-in sheet at the front, so I'll know who's attending. No one gets in without proof of being an accredited journalist or member of the press."

Rego's face was grim as he nodded.

"If you wait off-stage," she continued, pointing to a door where a wedding party would enter, "I'll bring the reporters in and seat them now."

"Well done, Isla. Thank you."

She smiled but was already hurrying away.

A minute passed, and Rego could hear a number of voices in the room beyond. He counted to 30, then entered, the noise level dropping to a murmur as he strode towards the table placed on a small, raised platform.

He was surprised to find that Lloyd had followed him into the room and slid into a chair before Rego could say anything.

Rego decided to stand in front of the table and saw Lloyd's smug smile wither.

Cameras clicked and flashed, making him blink.

"Good evening," he said. "I'm Detective Inspector Robert Rego, Senior Investigating Officer. This evening, at 9.27pm, a 31-year-old woman was found unresponsive and floating in the sea by a member of the public. That same person attempted CPR, and an ambulance arrived within minutes, but unfortunately the woman was declared dead at the scene. There is a lot of online speculation about her identity, but it's believed to be Erin Viljoen, a Dutch national, here to take part in the Boardmasters surfing competition. At present, we are treating this as an unexplained death. I would ask any members of the public who have spoken to Ms Viljoen in the last couple of days to contact Devon & Cornwall Police on the hotline number you'll find in your press packs."

He cleared his throat and continued.

"At this time, my thoughts are with Ms Viljoen's friends as we try to understand what led up to this incident. We are keeping an open mind as we work to establish the facts, as we would normally do in these circumstances. A team of dedicated detectives will be gathering evidence over the coming days, and we'll keep you updated as soon as we are able to say anything further. I won't be taking any questions at this time. Thank you."

A barrage of comments and shouted questions were tossed in his direction, but Rego was already out of the room, breaking step only to glance at Lloyd who followed him reluctantly.

"What was that about?" Rego demanded. "When I

discussed the press conference with Isla Forrester, we did *not* discuss having you there."

Lloyd looked just as annoyed.

"I'm not your bloody sidekick, Rego! And you shouldn't have ended the press conference so abruptly. You re supposed to be getting the press onside."

"I'm the SIO on this – Force policy is to have the SIO do the press conferences so that..."

"'*Other officers from the investigation team may also participate to answer specific questions*'," Lloyd interrupted, quoting the D&C guidelines from memory.

"There are no 'specific questions' for anyone to answer at this stage," said Rego. "We just needed to give the press a single point of contact. Now they'll be wondering what an MCIT officer is doing there."

"I didn't identify myself," said Lloyd.

"They're *journalists*," snapped Rego, mentally adding, *you utter tool*, to the sentence. "Finding out things is what they do."

Lloyd shrugged.

"If I'd known it was that important to you, I'd have asked nicely first," said Lloyd, sarcasm dripping from every word.

Rego shook his head in frustration, then glanced at his watch.

"I don't have time for this. I need to check out Viljoen's room."

"I'll come with you," said Lloyd, a sly smile oozing across his face.

"Great," Rego said under his breath.

A team of Crime Scene Investigators were still processing Viljoen's room, a painstakingly tedious job that involved documentation of the conditions and the collection of any physical evidence that could help detectives work out what had happened: fingerprints, hair, bodily fluids; as well as IT analysis of the deceased's phone and laptop – in other words, all the protocol on dealing with the pathology aspects of an investigation into a sudden and unexpected death.

At least Lloyd stayed out of the way this time.

The leader of the CSI team looked up as Rego pulled on one of the forensic suits and a set of booties which had been left at the suite's door.

"Anything?" Rego asked, hovering at the entrance.

"Not yet, Inspector," came the curt reply.

Rego sympathised: it was early days, and he knew that the scene would be thoroughly photographed. In fact, D&C Police had recently started working with 3D cameras so that Rego could later do a virtual walk-through of the scene, but nevertheless, he wanted to go and have a look now. Just looking, no touching, but trying to get a sense of who Viljoen had been.

The suite was large and airy, with a wide balcony that held four sun loungers and a coffee table. It was twice the size of Rego's first flat.

Rego didn't think he knew the CSI tech, but it was impossible to be sure beneath the full forensic suit and mask.

"Okay, thank you ...?"

"PC Janet Aspen," the tech replied.

"Thank you, PC Aspen," said Rego, thinking how unflattering forensic suits were and that he was lucky he hadn't made a major gaffe when he'd thought she was a man.

Devon & Cornwall Police's CSI teams were not all warranted officers. In fact, the majority were civilian staff members with expertise in evidence collection and analysis. The fact that PC Aspen had been sent showed that the Chief Constable was pulling out all the stops, probably in case of future scrutiny or a court case.

"Hot briefing, sir?" Aspen asked.

"Yes, please."

"Are you looking for anything in particular?"

"Is there any sign of criminality occurring in this suite?" Rego asked.

"Too early to say, sir, but it looks like only one person was staying here."

"Okay, well take everything and swab everything – we don't know what we'll need."

Lloyd called out from the door, "I hope you're going to put this in your policy book, what you've instructed the CSI to do."

Rego counted to ten: doing what Lloyd suggested was a matter of course, and Rego didn't need to be reminded.

"One thing you should see, sir," said Aspen, her eyebrows lifting as she glanced across at Lloyd.

She turned back towards Rego and held up an empty pill bottle that had been logged and placed in a numbered evidence bag.

"Empty pill bottle in the wastepaper basket. No prescription label, but bought in South Africa. Doxylamine: it's an over-the-counter sleeping pill. I'm no doctor, but it looks like a pretty strong dosage. I'll check it for prints back at the lab."

Larger surfaces such as tables, walls, and doorframes would be dusted at the scene. Anything that could be removed would go for superglue analysis at the lab. The cyanoacrylate fuming method detected latent fingerprints. Fumes were attracted to sweat and oil from finger ridges, crystalising to leave behind a white residue that revealed the presence of prints.

"Suicide then," said Lloyd, folding his arms as he leaned

on the wall outside the room. "Like I said. You owe me a tenner, Rego."

Rego didn't necessarily disagree with Lloyd's assumption, but the bloke was irritating him, and it was far too early to conclude suicide or any other cause of death, and certainly not where other officers could hear him. Apart from anything else, Rego needed to show that he was keeping an open mind and go where the evidence led – not form a theory and choose the evidence that fit a particular scenario. Rumours started all too easily.

"There's also a water glass with a residue around the rim," PC Aspen added. "Bagged and tagged."

"Phone? Laptop?"

"Just a laptop. It's on the way to our IT people."

"No phone?"

Aspen shook her head and this time, Lloyd didn't comment.

Rego looked up to see that the man had walked halfway down the corridor to make yet another phone call. *Probably calling his agent about the film rights*, Rego thought sourly.

Rego glanced around the suite again, suddenly realising what was missing.

"Where's the rest of her surfing kit? She must have had more than one surfboard and the wetsuit she was found in."

PC Aspen muttered something under her breath that might have been, *Oh, shit.* Rego let it go, not asking her to repeat what she'd said – it had been a long night for everyone already.

"A beach hotel like this probably has a secure area for storing surfboards; probably a drying room for wetsuits, too," he added.

"I'll check it out personally," said PC Aspen, clearly annoyed that she'd missed something important.

Rego nodded and left the team to finish processing the room ... and the surfboard storage area.

Lloyd was talking animatedly on his phone and kept glancing at Rego.

He wondered who the little twerp was talking to. Then decided he didn't care.

Which was a mistake.

CHAPTER 3

Rego wanted to speak to Viljoen's manager and his wife, preferably without Lloyd hanging around and butting in, but the man followed him like cheap aftershave.

He tried not to let his growing irritation distract him as he knocked on Ford's door.

"What's your interview strategy?" Lloyd asked.

"Ask them questions," Rego replied, deadpan.

Lloyd's lip curled in a sneer.

"Funny."

The hotel room was another suite, side by side with Viljoen's.

When Phil Ford opened the door, some of his normal colour had returned to his face. He introduced his wife who was slumped in an armchair that seemed too large for her small frame, a soggy tissue pressed to her nose.

Rego introduced himself to the woman and waited for Lloyd to do the same.

"I can't believe Erin's gone," she said, repeating her husband's words.

"I know this is hard for you," Rego said, his voice kind,

"but it's good to get as much information from you as quickly as possible while it's all fresh in your mind. My colleague and I have a few questions."

Lloyd pulled out his pocket book but Rego didn't. He'd learned not to make notes straightaway, because it often put people off. He preferred to sit and listen to what they had to say.

Lloyd looked as if he was taking dictation, the opposite of Rego's technique for getting the best out of people. His wife always said he was good at chatting, a real people person. So, he would sit here, have a conversation with the Fords, then gently bring it to where he really wanted it to go.

He faced Julie Ford and leaned forwards in his chair.

"We will get to the bottom of this, Mrs Ford."

Fresh tears trembled in her eyes as she nodded, unable to speak.

"How did Ms Viljoen seem the last time you saw her?" Rego asked gently, but it was Phil Ford who answered.

"There were awful things said about her online," he gestured helplessly. "Vicious, cruel shit. I've printed off some of the worst for you."

"I know this is a very difficult time for you both," said Rego, "but everything we can find out about Erin will be really useful."

"Whatever helps us to understand this terrible tragedy," said Ford quickly.

And he picked up a thick manilla envelope, then seemed uncertain who to hand it to.

Rego held out his hand for the envelope, scanning through some of the transphobic messages with associated threats of violence, and several declarations that Viljoen was a cheat and shouldn't have been allowed at Boardmasters.

He passed it to Lloyd without looking at him.

"These are just some of them," said Ford. "The trolling has been on-going while we've been travelling internationally."

"We'll have our IT techs look into them," said Rego. "Mr Ford, is it usual for a surfer's manager to travel with them to events? Or do you manage several surfers?"

Ford shook his head, sharing a small, secret smile with his wife.

"No, just Erin, but she was special," Julie Ford replied, her voice steadier. "She was going places. French *Vogue* have ... had ... booked her for a cover shoot. She was so beautiful."

"She was about to sign an important deal with a major surf apparel company," said Phil Ford. "She could have gone all the way."

Julie Ford nodded in agreement.

"Yes, people loved her."

"Not everyone," Lloyd interrupted, holding up the file. "Some of these comments are pretty unpleasant."

Julie Ford's lips quivered and she looked down at the carpet.

"Was it all online threats, or were any made in person or by letter?" Rego asked. "Text? Email?"

"All of the above," said Phil Ford. "We even had several letters delivered by hand to the hotel." He gestured at the file. "They're in there, too. Perhaps you can get fingerprints?" He sighed. "We kept changing her phone number and email address, but the trolls kept finding her."

"The same person?" Rego asked.

Ford shrugged. "Who knows with these animals."

"And how did Erin ... cope with it?"

"I didn't show her most of them," Ford said firmly, "but she wasn't stupid – she knew it was happening. She ignored it."

That contradicted the man's assertion that Viljoen had killed herself because of trolling, but Rego kept the thought to himself for now.

"Have there been any specific threats since you've been in Cornwall?"

Ford nodded then seemed to change his mind.

"Not threats, but the usual comments. And some of the women surfers have been unhappy about Erin's inclusion in the competition."

"Oh? Why's that?"

"Because Erin would have won."

Rego waited.

"Because until the International Surfing Association made a ruling allowing her to surf in women's competitions, the top woman surfer at Boardmasters would have been Alana Bright, a British woman. She was very outspoken about Erin being allowed to compete."

Rego made a mental note to speak to Ms Bright.

"But Erin met the ISA's criteria of having a concentration of testosterone in her serum of less than five nanomoles per litre continuously for the previous 12 months," Ford continued. "It's been ... challenging for her to surf in US competitions because of President Trump's executive order that prevents transgender women from competing in female categories of sports. The WSL are standing up to him so far, but that battle is far from over."

"WSL?"

"World Surf League – it's for professional surfers, and they adopted their transgender policy from the International Surfing Association."

"Have there been any specific incidents in Cornwall?" Rego pressed. "Anything that's been reported to the police?"

"No," said Ford. "We didn't want to involve the police – the press would have killed Erin."

His mouth dropped open when he realised what he'd said.

"You may as well say it," Julie said fiercely, "because that's what happened! Erin was hounded to death. They as good as murdered her – we all know it!"

Her husband tried to wrap his arms around her but she batted him away and hunched down into the chair, her face turned away.

The tension in the room built palpably, but Rego didn't speak. Many people couldn't stand the vacuum of silence and found the need to fill it, but neither of the Fords spoke; they simply stayed lost in their separate thoughts.

At least Lloyd didn't try to interrupt this time.

Finally, Rego let the tension in the room slacken, waiting, appearing to be relaxed, before he asked his next questions: when was the last time they'd seen Erin, how had she seemed, what had she said, and so on.

"Who were Erin's sponsors?" Rego asked, circling back to the issue of money again.

"Well, this was her first season on the women's circuit," said Ford. "We had some of the usual surf apparel brands: Mami Wata, Instinct, Komsurf." He cleared his throat. "They're all South African companies, but we were in talks with all the big brands like Quiksilver, Rip Curl, Billabong – Roxy were very keen."

"Who was her biggest sponsor?"

"Mami Wata: they're small now but growing fast, and they're in talks about partnering with Billabong," he said.

Rego stayed quiet, letting Ford find the words in his own time.

"When she won at Boardmasters, all the sponsors would

have..." his voice petered out. "What happens now, Inspector?"

"Erin's body is with the coroner and a post-mortem will be carried out to establish cause of death."

"She'd hate that," Ford said softly. "She was proud of her body, but she hated her scars."

His wife threw him a look that Rego couldn't interpret.

"She will be treated with respect," Rego said gently.

Which was true, but post-mortems were also brutal, no matter how respectful the pathologist would be.

"Would you be willing to formally identify Ms Viljoen?"

Ford swallowed then nodded.

"Yes, of course."

"Thank you. It'll be tomorrow morning sometime. I'll be in touch."

Phil Ford put his arm around his wife's shoulders, and this time, she let him.

"I've got a good team of people working for me that I trust," Rego said to the couple, trying hard to avoid glancing at Lloyd. "My phone is always on."

He laid another business card on the table, then looked at Lloyd, giving him the courtesy of allowing any questions the man had, but Lloyd was uncharacteristically silent.

He wondered what Lloyd would be reporting back to ACC Gray, a man who was no fan of Rego's.

He ran his fingers over his short hair. He just wanted to do his job without playing politics, but the more his career advanced, the more times he had to watch his footing, even if he was reporting directly to the Chief Constable ... or maybe *because* he was reporting directly to the Chief Constable.

As Rego left the room, he glanced at his watch: 10.45pm. It was probably too late to interview Alana Bright, Viljoen's rival in the women's competition, but it was worth a try – and if not, he wanted to make sure that he spoke to her first thing in the morning.

He texted his sergeant, saying that he needed Bright's phone number from the Boardmasters' organisers. If he was lucky, she'd be awake; if he was very lucky, she'd be awake and sober; and if God loved him, she'd be awake, sober, staying at this hotel and prepared to talk to him right away.

"She's a local, boss," Stevens said, a few minutes later. "Lives with her parents in Newquay. She was out partying when I called her and we couldn't hear each other that well, but she agreed to come to Newquay nick first thing tomorrow morning. I told her that 'first thing' meant 8.45am. She didn't sound too happy about that, but I'm confident she'll be there."

"Good work, thanks, Tom."

"I've got Jen over there setting up an incident room," Stevens continued.

Rego normally worked out of Penzance police station, but it made sense to use the nearest station instead.

Detective Constable Jen Bolitho was an important member of Rego's team, excellent at interviewing suspects and intuitively analysing what made people tick, but organising all the data that came in on a complex incident was not one of her strengths.

"Have you spoken to Mimi tonight, Tom?" Rego said immediately. "I need her as the data analyst on this, starting with a timeline of Viljoen's movements."

A good analyst could make or break a case: their job was to read and collate statements, and all other intelligence such as telephone billing, internet usage, maybe CrimeStoppers and Neighbourhood Watch programmes – you never knew where intelligence was going to come from – then assess the questions that needed to be answered and run the data through sophisticated software programs.

The analyst would differentiate between single strand intelligence, their source and their credibility: had it been corroborated? Was it intel that wasn't disputed? They'd need to follow the national intelligence model, known as 5 x 5 x 5 which scored the credibility of the intelligence, as well as pulling together all the strands and disseminating it appropriately.

When Rego had a complex case, he always requested DC Mimi Eagling from Camborne nick – he thought of her as part of his team, but the truth was, he couldn't get her nearly as often as he wanted.

Mimi was a whizz at producing charts, a sort of Venn diagram linking overlapping areas of intelligence. The charts were documentary exhibits, which meant that they could be challenged by the defence if the case came to trial.

She'd never let Rego down.

And she wasn't available.

"Sorry, boss," said Stevens. "She's on leave till next Monday."

Rego groaned.

"You know she finally got engaged to that Polish boyfriend of hers. They've been seeing each other for years. Wossisname? Luka something. You must have heard about what they're doing to celebrate?"

A vague memory stirred in the depths of Rego's brain, but he had more pressing matters to think about.

"Tom, I..."

"They're only driving to Ukraine! With an ambulance full of baby food and clothes donated by D&C Police. Ukraine! How insane is that? Well, as far as the border with Poland. Mimi's fella has family over there. Didn't you read about it on the intraoffice newsletter? ACC Gray made a big noise about it, got it in the newspapers and on the radio."

"Oh, that's right." Rego sighed. "Damn it."

He'd put fifty quid in the collecting tin.

"How about Jen?" Stevens offered hesitantly.

Rego sucked in a deep breath.

"Okay, Jen's our analyst – give her all the help she needs. I don't want any details slipping through the net."

"Jen has a mind like a steel trap," Stevens objected.

"Yes, she does," Rego agreed, "but she doesn't always remember to share what she knows or put it in a report."

Stevens was silent.

"I'll give her a hand, boss."

"Thanks, Tom," Rego said to his sergeant. "And tell her to phone me. I want you to talk to staff working at the hotel: did Viljoen drink at the bar, socialise with anyone, eat at the restaurant? Check CCTV: where the cameras are and how the footage is stored. If we're lucky, it'll be a cloud-based system that we can access remotely, if and when we need it. The residents can be allowed back in now and we'll talk to them in the morning. But keep it all low key."

"On it, boss," said Stevens.

Rego glanced over his shoulder and saw that Lloyd was listening to every word he said, and not trying to hide it.

"Look, Rego," he said, breaking Rego's chain of thought. "I know you're reporting back directly to the Chief, but I've been ordered to report back to ACC Gray. Let's just cut through all the crap and do the job right, okay?"

It was pretty much what Rego had been thinking, but Lloyd hadn't earned his trust – far from it. He decided that there was too much going on to worry about it now.

"Sure," said Rego. "I've got my team setting up an incident room at Newquay nick now, and Alana Bright has agreed to come in to speak to us tomorrow morning."

Lloyd nodded, falling into step with Rego as they headed to the hotel's car park.

"You know that we're taking a lot of shit about this," said Lloyd.

Rego raised an eyebrow.

"The press are reporting that the police failed to act on the threats against Viljoen because we're all transphobic." He rolled his eyes. "We're supposed to be mind-readers and investigate crimes that haven't even been reported. That's why the top brass has got the wind up their skirts."

He grinned at Rego conspiratorially, inviting him to join in dissing their senior management team.

Rego wasn't falling for that old chestnut.

"This is my car," said Rego pointing his fob at a dark blue Vauxhall Astra, praying that Lloyd would make his own way to the police station.

Lloyd paused, as if waiting for an invitation that would be a helluva long time coming, then nodded and walked towards a similarly bland pool car.

Rego was glad to have a moment alone to gather his thoughts. He wanted to know more about the Fords, more about their business arrangement with Viljoen and how they were paying £1400 per night for two suites without a major sponsor.

No matter what they'd implied about what Viljoen *could* earn, there was nothing concrete about the potential sponsors.

Rego had been in Cornwall for over a year now, and he'd heard of all the big brand names in surfing, none of which had signed with Viljoen.

It might not be significant, but it had raised a red flag in his mind, especially with Ford's equivocation about the lack of big brand sponsors. Although, he admitted that if Viljoen had topped the women's WSL circuit this year, the sponsorship deals would have no doubt come.

Everyone loves a winner.

CHAPTER 4

Cassie and the kids were asleep by the time Rego got home to the cottage in Newlyn that he'd been renting since he first arrived in Cornwall.

Only Bill, their Labrador puppy, was awake, his bright hazel eyes, lolling tongue and wagging tail saying that he was happy to see his dad, no matter how late it was.

Strictly speaking, the rental property didn't allow dogs, but Bill was just visiting. Except for school holidays, he lived up in Manchester with Cassie and the kids in Rego's old house. Rego was very much hoping to change that situation and move the family to Cornwall, but so far, Cassie wasn't keen.

Rego slumped into an old armchair, and Bill tried to climb on his knee, forgetting that he was now eight months old and ten kilos too heavy for that to be comfortable for either of them. Groaning, Rego lifted the puppy off him and took Bill outside for a comfort break and a sniff round the small yard, then brought him back inside and shared the ham sandwich that Cassie had left out for him.

Rego still needed some time to unwind from the busy

evening, so he sat back in the armchair with Bill's heavy head on his knee, then spent 20 minutes scrolling through Alana Bright's social media and what the surf magazines said about her.

He learned that she was 26, an up-and-coming surfer from Cornwall who was sponsored by Range Rover, Coca Cola and Ralph Lauren, among others, even though she hadn't made it to the top 50 on the women's WSL rankings. And yet, Erin Viljoen, who would have won easily at Boardmasters – according to Phil Ford – had nothing like that quality of sponsorship. It didn't add up.

But it was still at the very early stages of the investigation and making snap decisions without evidence was not how Rego worked.

Finally, he settled Bill in his dog bed, and plodded upstairs, trying not to wake Cassie as he dropped his clothes onto a chair.

"What time is it?" she yawned.

"Late – go back to sleep." He kissed her cheek. "Thanks for the sandwich," he whispered.

She smiled drowsily as he slipped in beside her, snuggling into his chest. He wrapped his arms around her, but she was asleep again in seconds.

He watched as her breathing became light and even. Rego's busy brain began to quiet and he started to drift...

Too early the next morning, Rego was shaved and dressed, disappointed to miss seeing the kids before he left for the station.

"I'll call you from Mum's," Cassie said yawning.

Her nightdress had slipped up to her waist and her voice was heavy with sleep.

"Stop staring at me," she said, without opening her eyes. "It's creepy."

"Then stop being so sexy," Rego replied.

"Go and solve some crimes!" she snorted, but she was smiling.

When he arrived at Newquay police station, he found Lloyd waiting for him in the incident room.

That pissed him off and the day had only just started.

"I've been reading up on the Bright woman," said Lloyd. "Local girl, 26 years old, trying to be a professional surfer." He paused. "Can't imagine there's much money in that, but she's a bit of a looker, so maybe she does some modelling on the side."

Rego didn't bother to answer, instead helping himself to a cup of coffee that was strong enough to do push-ups, then reviewed everything he knew on the case so far.

Lloyd carried on talking, either unaware or uncaring that Rego was barely listening.

DS Tom Stevens arrived a few minutes later.

"Morning, boss. Sorry I'm late. Just been up at the Watergate Bay Hotel, but the Fords weren't awake so I'll go back later." He glanced at DI Lloyd. "Sorry, sir, didn't see you there."

Rego smiled to himself.

"And Alana Bright is waiting in reception with her fiancé. He looks a bit poorly, boss – must have been a heavy night."

"Thanks, Tom. I'll be there in a minute."

Rego re-read his list of questions for the couple, made a couple of notes, then walked to the front desk to find the pair.

Alana Bright reminded Rego of an older version of Tamsyn: the same willowy build, the same summer tan and sun-streaked blonde hair.

With her was a man in his late twenties, wearing the surfer's uniform of board shorts, flip flops and a faded t-shirt with a surf logo on it, sporting a man-bun and scruffy beard.

He was wearing sunglasses, and when he took them off, he looked very hungover.

Rego turned his attention back to the woman.

"Ms Bright?"

She nodded as Rego introduced himself, and Lloyd did the same.

"This is my fiancé Danny Stewart," said Bright, gripping the man's hand tightly. "I want him to come in with me."

"That's fine," Rego nodded, leading them to an interview room and pointing at a pair of chairs. "If it's okay with you, my intention is to record this interview so there's no discrepancy about what's said here this morning. You're not under arrest and are free to leave at any time, but I would like to ask you about your relationship with Erin Viljoen."

Bright's brown eyes widened and her forehead wrinkled with concern.

"Is it true that Erin's dead?"

"Yes, I'm afraid so," Rego replied.

He noticed her fiancé squeeze her hand, and if Rego wasn't mistaken, he seemed to be trying to hide a wry smile.

"You would have beaten her anyway, babe," he said, but Bright looked doubtful.

"I can't believe any of this," she muttered.

"How well did you know Ms Viljoen?" Rego asked.

"I didn't," she replied, "not really. I met her, like, maybe twice?"

Her voice went up at the end as if she was asking a question.

"Where did you meet her?"

"Um, so, we were both at Gironde last month? That's, like, the Caraïbos Lacanau Pro in France? On the Women's Qualifying Tour?" She frowned. "That's when I heard she was getting a Dutch passport and that she'd be at Boardmasters."

"And the second time?"

"Yesterday?"

Rego waited for more and Bright shrugged.

"We were doing a paddle-out for the start of the competition?"

"Did you speak to her?"

"I said hi?"

"That's all?"

Bright nodded.

"You didn't like Ms Viljoen?" Rego asked.

"I didn't know her," Bright repeated, shaking her head.

"But I understand there was some animosity between you?"

Bright pulled a face.

"Look, it was nothing, right? The online forums made it into a total, like, thing!"

Rego waited, hoping that Lloyd wouldn't break the silence.

After several long seconds, Bright spoke again, tugging on the fraying ends of a friendship bracelet, not unlike the one Rego's ten-year-old daughter wore.

"So, Erin has, like, always dissed surfing in the UK and said that Boardmasters shouldn't be on the WSL circuit. She said the waves are rubbish. I mean, like, she's not wrong, but that's because they always have the competition in the summer to pull in tourists for the festival. Our best waves are in the winter but the event organisers want sunshine, shorts and sandals, so screw the waves. That's all it was about!" she said vehemently.

"You're saying it was nothing to do with Ms Viljoen being

a transgender athlete, or the fact that she was favourite to win the women's event at Boardmasters?"

It was her fiancé who answered.

"Yeah, no! I surfed against her when she was still Ryan Kloppers, like, three years ago in SA. He was mediocre at best." Stewart looked down. "Same as me. He was never going to make the top 100 let alone the top 10 ... but as a *female* surfer." He paused. "Look, yeah? I'm not transphobic, but male-bodied athletes shouldn't be competing in female sports – it's not fair, is it? I mean, like, it's almost fashionable or some shit like that – and anyway, it wasn't a forgone conclusion that he ... that *she* would have won. Alana is an incredible surfer."

They smiled at each other, sharing the supportive and unconscious gesture of a long-term couple.

Rego paused, mentally cataloguing Stewart as another 'person of interest'. His animosity toward Viljoen was obvious and Rego couldn't help wondering if the man was behind some of the online trolling, maybe even the hand-delivered letters to the Watergate Bay Hotel.

Could the fiancé have done more than hedge his bets to improve Bright's chances? Maybe he thought that the trolling would be sufficient pressure to put Viljoen off her best, which would give Alana Bright a better chance.

Rego tore two pieces of paper out of his notebook and pushed them towards the couple, glancing at Lloyd who pulled two pens from his jacket pocket and handed one each to Bright and Stewart. Rego nodded his thanks.

"What's this for?" Stewart asked.

"I'd appreciate you both giving me your social media information: Facebook, Instagram, Twitter, TikTok, Snapchat, anything else that you might have, and the names of the surfing forums that you mentioned."

He spoke directly to Bright.

"And if you have professional pages as well as personal accounts for any of them, I'd like to know both of them, and your website, if you have one."

He already knew that she had a website because he'd studied it the night before; he'd asked simply to see if she'd tell him the truth.

Stewart scowled and folded his arms.

"What for?"

"Because you said Viljoen's inclusion at Boardmasters was discussed on social media forums. That information could be useful to our inquiries." He quoted Bright's comment back at her: "'*It was nothing, right? The online forums made it into a total thing*'."

Bright's face reddened, but she grabbed a pen and started writing down information. A second later, Stewart began to do the same.

Rego watched them. Of course, the troll or trolls generally used anonymous accounts, but he needed somewhere to start.

The two wrote the information slowly, occasionally conferring on which sites they'd both used, then grudgingly pushed the scrawled pages back towards Rego.

Lloyd scooped up the pens without comment.

"Thank you," Rego said pleasantly. "And if you could tell me where you both were yesterday evening, from 4pm onwards."

The couple exchanged startled looks, the seriousness of the situation beginning to sink in.

Bright chewed her lip nervously.

"So, I did that paddle-out, yeah? That was at high-tide and I was there till, like, six o'clock, right?"

She looked at Stewart who nodded.

"Yeah, and I was helping out at the sponsors' booth all afternoon," he added, his voice far less bolshie now.

Rego made a note to check both statements.

"And then?" he asked.

"We went to my mum's and had chicken salad with sweet potatoes," said Bright. "Slow-release carbs, right?"

"Both of you?"

They nodded quickly.

"And your mother will confirm that?"

"Well, yeah!" Bright said, sounding surprised. Then as an afterthought, "It'll be on her door-cam, yeah?"

Rego jotted a note to himself: he loved door-cams for police work.

"And then?"

"We got ready to go out?" Bright pushed her hair behind her ears. "We wanted to see the Wombats."

Rego used his extensive experience as a police officer to deduce that this was a band and not a group of small marsupials.

"Show them the vids, Al," Stewart said, suddenly brightening as he realised this would prove where they'd been.

Rego and Lloyd stared at the small screen of the couple dancing and laughing, the time stamp clear on the video.

"We weren't raging or anything," Bright offered.

"Yeah, because Al doesn't drink," Stewart said proudly. "She's a professional athlete. She looks after her body," and he gave his fiancée a lascivious look that made her grin. "I might have had a few Rattlers though."

Taking into account the bags under his eyes, it must have been more than a few cans of cider.

Rego asked for a copy of their festival videos then changed tack.

"I understand that you're sponsored by some pretty big names," he said to Bright. "Does that bring in much money?"

She sighed and scrunched up her face.

"Well, I'm not, like, rich, yeah? But I get my boards, surf apparel, gym membership, and some travel expenses. Unless you're in the top ten in the world, yeah, not so much. I'll do the circuit for a few more years, then I'll have to get a real job."

She laughed ruefully.

"I heard that Erin was about to pick up some big sponsorship contracts," said Rego.

"Maybe?" Bright shrugged. "I don't really know. There were rumours, but then there always are? I mean, Rip Curl sponsored Sasha Jane Lowerson, put an ad out with her, then pulled the ad six days later? They even apologised for it. It was totally a thing."

"Who's Sasha Jane Lowerson?" Lloyd asked, leaning forwards.

"She was the first transgender athlete to surf in a pro competition when she'd previously competed in the men's division. It's a pretty new thing in surfing. Everyone thinks we're so, like, rad," she said sarcastically, "but it's still run by a bunch of old guys."

"Look," said her fiancé, crossing his arms defensively, "I know why you wanted to speak to Al, but she's a good person; she's never said a bad word about anyone – not even Erin. All she said was that Erin should try surfing in Cornwall before rubbishing it. That's it! That's the whole thing. It got blown up into crazy-ville."

Rego changed tack a second time.

"Do you know Ms Viljoen's managers, Phil and Julie Ford?"

"No, I'd never heard of them until this year. Have you, babe?" asked Bright, turning to her fiancé.

"Nah, and Ryan ... Erin ... didn't have a manager in Durban three years ago."

Although they questioned the couple for another 30 minutes, Rego and Lloyd learned nothing new.

Out of politeness, Rego glanced at Lloyd to see if he had any further questions, but the man shook his head.

"Thank you both for your time," said Rego. "I'd like to ask if you'd both submit your DNA and fingerprints for elimination purposes."

He asked for two reasons: in case they were the authors of the vile letters that had been delivered to the hotel, but also so he could see their reactions.

Of course, there was no obligation for them to provide either, but it was one of the enquiries he had generated for all the hotel staff and where possible, anyone who had come into contact with Viljoen.

They looked startled, and for a moment Rego thought that Stewart would object, but in the end, they both agreed without any fuss.

"Is it true that Erin killed herself?" Bright asked as Rego escorted them from the room.

"At the moment, it's an unexplained death," he replied.

Bright shook her head.

"I don't get it. Win or lose, she had a manager who was paying for everything including first class travel. I mean, she was staying at the freaking Watergate Bay Hotel – most of us are lucky if we're not sleeping on someone's floor." She shrugged again. "I don't get why she'd kill herself. It doesn't make any sense. I guess she was pretty messed up, yeah?"

This time, there was a real question in her voice.

CHAPTER 5

Tamsyn had been worrying that a police presence for an unexplained death might scare off the toerag criminals she was trying to get locked up, but it seemed to be having the opposite effect. In fact, Rego was right when he'd said that everyone would want to talk to her.

Some people were subtle about it; others came right out directly and asked her what it had been like finding a dead body. Tamsyn tried to make it sound as though she was just one of the people at the bonfire until she learned that she'd been videoed doing CPR.

"That's you, yeah?" said a girl a few years younger than Tamsyn, thrusting her mobile phone in her face. "On TikTok? It's gone viral. That's well cool, even if she died anyway."

Tamsyn was so surprised to find out that she'd been filmed, she simply stared at the footage of herself, watching the person on the small screen as she tried – and failed – to re-start Erin Viljoen's heart.

There were dozens of comments already. Her own heart triple-timed. Had anyone recognised her? Maybe identified her as a police officer?

It definitely compromised her TPO role and she was afraid she'd be pulled off the job.

The girl was still staring at her, clearly impatient to get her phone back. Finally, Tamsyn managed to mutter something about lots of surfers knowing CPR, which was only half-true.

Her subconscious brain suddenly bullied its way to the forefront, pointing out two things that had caught Tamsyn's attention without her realising it: something in the video, and something that *should* have been in the video but wasn't.

She remembered now – when she'd paddled out for her surf, there'd been a fishing boat out on the water, only an hour before low tide. Could they have seen or heard anything?

And the second thing: where was Erin's surfboard? Tamsyn hadn't seen it after surfing over the woman's body. The leash hadn't snapped because there would have been a trailing edge and the Velcro strap would still have been secured around Erin's ankle. Which meant she must have taken it off herself.

Tamsyn's eyes closed briefly. That added to the suspicion that Viljoen had killed herself.

She needed to tell Inspector Rego.

"Thanks for showing me this," she said to the girl who was still watching her. "Must be my fifteen minutes of fame."

"Oh no," said the girl. "They only got, like, five minutes – maybe the battery on their phone died. Bummer."

Tamsyn gave her a half-hearted smile.

"Oh well, thanks anyway. What's your username? I'll give you a follow."

"Yeah, no worries," the girl said, tilting her phone so Tamsyn could see the name *ShazamGal*. "I can't wait to show my friend Viv. She met Erin loads of times before she was dead. She works in housekeeping at Watergate Bay Hotel. She'll be totally buzzed."

"Wow," said Tamsyn, hoping that was the appropriate response.

"I know, right? Viv said she was a total headcase and trashed a load of surfboards right in her room! Like, totally smashed them apart. She was hoovering up foam and fibreglass forever. Crazy shit!"

"I think I know her," Tamsyn lied. "Viv Taylor ... long brown hair?"

"No." The girl gave Tamsyn a puzzled look. "Viv Jenkins and she's got a bleach pixie-cut."

"Oh," said Tamsyn. "Must be someone else."

The girl wandered away, and Tamsyn quickly headed for the privacy of the TPO van to make her call.

She was disappointed when Rego's phone went straight to voicemail.

"Sir, it's Tamsyn. Look, I don't know if it's important, but there's a video on TikTok of me administering CPR to Erin Viljoen. And in it, I can see a fishing boat in the background. Maybe they saw or heard something?" She paused. "And if they were heading for Newquay Harbour, I don't think they'd do it two hours after slack water because that's when the tidal flow is pretty much at its fastest. Although they could have been going somewhere else..."

Her words trailed off. It was the kind of detail she needed to run by her grandfather. He'd fished the Cornish waters for more than seven decades, and there was nothing he didn't know about time and tides.

"And I thought of another thing," she continued. "Erin went out with a surfboard, one of the glittery ones that she's kind of known for. But it wasn't with her when I found her, and she didn't have the leash around her ankle." She took a breath. "And when I talked to the girl who showed me the video ... her TikTok username is *ShazamGal* ... she said that a friend of hers, Viv Jenkins, works in housekeeping at Watergate Bay Hotel..."

She finished her message, knowing that she needed to get back to work. There could well be more people who'd want to talk to her about the events of last night. What she'd found out already could be really useful to the investigation.

And it was better to be useful than to have the woman's death preying on her mind.

Her personal phone rang, and she sneaked a look then answered quickly.

"Hey, Joe."

"Hello, beautiful," said her boyfriend, making her smile for the first time that day. "I heard it's all kicking off down there. Are you alright?"

Joe Quinn lived in London and the long-distance relationship didn't always make for a smooth ride, but Tamsyn thought that a few bumps in the road were worth it, so far.

It helped that Joe was also a police officer and understood the pressures of long hours, shiftwork, shit-work, and unpredictable job patterns. It didn't help that he was a Firearms Officer in London's Metropolitan Police, a frontline officer for the capital's most serious crimes – it made her anxious. She felt as if him being with her was a giant jinx that put him in even more danger. She couldn't stop the feelings tugging at her even though she knew it was stupid.

But still, she'd needed to hear his voice today.

"I heard that my gal's a bit of a hero," Joe said proudly. "Cal saw you was on TikTok."

"Really? Wow, I've only just seen that video myself." She paused, her voice dropping. "How is Cal?"

She heard his drawn-out sigh across the long miles.

"Doing the best he can," Joe replied at last. "You know."

Tamsyn did know. Just before Christmas, Cal's girlfriend, an officer from Penzance police station, had been murdered by the boss of an organised crime gang. The loss had marked them all.

"Give him my love," said Tamsyn.

"What about me?" Joe asked, pretending to be miffed. "Do I get any?"

"I'm thinking about it," Tamsyn laughed, her answer more truthful than she'd meant it to be.

"You're a tough nut to crack, Cornwall," Joe laughed with her. "But my nuts are tougher."

Rego was massaging his temples, trying to ward off the headache that threatened. DC Jen Bolitho wasn't happy having been nominated as the analyst on the Viljoen case, but she was the only officer available.

"I'm too old for all this computer stuff," she sighed. "Give me a notebook and pen and I'm fine. Can't I do it that way, make a checklist?"

"It'll be easier in the long run if we get it all digitised from the start," Rego replied, forcing a smile he wasn't feeling. "Let's go through it one more time."

"Okay, she sighed. "Show me again."

"Start with a time line of events up until Viljoen's death – that's this section here on the database," and he pointed to the screen in front of them. "It's your basic chart with 'time' running along the top and 'events' on the vertical plane. With me so far?"

She cut him a look that said she wasn't a complete idiot.

"Okay, so the point is that this will identify any holes in

the intelligence picture so we can direct where further enquiries need to be made to fill the gaps. For each piece of information, you need to log where the intelligence corroborates from different sources..."

"...and identify where accounts differ," she said. "I know what I'm doing, boss, I'm just not as quick as Mimi on the computer side of it."

Rego held up his hands.

"Okay! I get the message. I'll leave you to it, but for God's sake shout if you need help. And as soon as the phone records come in for Viljoen and the Fords, check for numbers in common and mirroring."

'Mirroring' allowed the data analyst to see if all three phones were pinging on the same cell phone sites at all times, giving their relative locations.

"I just need to get started and organise it all in my head first," Jen stated.

Rego wanted to groan: *organising it in her head* was the last thing he wanted. The whole point of the data analysis software was that you *didn't* keep it all in your own head.

But Jen said she knew what she was doing, so Rego would have to trust her. Besides, he was too busy to be breathing down her neck while she got to grips with the case, and any way, no one liked someone looking over their shoulder the whole time.

But Rego was in no doubt that he'd given her a big job. For a start, she'd have access to every piece of information that had been gathered so far and every new piece as it came in.

Which reminded him, as soon as Rego spoke to the Fords, he'd ask them to provide a full account of the time they arrived in the UK with Viljoen, including the time and method by which they travelled to Cornwall. This would need to be corroborated by flight times, car hire times, ANPR on the hire vehicle, and cell site analysis of both of their mobile phones and Viljoen's, which hadn't yet been recovered.

If any of them had made phone calls along the route from Heathrow to Cornwall, billing from the calls would identify who was called, and cell sites would provide the location.

All of this needed to be added into Jen's database.

Then, she'd also need to chart the times they'd booked in at the hotel, which would need to be corroborated by the hotel checking-in system, CCTV at the hotel, and intelligence from door key swipes, both in and out, as well as any calls from the hotel or drinks purchased from the bar, giving as full a picture as possible of their movements.

There would be hundreds of strands of intelligence, maybe even thousands when multiple mobile phones were involved.

A good analyst's chart would identify if Viljoen had left the hotel on her own and at what time, but it would also indicate if there were any time gaps where they didn't know where she was, who she was with (if anyone), or where she went.

Once this sort of intelligence gap had been identified, Rego would then be able to direct staff to trawl local CCTV or make enquiries with taxi companies, local cafés, and so on.

As SIO, Rego needed to have a complete picture of where Viljoen was at all times in the days leading up to her death, and because suicide, death by misadventure, accident, or act of violence had not been ruled in or out, if any suspects were later identified, Rego would need to see where they were at any significant points on the timeline.

Further, Jen's chart would also identify witnesses who could have more information to offer, and 'significant witnesses' that may have to be re-interviewed – and every piece of intelligence would have to be supported with a document such as a witness statement, phone billing, cell site analysis, and so on.

In other words, the timeline of events could potentially be an enormous and complex document, but the software available would build the charts for Jen. Assuming she could get to grips with the software in the first place and didn't rely on pencil and paper.

Rego was putting his faith in her: the timeline was likely to be a foundation block in the investigation.

Leaving Jen to battle through, Rego headed out.

A uniformed officer had collected Ford and brought him to meet Rego at the mortuary's viewing gallery, located in Treliske Hospital.

Rego made sure that his phone was turned off: he wouldn't risk it ringing at such a sensitive time.

Ford was grim-faced when Rego met him at the hospital.

"Julie wanted to be here, but..."

His words trailed off.

Rego nodded in understanding, and he led Ford to the mortuary, trying to make small talk to keep the man's mind from what he was about to see. A couple of times in his career, Rego had been with people who'd got this far, then refused to continue with the formal ID; he definitely wanted to avoid that.

When they reached the mortuary, they were taken to a slightly elevated mezzanine floor, where Erin Viljoen's body was lying on a table beneath them, a white sheet pulled up to her neck respectfully.

Rego heard Ford's breath hitch.

"Yes, that's her," he said softly. "That's Erin."

"Thank you, Mr Ford," said Rego. "I'm very sorry for your loss."

The man nodded without speaking, his lips pressed together.

"I'll have one of my officers take a quick statement from you as having identified Erin. It's a formality but it will be needed for the coroner. It won't take long," Rego added, "then I'll make sure you're taken back to your hotel."

"What will happen to her ... to the body?" asked Ford.

Rego was truthful, knowing that sugar-coating things too much could be counterproductive.

"A post-mortem will be performed to find out as much as possible about how Erin died. Her body will be retained until the investigation has been concluded. We'll be trying to find any next of kin, so if you remember anything else about that third cousin Erin mentioned to you...?"

Ford shook his head wordlessly.

Rego didn't say that the police would be exploiting the South African press and social media to find out if there were any living relatives. They'd connected with authorities from Durban and had also gone to some lengths to find relatives in other parts of South Africa, including posting on Facebook groups in the towns closest to where Viljoen had been born, as well as some of the well-known surfing areas.

"Erin didn't stay in touch with anyone from her old life," Ford insisted. "She always said that we were the only ones who understood her. Why can't Julie and I take care of her now?"

Rego hated this part of his job.

"Did Erin make a Will?" he asked.

"She was 31! What do you think?"

"If we don't find any next of kin," Rego said carefully, "you can apply for a Grant of Letters of Administration. This would give you the legal authority to handle Erin's estate and make decisions about her funeral."

"Thank you," said Ford, looking relieved. "I could set up a crowdfunding page to help pay for her to be flown home."

Rego guessed that 'home' would be South Africa, not the Netherlands, even though Erin had recently received a Dutch passport. He had no idea how complex it would be transferring a body like that, but somehow, he wasn't surprised that Ford was going to use his client's death to set up a fundraising page.

The Fords were putting on a good show but their expenses on Erin's behalf seemed to vastly outweigh any income so far. And if they were as well off as they seemed, why were they considering crowdfunding her body's repatriation?

"I'd only ask that you stay in the area for now," said Rego.

Ford's face creased with annoyance.

"You don't expect my wife to stay here, do you? She's been through enough!"

"It would be helpful," Rego said mildly. "It doesn't have to be the Watergate Bay Hotel – just stay within the county, please."

Ford twitched a shoulder, which could have meant something or nothing.

"You have my number, Inspector."

Rego was beginning to think that he did.

As soon as Ford had left the area, Viljoen's body was taken back to the mortuary for the post-mortem.

Chief Constable Stephen Evans had insisted on a forensic post-mortem, happily signing off on the extra cost. No doubt it was an arse-covering exercise, but Rego couldn't blame him – the press were already saying there'd been a police cock-up. Although that accusation was nothing new.

Rego had met forensic pathologist Dr Manners on several occasions. She was in her late 50s with iron-grey hair and a ramrod posture, good at her job, didn't suffer fools, and didn't do small talk.

"Inspector Rego, good morning," she said, pulling on a pair of nitrile gloves and placing protective safety glasses over her eyes. "Are you going to watch from the viewing gallery or would you like to join me?"

"Uh, I can see better here," Rego said hurriedly.

Dr Manners glanced up, her eyes twinkling.

"The press are already ruling this a suicide – let's see if I agree with them."

Rego stood with his back to the wall of the mezzanine area, his face expressionless, his body screaming at him to run. The room was cold, white, clinical, and smelled strongly of disinfectant. Two stainless-steel tables were arranged in the centre of the room, with shallow rims and drains to catch bodily fluids, and a row of stainless-steel sinks running along the far wall. Dr Manners' assistant had laid out a set of surgical tools that she'd use during the two-hour procedure: autopsy saw, knives and scalpels, dissecting hooks enterotomy scissors, needles, forceps and a skull breaker which looked like a miniature hammer.

A CSI photographer was present, ready to document everything.

Dr Manners started the digital video recording as her assistant slipped into the room, and began the process by weighing the body.

"The deceased is 31 years-old, well-nourished, weighing 75.2Kg, 188cm in height."

Rego scribbled down the numbers then googled them to find out that meant 6'2", 11 stone and 10 pounds.

"The deceased has been identified as Erin Viljoen, a male to female transgender Dutch national."

The autopsy assistant cut the neoprene wetsuit from the

body using long, thin scissors. Rego peered forwards to see if Viljoen had a waterproof case around her neck for her phone and hotel room key, but there was nothing. He made a note to find out where that missing key card had gone, and the last time it had been used. And where the hell was her phone? Could she have left it on the beach? It seemed unlikely but it needed to be checked. And it was worth asking if anything had been handed in at the hotel's reception.

Dr Manners made an external exam of the body then glanced up at Rego, and for a horrifying moment he thought that she was going to insist he come closer.

Instead, the pathologist drew his attention back to the body as she pointed out several small scars.

"These are from the deceased's transgender surgery, and these are from her breast augmentation. You can also see that her musculature is unusually well developed, which is what I'd expect from a professional athlete."

"Have you done post-mortems on surfers before?" Rego asked.

"I practise pathology in Cornwall," said Dr Manners without looking up, in a tone that clearly meant, *Of course, you idiot.*

Having finished the external examination, Dr Manners pulled on a lightweight chainmail glove to protect her left hand from the sharp tools she'd be using to cut open the deceased's skull and sternum.

Dr Manners started at the head, working methodically. Rego looked at his shoes and took shallow breaths through his paper mask, pressing his back to the wall, wishing he could sink through it and into the corridor beyond.

An eerie groan escaped from the corpse's mouth and Rego jumped. Dr Manners glanced up, and Rego could have sworn that she was smiling behind her paper mask.

"Just gas escaping from the body, Inspector. I don't do post-mortems on the living."

She chuckled at her own joke as the scalp was peeled back. Then the saw did its grizzly work and a large piece of skull was removed with a squelch and a pop.

Rego swallowed, trying to control the roil of his guts.

It was the sounds that got to him: the buzz of the saw, the wet snick of the scissors, the sticky peeling sound as the scalp was retracted and the sucking sound as a section of skull was removed, and worst of all, the firm *clunk* of loppers which were used to open the ribcage. Rego had a pair just like them in the shed of his family home. Except that his were used to trim trees and shrubs.

"I see a number of small bruises on the top of the head and at the back of the neck," said Dr Manners, examining the underside of the scalp. "Perhaps as many as eight – I'll check for extravasated blood cells within the tissue, but I do not believe these are the result of postmortem lividity."

"So, something hit the top of her head and the back of her neck repeatedly while she was alive?"

"Yes."

"Could she have knocked her head against her own surfboard?"

"The shape and positioning would suggest not," said Dr Manners, but didn't comment further, and Rego knew better than to ask any more questions at this point.

Dr Manners moved onto the brain itself – in fact not entirely grey, the deepest parts being white – even though it was widely referred to by lay people as 'grey matter'. Dr Manners examined everything minutely, looking for signs of haemorrhage and intracranial bleeding.

Once satisfied that she'd drawn every piece of diagnostic information that she could from the brain tissue, noted the injury on the posterior where the fin of Tamsyn's surfboard had bruised the skin, then the rest of the organs were removed and weighed in the kind of pan that Rego's wife used when she made brownies with the kids.

He really wished he hadn't had that thought.

Then further samples were taken for histology.

"The lungs show evidence that the victim drowned," said Dr Manners.

"Is that the official cause of death?" Rego asked.

"I don't like being rushed, Inspector," she replied with asperity.

The next revelation came ten minutes later, as the odour in the room grew worse from the stomach and bowel contents, both of which were minutely examined.

"I can smell alcohol in the stomach contents," said Dr Manners, glancing up. "Champagne?"

"I'll take your word for it," Rego said, his own stomach lurching in protest.

"The deceased ate a meal of baked salmon and broccoli with new potatoes, and a chocolate brownie and ice cream for dessert. But you should see these minute pieces of white powder in the stomach contents, Inspector."

"Aspirin? Paracetamol? Maybe, um, hormone pills?" Rego paused, remembering what had been found in Viljoen's room. "Sleeping pills? An empty bottle of doxylamine was in the deceased's room – no prescription and bought in South Africa. Could the powder you're seeing be that?"

"That's a question for the lab," Dr Manners answered. "However, I have noted what appears to be a transdermal oestrogen patch on her right arm, although anti-androgens would likely be in tablet form." She paused. "But I make two observations which are unusual: firstly, the quantity – more than three or four tablets have been ingested, perhaps as many as seven or eight; secondly, the tablets have been ground up and added to the food, not taken whole."

Rego's antennae twitched: he didn't like the word 'unusual' when it came to apparent suicides. He didn't like unexplained bruising, and he didn't like that Viljoen's hotel key card and phone were missing.

It was more than an hour later when he finally had a chance to listen to Tamsyn's message about the missing surfboard and leash, and the unknown boat that had been so close to shore the night before. His bad feeling intensified. He was also furious with himself for not considering that all the rubberneckers on the beach would have recorded the whole thing on their mobiles. Maybe there was more footage on social media that would offer additional information.

He needed to get an officer looking for it immediately, and he needed to know whether or not the missing surfboard was listed in evidence.

"No, boss," Jen replied when he phoned her. "And there's still no sign of her hotel room key or her mobile phone either."

He heard her scratching a note that he really hoped would get entered into the data analysis software.

"And find a spare body to look at social media posts," said Rego.

"Jack's good on the socials," Jen replied. "He's never off that phone of his."

Jack Forshaw was the second youngest DC on the team, and Jen was right – he could run rings round all of them when it came to things he could do with a smartphone.

Rego nodded in agreement then phoned his sergeant.

"Tom, I've just heard that the surfboard Viljoen was using last night is missing. Not just the surfboard but the leash as well. I have to consider that she removed it herself. We'll need a drone pilot to search the coastline to see if anything has washed up. Find out if Harry Joules at Camborne is available, but get him to check the pattern of currents and wind from last night so he's not searching in the wrong direction. I want to find that missing surfboard."

He then relayed the rest of Tamsyn's thoughts, the mysterious fishing boat, and the pathologist's comments about the bruising and ground-up pills.

"There were no bottles of champagne in her room, boss," said Stevens. "And she didn't order any from the hotel – I already checked."

Rego thought about that.

"I suppose she could have had a glass at the bar or somewhere else. Could a fan have sent some up to the room? But then why would the bottle have been removed," he said more to himself than Tom. "Speak to the hotel staff – see if any of them know anything, and confirm with the Fords whether or not they were drinking with her."

"I'll check again," said Stevens doubtfully, "but there definitely weren't any wine glasses in the room, just the water glasses, and the Fords say she ate alone last night."

"I suppose she could have drunk straight from the bottle," said Rego.

"Very rock 'n' roll," Stevens added cheerfully, but Rego didn't feel like laughing.

"Get someone – Jack if he's available – and find out if there are any videos, any evidence that Viljoen might have had a drink with one of the party goers on the beach before she went out to surf."

Stevens made a note.

"And find out if there's a Viv Jenkins on the housekeeping team. She's the one who allegedly saw Viljoen destroy several of her surfboards. If she's in, I want to talk to her asap; if not, get her phone number and home address."

"On it, boss."

An hour later, Rego was sitting in one of the hotel's empty business suites with a very anxious Viv Jenkins.

Her eyes were red-rimmed either from tiredness, a hangover, or doobies, a.k.a. whacky baccy. She looked as if she'd just rolled out of bed or somewhere more dubious.

"Viv, I just have a couple of questions for you, okay?" said Rego, trying to sound as non-threatening as possible.

She swallowed nervously but didn't reply.

"I understand that you're employed as a housekeeper here at the hotel. Can you tell me about that?"

"So, yeah, I just started at Easter."

Rego waited, but she sat slumped in an armchair, staring at the floor and sucking on her lip-ring.

"What time do you usually begin work?"

"So, yeah, I have to be here at 8am and I get, like, 20 minutes to clean each room or 30 minutes for a suite."

"What does that involve?" Rego asked.

Jenkins stared at him with a puzzled expression.

"I have to make the beds," she said, rolling her eyes.

"What else?" Rego prodded. "What else do you do in that 20 or 30 minutes?"

Jenkins sighed and pulled at her lip ring.

"Hoover and tidy up, empty the bins, put out fresh towels if they want them, clean cups and saucers, extra coffee and tea sachets, sugar, Cornish Fairings – you know, ginger biscuits – the usual shi— stuff. They're really fussy about the bathrooms. I even have to fold the ends of the frickin' toilet paper into little triangles."

She rolled her eyes again.

"But the pay is pretty good, better than a lot of places, so, whatever."

"It sounds like hard work," said Rego, thinking about how

his bachelor flat had looked back in the day, and cringing at the memory.

Cassie had made him shape up or threatened she'd ship out. She'd made it very clear from the first time she'd gone home with him that he had to raise his standards. The habit of tidiness had stuck ever since.

"People are pigs," said Jenkins, wrinkling her nose. "You wouldn't believe some of the gross shit I have to deal with. And I mean that literally."

"Even in a hotel like this?" Rego asked.

"Oh, yeah. Pigs with better styes," she laughed sharply. "There was this one time when I looked under the bed and..."

Rego had already endured an autopsy that morning; he didn't want to hear what Viv had found under a hotel bed.

She told him anyway. And for the rest of his life, Rego would check every part of a hotel's bed – in, on, and under – before he got in it.

"Tell me about when you cleaned Ms Viljoen's room two mornings ago."

Jenkins sank further into her chair and made a sound of annoyance.

"So, yeah, she wasn't sketchy or anything, and the first morning it was just a normal clean. But the second morning, she'd, like, gone all John Wick and trashed a load of surfboards."

Rego frowned.

"More than one?"

"Oh God, yeah! Like, maybe three? I saw at least five fins and a couple of noses. There was fibreglass and foam everywhere." She gave a quick smile. "My boyfriend's a shaper. He's got his own workshop and everything."

From which Rego deduced that her boyfriend made surfboards.

"How much would a professional surfboard cost?" he asked.

She shrugged.

"Kipper, my boyfriend, his custom boards start at £600 and go up to, like, maybe £1400?"

Rego was surprised. He'd seen them in local shops starting at just a couple of hundred pounds.

"What would a professional surfer pay for a competition board?" Rego asked.

"So, yeah, about that, I think," she shrugged again. "But her boards were extra custom – she had all that sparkly shit in them." Viv frowned. "They were cool, and she just trashed them like they were nothing. One of my friends is on the tour and he has to sleep on floors and scrounge food half the time. It's not fair. But *she* just goes out and buys a new quiver the next day – I saw them all lined up. They weren't even custom boards. I mean, like, really? She's about to compete at Boardmasters with untried boards? Like, what the fuck?"

Rego considered this: he'd always heard that athletes were superstitious before competitions, sticking to the same routines, wearing their lucky socks or lucky pants. Deliberately damaging custom-made equipment before a major event seemed odd.

He made a note to ask if there had been complaints about noise from Viljoen's room.

"After you'd cleaned her room that morning," he said, "where did you put the rubbish from her room?"

Jenkins stared at him blank-faced, as if she hadn't understood the question.

"You said you emptied the rubbish bins?"

She nodded.

"Into a bin bag?"

She nodded again.

"Then what?"

"Oh, right! I take the black bags to the big bins at the back of the hotel."

"Do you know if the bin men would have emptied those yet?"

She pulled a face.

"Like, I don't know? Maybe?"

Rego would get it checked out. If the rubbish bags were still on site, he'd get a CSI to check it out, but if the bin men had already collected the rubbish, he couldn't afford to tie up anyone looking for it without a better reason for doing so. Which he didn't have. Yet.

But Rego's gut was insistent: this was another question pointing to things not quite adding up.

Gut instinct wasn't proof. He needed a few tiny little extras ... like evidence.

But when it came, it wasn't what he was expecting.

CHAPTER 6

PC Harry Joules was the drone pilot brought in from Camborne police station and he clearly loved his job. He could bore for Cornwall on high resolution cameras, thermal imaging, flight time, live video transmissions, wind and speed resistance, obstacle avoidance and zoom capabilities. He was delighted to be pulled off his regular duties of monitoring the Boardmasters crowds to search for Viljoen's missing surfboard.

"I heard PC Poldhu was involved with the case," he said casually, glancing around him as if Tamsyn was about to pop out from behind a bush.

"Mind on the job, constable," Rego replied. "She's also a TPO here, so don't approach her if you see her."

"Yes, sir. Sorry, sir," Joules said quickly, turning his eyes back to his drone kit.

"You're looking for a surfboard that is approximately eight feet in length, and apparently it has 'sparkles' in it."

"Shouldn't be too hard to find then, sir," Joules said cheerfully, the reprimand already in the past. "I've spoken to the Coastguard and they reported that the wind was offshore last night, approximately 15mph, but now it's swung around to sou'-sou'-west."

Rego was still getting to grips with the nautical terms he came across since his transfer to Cornwall, and only had a vague idea of what the vagaries of wind and weather would do to an item built to float, as opposed to, say, a body in the water. But the relayed information clearly made sense to Joules.

"And I've advised Air Traffic Control at Newquay Airport that I'll be working the coastline, although I won't be in their flight path."

"Do they get many problems with people using drones up there?" Rego asked out of interest.

"Yeah, some, but not as many as they used to. Lots of hobbyists use apps now like *Drone Assist* so they know the restricted areas and where they can fly safely, as well."

Joules ran through his pre-flight checks: a visual inspection for cracks, obstructions, anything loose; battery voltage and charge level; checked the remote's controls, then finally launching the drone, watching it hover for a moment, a large, black insectoid machine that buzzed loudly.

Rego squinted, then shielded his eyes as it soared upwards and out across the sea. He was still watching the black speck when his phone rang.

"Hiya, Vik? How are you? Kamla kicked you out yet?"

"She sends her love," his friend paused. "Well, she would if she knew I was calling you."

"Not a social call then?" said Rego, walking further away from Joules even though the officer looked like he was fully engaged with concentrating on the drone.

Rego had known Vikram Verma for more than 16 years –

friends from their first day as raw recruits in Greater Manchester Police.

Rego liked to think that he had more than a couple of brain cells to rub together, but Vik's brain was approximately the size of a planet and spun faster than most computers. These days, Vikram's salary was paid by the National Crime Agency but more recently, he'd been seconded to the grey shadow-world of MI6, and Rego could only hazard vague guesses as to what he did there. But Vikram was the man with his finger on the pulse. More importantly, Rego trusted him with his life.

"'Fraid not," Vik replied, his broad Brummie accent unchanging over the years. "I heard on the news about the unexplained death of the transgender surfer and saw that you'd caught the case: Erin Viljoen, right?"

"Yes, what about her? I haven't found anything much except a whole load of questions and no answers."

"I'm interested in the South African angle and..."

"Shit, sorry, Vik! I'm getting a call from HQ. I'll have to take this."

"Okay, Rob. Call me when you've got a moment."

"Will do."

Sighing, Rego answered the call from Middlemoor, Devon & Cornwall Police headquarters.

"Good morning, Detective Inspector Rego," came a woman's voice. "This is Maggie Tyacke from Chief Constable Evans' office."

"Hi, Maggie," said Rego, surprised to receive a call from the Chief Constable's PA, and even more surprised that she was speaking so formally when he'd met her a number of times. "How are you?"

"Very well, thank you, Inspector." She paused, the silence

uncomfortable. "The Chief would like to see you in his office as soon as possible."

Rego frowned. He was in the middle of a high-profile investigation, but when the Chief requested your attendance, there was only one correct answer.

"Of course," he said. "I can be there at 8am tomorrow and..."

"I'm afraid it will have to be today," she said quickly. "In fact, the sooner you can get here, the better, Inspector."

Yep, zero choice in the matter.

"I'm on my way," said Rego.

Tamsyn was gasping for air, she couldn't breathe. She clutched her throat but there was nothing, no air, and the pressure on her lungs grew unbearably. The sea crashed over her head, the force of the waves pushing her down, down, down. Her lungs screamed as darkness surrounded her. Which way was up? Which way! She struggled desperately, clawing her way, trying to reach the surface.

Her brain woke enough to realise that she wasn't in water, and was still lying on her sleeping bag. But she wasn't safe there – she could feel a dark, malevolent force standing over her as she sank further and further into the ground, into the dark earth, helpless as she was pulled deeper and deeper down.

"No! No, I won't go!"

She screamed.

Someone shook her shoulder: her eyes flew open, arms flailing wildly.

There was a sharp crack and a yell.

"Bloody hell, Tam," said Jamie, his eyes screwed up as he

held a hand to his cheek where she'd caught him with a stray elbow.

She sat up, shaken, the dreams too real.

Oh, God! Did I scream? She pressed her hands over her eyelids.

She'd been so tired after being up most of the previous night, she'd been given permission to take a short nap.

Andy appeared at the entrance to the stuffy tent with Sully on his heels.

"What the hell's going on in here?" he snapped, his eyes flicking between Jamie and Tamsyn.

"She hit me!" Jamie croaked, his voice higher-pitched than usual. "She was screaming shit and I was just trying to wake her up."

"I don't know who screamed louder," Sully laughed. "It sounded like two girls anyway."

"You two wait outside," Andy said, backing away so Jamie had room to squeeze past him, probably very happy to be outside and away from his crazy colleague.

"Are you okay, Tamsyn?" Andy asked, his eyes running up and down her body, assessing, as if searching for an injury.

"I'm fine," she said weakly. "It was just a bad dream."

"You sure you're not hurt?"

She nodded again.

"I'm fine."

Andy crouched down next to her.

"Look, I promised the sarge that I'd keep an eye on you but he said that if there was anything which affected the operation, I had to withdraw you straightaway. He's also got someone checking to see if you've been identified as an officer or by name on that video." He sighed, rubbing a hand over his scruffy beard. "But enough's enough. I'm sending you home, Tam."

She started to argue.

"No, I'm sorry. I had my doubts after you found Viljoen's body. I thought then you should have taken a couple of days off."

"Andy, I'm fine!"

"You're not, Tam. You need to speak to a counsellor. This isn't just about Viljoen, is it?"

"I'm fine," she said again, more emphatically. "And I've already spoken to a counsellor. Anyway, Inspector Rego wanted me to stay on because he said I'd be useful – people want to talk to me; I hear stuff."

He shook his head.

"I'm sorry, Tam. It's not your call – and it's not his either."

Tamsyn was silent, trying to find a way to convince Andy that she should stay, but he was already reversing out of the tent.

She lay back on her sleeping bag, her eyes open as she stared at the canvas above her. She could hear music from the arena in the distance, people laughing and talking, the world beyond this tent still spinning.

Her heart was gradually slowing, beating with its usual steady rhythm. She felt oddly disconnected here, the light muted, the sounds muffled, everything a degree less certain. It was peaceful as she recovered from the darkness, from her nightmare, grateful she was awake, grateful she was alive. Dear God, the memories ... the memories of that twilight winter evening when a maniac with a gun had nearly killed her. Instead, she'd wrapped an anchor rope around his neck and watched him plunge to the bottom of the sea.

She'd saved herself and she'd saved DI Rego, but those seconds haunted her, and they came flooding back too often, sometimes night after night, the power of the memory pulling her back to that moment frozen in time.

But she'd never suffered from sleep paralysis before – knowing she had to fight but being utterly unable to move, simply being pulled further under.

She sat up suddenly, determined not to give in. She wasn't going to be sent home like some hysterical idiot.

She'd go directly to Inspector Rego. No matter what Andy said, Rego was a Detective Inspector and had a lot of clout. He'd said she was useful. He'd want her to stay at Boardmasters. She was sure of it.

Rego didn't think it was a good sign when he arrived outside the Chief Constable's office and saw his arch nemesis sweep past him, a smug smile on his face.

"Go on in," Maggie said to Assistant Chief Constable Gray, "he's expecting you."

Rego followed the man's progress with his eyes until the door was closed firmly behind Gray, then he glanced across at the Chief's PA, but Maggie refused to meet his gaze.

It was beginning to feel like an ambush. But why?

He only had to wait another minute before he found out.

Maggie's desk phone buzzed and she answered it immediately.

"Yes, sir," she said, then replaced the phone on the hook and finally looked at Rego. "You can go in now, Inspector."

"Thank you, Maggie," he said, straightening his tie.

The Chief was seated behind his broad oak desk, dressed in an immaculate uniform with a row of colourful service ribbons denoting good conduct, long service awards, and the King's Police Medal. His epaulettes had crossed tipstaffs in a laurel wreath with one crown, signifying his rank. His dark hair was greying at his temple, and glasses with thick lenses had slid down his nose, but his expression was full of annoyance as he glanced up at Rego.

DCS Richards was there too, his arms crossed over his chest, his countenance stormy.

ACC Gray, on the other hand, was all but beaming.

Rego continued to stand as he hadn't been invited to sit, but the Chief waved a hand as if swatting a fly.

"For God's sake, Rego, take a seat, man."

There was another person in the room, an older officer probably nearing retirement who was unknown to Rego; this one in plainclothes with a folder full of documents that he pulled from a battered briefcase and placed on the chair next to him.

"Thank you, sir."

"Well, I'll get straight to business. This is DCI Boyd from Professional Standards."

"Inspector Rego," said Boyd, "I'm a Complaints Investigator and I'm here to serve you with a Reg 9 notice."

For a second, no one spoke: the air in the room was charged, and Rego felt as if he'd just been struck by lightning.

He glanced at DCS Richards who seemed like the only person in the room on his side, but the man just gave an imperceptible head-shake, as if to say, *it's out of my hands*.

Rego's heart beat faster as Boyd slid a document across the desk to him – someone had made a serious complaint about Rego.

Regulation 9 of the Police (Conduct) Regulation 2004:

As soon as practicable, the officer concerned should be given a written notice:

a. *that there is to be an investigation into the case*
b. *the nature of the complaint or allegation*

c. *informing him that he is not obliged to say anything concerning the matter, but that it may harm his defence if he does not mention when questioned or when providing a written response something which he later relies on in any subsequent proceedings under these regulations*
d. *informing him that he may if he so desires make a written or oral statement concerning the matter to the investigation to the appropriate authority and that if he makes such a statement, it may be used in any subsequent proceedings under these regulations*
e. *informing him that he has a right to seek advice from his staff association or any other body*
f. *informing him that he has a right to be accompanied by a police officer who shall not be an interested party in any interview or hearing.*

Rego scanned the document with growing disbelief, the allegation serious, career-ending and criminal.

It was bad. Really fucking bad.

He continued reading, taking his time, forcing back his anger and yes, his fear; forcing his brain to engage, not to react but to think calmly.

"A serious allegation has been made against you," said DCI Boyd when Rego finally looked up.

"So, I see," Rego replied, keeping his voice steady.

"We'll get to that in a minute," said the Chief, as if something that could be career-ending was of little matter. "The point is that the Viljoen case is a priority, and with the press spotlight on us, we've got to be shown to be beyond reproach. I can't have an officer who is under investigation as lead."

"Detective Inspector Lloyd will be taking over as SIO," Gray said smoothly, clearly enjoying the moment.

"I still think this is the wrong move," DCS Richards said between gritted teeth.

The Chief cut him off with an annoyed look; he didn't contradict ACC Gray either.

"But we're making progress on the case," Rego argued. "The team has found some good leads and..."

"I've made my decision," said the Chief, a note of finality in his voice.

Rego drew in a breath, silencing his anger and forcing himself to maintain a professional demeanour as the Chief steepled his fingers on the desk, peering over his glasses and giving Rego the look of a stern headmaster to a troublesome pupil.

DCI Boyd raised an eyebrow and the Chief nodded for him to continue.

"The allegation is that on 24th December last year, you conducted an unlawful interview with a Portuguese national, Aderito de Jeles, on the island of Bryher. You failed to advise him of the grounds and necessity for his arrest, nor did you inform him that he was suspected of another crime. The only question you should have asked him was his name."

Rego leaned back in his chair, trying to look unimpressed. It sounded like a fishing expedition; he wasn't sure why, but he could make a damned good guess where the allegation had originated.

But DCI Boyd hadn't finished yet.

"Furthermore, you removed his personal wallet which contained €10,000. When his wallet was entered into evidence, the money was missing."

"No!" the words shot out of Rego's mouth before he could stop himself. "No," he said again, more calmly this time even as rage bubbled lava-hot inside him. "I talked to de Jeles on the harbour in plain view of everyone. I didn't search him and I certainly didn't remove any evidence from the scene. At no point was I alone with him: I was in full view of several police officers at all times."

"You're lucky you're not being suspended," said the Chief, but his gaze was troubled.

Rego was an officer who brought results, and since his arrival, Penzance's crime-solve rates were higher than every other station in Devon and Cornwall proportional to its size.

Chief Constable Evans was also aware that Rego had friends in the Secret Service; he wasn't sure who exactly, but someone had been sent to extract Rego from a very sticky situation the previous summer, and the Chief was still reeling from that unpleasant challenge to his authority.

For his part, Rego was seething. He knew exactly what this was and had a strong suspicion who had coerced de Jeles into making this false accusation.

The shadowy menace of the Hellbanianz organised crime gang was all over this, with Albanian crime boss Dritan Domi at the heart of it, reaching out from his comfortable cell in *HMP Manchester*, finding a way to jam him up and ruin Rego's career. It was revenge for the death of his little brother on Bryher last Christmas.

The fact that Domi junior had been trying to kill both Rego and Tamsyn wasn't of interest to anyone, it seemed.

"Sir, this allegation is entirely without credibility – it's nothing more than a cheap shot, a deliberate attempt to damage my reputation."

"It's very disappointing, Rego. Very disappointing indeed," said the Chief as he glared at Rego.

Rego's vision went red. 'Disappointing' was not the word he'd bloody well use.

"However, while this matter is thoroughly investigated," the Chief continued, waving in Boyd's direction, "I can't have you on a high-profile case, and that's that."

ACC Gray crossed one leg over the other, inspecting the immaculate crease of his uniform trousers.

"Inspector Lloyd will be SIO and he's expecting all your notes," said Gray for the second time, clearly enjoying saying the words.

Rego's voice could have frozen helium.

"DI Lloyd was apprised of this allegation before I was afforded that courtesy?"

The Chief's eyes narrowed, his face flushing with annoyance as his gaze flicked to Gray, but the man was without shame.

It was clear to Rego that Gray had been all too delighted to spread the happy news of the serious complaint which had been brought against him.

"While the investigation is pending, you're lucky you're not being suspended," the Chief repeated coolly. "Go back to Penzance station and continue with your role there. Professional Standards will be dealing with this."

The Chief leaned back in his chair, and Rego wasn't sure if it was his boss or the chair creaking loudly.

"You've been in the job long enough to know how this works," said the Chief. "There's a process to follow and we can't be seen to make exceptions for anybody, Rob. This is a criminal complaint of theft which has come from de Jeles' solicitor." He sighed. "There's a lot of work to be done, but we have a robust procedure for this sort of thing."

Rego knew that. He also knew that it could take months to resolve, and until that moment, maybe even longer, he'd be under a dark cloud of suspicion, no matter how spurious the accusation.

But then he wondered. De Jeles hadn't seemed very fond of the late and not-great Besnik Domi, the opposite in fact. He'd been relieved that the man was dead and almost happy to be taken into custody. So why had he made this accusation more than six months after the event? It must be that Domi senior had found a way to put pressure on de Jeles to make the accusation.

That definitely seemed plausible.

And it needed to be investigated.

Rego's gaze hardened: he wasn't going to take this lying down. He'd come out of the ring fighting ... or rather investigating. And he wasn't going to leave that to DCI Boyd or anyone from Professional Standards.

"I'll be speaking to my Federation rep," Rego replied. "Sir."

He stood up and pulled open the office door.

"We'll get to the bottom of this, Rob," said DCS Richards, trying to sound encouraging.

"Thank you, sir. I appreciate that." He turned back to the Chief again. "And I'll be speaking to the Federation solicitors – Slater & Gordon, I believe, sir."

He strode from the office, yanking off his tie and stuffing it in his pocket.

His fury rose with each step. He'd never been kicked off a case in his life, and he'd certainly never been accused of stealing, let alone with such flimsy evidence.

Although, it was true that he shouldn't have questioned de Jeles.

And it was true that the sergeant from the Isles of Scilly hadn't been with him for the entire time Rego had talked to de Jeles.

And there was no CCTV at Bryher harbour to

corroborate Rego's story. Which meant it was Rego's word against de Jeles's, a fact which could work in his favour.

Or not.

"Shit!" Rego yelled, startling a few seagulls. "Shit!"

He felt his phone vibrate in his pocket and he pulled it out, frowning as he read Tamsyn's text.

Damn it! He knew she should have had some time off after the way she'd found Viljoen's body and so soon after Domi's murder attempt. She was too young in service to cope with all the crap that had been heaped on her. He'd put the investigation above the health of a junior officer, and that was unforgiveable.

He tapped out a quick message: *Take the time off.*

And then he shoved the phone back in his pocket and sat in his car thinking.

He wasn't taking this accusation lying down, and he wasn't being pushed off the case so a twat like Lloyd could stuff it up. It was beginning to look more and more like a wrongful death than a suicide, but Lloyd would want to clear it up as quickly as possible so he could look like a boy scout and the Chief could get the press off his back.

Rego saw the guiding hand of ACC Gray in this, wielding the knife that was currently sticking out from between his own shoulder blades.

He turned the key in the car's ignition, checked the rearview mirror, and headed southwest, back to Penzance.

As soon as he was on the A30 dual carriageway, he used the hands-free phone to call the one person who was guaranteed to help him.

Vikram answered on the first ring.

"Thanks for calling me back, Rob. Eh, everything alright, mate?"

Vikram's broad Brummie accent brought a smile to Rego's face, and the tension in his body eased just a fraction.

"Not really. I need a favour, Vik."

"Name it, brother."

Rego told him all about the allegation and that he believed it had originated from Dritan Domi.

"And I need to find out everything you've got on Assistant Chief Constable Ian Gray," he said.

"That limp-dicked pencil-pusher still giving you grief?" Vik asked sharply.

"Let's just say he was way too happy to hear about this allegation," Rego replied.

There was a short silence.

"I know there's no credibility to what's being said, Rob, but it won't be easy going through the process because everyone will be looking at you," Vik sighed. "And you know that someone working in Professional Standards often uses it as a step for promotion."

"I know," Rego said grimly. "But Boyd must be nearing retirement, so I don't think it's that with him. God, I don't know..."

"I've got your back, I always will." Vikram's voice became serious. "And anyway, I owe you one."

Rego was fairly certain that he owed Vikram far more than he could ever repay already.

"Thanks, Vik."

"Hang on in there."

Rego had no choice.

"By the way, what did you want to talk to me about before?"

"Nothing specific," said Vikram. "It's just that I'm hearing a lot of chatter about links with OCGs from South Africa – I heard that your dead surfer was originally from SA. I was just wondering if you'd got any thoughts on the case yet?"

"Lots of thoughts," said Rego. "Almost zero evidence. But my gut tells me it isn't suicide – I just don't know what it is. And now I'm off the case..."

"I'll help you any way I can, Rob, you know that."

"Yeah, Vik. I know. Thanks, brother."

But Rego had no idea how Vikram could help him.

How could he prove that de Jeles hadn't had any money when they'd spoken at Bryher?

How could he prove a negative?

CHAPTER 7

Tamsyn was furious. Worse still, she felt betrayed.

She'd been so sure that Inspector Rego would side with her and insist that she continued to be involved with Boardmasters, working the Viljoen case as well as carrying out her TPO duties.

Instead, she'd been sent straight home and by the afternoon, she found herself on duty at Penzance station, going cross-eyed with paperwork while the rest of her team were all out on calls or enjoying the sunshine in Newquay.

'Enjoying' might be too strong a word as half the work was dealing with members of the public who were a) lost, b) drunk, or c) lost and drunk.

At least they were doing something more than sweltering in a stuffy office. If she'd wanted to type reports all day, she'd have...

I'd have what? Become a bank manager?

She snorted at the thought. In all honesty, becoming a police officer was the only career she'd ever wanted. For years, it had seemed out of reach for someone like her, but now she couldn't imagine doing anything else.

And she wasn't like many of the new recruits who were enticed by the prospect of a cheap way to pay for a degree; she'd joined because she believed in what the police did and what they stood for. She'd thought of herself as a lifer, so being side-lined by Inspector Rego – that stung.

God! She was being treated like a complete newbie when she'd been 17 months in the job and had seen more and done more than some life-long officers. How many times had she been told that she was 'young in service'? Even when there were several other rookies who were younger than her. Sure, she hadn't seen everything, but she'd seen a lot – and she hadn't crumbled yet. It rankled that they thought she couldn't cope.

Tamsyn stared moodily at the pair of computer screens mounted at her work station. Completing reports was the bane of every officer's life. There was always a mountain of paperwork, filing, and even more typing to be done.

She closed her eyes and spun her chair so she could glimpse the sky from the grimy window above her desk.

Just to rub salt in her wounds, Tamsyn's grandparents were pleased that she was no longer involved in a murder case, and even Joe had said that she should take a step back. In fact, he'd told her straight that he fully supported the decision to pull her off the case. He didn't get a chance to explain his reasoning because she'd hung up on him and refused to take his calls or answer his messages ever since.

She knew that she was being childish and she almost didn't care.

Only her best friend Jess wasn't irritating the hell out of her.

For months now, they'd been planning to rent a flat together over the Turkish barbers in Penzance. The refurbishment was finally finished after a long delay caused by a leak in the roof. Jess's job as an estate agent meant that they had first dibs at the new rental. But Tamsyn had been dragging her feet when it came to telling her grandparents, and Jess was growing impatient.

At that moment, her phone rang, as if Jess had been listening in to her thoughts.

"Have you told them yet?"

"No," Tamsyn admitted. "They were pretty shaken up by everything that happened at Christmas."

"It's August," Jess said, and Tamsyn could almost hear her eyeballs swivelling in their sockets. "You've got to do it soon, Tam. We need to put down the deposit this week or we'll lose it."

"I know, I'm sorry. I will. I'll do it as soon as I'm home. God, I really need my own space."

"And a double bed, right?"

"Not at the moment," Tamsyn admitted moodily.

"What? No! You've kicked Mr Sexy-pants into touch?"

"Not exactly."

"Then what?" Jess asked.

"I'm just not speaking to him."

Jess laughed. "Very mature."

Tamsyn smiled despite herself. "I know. I'll talk to him when he's not being an asshole."

"What assholish thing is he doing this time?"

Tamsyn could hear the smirk in Jess's voice.

"He agrees with Rob Rego that I should be pulled off the undercover Boardmasters stuff, so I'm stuck in the office doing fucking filing."

"I feel your pain," Jess sighed. "I seem to spend half my life doing filing. Oh, well, you'll forgive him," Jess sang.

Tamsyn didn't know if she was talking about Joe or Inspector Rego.

"Probably."

"Yeah, yeah. You say that but you miss Joe, don't you?"

Tamsyn didn't answer.

"Whatever. Just promise me you'll tell your grandparents tonight."

"I promise."

"Really?"

"One hundred percent."

"Oh my God!" Jess squealed. "We'll have the best time ever! Call me when you've done the deed."

Jess rang off and Tamsyn stared at the computer screens, her pulse just a little too fast. Jess was the sister of her soul and she loved her, but she was worried about moving in with her. Not that she worried about fights over Jess's epic messiness, but because the last person she'd shared a house with had been murdered. Because of Tamsyn.

The death of PC Rosie Flowers had been a case of mistaken identity; it should have been Tamsyn instead. And God, that was a terrible feeling, knowing that Rosie's parents had lost a daughter, knowing that nine-year-old Karenza had lost a sister. Feeling, *knowing* that she was to blame.

The murderer was dead. And Tamsyn lived with the guilt.

There was another reason that she'd been dragging her feet – telling her grandparents that she'd be moving out was not going to go down well, even though she planned on still giving them some of her wages to help make ends meet.

But that wasn't the bigger part of it – her grandparents were crazy protective about her. Tamsyn's mother had left before she'd started school and her father had died when she was ten. Her grandparents had been everything; always there for her. She felt like she was abandoning them, even though she knew that flying the nest was normal. Maybe they even expected her to leave, although they'd never said anything about it.

She was pensive as she walked home, feeling older than her 22 years, raising her face to the sun and tasting salt on the soft summer breeze. The shops had closed but the pubs and restaurants were doing a good trade, with customers spilling outside onto tables and benches, enjoying the warm evening. It could have been somewhere in the Mediterranean except for the advertising boards that encouraged tourists to try a Cornish pasty or a clotted cream tea – jam first.

The village of Gulval was almost an extension of Penzance these days, separated only by the elevated section of the A30 bypass that soared overhead, the low rumbling of cars and lorries a constant undertone.

The narrow lane where Tamsyn lived with her grandparents was quiet, with only a few cars parked nose to nose on the dusty verge, and each stone-built cottage taking on the demeanour of a miniature fortress with granite walls two feet thick and panes of glass so old that they distorted the view through them.

It was as familiar to Tamsyn as breathing.

When she opened the front door, a furry bullet shot past, coiling herself around Tamsyn's legs like a cat.

She reached down to pet the small dog who was almost frantic with excitement, but Morwenna had other ideas and leapt into Tamsyn's arms, scrambling and wriggling until she settled with her front paws on Tamsyn's shoulder and her head nuzzled against Tamsyn's neck.

"Hello, scruffalicious," she said, kissing the scruffy little dog on the head as she walked inside, then depositing little Mo back on her grandfather's knee, bending to kiss him, too.

He sat in his favourite armchair, something almost biblical about his long white beard and deeply-etched cheeks: he smelled like pipe tobacco, diesel, salt, and faintly of fish – the scents of her childhood, familiar and comforting.

Sadness rippled through her. He'd aged in the last two years. He'd always seemed so unassailable, ageless, as defiant as Cornwall's soaring cliffs. But now he had a stoop in his shoulders and his blue eyes, once as bright as Tamsyn's own, seemed shadowed.

"Tammy," he nodded, his unlit pipe clenched between his teeth.

"Hello, Grandad. How was the catch today?"

"Could be worse," he grumbled, as he always did.

Tamsyn smiled at the familiar reply.

"Where's Gran?"

He jerked his head toward the kitchen and went back to reading his newspaper. Morwenna immediately hopped down to follow Tamsyn.

Andrea Poldhu was sitting at the kitchen table, a mug of tea forgotten as she gazed out at the sweet peas growing along bamboo canes in the back garden.

Long shadows spilled across the narrow patch of grass and the abundant beds of soft fruits, tomatoes and lettuces, netted against the thieving birds, her labour and her joy.

"Tammy! There you are." She stood up, immediately filling the kettle. "We've been waiting for you. Do you want a cup of tea?"

"That would be great. Thanks, Gran."

Tamsyn slumped at the kitchen table, the boredom of the day washing over her, the frustration of being relegated to office junior, the irritation of Inspector Rego's blunt response, and a flutter of apprehension that she had to tell her grandparents something which would hurt them. Morwenna jumped onto her lap, curling into a ball of fur with a contented sigh.

"How was your day?" her grandmother asked.

"Bit boring this afternoon," Tamsyn admitted, then steeled herself. "Actually, there's something I've been wanting to talk to you and Grandad about," she began.

"And we'ens been wanting to talk to you, too," said her grandmother with a broad smile.

"Oh?"

"Ozzie, come and tell Tammy our news!" Andrea called out to her husband.

"Good news?" Tamsyn asked tentatively.

"The best!" her grandmother beamed.

Tamsyn's eyebrows rose, a matching smile hovering on her face. Lord, she needed some good news.

Ozzie Poldhu eased himself onto a wooden chair at the head of the table and nodded at his wife to continue.

"Your grandfather and I went to see a solicitor today," Andrea said. "And not for the first time."

Tamsyn didn't know what to say. The only profession her grandparents avoided more than lawyers was the doctor.

"We've put the cottage in your name," her grandmother said proudly, reaching across and taking Tamsyn's hands in hers. "We only have to live another seven years," and she smiled at her husband, "and it's all yours, tax-free. You'll always have your home; you won't ever have to move away or worry about not being able to buy a house in Cornwall, what with the way prices are rising. Mr Croft, the solicitor, he talked us through it and we all agreed it was the best thing for us to do. Isn't it wonderful?"

Trapped.

That was the first word that came to Tamsyn's mind, but after a second of shock, she gave them the response they were so obviously looking for.

"Wow!" she said. Then tried again. "Wow! I can't believe ... that's amazing! Thank you! Are you sure? I mean, is it okay to do that?"

"It's all legal," her grandmother confirmed. "And we wanted to make sure that Alexandra couldn't get her grubby little paws on it, no offence Morwenna."

Morwenna wagged her tail, not concerned by the unflattering comparison with Tamsyn's feckless and long-absent mother.

"Has she been in touch?" Tamsyn asked sharply.

The last time she'd been face-to-face with her mother, Tamsyn had been five years old. She had only a fuzzy recollection of the woman, until last winter when Alexandra Poldhu had sold her 'story' to a tabloid newspaper because Tamsyn had been in the national press.

"She wouldn't dare," Andrea snapped, pressing her lips together. "Not if she knows what's good for her." Then her gaze softened. "But we aren't getting any younger, Tammy, and we want to do right by you." Her eyes grew wet. "Your father would have wanted that."

Andrea brushed a tear away, then forced a wide smile.

"How does it feel to be a homeowner, Tammy?"

"I don't have the words," Tamsyn replied honestly.

And when she'd finally hugged and kissed them even to her grandmother's satisfaction, she made an escape to her bedroom.

Morwenna followed her cautiously, her expressive eyes clearly picking up on her owner's real feelings.

Tamsyn stared around the tiny room that barely fit the

single bed tucked into the eaves. Her grandparents had given her a great gift, but it felt more like a prison sentence.

She wanted to scream in frustration, but instead she held her tongue. They could never, ever know how she really felt.

She picked up her phone, her finger hovering over Jess's contact details before she finally dialled.

"Hey, Jess. It's me..."

CHAPTER 8

The next day, it was all over Penzance nick: Inspector Rego had been pulled off the Viljoen case and replaced with a DI from Camborne MCIT.

News spread quickly that Rego had been summoned to Middlemoor HQ for an urgent meeting with the Chief Constable the day before, but no one knew why, and it seemed that DI Rego was keen to keep it that way for as long as possible and was remaining tight-lipped.

Speculation was rife with various theories abounding – and whatever theory was being touted currently, there'd always be someone who trotted out the old adage, *there's no smoke without fire.*

Tamsyn couldn't deny that when she heard the news, she'd enjoyed a moment of vindictive pleasure, thinking that by being yanked off the case, he'd got a taste of some of his own medicine.

He'd treated her as if she was a stupid little girl who needed to have her hand held every step of the way. She'd saved his frickin' life – she wasn't fragile and she wasn't prepared to be treated that way.

The feeling of schadenfreude didn't last long, not when she was called into Inspector Maura Walters' office.

Rego was head of CID at Penzance station, but Inspector Walters was in charge of all the uniformed staff, including Tamsyn.

"Ah, Tamsyn," Inspector Walters began. "Take a seat."

"Thank you, ma'am."

Tamsyn sat stiffly, feeling unreasonably anxious. Walters leaned back in her chair, frowning across the desk.

"You were on Bryher last December with Inspector Rego and you provided a statement of events at that time," Walters said, staring straight at Tamsyn. "You should know that Inspector Rego is currently under investigation. As you were there that day and are a potential witness to those events, Professional Standards will almost certainly want to speak with you about the incident and re-interview you."

Tamsyn felt sick. God, they'd both nearly died – a crazed crime gang enforcer had threatened them with a gun, and then they'd almost drowned in the freezing wintry seas. Inspector Rego had only been there because he was concerned that she was in danger. He'd *saved* her.

"Is there anything you want to add to your statement at this time?"

"No, ma'am."

Walters' frown deepened.

"I'm assuming you've heard that Inspector Rego is no longer SIO on the Viljoen case?"

Tamsyn gave a quick nod.

Walters' nostrils flared, and she seemed to be coming to a decision about something.

"It has been alleged," she said at last, "that Inspector Rego removed key evidence from a detained person, Aderito de Jeles, evidence which has since disappeared."

Tamsyn's eyebrows flew up. She certainly hadn't seen anything like that, but then again it had been a confusing and chaotic time.

What sort of evidence could Inspector Walters be talking about? It didn't make any sense. Loads of people had been on the quay that morning: men from the lifeboat and two police officers from Bryher, and probably civilians. Had her cousins been there? She couldn't remember. She wracked her brains, but her memories were hazy – and she'd still been in shock.

Even so, she couldn't, wouldn't believe that Inspector Rego had done anything wrong that day. Why would he remove any evidence? No, it didn't make sense. They were wrong. Whoever said he'd taken something, they were wrong.

Inspector Walters folded her hands together on the desk.

"Tamsyn, let me give you some advice – discuss this with your Federation Rep, and when Professional Standards ask to speak to you, I strongly suggest that you tell them you want your Fed Rep present during that interview." She gave Tamsyn a speaking look. "Anything that you might have to add, well, I wouldn't want anything that you say to be ... misrepresented."

"Thank you, ma'am," said Tamsyn, now even more concerned.

Walters gave a quick nod but was still studying her.

"Well then, Tamsyn. I shall ask you again, do you want to amend your statement about what transpired on the 24th of December at Bryher?"

Tamsyn lifted her chin.

"No, ma'am. I have nothing to add at this time."

"If the complaint is upheld and there's a trial, potentially, you could be called as a witness."

Tamsyn licked her lips. Surely, surely it wouldn't come to

that? What evidence could they possible have against Inspector Rego?

It felt like a re-run of the previous summer when both she and Rego had been arrested then suddenly freed after he'd talked to the Chief Constable[1]. She'd been told it was some sort of 'training exercise' but she knew for a fact that wasn't true. She'd never been told the full story then either.

"I see, ma'am. Thank you for telling me."

Walters continued to study Tamsyn's face, then gave a curt nod.

"You will not discuss what I have disclosed in this office today with anyone other than your Federation rep. Is that clear?"

"Yes, ma'am."

Walters closed the folder in front of her, then leaned back in her seat.

"A police presence has been requested at this evening's football match in Mousehole. Sergeant Terwillis has the details. Dismissed."

Feeling shaken, Tamsyn left the office and went to stand outside. She needed fresh air; she needed to feel the sun on her face and hear the herring gulls wheeling overhead.

Gradually, her brain cleared and her agitation sank to a manageable level. She didn't want to admit that sometimes she felt overwhelmed by the responsibility of her job.

She gave a wry smile. Yesterday, she'd been getting bent out of shape because they *wouldn't* give her more responsibility.

Taking one last breath of salty air, she headed inside to find Sergeant Terwillis.

He was sitting at his desk, as usual, peering at a pair of

1. Told in *Dead Man's Dive*

computer screens and hemmed in by a stack of files at least a foot high.

"Hi, sarge," said Tamsyn. "Inspector Walters told me to see you about policing a football match this evening."

"Ah Tamsyn," he said grinning at her. "Looks like you caught the short straw. God knows why, but it's come from HQ, well, from Inspector John Casey who is ACC Gray's Staff Officer ... and it appears that ACC Gray is endorsing some sort of co-operation between a local supermarket, Mousehole Football Club, and Devon & Cornwall Police. Maybe a couple of new vehicles will turn up in our yard with the D&C logo and a picture of a Cornish pasty on them."

Tamsyn gave a smile appropriate for a senior officer who'd made a lame joke.

"Anyway, don't shoot the messenger," Terwillis continued, "and I know you should be off at 4pm today, but a few hours' overtime won't hurt."

He paused, but Tamsyn had nothing to say. Her life sucked and she'd rather work than go home.

"Anyway, HQ would like a police presence at this evening's match between Mousehole AFC and Evesham United, so the Robins are playing the Seagulls."

This time, Tamsyn looked blank because she had no idea what he was talking about.

"Chuffin' hell, Tamsyn! You're a local – you should know that Mousehole Football Club's mascot is a seagull!"

"Oh, right. Sorry, sarge," she said. "We don't follow football in my house, just rugby."

He gave her a look that said, *Fair enough.*

Rugby had long been more popular than football in Cornwall.

"I don't know who you pissed off, but you've been

specially selected to be D&C's presence at the match with Evesham, along with a PCSO."

"Yes, sarge. Um, where's Evesham?"

"Well, that's your first task. Google Evesham and read up about the town, then you can engage with the local supporters. Kick-off is at 7pm, so get there an hour before. Make sure that you park so you can get out quickly if we need to send you anywhere else. It'll probably be a bit boring if footie isn't your thing, but I know you'll do this with a smile on your face, won't you? Good PR for us and all that."

"Yes, sarge," she said, practising that PR smile.

She'd much rather be policing Boardmasters than a frickin' football match, especially as any one of the guys on E-team would have loved a couple of hours watching a game.

"Who's my PCSO?"

Police Community Support Officers worked with warranted officers and shared some but not all of their powers. They were a useful addition to the team, not least because their knowledge of local communities was usually greater than that of regular officers who had a much wider area to patrol.

"I'll let you know when I know, Tamsyn."

"Okay, thank you." Tamsyn turned to go.

"One other thing, Tamsyn. I don't know if you've heard the news, but I'm retiring at the end of the month."

Tamsyn's eyebrows shot up. "But you're not that old, sarge!"

Then she blushed bright red.

Terwillis laughed, a broad smile on his face.

"Despite my boyish good looks, I've been at this game for 30 plus years. It's time."

"I'll be sorry to see you go, sarge," she said.

Tamsyn was genuinely disappointed because she really

liked the man and had learned a lot from him: from his experience, wisdom, patience, and his decency. All the new recruits had only good things to say about him.

"Are they promoting someone up?" she asked.

"Nah, you'll be getting someone down from Plymouth, I think."

Tamsyn was quiet, wondering what changes the unknown quantity would bring.

"I'll really miss you, sarge," she said.

"Steady on, Tamsyn – I'm retiring not turning up my toes." His smile softened. "But it's good of you to say. The boys and girls are giving me a send-off at the *Admiral Benbow* at the end of the month. Drop in for a brew, if you can get the time off."

"Thanks, sarge. I will."

As she left his office, she hoped that the new sergeant in charge of all tutoring recruits was as great as Sergeant Terwillis. He was always ready to listen, explain, educate and reassure, and he was really good at bolstering your confidence when you most needed it.

Damn it. Why did things have to change? Why did all the best people leave?

Tamsyn sighed then shook it off. Maybe the change would be a positive one.

She headed for the break-out area, phone in hand, googling Evesham.

Founded in the 8th century, Evesham is a market town in the Wychavon district of Worcestershire, located equidistant between Worcester, Cheltenham and Stratford-upon-Avon. It has a population of 27,000.

Then Tamsyn Googled, *distance between Evesham and Mousehole.*

The answer surprised her: 245.4 miles.

"Who the hell is going to travel five hours to watch Mousehole against Evesham?" she muttered to herself.

It was hardly Tottenham versus Arsenal, but she also knew that sports fans could be rabid in support of their teams.

By the time 6pm rolled around, Tamsyn still hadn't heard about getting a PCSO, so she headed over to the tiny fishing village of Mousehole, pronounced *Mowzel,* and parked her police car at the far end of the car park, bonnet facing out. Then she radioed the control room to inform them that she'd arrived at the football club and was going into the ground.

Just as she stepped out of her patrol car, an ancient minibus wheezed and bounced into the car park. *Evesham United Supporters Club* was emblazoned in bold letters on the sides and back. The windows were dirty, but she could see that the occupants appeared to be in very good spirits.

Tamsyn stood back and watched as a jumble of colourful individuals staggered off the minibus, obviously having enjoyed the hospitality of a local pub or two along the way. But they seemed happy enough as they wandered into the grounds singing,

"I am a cider drinker

I drinks it all of the day."

She didn't think that twenty pensioners were going to cause her too much trouble. But then two more minibuses arrived, and ragged cheers rang through the car park.

By the time kick-off neared and the small ground gradually filled up, she estimated that some 250 Evesham supporters had arrived, and about the same number of locals.

And still no PCSO.

She radioed Control again but was informed that there was no one available to help her. She was on her own.

Tamsyn hoped that nothing was going to kick off – no pun intended – and that they'd all behave themselves.

Mousehole was the first team to run out to loud applause. Evesham followed, led by a tall guy with bright ginger hair. There was some jubilant shouting from the away-supporters, one of them turning to Tamsyn and saying, "Thats my lad, Jackson – they call him the Ginger Prince. He's single, by the way."

Tamsyn smiled politely and moved to a different part of the stands.

By half-time, the score was a thrilling 0-0 and Tamsyn was bored to tears. Unfortunately, she still had another 45 minutes of mind-numbing football to watch before she could finish her long shift and go home.

Supporters from both sides streamed towards the tiny bar, thirsty from shouting and singing, and eager to top up their liquid intake with a few pints of the local Rattler cider.

Over the PA speakers, she heard the announcer clear his throat and smiled when she recognised the gravelly tones of one of her grandfather's fishing buddies.

"We're very grateful to Pengelly's of Porthleven for the donation of pies and pasties – don't forget to take one home for the missus," he said. "And we're very happy to see Devon & Cornwall Police in attendance. Well done, Tammy. Looking beautiful, my lovely!"

She felt 500 pairs of eyes focusing on her, gave a rather self-conscious smile and a brief wave as the small field echoed to loud cheers and wolf-whistles.

Thankfully, the sound was drowned out by music pouring from the speakers, the Wurzels' other big hit, *I've got a brand-new combine harvester*.

A 2025-registered Ford Ranger pickup nosed through the crowd and drove onto the pitch as music continued to thump from the PA system. Standing in the back of the pickup were two women about Tamsyn's age, dressed in a very skimpy approximation of Mousehole's football strip. Tamsyn didn't recognise either of them, and they didn't acknowledge her.

Tamsyn walked over to have a chat with the driver who was her grandfather's friend and also the part-time match announcer.

"Hello, Alf. How are you?"

"Fair to middlin', Tammy. How's you, maid? Joined the police, is it?"

"Did the uniform give it away?" she smiled. "Nice truck. Did you steal it?"

She wasn't entirely joking. Alf Worth had never had two pennies to rub together, so she didn't know how he could afford a brand-new vehicle worth more than £35,000.

"Now, now, Tammy," he said, tugging nervously at his short beard. "Don't you be making jokes like that, maid. Bought it fair and square, I did."

She raised an eyebrow.

"'Iss!" he insisted. "I sold my punt to a couple of foreigns."

Tamsyn laughed out loud.

"That old tub wasn't worth the price of a new pickup!"

"I knows that, Tammy. But I swear to you, they wanted it and I sold it."

Tamsyn's expression was doubtful.

"Grandad didn't tell me you'd given up crabbing."

"No, well," he sighed. "None of us are getting any younger and I've got the arthritis in my knees, see. Can't get to my crab pots anymore. They made me an offer I couldn't refuse," and he grinned at her, flashing the single tooth still attached to his upper gums.

"Really? How much did they pay you?"

"Is this official?" he asked, licking his lips.

She stared back at him.

"Well, they paid cash," he admitted. "I didn't ask no questions."

"What did they want with your old punt?" Tamsyn asked.

"Couldn't say. A fool and his money are soon parted. But I heard that my old *Penrose Pride* was seen up Newquay way."

That definitely caught Tamsyn's attention.

"When was this?"

Alf pulled off his woolly hat and scratched his matted hair.

"Couple of nights ago. Jonas Jedna tole me and someone 'ad tole him. You know ole Jonas, do 'ee?"

Tamsyn nodded. Jonas Jedna was the nightwatchman at Newlyn Harbour. He didn't chat much, as a rule, but he always had a finger on the pulse of the fishing community. Tamsyn made a note to check what Jonas might have heard.

"Where were these foreigners from?" Tamsyn asked. "Do you have a phone number for them? How did they contact you?"

Alf held up his hands.

"Steady on, Tammy! Let a man think."

She waited impatiently while he pulled out a battered mobile phone with cellotape criss-crossing its cracked screen.

"I don't know how they heard about the *Pride*, but that's the number they called me on. They was young, perhaps 40 or so, tanned faces, but they weren't no fishermen, I can tell you that much."

Tamsyn wrote down the brief descriptions. She was so intent on making notes, she didn't notice that the level of noise in the football ground had risen sharply.

A mixture of drunken rivals and barely-dressed women was not a great combination at the best of times. But when the two women started lobbing pies and pasties into the crowd as a giveaway for the supporters, Tamsyn was too late to stop them.

It might have been okay if the ensuing food fight just meant the destruction of a few pies, but unfortunately, the pies and pasties were still frozen and had quickly been turned into missiles.

All hell broke loose: pies were being thrown at the women in the pickup, they were screaming, Alf was screaming as dent after dent marked his new truck. He put the truck into gear too quickly, and both of the women fell backwards with their legs waving helplessly in the air. The sight of this set the crowd off to a new level of vulgarity and determination to throw the food further.

The football ground resembled a war zone: Seagull supporters were throwing pasties at the Robins supporters, who in turn were throwing them back. Others had their phones out filming, and Tamsyn was stuck in the middle.

A pasty missile hit her helmet as she pushed her PTT and shouted into her Airwave radio, "ASSISTANCE! ASSISTANCE REQUIRED AT MOUSEHOLE FOOTBALL CLUB! THE CROWD ARE RIOTING WITH PIES AND PASTIES!"

CHAPTER 9

Rego had spoken to his Federation Rep who asked him to send him over a copy of the complaint notice, and then made an arrangement to meet up with him so they could discuss the allegations.

But Rego knew how insidious an allegation of theft could be. He'd seen good officers worn down by the side glances, the innuendo, and their inability to disprove something that had never happened in the first place.

At least he hadn't been suspended. But it pissed him off no end to hear how that knob, Lloyd, was ruining his case. If it carried on the way it appeared to be currently going, Viljoen's death would be ruled an 'accidental drowning', implicitly agreeing that the woman had committed suicide. But for Rego, there were too many loose ends, too many questions that remained unanswered – and he didn't even have the distraction of being with his family to take his mind off it.

Cassie had gone back north, taking the kids to stay with her mother for a few days. His rented cottage was lonely without all their noise, clutter, chaos and laughter, and there was only so much admin he could do and reports he could read at work before his eyes crossed and his brain melted.

Bloody Lloyd! The man would be out of his depth in a puddle.

Fed up and eyes aching, Rego hooked his suit jacket off the back of his chair and left the station on foot.

It was pleasantly warm as he strolled through the tangle of tiny alleyways called *opes* towards a backstreet in Penzance where he knew he could find a quiet curry house. He intended to enjoy some good food, and brood, well away from curious gazes.

The restaurant was empty this early in the evening, so he had his choice of tables. He chose one towards the rear where no one could sneak up behind him, and where he could see everyone entering before they saw him. He wasn't expecting any trouble, but it was a habit that he had no intention of breaking.

His top button was already undone and his tie loose. He yanked it off without unknotting it and shoved it in his pocket, then slung his jacket over the chair next to him.

The owner of the restaurant walked across with his hand outstretched in a genuine welcome, and Rego thought again that there were bonuses to being a regular, although he came to the Taj Mahal less often when Cassie and the kids were at the cottage.

Rego half stood, offering his hand, but winced as he caught his thighs on the table, shifting it about six inches forward.

"Good evening, Inspector Rego. How are you, sir?"

No matter how many times Rego had asked Suresh to call him by his first name, the older man never did.

"Hungry," Rego admitted with a smile. "I've been craving your Chicken Balti and Keema Naan."

"And a Cobra beer?"

"Not tonight. I'll be driving later."

"Of course, Inspector."

"How's business, Suresh? The world treating you well?"

The man bowed his head.

"The elephant came, but there is no bridge," he sighed. "Not as many tourists this year."

Rego commiserated for a few minutes then placed his order. He knew what he wanted and didn't even have to glance at the laminated menu.

Suresh hurried away to the kitchen as soon as he'd placed four poppadoms with sauces in front of Rego.

Missing his family but enjoying a solo brooding session, Rego took a guilty pleasure in smashing the poppadoms into pieces with the flat of his hand and generally making a hell of a mess. Cassie went mad when he did that, especially as their son had started copying him. But tonight, he was in the mood for a small if childish rebellion.

The steaming food arrived and Rego ate hungrily, using his fingers to dip the wafer-thin pieces into each of the sauces in turn.

Once he'd taken the immediate edge off his hunger, he wiped his hands, pulled his mobile phone from the inside pocket of his suit jacket and propped his phone up against the sauce server.

Part of the reason for wanting a bit of solitude was to FaceTime Vikram. He pushed his earbuds into place and dialled.

Vikram answered on the fourth ring.

"Bloody hell, Rob, FaceTime? What are you, thirteen?"

"I wanted to see a friendly face."

"Where are you?" Vikram asked, squinting to see the background.

"Out having a Cornish curry," Rego said smiling. "Chicken Balti, half rice, half chips, Keema Naan and egg fried rice."

"You heathen," Vikram grimaced. "I thought I'd taught you better than that half rice, half chips malarkey. All those times we were out on Ladypool Road in Birmingham, the Balti capital of the universe and you've learned nothing! I took you to proper curry houses."

Rego laughed for the first time since he'd been made aware of the complaint against him.

"I know, Vik, they were bloody hot! I had to put the bog roll in the freezer before I went out." He sighed. "But this is Cornwall, and I'm starving and pissed off. I know, I know, whinging git! I think I'm just feeling sorry for myself. I'm missing Cassie and the kids, *and* there's been this suspicious death *and* I've had the investigation taken off me *and* I've got a knob of an ACC who's..." Rego paused. "I'm trying to think of a word that describes him – you know, someone who got to the top on the back of other cops' hard work. I'm properly fucked off, Vik."

Rego looked around, checking that Suresh or none of the other staff could hear him, his voice rising with his aggravation.

"Sometimes I think about going back to Manchester."

"Seriously? I thought you loved living in the land of cream teas and pasties."

"Mostly, but sometimes ... it's not always easy being the only gay in the village."

"Did you call me to say that you fancy me, Rob, cos you're not my type."

"You'd be so lucky, mate. No, I just mean that I get why Cassie is worried about the idea of moving the kids down here – it's not exactly the most ethnically diverse place. She's worried about the kids getting bullied and she might not be wrong."

"Kids are feral wherever they are," said Vikram with the certainty of someone who didn't have kids and wasn't bothered by the fact. "If a kid's going to get bullied, the bullies will find a reason: too short, too fat, rubbish at sport, wrong clothes, short-sighted, too black, too white, too whatever. Max and Maisie will be fine. Maybe it's really about Cassie – maybe she doesn't want to leave Manchester and her mum. Your mum's up there too, mate. Look, you've done nearly 18 months in Cornwall – you went there to get a broader experience of policing. You've done that – if you want to go home, you can go with your head held high."

Vikram paused.

"Or is there another reason that you're suddenly feeling homesick?"

Rego smiled. There were no flies on Vik.

"Might be," he admitted. "Do you remember Trevor Albutt?"

"Course I do. He was a top bloke."

"Yeah, he was. And he finished up Detective Chief Superintendent Operational Support just after you left GMP. Trev got to the top by bloody hard work; everyone loved him. Anyway, he sent me a message the other day saying there's going to be a get-together in September for my old team. He wanted to know if I could make it. I was halfway through messaging him back when I thought rather than play text ping pong, I'd give him a ring. Trevor was always good at listening and he was in the job a lot of years. I sounded off to him about the de Jeles complaint and being taken off the Viljoen investigation, and he said to take a positive from it, in that when the enquiry stalls or gets fucked up, they'll soon come running. Then he says, 'crime ain't going to stop in Cornwall with this job – there's lots of dirtbags around the next corner'."

They both laughed, remembering more of Trevor Albutt's salty sayings.

"Are you going to the reunion?" Vikram asked.

"It wouldn't hurt to show my face and perhaps reach out to see if there's still a job for me if it doesn't work out down here. I'll have a few beers and get to see Cassie, Bill, and the kids. I'm not sure if that came out in the right order though!"

"At least you put Cassie at the top of the list. If she'd come after the dog, well I hate to tell you, mate, but people have been divorced over less."

Rego laughed, but he knew that he owed Cassie a lot. It hadn't been easy on her, keeping the family together when he'd taken a promotion three-hundred miles away in Cornwall.

"Go for it, Rob," Vikram advised. "Blow off some steam. There'll be loads more cases that come your way – our work is peaks and troughs, you know that. And we make ourselves better by questioning ourselves. We get so engrossed in what we do, we get blinkered and sometimes don't see the bigger world. Bollocks to your bloody ACC Gray! You have the support of the Chief, that's what counts. And now you've got the measure of the ACC, you can deal with him."

Rego lowered his voice.

"Do you have any news for me?"

"Not about your ACC, I'm still working on that, but I have something on the Viljoen case."

Rego ran a hand over his short hair, frustrated and impatient.

"You couldn't mention that first?" he asked sarcastically.

"You've just spent half-an-hour moaning at me because you're off the case," Vikram pointed out.

"Fuck's sake, Vik!"

"Hear me out, buddy. There were no hits on the Law Enforcement Database or anywhere else when you checked out Viljoen's name, right?"

Rego nodded.

"But when you entered his cisgender name, Ryan Kloppers, it raised so many red flags, I thought I was watching a Millwall game."

Rego sat up straighter.

"And?"

"As Ryan Kloppers, he'd come to the attention of the Hawks in Pretoria."

The Hawks were a specialist police unit in South Africa; they'd been established after the political transition of 1990, specifically to deal with the unchecked rise of organised crime.

"The Hawks were watching Kloppers?" Rego asked quietly.

Vikram shook his head.

"No, mate. Kloppers was one of their assets. He was a confidential informant who was working for an OCG called Black Axe."

Rego lowered his voice still further.

"I've heard of them, but I thought that Black Axe were the Nigerian mafia, not South Africa?"

"Yeah, but they've been expanding right across the whole continent," said Vikram, his expression worried.

"Drugs?"

Vikram shrugged.

"Drugs, prostitution, gambling, people-trafficking, cybercrime, guns: buying, not selling. The Hawks have been trying to infiltrate them for years."

"Holy shit!" Rego murmured.

He sat back, his mind whirring as he considered the intel Vikram had just dropped in his lap.

"It would be a hell of a coincidence if Viljoen really did kill herself."

"Maybe yes, maybe no," said Vikram thoughtfully. "Maybe the pressure got to her and what with the online trolling as well, it all became too much."

Rego shook his head.

"I hear what you're saying, Vik, but my gut says otherwise."

"I'm inclined to agree with you," Vikram said quietly.

"What I don't understand is Viljoen's role in all this," Rego said thoughtfully. "Black Axe is a predominantly black crime gang. Why bring in a transgender surfer who's white? You can't get much more high-profile than that. Unless..."

"Unless what?"

"Overt to be covert."

Vikram whistled between his teeth and nodded in understanding.

"Of course! Because she's so high profile, no one would think she's involved with an organised crime gang. Mate, I think you're onto something. And Black Axe have been taking some heavy hits over the last few years. I've spent the day looking into them – they were badly damaged by Ireland's Garda National Economic Crime Bureau in 2020."

"Of course! That's where I've heard about them. But I thought only a handful of Black Axe members were arrested there?" Rego said.

"True, but the operation paved the way for the exposure of a far wider network. Last summer, Operation Jackal III was coordinated across 21 countries, made more than 300 arrests, and seized assets in the millions." Vikram shrugged. "They're always looking for new business opportunities."

Rego considered for a moment.

"But I still don't get how Viljoen ties into all this. What exactly was she doing for Black Axe?"

"Reading between the lines," said Vikram, "I get the feeling that the Hawks had lost control of her. Maybe she had the opportunity to make real money in her own right as a transgender surfer winning women's surfing events; maybe she just wanted out, like you said."

Rego gazed at his friend. He could tell that Vikram's massive computer-like brain was working on another idea.

"Or?"

Vikram grinned at him.

"Maybe Viljoen was a token."

"Token what? Token transgender athlete?"

"Nah, mate. Trust between criminals has to be earned over many years, yeah? But with all the hits on Black Axe recently, they've had to rebuild their organisation in a hurry, so maybe there's a trust issue with their new suppliers. And with the value of commodities that they're dealing in running into hundreds of thousands of pounds or millions of pounds, you have to make sure that the commodity is going to the person that ordered it."

"Okay, and...?"

"As a general rule, the person who's got the commodity in their possession is responsible for it, so if it gets stolen or seized by law enforcement, you'll be responsible to reimburse the seller."

"Or things get violent quickly," Rego said grimly.

"Too bloody right," Vikram said darkly.

"And they need a system to ensure the person receiving the commodity is who they say they are," Rego added, nodding as he followed Vikram's reasoning.

"Got it in one. So, they exchange a 'token' like a serial number from a bank note, because those are totally unique."

"Yeah, I know all this, Vik," Rego said impatiently.

Vikram did his best (worst) Yoda impersonation: "Patient must you be," ignoring Rego's muttered comment of, "Fucking get on with it."

"Black Axe are known for using encrypted message platforms to send a picture of the banknote's serial number so when the courier meets the buyer, the buyer will hand the original bank note to the courier, who, when satisfied, will hand them the commodity. If the note isn't handed over, the deal is off. The courier will have a copy of the image of the bank note on their phone."

Rego sat up straighter.

"We haven't found Viljoen's phone. It wasn't on the body or in her room. I asked her manager, Phil Ford, about it but he denied knowledge. There was something off about him though. He seemed a bit too..."

"Too what?" asked Vikram.

"Let's just say that the Fords were very keen to say that Viljoen had committed suicide. And one or two things about them didn't add up."

"Such as?"

"They kept saying that Viljoen was making some serious money, but when I asked about sponsors, they couldn't pull any big names out of the hat, and when I checked, her prize money was only a few thousand Rand to date, but they were paying for two hotel suites at £700 a night each ... and then they started a crowdfunding page to pay for repatriation of Viljoen's body. I need to question them again and..."

Then Rego remembered that he wasn't on the case anymore and lapsed into silence.

Vikram gave him a moment, then continued.

"Viljoen's phone could be the key to this, Rob. Especially if Black Axe were paying for their *commodities* in Bitcoin. In circumstances where it's a new customer or there's a lack of trust, a further level of security is built in. The OCG providing the commodity would probably send two trusted members of their gang. One will carry the commodity – the 'dirty car' and one will be 'clean'. At the initial point of contact, the 'clean' car will meet the buyer at a pre-arranged location. The 'dirty' car with commodity will be parked nearby. So, the 'clean' car will meet the buyer and check the token number is correct. The buyer will then be redirected to the location where the 'dirty' car is, where the exchange will go ahead. This system ensures that at the initial point of contact the courier isn't robbed."

"You keep saying 'car', Vik," Rego said quietly. "But what if it's not a car? What if it's a boat?"

Vikram's eyes widened.

"Bloody hell!"

"A boat was seen close to the shore the night Viljoen died," Rego said slowly.

Another idea tickled at the back of Rego's brain. It seemed crazy, but still ... exchanging a commodity on a boat would be a really clever and very safe option for anything criminal. No one would be able to surprise them, so they wouldn't get jumped and robbed by a third party, and if the police were on to them, they'd have a nifty way of getting rid of anything at the bottom of the sea in a location that was very tidal. But then again...

If Viljoen was making a living with her surfing, and also had some side gig with the people on the boat and had successfully made an exchange, killing herself made no sense.

What did make sense? That her cover as an informant was blown? That one of the competition surfers killed her?

Had someone else been on the water that night, someone Tamsyn hadn't seen?

Where was her surfboard and why had she unleashed it? Where was her phone? The lab had confirmed that the white powder in her stomach was sleeping pills, but how had they got into her system? Had she done it herself or had someone tampered with her food? So many loose ends...

"Just playing Devil's advocate," Vikram interrupted Rego's unfinished thoughts. "You need to get back on the Viljoen case, asap."

Rego gave a bitter laugh.

"I'd love to, but Dritan Domi has got me stitched up tighter than a kipper."

Vikram smirked at him.

"Come on, Rob! Use your head for something other than hanging your hat on. Aderito de Jeles worked for Besnik Domi, the baby brother of the Hellbanianz crime boss, who you just happened to bump off..."

"That was Tamsyn," Rego interrupted moodily.

"...and de Jeles makes the allegation about you after seven months in prison, and you don't smell something fishy about it?"

"Jesus, Vik! I know Dritan Domi is at the root of this, but I can't *prove* it!"

"No, but ask yourself why de Jeles is coming out with this bullshit now. Who has Domi senior put pressure on? De Jeles himself? His wife? Kids? Mother? Pet dog? You find out the pressure point, and you can get him into witness protection."

"I don't have that kind of clout," Rego scowled. "Especially now."

"Maybe not, but I'm hearing whispers that the Secret Service are pressing hard to make a deal with de Jeles for more intel on the Hellbanianz's smuggling routes." Vikram nodded at the interest on Rego's face. "Yep, and de Jeles is currently in Exeter prison so Devon & Cornwall Police can interview him with his solicitor about his allegation against you..."

Vikram left the sentence hanging.

"There might be a way to make him withdraw the allegation," Rego finished for him.

"Bingo!"

CHAPTER 10

Tamsyn didn't know what to do with the information she'd learned at the football match. If Inspector Rego had still been on the Viljoen case, she would have spoken to him immediately.

Of course, she knew that she could, that she *should* take what she'd learned to DI Lloyd, but she hadn't liked him when she met him and she hadn't felt heard by him. He'd been curt and dismissive while she'd been reeling from shock and exhaustion.

As for her other options: her best friend, Jess, still wasn't speaking to her; and Tamsyn still wasn't speaking to Joe; Rego was off the case; and Sergeant Terwillis had one foot out of the door prior to his retirement. All her colleagues on E-Team were in Newquay, either at Boardmasters or patrolling in the town; and she preferred to avoid talking about her work with her grandparents – they'd been pulled into enough of it in the past.

The decision was made for Tamsyn when her phone rang again and Joe's name showed on the screen, a FaceTime call. She let it ring three times before she decided to answer it.

"Hi," she said shyly.

"You're talking to me again! Thank fuck," Joe laughed.

And just like that, Tamsyn let go of her anger at him. She knew that she'd been wrong, childish, to ghost him just for agreeing with Inspector Rego that she needed time off. She'd expected him to be holding a grudge because sometimes she forgot that Joe was a fully formed adult, not one of the man-boys she'd dated in the past. Joe had been a Royal Marine before he'd become a police officer, plus he was a hands-on uncle to two little boys, held a dangerous and responsible job, and had a range of life experiences that made him resilient, determined and compassionate.

She wanted to talk about what she'd learned at the football match; she wanted to hear his thoughts about the Viljoen case; she wanted to feel his arms around her and his warm, strong body pressed against hers in bed.

And for reasons that escaped her, he seemed ready to put up with all her insecurities, lack of confidence and lack of experience; he seemed to understand her, to want her. And although he'd indicated that he'd wait for her to catch up, he was also gently pushing for a commitment and intimacy that scared her.

For once, she voiced something of her real feelings.

"Why do you put up with me, Joe?"

"Wow, that's a deep question for a Tuesday lunchtime," he said, smiling.

"It's Saturday."

"Is that right?" he chuckled.

"I'm sorry," she said immediately. "My head's all over the place. Forget I said anything."

He looked at her thoughtfully, his grey eyes serious.

"What's going on, Tam? What's going on in that beautiful head of yours?"

"Jess won't talk to me," she blurted out. "She's so mad that I let her down about moving in with her."

"That wasn't your fault," he said reasonably. "She knows that and she'll come around."

"I don't know, I don't think so. She said I didn't do anything except let her down. And she's right! I'm always cancelling doing things with her because I'm working overtime or on shitty night-shifts and I'm tired and moody."

"She'll come around," he repeated. "She's just disappointed. She loves you, Tam. You've been best friends your whole lives."

"She's better off without me," Tamsyn said, her throat tight. "I'm tired of losing people I love. I can't do that anymore. I'm sorry."

"What are you saying?"

"I don't know. I'm a mess right now."

He was silent, pensive, his face grave.

"You haven't lost Jess. And Rosie dying, well, that was shit, but it wasn't your fault."

"Wasn't it? Cal thinks so. She was killed because of me – because someone thought she *was* me."

"That's on the evil bastard with the knife, Tam. It isn't your fault and Cal doesn't blame you."

"I wish I could believe that."

"Tam..."

"It's not just that – it feels like everything is falling apart, and I feel trapped."

"Is this about the cottage?" he asked. "Just because your grandparents put it in your name, it doesn't mean that you have to live there forever; they just want to give you a safety net. Anyway, you could get sent to Plymouth or Exeter to experience a different type of policing, and you have to live within half-an-hour of your nick."

Tamsyn paused to consider that, and Joe continued talking.

"I mean, I could apply for a transfer down there too, and we could spend more time together."

Tamsyn's shock was very real, and her voice was very small.

"You'd do that for me?"

"In a heartbeat ... if you asked me to."

Tamsyn was taken aback. The conversation had started in one direction then gone in another direction entirely. She'd never thought of leaving Cornwall and she'd never thought that Joe would be prepared to leave London, and yet here he was, offering to change his world for her.

"What if it didn't work out?" she said quietly.

"What if it did?" he countered. "Look, I know that since Rosie died..."

"Rosie was murdered because they thought it was me!"

He continued talking over her outburst.

"Since Rosie died, you've been treading water, but she wouldn't want you to stop living your own life. Dying is just the end of living. Are you saying you'd rather not have had Rosie in your life even though it wasn't for very long?"

"No, I'm not saying that."

But maybe I am.

"Then what?" he asked gently. "You and me, we do a job that has risk to it every day, but people get killed crossing the road or falling off a ladder clearing their gutters, but it doesn't mean you don't cross the road or let the gutters get blocked." He paused. "Or are you saying it's me you don't want?"

Tamsyn's heart jolted and she swallowed hard.

"No, I'm not saying that."

He gave her a relieved smile.

"I'm glad we've got that sorted out. I'm not going

anywhere, Cornwall. Now, apart from Jess and the cottage, what else has got your knickers in a twist?"

Despite herself, she smiled, and went on to tell him about what she'd learned at the football match.

When he'd finally finished laughing at her description of being pelted by half-frozen pasties, seagulls clearing away the evidence of mayhem, and the other officers in Penzance police station who'd greeted her by singing,

"I am a pasty eater!

And I eat pasties all day"

Joe told her to take the intel to Inspector Rego.

"He's a good bloke, Tam. He'll take you seriously."

"But what about this allegation that he withheld evidence? I just can't believe it."

"Then don't," he said sagely. "It sounds to me like he's being stitched up. It happens more often than you'd think – some jumped up snot-rag of a crim tells his brief that he's been bopped on the conk or had his feelings hurt by being called a nasty name, and every bleeding-heart liberal with a law degree is calling for your suspension. Just about every copper has to go through it, Tam. All the good ones – especially the good ones. I shouldn't think that more than one per cent of them ever have reasonable doubt, let alone grounds for a criminal charge. It'll happen to you if you stay in the job long enough."

He paused.

"Your Inspector seems on the level. Take what you've found to him – he'll know what to do with it. And I know you're off today and tomorrow, but it's not something you want to leave too long."

Tamsyn nodded slowly.

"You're right. As long as I've told him, it's up to him or

MCIT what they do with the information." She smiled. "Thanks for listening, Joe. Sorry I've been such a bitch."

"Yeah, but you're my bitch, right?"

Tamsyn laughed out loud.

Half-an-hour later, she was knocking tentatively on Inspector Rego's office door. Even though it was a Saturday, he was sitting behind a column of towering files, looking tired and more pissed off than she'd ever seen him.

"Is this a bad time, sir?" she asked, already backing out of the door.

"God, no! I need a break from all this paperwork," he yawned, stretching out his back and massaging his neck. "Come on in, Tamsyn. Sorry I can't offer you a Cornish pasty," and he grinned at her.

She rolled her eyes and smiled. "You heard about that?"

"Are you kidding? The whole of D&C Police has heard about it. There's even a meme somewhere – hashtag *#pastypolice*."

"Great," she sighed.

"So, what can I do for you?" he asked, leaning back in his chair.

"It might be nothing," she said cautiously, "but when I was at the football match, I bumped into a friend of Grandad's, Alf Worth, and he was driving a brand-new Ford Ranger pickup truck. He said he'd sold his punt and bought that instead."

"Okay, and...?"

"And his punt was worth a few thousand pounds – a new Ford Ranger is at least £35,000. I checked."

Rego leaned forwards, his gaze narrowing on her.

"He told me that the people he sold it to were 'foreign', in their forties, and definitely not fishermen. This is the number they called him on to make the deal."

She slid the number across the desk to Rego.

"And then he told me that his punt, *Penrose Pride*, had been seen up Newquay way by someone who told Jonas Jedna, the nightwatchman at Newlyn Harbour – and Alf thinks it was on the night Erin Viljoen died. So, I couldn't help wondering why anyone would pay six or seven times over the odds for Alf Worth's old punt, cash in hand, and they weren't even fishermen. It sounds hinky to me – you know – dodgy."

"Did you show him the video from that night with the boat in the background?"

Her cheeks flushed.

"I'm sorry, I didn't think ... and it all started kicking off..." She paused. "Do you think it could be important?"

Rego met her eyes across the desk.

"Where can I find Alf Worth?"

Rego waited until Tamsyn had left his office and closed the door behind her.

Her instincts were good: the deal was definitely 'hinky', and he'd very much like to know why someone would pay way over the odds for a knackered old fishing boat, especially if they weren't local and weren't fishermen.

Rego stared at the phone number Tamsyn had given him. Much as he'd like to call the number that Alf Worth had provided, he knew that he couldn't. If he rang the number and it was answered, what could he say other than 'sorry, wrong number' and risk a potential criminal knowing that the number had been 'made' and ditching the phone.

No, he had to be cleverer than that – and he also had the advantage of a great team that he had learned to trust.

He called his DS and Tom Stevens answered immediately.

"Boss, this is completely shit! I can't believe they've kicked you off as SIO for that muppet Lloyd. He's making a complete Horlicks of the case!"

Rego smiled at the indignation in his sergeant's voice.

"Thanks, Tom, I appreciate your support but that decision came straight from the top. Although ... there is something you could do for me. I need you to run down a phone number..."

And he explained about the origin of the phone number, the *Penrose Pride*, and Tamsyn's concern.

"Run the number through telecoms and if it's a pay-as-you-go with no subscriber – as I'm guessing it will be – then that may well be a further line of enquiry where we could track it by cell site."

"You really think this is connected to the Viljoen case?" Stevens asked, lowering his voice as if he didn't want to be overheard.

"It's a line of enquiry," Rego said again. "If it's a coincidence, it's a damn strange one."

"I thought you didn't believe in coincidences, boss," Stevens said lightly.

"I don't," Rego replied.

Next, he called Vikram.

"You know it's a Saturday, Rob," he said grumpily.

"Yeah, yeah," Rego said impatiently and went through the same explanation.

"I've got my DS running it through telecoms, but I'd really like to know if it appears on your intelligence database or as a number that's cropped up on your phone intercepts," he said.

"Hmm, interesting," Vikram said slowly. "I'll look into it,

but you know that my involvement could make things difficult if you're able to bring the case to trial."

Rego sighed.

"I know, Vik, believe me I know. But it's a solid lead."

"I'm on it, brother," Vikram said and rang off.

Rego knew that his friend would be limited by what information he could legally pass on.

Whilst phone interception in the UK was lawful, it could never be evidential. When there was a live investigation involving phone interception, unless you were specifically trained to have the intelligence that came from it, you couldn't be told the information. It was against the law and could involve a prison sentence.

Which led to the frustrating situation where intelligence could only be released in a very raw state.

If the intercept heard that two people were planning a meet, and one says that they're driving a black Audi with a 21 plate and the other party says they have a grey BMW with a 68 plate, and to meet at 2pm on 1st July on Victoria Street, the intelligence released would be something like:

It is believed that there will be a criminal meeting between two unknown persons on or around the 1st July in the general area of Newtown.

And Victoria Street was in Newtown district.

The SIO would know the full intelligence, and it would be up to them to place staff in the general area of Victoria Street and ask them to commentate on any vehicles of interest. Then it would be up to the skill of the observing officers to use their street craft to ID the criminal meeting.

It was time-consuming, wasteful, and basically a shit way of trying to do the job, in Rego's opinion.

Most other police forces in the world were using telephone interception in evidence. He was of the belief that the UK could put a serious dent in organised crime gangs if they were able to use telephone interception in evidence. At this point in time, they could listen to all those calls involved until they were blue in the face, but couldn't use any of it.

This situation had solidified Rego's belief that Tamsyn had stumbled onto something – whether or not it was the mysterious fishing boat seen in the video footage, he didn't know and would definitely check, but even if it had nothing to do with the Viljoen case, it was certainly shady.

Probably nothing to do with Viljoen. Nothing that he needed to pass on to Lloyd.

Yeah, right.

A shady deal, proximity to a possible crime, at the very least a potential witness – Rego knew that he should pass on the lead to the SIO.

He spun around in his chair again, thinking, considering, maybe hoping for inspiration or some sort of justification for what he was contemplating.

Should, could or would?

He spun his chair a few more times, only stopping when it creaked ominously. Then he had another *fuck it* moment: he seemed to have had a few of those since he'd come to Cornwall. Maybe it was something about all the space here, the literal freedom of a rural and maritime county; maybe it was the metaphorical freedom that came with being an inspector.

Yep, decision made: Mr Alf Worth was going to get an up close and personal visit.

Rego was about to head out of the office and make enquiries about Mr Worth's purchase of his new pickup truck, how the 'foreigns' had heard about him in the first place, confirmation that the boat in the video was his, and anything else the bent old bugger might know about the people who'd financed his windfall.

But as he was pulling on his suit jacket, there was another knock at the door. Rego was surprised to see Assistant Chief Constable Sue Nash standing in front of him.

This couldn't be good. Assistant Chief Constables didn't visit lowly DIs in their office on a weekend unless it was serious. Was she going to suspend him?

"Ma'am," he said, leaping to his feet and straightening his tie.

"Sit down, Rob," she said. "Apologies for dropping in, but this had to be said face to face."

Rego swallowed hard.

In the seven months since ACC Nash had been part of Devon & Cornwall Police, she'd developed a good reputation, a copper's copper who'd come up through the ranks: tough but fair, strong but compassionate, never overbearing but commanding respect. Her reputation for integrity had followed her from West Mercia Police. In other words, she was the complete opposite of ACC Gray.

Rego held his breath.

"Now then, Rob," she said, folding her tall frame into the chair opposite him. "What's all this bollocks about €10,000 going missing on the de Jeles case?"

"Ma'am, I..."

She waited while Rego tried to order his thoughts.

"In your own time."

With as much clarity as he could muster, Rego explained the facts of the case, what he knew and what he suspected. Then he told her about Vikram's theories without naming the source of his information.

He hadn't planned on telling her about his own thoughts on the Viljoen case but found himself opening up to her. She listened without interruption and without judgement, leaning towards him, alert and fully engaged in what he was telling her.

"Anything else?" she asked at last, her penetrating gaze seeming to drill through him.

Rego shook his head.

"Right. Well, this is the situation: I was brought to D&C because the PEEL report downgraded us for our investigative and detection rates: they're shit. I told the Chief that he shouldn't allow a spurious complaint, with zero credibility, mean that one of our best investigators is taken off the Viljoen sudden death. His argument is that he can't have an officer with a serious complaint against him doing the investigating because the reporters might pick up on it. I told Chief he was being a knob and to grow a pair, but the optics don't look good."

She paused to draw breath.

"I had a chat with a former colleague of mine this morning," she said. "He happens to have a contact at *HMP Manchester* who's been tasked with monitoring Dritan Domi's calls," she said. "You and I both know that Domi wouldn't have any problem organising this attack on you from prison. The clever bastard speaks at least three languages plus his local Tosk dialect, so the theory is that he's been making the arrangements by dialling out to platform numbers and talking in all his languages which makes detection of this scam difficult. Prisoners are only allowed a certain number of contacts; the numbers must relate to family or friends, and must have dialling codes relevant to the region where they live. But I doubt all of the numbers have been checked out."

She gave an irritated shake of her head.

"Of course, all telephone conversations are recorded, and prisoners know this. However, Domi is almost certainly using a platform number which looks like a UK number because it has a UK dialling code. In reality, he could be dialling anywhere in the world, and since he's also speaking three or four different languages in each conversation, it's made translation very expensive and frustratingly slow. We also know that on several occasions he's called his mother in Albania, and his dear old mum has had another mobile at the ready so that he can hold a conversation with anyone he bloody well likes."

She huffed in frustration.

"Because of these tricks, I'm hoping to convince the Home Office to upgrade him from the Category B block to Cat A, preferably at a different prison, but don't hold your breath."

"Thank you for trying, ma'am," Rego began.

"I'm not finished," she said sharply.

"Here's what's going to happen. While we're waiting for the Home Office to wake up and smell the shit, I'm going to personally interview Mr de Jeles and find out who's been leaning on him – although we both know the answer to that, we need it on the record. Then I'm going to make him a deal he can't refuse, providing he withdraws the complaint against you."

"I might be able to suggest something else that might help, ma'am," Rego added. "I heard from ... a friend ... that the Secret Services are trying to get more intel on Hellbanianz smuggling routes, and I'm sure de Jeles must know more than he's said so far."

"How good is this intelligence?" she snapped.

"It's good, ma'am," he said, hoping she wouldn't ask him where it had come from because he couldn't, wouldn't tell her.

She gave him an appraising look, then nodded once.

"I want you back on the Viljoen case and so does DCS

Richards – as soon as possible, before it's completely cocked up." She pinned him with a look. "What *you* are going to do, Rob, is get your head out of your arse and follow up all the leads until we get a result. I'll make sure that Inspector Lloyd's reports make their way across your desk until you're officially back as the SIO. Clear?"

"Yes, ma'am."

"Good. Crack on then," and she barrelled out of his office.

Rego caught his breath as the door closed behind her, then smiled to himself. ACC Sue Nash had balls of steel.

CHAPTER 11

Tamsyn was determined to fix things with Jess, and seeing as her best friend was currently ghosting her, refusing all calls and texts, she decided to make an in-person, impromptu visit to her office.

She knew that Jess was hurt and felt let down, so Tamsyn deployed her best weapon in the struggle for reconciliation – underhand tactics: she brought Morwenna with her.

Jess had never been able to resist when the little dog turned those soulful, hopeful eyes on her.

Morwenna was delighted to go for a drive. She loved sitting in the front seat, her paws on the window sill, her head hanging out with her ears flapping furiously in the breeze, shaggy fur windblown into a go-faster look. And when they slowed down as they neared Porthleven, only her dog harness stopped her from diving out of the window to chase seagulls.

Tamsyn squeezed into a parking spot on Fore Street, praying that the handbrake of her ancient Fiat wouldn't let her down on the steep hill.

She lifted Morwenna out of the car and smiled as the little

dog danced down the street, heading straight into the estate agents which Jess's parents owned.

The shop didn't have any customers, only an older couple who stood outside studying various property details displayed in the windows.

By the time Tamsyn caught up with Morwenna, she was already sitting on Jess's knee, looking very pleased with herself.

"What do you want?" Jess snarled as she looked up at Tamsyn from her desk.

"To grovel, beg, and to apologise to my best friend," said Tamsyn quickly, before Jess could tell her to fuck off.

"And you thought sending Morwenna in first would soften me up?"

"Is it working?"

For a second, Jess's stony expression refused to crack, but then she let out a long sigh and gestured to the chair opposite, allowing Tamsyn to sit down.

"Bitch," Jess mumbled, as she continued to stroke the little dog who'd curled up on her knee.

"Cow-bag," Tamsyn replied.

Jess gave a reluctant laugh.

"I've missed your face. I hate it when we argue."

"I missed you, too," said Tamsyn. "And I'm sorry I let you down. I was completely blindsided by what my grandparents did – I honestly had no idea that they were going to put the cottage in my name."

Jess studied her minutely, then nodded.

"I know. I'm sorry I got all up in your grill."

"You've got to stop watching American films," Tamsyn teased her. "You're starting to sound like Al Capone."

Jess frowned. "Who's she?"

Tamsyn gaped at her.

"Seriously?"

"Ha ha! Gotcha," Jess grinned.

"Oh, very funny!" Tamsyn sighed. "God, I've missed you."

"Me, too," Jess admitted. "But guess what?"

And she pulled a set of front door keys out of her handbag.

The jangling noise disturbed Morwenna, who jumped down looking affronted then trotted off to the back of the shop to see if there was anything interesting in the agency's small kitchen.

Tamsyn cocked her head on one side as she gazed at the keys, then sudden realisation sent her eyebrows soaring.

"You're taking the flat anyway?"

"Yep!"

Jess popped the 'p' loudly.

"How can you afford it? Did you ... did you find someone to share with?"

"I did!" Jess grinned. "Me and Jason are moving in together next week!" and she squealed so loudly, the dog next door began to bark which set off Morwenna.

A sharp spike of envy seared through Tamsyn. And then she remembered what Joe had said to her about the cottage not being the prison she'd started to imagine.

"Wow! Congratulations!" she managed to say, summoning every ounce of enthusiasm that Jess deserved. "I'm so pleased for you guys. Jealous as hell, but really, really pleased. I didn't know it had got that serious between you two."

"Nor did I," Jess admitted. "But I was whinging to Jay about you letting me down," and she shot Tamsyn a rueful look, "and then he said why didn't he move in with me. I'm so excited!"

"Jason is a good guy," said Tamsyn. "I'm really pleased for you, Jess. I hope he knows how lucky he is."

She meant it: Jason was a good guy, a good officer, a good colleague. He'd started as a student officer on the same day as Tamsyn; and he'd known Joe when they were both in 40 Commando, the Royal Marines.

"He does," Jess grinned. "But I intend to remind him how lucky he is every frickin' day."

"What did your parents say?"

Jess shrugged.

"A bit surprised because they thought that you and me would be renting together, but they like Jay, so they're cool. What about you?" she asked, still smiling. "Have you forgiven Mr Sexy-pants yet?"

Tamsyn rolled her eyes.

"Yeah, but it was more me apologising to him." She cast a look at Jess. "I've been doing a lot of that lately."

Jess gave her a thoughtful look.

"You've changed since you joined the police. You're more..."

Tamsyn waited.

"You're more direct, like you won't take anyone's shit anymore. You used to be like a Golden Retriever, all smiley and eager to please. But now you've got this hard stare, like a Rottweiler or something, and you look like you're ready to bite. No offence to Morwenna."

"Um, thanks?" Tamsyn laughed uncertainly.

Jess shook her head.

"I'm saying it wrong. You know, you can be a little bit scary sometimes," Jess admitted, "but I'm so fucking proud of you, Tam. I've always been proud to call you my friend but now you're totally badass."

The words were heartfelt and touched every part of Tamsyn's being.

"God, I don't know what I'd do without you, bestie," Tamsyn murmured, emotion thickening her voice

Jess threw her arms around her.

"You'd be a dried up, miserable old hag with no friends."

"Probably," Tamsyn laughed, all too aware that it could be true.

"Anyway, make sure that you invite Joe to our house-warming party – Cal, too, if he'll come. It's going to be epic!" She looked at Tamsyn slyly. "And you and Joe can have the spare bedroom because Jason won't be using it, if you know what I mean."

The two women high-fived and Morwenna reappeared, crumbs around her mouth, and finally Tamsyn felt that all was well with the world again.

She wondered if the information she'd given to Inspector Rego had been useful. He'd told her that she had good instincts, but she knew that wasn't always the case.

Alf Worth had peered at the video from the night of Viljoen's death, then pulled on a pair of smeared spectacles and peered again. He scratched his beard, inserted a dirty finger under his minging woolly hat, scratched again, checked his fingernail for trace evidence, then conceded that, "Might be 'er.'

"Take another look, Mr Worth," Rego said, showing him an enlarged still taken from the video.

"Lookee, Inspector," the old man said anxiously. "It's not my fault theys a bit tuppence-ha'penny, if you know what I mean," and he tapped the side of his head. "The deal was fair and square – theys can't be complaining 'bout it now."

"I'm not interested in how you made your deal, Mr Worth," Rego said patiently. "But it's possible that your boat could have been involved in a serious crime."

"Geddon!" said the old man, his soft-boiled eyes widening in surprise.

"Confirming whether or not the boat in the picture is yours or was yours could be very useful to our enquiries." He paused. "After all, you have sold it, so it's nothing to do with you now, is it?"

"This an't 'bout the taxman then?" Worth asked suspiciously.

"I'll leave that to your conscience and I'm sure you'll do the right thing," Rego replied.

The old man gave a wide smile, flashing pink gums and a single snaggle-tooth.

"Fools and children tell the truth, Inspector."

Rego continued to stare at him.

"A'right, a'right. 'Iss! That's my boat. That's *Penrose Pride*, leaking wet ole tub, and I'm well shot of her."

"Thank you, Mr Worth."

It took every ounce of skill and patience that Rego possessed to extract each morsel of information about the men who'd paid over the odds for Alf Worth's old punt, but by the end, Rego was more convinced than ever that the 'foreigns' were involved in something shady, probably illegal, which may or not be connected to the Viljoen case.

He learned that there were two men: one was 'daft' and the other was 'teasy' or bad-tempered; he was the one who did all the talking and was probably the boss. Both were 'emmets', so not Cornish, and deeply tanned,

"But not as black as you, boy."

Rego didn't think the old man was trying to offend, so took no offence.

But no matter how many different ways he framed the question, Alf Worth consistently denied knowing how the men had known to contact him in the first place; he only knew that they'd called him on his mobile.

As Rego drove back to the station, he made three phone calls: one to the harbourmaster at Newquay to see if *Penrose Pride* had used the harbour in the last week, but after he was put on hold for several minutes, the answer came back as a negative.

Next, Rego left a message for the nightwatchman at Newlyn Harbour to find out who he'd spoken to about seeing Worth's old boat on the north coast.

And thirdly, he left a message on Tamsyn's phone, enlisting her help in talking to her grandfather.

"Ozzie has his ear to the ground. Ask him if the 'foreigns' that Alf Worth talked to have been seen hanging around at Newlyn. Worth says he has no idea how they got his mobile number or knew to contact him in the first place. That sounds dubious to me, so if you could sound out your grandfather, that would be helpful."

Tamsyn listened to Inspector Rego's message with a feeling of satisfaction: the information on Alf Worth must have been useful if he was asking her to follow up on it.

With nothing else to do and still feeling restless even after having fixed things with Jess, Tamsyn headed to Newlyn to speak to her grandfather.

The harbour was quiet at that time in the morning. Most of the fishermen landed their catch ready for when the fish market opened at 4am each morning. The graders and sorters would organise the day's catch by size and species, then prepare it for auction to restaurants throughout Cornwall and even further afield.

But for now, the working part of the harbour was all but empty, just a couple of leisure yachts bobbing on the sparkling water, their small crews making ready to cast off.

Morwenna ignored the sign that said 'no dogs' and trotted down the pontoon towards the *Daniel Day*.

Ozzie was staring out across the water, a crab pot at his feet. His powerful hands, gnarled and tanned to the colour of tea, were stilled, and he seemed lost in thought.

Oh, Grandad, when did you get so old?

Tamsyn stood in silence, her heart squeezing painfully. Gifting her the cottage he'd been born in was her grandfather's way of trying to protect her, to watch over her even after he was gone. For his whole life, he'd worked hard, gone out in all weathers to provide for her. Her grandmother scrubbed floors for other people and did twenty other jobs to make ends meet.

Tamsyn felt the weight of guilt. She hadn't wanted the cottage, still didn't in some ways, but she recognised it for the priceless gift it was: her future.

Morwenna trotted a few steps, then looked over her shoulder at Tamsyn, giving a short whimper of concern.

Tamsyn squared her shoulders and fixed a smile on her face.

"Coming, scruffalicious," she said.

Reassured, the little dog trotted along the pontoon, the tip of her tail waving like a flag.

Tamsyn's grandfather murmured something as Morwenna circled him, leaning down to give her hairy backside a good scratch.

"I wonder what brings my granddaughter down this a'ways?" he said to little Mo.

"She thought she'd come and see her grandfather," Tamsyn smiled.

He tugged at his long beard.

"Did 'er now? 'Spec she's got 'er reasons."

He ducked his head as she kissed him on the cheek, uncomfortable with public displays of any type of affection.

"Okay, fine," she said. "My DI has asked me to follow up on Alf Worth and *Penrose Pride*."

"Is that right?"

"Yep, so come on, Grandad. You know everything that goes on around here."

"Maybe I do and maybe I don't, but I minds my own business, maid," he said gruffly.

"I wouldn't ask if it wasn't serious," she said. "It won't get your friend into trouble..."

He gave a snort of amusement.

"Alf Worth can do that all by 'isself. He's been backsyfore ever since 'e was a chile." He cast her a look. "Alf an't never been one for the rules."

"Which means?"

"If you was a certain type of businessman," he said thoughtfully, "you'd know that Alf could do you a turn, no questions asked."

Tamsyn translated his elliptical way of speaking.

"He's bent."

"As a nine-bob note."

"So, if you wanted something dodgy doing, it wouldn't be odd for Alf Worth's name to come up?"

"Alf Worthless'd be top o' the list," Ozzie acknowledged.

Tamsyn thought about this for a while.

"Have you seen anyone down the pontoon who doesn't belong?" she asked.

"Tourist season," he muttered, a frown carving his lined forehead.

"Other than tourists."

He leaned back and clamped his unlit pipe between his teeth.

"There was this one fella come by, all-overish, he was."

"Nervous?"

Ozzie nodded.

"A foreigner?"

This time Ozzie shook his head.

"Don't reckon so. But not one o' us." He nodded to himself. "Not one o' us."

Tamsyn knew that could cover a lot of ground.

"How long ago was this?"

"'Bout a month before Alf got isself that new toy."

"What did he look like?"

"Black hair, thin face, all leary like."

"Beard? Glasses?"

"Not a proper beard – just that nasty rash o' hair that men wear nowadays."

"How old was he?"

"He wan't old, mebbe 30, 35?"

"What was he wearing?"

"Fashion police now, is it?" Ozzie asked, making Tamsyn smile. "Blue jeans and a white shirt." He paused. "Long sleeves rolled up, and a collar but no tie."

"Have you seen him since?"

"No."

"Any other strangers asking for Mr Worth? Anyone else I should know about?"

Ozzie considered the question for a moment then finally shook his head.

"Thanks, Grandad. Oh, one more thing – do you think you'd recognise the stranger again?"

He nodded slowly.

"Reckon I would, maid."

By the time Rego arrived back at his desk, he'd been given digital access to all of DI Lloyd's reports. ACC Nash didn't hang about, that was for sure.

There were already over a hundred new reports to read, including interviews with hotel staff, people on the beach that night, telephone analysis, CCTV, personal videos with a separate list of viewing logs: dates, times, and all the witnesses who'd been at Watergate Bay that night. Rego rolled up his sleeves and got stuck in.

He needed to conduct a forensic review, looking at all the evidential gathering opportunities to make sure they'd been maximised. Rego started reading, his frown deepening with each line.

The investigation wasn't bad as such, but Lloyd hadn't been good with some of the details and had let a few things slip through the net. There was a memory stick from the hotel's CCTV that hadn't been looked at properly; some fingerprints and DNA found in Viljoen's suite hadn't yet been sent off to the lab, and neither had fingernail scrapings taken from the deceased. But more damningly, the coroner had suggested to Lloyd that the bruising on the back of Viljoen's head and neck was from a shaped object and had specifically requested that a member of Lloyd's team search the suite for this. It hadn't been done and Lloyd hadn't thought it needed prioritising either.

Rego suspected that Lloyd hadn't followed up on these

things because he'd been single-track focused only on evidence that fit in with his theory of Viljoen's suicide.

That was short-sighted and sloppy.

After Rego had made a list of tasks to be acted upon or followed up, he began wading through Viljoen's social media. The trolling was absolutely vile with a number of anonymous posts saying that she deserved to be raped, sodomised, and murdered. Rego felt sickened by the people who thought they could post this hateful material with impunity.

Again, he made lists of Twitter posts to be analysed as part of the investigation. It was possible that the level of malice had pushed Viljoen into making a bad choice, but there was no doubt that the transphobic comments constituted a hate crime and would need to be investigated.

He made a note to put DC Jack Forshaw onto that.

But it wasn't cut and dried either. Some 80-90% of online posters supported Viljoen's choice and her right to transition, but that approval rating fell to around half when it came to allowing her to compete in women's sporting events. Although in the US, that sort of support for trans athletes fell to less than a quarter of people, if the polls were correct.

But Rego's overall view was that Viljoen had received far more support than not, which made blaming social media for a potential suicide even more spurious.

DI Lloyd had been pushing the coroner to record a verdict of 'death by misadventure'. Whilst that stopped short of Viljoen's death being recorded as a suicide, there was blame implicit – that Viljoen had voluntarily undertaken a risk that led to her untimely end, ie. taken a quantity of sleeping pills prior to going surfing, alone, at night.

Reading between the lines, Rego saw that everyone from the Chief Constable to the mayor to Viljoen's manager would be happy with that result. The coroner, however, was withholding a final ruling until his questions were answered to his satisfaction. The coroner made his ruling based on the post-mortem, not DI Lloyd's rather shaky assumptions.

Right from the start, he'd gone into the case assuming that Viljoen had killed herself, but that was a poor way to conduct a case because he was choosing the facts that supported his belief and ignoring the ones that didn't fit.

Lloyd had even put his thoughts in writing:

In my opinion, the death was a pure accident after the deceased had ingested a large quantity of sleeping pills.

The coroner had not been swayed and had written a report to that effect:

If the death of Ms Erin Viljoen is a result of suicide, I would have expected to see a note giving the reasons for her choice, especially in light of her celebrity and what has been found on various social media sites. Although she had ingested alcohol within an hour of her death, her blood-alcohol level was low, less than ten milligrams of alcohol per 100 millilitres of blood, which was not enough to cause significant impairment. The sleeping pills, however, were of such a high dosage, that she would have started to feel the effects within 20-30 minutes of ingesting them. Further, there is unexplained bruising on the top of the deceased's head and at the back of her neck; PC Poldhu's conversation with the deceased immediately prior to her going surfing showed no indication of suicidal tendencies; and the hotel manager, Mr Martin Caterham, stated that a member of his staff had taken an order for hot chocolate to be delivered to the deceased's room at 11.30pm. With all of these inconsistencies and unexplained points in mind I am not prepared to make a ruling at this time, and believe that the death of Ms Erin Viljoen needs further investigation.

More damningly, the coroner had complained with some asperity that he was, *not prepared to give a political verdict for the convenience of either the town of Newquay officials nor Devon & Cornwall Police.*

He was clearly unhappy at being put under pressure by Lloyd to make a ruling.

Rego couldn't help a grim smile, feeling vindicated in his suspicions.

And that was all before Rego had made the connection between Erin Viljoen and Ryan Kloppers: he'd just thrown the investigation wide-open again.

When Tamsyn texted him with her grandfather's description of the stranger who'd been looking for Alf Worth, he added it to the file along with the intel on Kloppers.

Then sat back and waited for more shit to hit the fan.

CHAPTER 12

Rego's suspicions about the Viljoen case were proving correct, but his satisfaction didn't last long when he realised that he had two months' worth of crime complaints to read through. If the files had been printed out, it would have meant the death of several trees.

It was a self-imposed task because Rego wanted to see how many had been filed where evidence-gathering opportunities had been missed. If he could establish some sort of pattern of a particular offence where nothing was ever done, then perhaps he could put in place a plan to get things changed.

He started with garden shed-burglaries between 10pm and 2am but not on weekends, where a number of tools, chainsaws and lawnmowers had been stolen. He made a plan of the geographical area, and suggested an increased police presence in those streets and a review of doorbell cameras, then emailed the information to Inspector Walters who was in charge of the uniformed officers and suggested they have a meeting.

What would help even more would be to get a trained analyst on the crime reports.

Not doing these sorts of analyses and the lack of lateral thinking had been at the heart of the criticisms from His Majesty's Inspectorate of Constabulary in their most recent report on Devon & Cornwall Police. But it was always a battle of time and resources against the sheer volume of crimes.

DC Mimi Eagling was the only trained analyst in west Cornwall, and although she'd be back at work soon, there would be more urgent demands on her time. No one else was available in the whole county, and if they were, they'd be working at full capacity already – good analysts were already as rare as rocking horse shit.

Rego wondered how Jen was getting on with the data analysis in the Viljoen case.

He leaned back in his chair and rubbed his eyes.

When Rego had started as a copper back in the dark ages a few years into the new millennium, crimes were still being recorded on self-carbonating paper documents, handwritten, with different copies going to different departments. Each document had character, a coffee stain, errors, crossings out, spelling mistakes, shocking handwriting that was sometimes barely legible, and making all the reports unique. But he also knew that the availability of digitised documents had been a massively positive progression.

Those that churned out stats loved it because they could produce charts at the click of a button. The downside was the sheer volume of data that needed to be analysed after collection, which didn't always happen: hence the need for more analysts. It was an ever-decreasing circle of frustration.

But as he trawled through files, Rego thought that there was another part of the pattern of thefts which was missing:

looking at low-value-high-volume crimes in a specific area … which had suddenly stopped. Shed break-ins, bike thefts – these were crimes typically perpetrated by drug addicts – so Rego decided to look at who had been arrested in that locality for similar crimes, then he'd get a detective to visit them in prison to try and identify if they'd committed those crimes but not admitted to them. Jen was particularly skilled at this – there was something warm and motherly about her that got the crims confessing to her while they were banged up.

The carrot dangled in front of the prison inmate was that if they owned up to the crime, it would be added to their sheet but without additional time added to their sentence – which also meant that the crime could be 'written off' as having been detected.

But if they didn't own up and additional evidence was subsequently found, they could be charged with additional offences which meant additional jail time, or affect their ERD, earliest release date.

It was a solid plan which the Chief could roll out to other detective teams across the county; and the Chief would probably get an OBE if he could show that crime-solve rates were climbing.

Rego's old boss used to say that the chivalry award Order of the British Empire colloquially stood for *Other Buggers' Efforts*; an MBE, Member of the British Empire was *Many Buggers' Efforts.*

Rego emailed Jen first and asked her to look into it when she'd finished with the Viljoen case – whenever that might be.

Sighing, he went back to work, this time plotting high-value car thefts in the area, and the way Major Crimes out of Camborne had been reporting the thefts. Land Rovers, Mercs, Beemers – all so nickable – and it didn't take that many thefts before adding up to a million pounds worth of property that had been stolen. Looking at them in isolation was a mistake and he soon spotted a pattern but needed to examine reports from a longer period of time to be sure. He was tempted to throw the work back to Lance Lloyd seeing as he was based at Camborne. Maybe he'd be able to scare up an extra analyst – after all, from the way the Viljoen case was going, Lloyd was about to have some spare time on his hands.

Nah, he'd have a chat with a colleague in Traffic and get them involved, maybe also suggest that Regional Crime take a look.

Just last month, Rego had been to a meeting of senior officers where the Chief Constable was obviously not impressed by the latest report that stated D&C Police were under-performing investigating crime. He thought the Chief was going to lose it during the presentation; Rego had watched him turning red, and he was making bets with himself whether or not they were all about to see an impersonation of Vesuvius, but in the end, the Chief had disappointed him by keeping the meeting professional.

To be fair, Rego knew that the police service was still trying to recover from Government spending cuts more than a decade earlier. The police had been hit hard, very hard, and as employees were the most expensive commodity, many forces, including Devon & Cornwall, used a police regulation rarely used before, Reg A19, to force police officers with more than 30 years' experience into retirement, aiming to reduce staff numbers. It meant that thousands of the most experienced officers were forcibly retired overnight.

It had been brutal.

But there'd been no public outcry, and Rego knew that a lot of those older officers were bitter about that. Nobody cared much about the police until they were a victim of crime or there'd been some major incident – then everyone wanted a police officer on hand.

The next blow had come from the College of Policing. Someone had decided that all new police officers must have a degree or an equivalent as part of their initial training.

Rego couldn't blame the kids who used this as a way to get a cheap degree then bugger off to make more money doing something safer elsewhere. Good luck to them, but it meant the force lost out again. And then, what could you do with a load of new graduate officers who were all looking for a quick promotion as soon as they'd earned their degree?

For sure, you needed the officers who could plough through the paperwork, enter and analyse the data, but you also needed the scufflers – the officers who were on the streets, nose to the scent, getting to know the local crims and where they did business. In other words, learning policing from the ground up.

When Chief Constable Evans had asked his staff how they could improve their crime response and solve rates, Rego wanted to put his hand up and say, "Stop promoting idiots, boss."

He was also tempted to suggest that the Chief reduce the amount of time that warranted officers could work from home. As his old sergeant had said when Rego was still wet behind the ears, "*You're not going to catch a thief while you're sat at home, son.*"

But Rego had enough sense of self-preservation to sit on his hands and keep his mouth firmly shut.

And if the work environment in the station was too distracting to be productive, then that was Rego's problem to fix. He couldn't create more space in the office, so he encouraged his team to wear headphones if they didn't want to be disturbed – it was a visual cue that they needed to concentrate. Besides, he trusted his team not to take the piss.

He sometimes wondered if he should have gone down the uniform policing route concentrating on Neighbourhood Policing. He'd have made every warranted officer do a day on the beat each month, ensuring that they maintained contact with people in the community. He fully approved of the concept of Neighbourhood Officers who were named, known, and available across a specified area. And for God's sake – promote Neighbourhood Watch! Nothing was more helpful to the reduction of crime than a nosy neighbour.

His mum had started a Neighbourhood Watch group in her street. Rego knew that his mother was a formidable woman who would move mountains to get her own way, and the local police had seen an immediate reduction in petty crime. Unfortunately, since Patricia Rego had been treated for cancer, she hadn't had her usual energy, and without her driving the project, the team had fallen by the wayside.

Rego's smile slipped – his mum was in remission and getting stronger each day, but she missed having her only son nearby. He felt shit about it, but short of calling it quits in Cornwall and moving back to Manchester...

And the truth was, although he loved Cornwall, it was hard having his family so far away. He thought Cassie was softening in her attitude to moving to the southwest, but she hadn't given in yet. She was thinking about it, but it was a big decision.

His thoughts drifted to Tamsyn and the tight bond with her grandparents. The Poldhus were a close-knit family – cut one, and they all bled.

Tamsyn was a good officer, but still young with a lot to learn. Her reaction when she'd been pulled from her TPO role showed it. He'd known that she'd be pissed off, but it was the right decision. She'd experienced more death in her short service than many other officers had in their whole career. He knew that she'd been seeing a police counsellor, but he wasn't her line manager and wasn't privy to whether or not the events leading up to the counselling had negatively impacted her mental health, and whether or not the sessions had helped her.

If he was honest with himself, he didn't really know her well enough to gauge with any certainty how she was faring.

Yes, they'd shared some intense cases, life and death moments, and he knew that she was resilient with real inner strength when it came to the crunch – but in his opinion, knowing someone, *really knowing* them, was about seeing if their behaviour had changed in the work environment and socially. And alongside that, she was less than two years in service, and Rego also acknowledged that being a police officer changed you. Although you probably didn't see it yourself, you had to toughen up. But he had no idea how she was coping outside of work.

He shook his head – she'd get over the disappointment, and there was always Boardmasters next year to hone her TPO skills. One day, she might even realise that taking her off TPO duties this year was in her best interests.

Although, to be fair, she'd passed on the information about Alf Worth, which was a good lead and showed that her head was still in the game.

Rego continued to trawl through files for two hours before he started to get a headache and knew it was time for a break. He caught his reflection on the computer screen and reckoned he looked even worse than he felt.

"God, I'm getting old," he grumbled to himself.

He was on the wrong side of 35, and if he would only

admit it to himself, he needed glasses to read the small print these days, but vanity had kept him from getting an eye test. Cassie had even gone so far as to book one for him, but he'd cancelled twice because something had come up at work. Of course.

Maybe he just needed to cut down on coffee and get some more exercise; maybe he should stop having a lie-in instead of going for a run, or maybe take up surfing. He and Max could learn together.

Rego promised himself that as soon as his kids were back from his mother-in-law's, he'd make the effort.

He leaned back, hands clasped behind his head, spinning his swivel chair round a couple of times, pushing it to the limit of collapse, before making up his mind to go for a stroll to clear his head.

The office was hot and oppressive. Usually, a sea breeze kept the air fresh, but for the last few days, Cornwall had sweltered in a heatwave that was sweeping the whole country. Flags in the harbour hung limply, the sea was flat as a millpond, and swarms of jellyfish were drifting onto the beaches.

Rego was reaching for his suit jacket when another email dropped in his inbox. He scanned the headline and couldn't resist sitting down again and reading the attached report.

Apparently, no one had informed the IT department that Rego was no longer the Senior Investigating Officer on the Viljoen case, so information obtained from her missing phone's number had gone straight to Rego.

If they had the actual phone rather than just the number, there'd be far more intel, but there was enough to pique Rego's serious interest.

Viljoen and the Fords had flown into Heathrow three days before Boardmasters, rented a car at the airport, then driven down to Newquay. But two days later, the day before the competition began, instead of checking out the local waves, Viljoen's mobile had pinged off a number of phone masts 250 miles away in the Midlands industrial heartland.

The IT tech had been able to show that from Birmingham's New Street train station, Viljoen had either caught a bus or was picked up by a car or taxi, but hadn't walked. Without CCTV verification, there was no way of knowing her mode of transport. If they'd had the phone handset, they could have checked for an Uber app.

The tech believed that Viljoen had been SIM-swapping – going back and forth between two SIM cards. Many phones were built dual-SIM so you could swap SIM cards within the phone settings. Even though it was becoming more popular for people to have one handset but be able to switch between personal and business calls, it was a possible red flag in Rego's mind.

He was still reading the report when Jen Bolitho phoned him.

"Boss, I've just had some intel come in from the IT department on the Viljoen case. I know you're not SIO, but ... could I just talk it through with you before I pass it on to DI Lloyd? I just want to make sure I've got it all straight in my head."

"Of course, Jen. Funnily enough, I'm looking at the IT report right now. I guess no one told IT that I was off the case."

She cleared her throat.

"I probably should have done that, boss."

"Don't worry, it's fine. And ACC Nash has already asked me to review all the files to date, so fire away."

"Does that mean you're back on the case?" she asked eagerly.

"It means I'm reviewing the files," he replied carefully.

There was a short pause where she heard what he wasn't saying.

Her voice was stronger and more confident when she spoke again.

"Okay, so the data shows that the Fords' cell site is stable around the hotel for the entire time up until Viljoen's death. But this is where it gets weird: Viljoen travelled to Birmingham two days before her death. I mean, what was she doing in the Midlands? She's just about to enter her first major surf competition in Europe as Erin Viljoen, and instead of getting used to the waves at Fistral, she goes to Birmingham. You can't get further from the sea if you tried."

"Yes, I thought that was odd. Do we know if she had friends or family in Birmingham?"

"We haven't been able to track down any family at all, and the Fords didn't even mention that she'd gone there."

"Didn't mention it or didn't know?"

"Unknown, boss." She paused. "I wondered if it was me; I wondered if I'd made a mistake, but I checked and rechecked the interviews with the Fords to date, and they never mentioned it."

"You're sure?"

"I'm certain! I went through it all three times – I thought I was going mad, but I'm 100% positive that they never mentioned it. I think someone should ask them about it again."

"Someone definitely should."

If the Fords had lied, that didn't look good. And surely they'd have known if their star surfer and only client had gone AWOL just before a major competition? They would have *had* to know that she'd vanished for nearly 14 hours.

"Are you at the station?" Jen asked. "Can I do screen-share with you?"

"Yep, go ahead, Jen."

A minute later, Rego was watching Jen's computer as an arrow darted around the screen. He was impressed with how speedy she'd become using the data analysis software. The adage 'you can't teach an old dog new tricks' flitted across his mind, then he winced. If he'd said that out loud in front of anyone, he'd have been whisked off for sensitivity training.

"Talk me through what I'm looking at," he said.

"On the left is a data set of times, dates, latitude and longitude coordinates, okay? The map on the right with the dots shows the plotting of the lat- and long- sites."

She scrolled up the map which showed a series of dots along the main trainline to New Street Station in Birmingham's city centre.

"Viljoen's phone ... the tech thinks she was SIM-swapping but maybe she had two phones – I'll have to check."

"And mirror numbers, check for those, as well," Rego added.

He heard Jen scratching out a note to herself.

"So, then the data moves from Cornwall to Birmingham's main station and Viljoen travels to an area called Hockley."

Jen enlarged the map to show more detail.

"Viljoen stays there for an hour before travelling a return route to New Street station and back to Cornwall. What was so important that she travels all the way to Birmingham for only one hour?"

"Good work, Jen," said Rego.

"So, what do you think, boss? Any ideas?"

Rego had been to Birmingham with Vikram many, many times, meeting his friend's family, enjoying the curries and maybe a few beers afterwards on Ladypool Road in Balsall

Heath. But there was another connection: while in Brum, Vikram had taken him to Hockley where Rego had bought Cassie's engagement ring from one of the tiny workshops that populated alleyways so narrow that you had to walk sideways; an unlikely place to find some of the best jewellers and best-quality diamond showrooms in the world.

Known as 'the Jewellery Quarter' since at least the 1770s, even today Hockley still had over 100 shops and businesses that produced some 40% of all the jewellery made in the UK: gold, silver, diamonds, watches, trophies and sporting cups, including the famous Venus Rosewater Dish, first presented to the Ladies Singles Champion for tennis at Wimbledon in 1886.

Apart from the fact that Hockley was world-famous for its long history of jewellery making and present-day revival, there was another reason that Rego knew so much about the area: it also attracted its share of criminal activity, with rogue dealers who accepted stolen gold and jewellery, the gold smelted, and jewellery remade into items which couldn't be identified if found.

Rego's brain somersaulted and that nagging, nascent idea that he'd had whilst talking to Vikram blossomed suddenly.

Diamonds.

Could this all be about diamonds?

What if Black Axe hadn't been paying for their 'commodities' with Bitcoin? What if they'd been trading conflict diamonds? Out of the top ten countries in the world for diamond mining, eight were in Africa.

Rego's pulse leapt.

"Boss?" Jen said again.

"I need to check something out, Jen. I'll get back to you."

He knew that he'd ended the call too abruptly, but he'd apologise to her later. He needed a moment to think; he needed to test whether he was completely barking up the wrong tree.

Because, what if the 'sparkles' in Viljoen's surfboard weren't just a gimmick? What if she'd been smuggling diamonds in plain sight? And what if the surfboards she'd trashed in her room had been to retrieve the diamonds.

"Overt to be covert," Rego said softly. "Bloody hell."

CHAPTER 13

Rego needed to clear his head. So many ideas were buzzing around in his brain, he wasn't sure whether or not he was imagining things. Could Viljoen really have been as blatant as that? But then again, criminals weren't always the sharpest knives in the drawer – how many drug dealers got spotted because they were driving brand-new BMWs and Range Rovers?

He strode down to the seafront, grabbing a takeaway coffee and muffin on the way. He was almost vibrating with energy but forced himself to think, to really think. He couldn't afford to go off half-cocked on this: he needed to plan what he was going to do next.

He walked along the wide promenade that ran from Rego's old fisherman's cottage in Newlyn all the way to the Jubilee Pool, a giant seawater lido on the edge of town. Then he leaned on the railings and stared out to sea.

If Viljoen's death was unlawful, was it because her food had been tampered with, or had somebody struck her on the head, or a combination of both? Food tampering was premeditated, so who had access to her food? Who could have laced it with sleeping pills? The Fords, obviously, but also anyone who worked at the Watergate Bay Hotel. Who benefitted from Viljoen's death? Well, that depended on *why* she'd been killed – and Rego was more certain than ever that it was a murder investigation. If Viljoen was or had once been an asset of the South Africa Police, had her cover been blown? Or had she been trying to run with the hare and hunt with hounds, working both the OCG and the police? Had she been skimming from Black Axe? Had the Fords been skimming? Were the Fords in danger or were they guilty of Viljoen's murder? Who were the men who'd given Alf Worth a crazy amount of money for a leaky old punt? Were they connected, and if so, how? Was it a coincidence that the Watergate Bay Hotel's manager was South African?

Or was Rego seeing connections where there weren't any?

He needed time to sort the wheat from the chaff, but he had the chilling sensation that time was a commodity in short supply.

He drew in a deep breath, then sat down in the sunshine, the information percolating through his brain. His seat was a giant pebble which the council had installed in a flight of whimsy as an alternative to wooden benches. Kids loved them and they made adults smile.

The polished granite was warm to the touch as Rego perched on his pebble, staring out at the aquamarine water, listening to the gentle lapping of the waves and the seagulls' piercing cries. He allowed his mind to drift, his subconscious working on the problems, the questions without answers. And even with all that going on, he couldn't help thinking, *You don't get this scenery in Manchester*.

The serenity was broken by his phone ringing.

"Rob, where are you?" Vikram asked. "I tried your office number. Bloody hell! Is that seagulls? Can you talk?"

"Anytime for you, mate. But listen, I've just had some intel that changes things on the Viljoen case in a big way, and I've been trying to decide what to do with it. Maybe I'm going crazy..."

"I've been saying that for years," said Vikram immediately. "Are you on the happy pills? You sound weird."

"Just enjoying the sun, sea and a salted caramel muffin. I needed to get out of the office."

"Well, I've got something that'll put a smile on your miserable face, so I'll go first."

Vikram always sounded enthusiastic about everything, and today was no exception. Rego could hear the frenzied shuffling of papers before his friend came back on the line.

"You remember the EncroChat investigation in 2020?"

Rego's ears pricked up.

"Yeah, the encrypted phone app that every organised crime gang started using."

"Right! Well, the server was based in France, and somehow the French authorities were able to penetrate its encryption and get hold of all the communications. Do you remember how stunned the law enforcement world was at the level of criminality? There were thousands of these encrypted phones in use, because the crims thought they were safe. The National Crime Agency took the lead while I was still working there, but the volume of criminality uncovered meant that we knew we wouldn't be able to cope, so we dished out the investigations in packages to all the police forces. Our lot got involved if it was thought there were EncroPhones being used outside of Europe."

Rego already knew this and was waiting for Vikram to get to the point: his buddy loved a good story.

"Well, this is the spooky thing. We sent several packages to South Africa."

That got Rego's attention. Another South African connection. He couldn't help sitting bolt upright on his giant pebble as if his body needed to focus on this new information.

"Each phone user was identified by a unique handle," Vikram continued. "We were able to separate the intel packages into crime gangs because we could see which phones were contacting each other, but we didn't know the proper name of the person who was using the device. One group we identified used the handles Globetrotter, Sparkles and Groot Hond. Well, when I was reading up on Viljoen, the press was all over the fact that she used a sparkly surfboard, and that caught my attention. I might be putting two-and-two together to make five, but I don't think so."

"Who did you send the intel packages to in South Africa?" Rego asked.

He wanted to hear if Vikram had come to the same bizarre conclusion that he had: he needed confirmation that he hadn't completely lost the plot.

"It was sent to the Directorate for Priority Crime Investigation," said Vikram. "Also known as the Hawks." He paused. "The same team who were using Ryan Kloppers, aka Erin Viljoen, as an asset. But get this, the phone number you gave me, the unknown males who paid over the odds for that old geezer's fishing boat..."

"Alf Worth's *Penrose Pride*..."

"Yeah, well, it's turned up on the Hawks' watchlist."

There it was: the connection that Rego had been searching for.

"Can you send that report to me urgently, Vik? That's too much of a freaky coincidence *not* to be connected with Viljoen's death."

"Are you back on the case, Rob?"

"No, but I think Lloyd is going to be moved from the

investigation. He's not following the intelligence; he's trying to impress the Chief by getting a quick result and pushing for a verdict of 'death by misadventure', but with your report – well, a heap more shit is really going to hit the fan and Lloyd has already been shovelling hard."

"You think they'll bring you back as SIO?"

Rego chewed that over.

"Maybe. I've got one of the ACC's going in to bat for me. She promised that she'd talk to the Hellbanianz gang member, de Jeles, to see if she could get him to withdraw the complaint against me. She seemed pretty certain that she could make him a deal he couldn't refuse."

"Bloody hell, mate! What's she going to do? Put a horse's head on his pillow?"

Rego thought about the ballsy ACC Sue Nash, and nodded.

"I wouldn't put it past her."

"I like the sound of her. Okay then, I'll send the intel packages over, then touch base with the SIO of the Hawks and pass on contact details. Oh, and by the way, Rob, the package includes some images: it's not just messages that were recovered. I know there are at least two pics with some diamonds in the open palm of someone's hand. The NCA have had some success in identifying people from the hands' ridge details in the photographs – it might be worth a follow up."

Then Rego told Vikram about where Viljoen's phone had pinged, with the assumption that Viljoen had been the one using it at the time, which could be confirmed by getting hold of CCTV from Birmingham train station. Hopefully, Rego would also be able to get CCTV of Viljoen visiting the diamond district, which could possibly prove his 'out there' idea that she may have been transporting diamonds inside her surfboards.

Vikram was quiet for several seconds.

"Bloody hell, Rob! I don't know if that's bloody brilliant or completely bloody bonkers."

Rego could hear him breathing heavily on the phone.

"Vik? You alright there, mate?"

"Yeah, yeah. Just looking something up ... here it is, a briefing that crossed my desk recently: the sale of conflict diamonds on the black market is massive all over the world. According to these figures, global trade in rough diamonds is approximately 112 million carats. I'll do the maths for you – that's about £1.3 billion annually."

Rego was stunned. He'd had no idea the sum was so large. Not that he'd had any reason to know, but this was off the charts.

"I was thinking smaller scale than that, Vik. I'm kind of mind-blown here," Rego admitted.

"It gets worse," Vikram said quietly. "There's been some uncorroborated intel that Black Axe are in the market for small arms, and there's been a flood of pre-loved guns coming out of Russia and Ukraine. Because of the influx of weapons, the price for AKs has dropped from around US $1,500 in 2023 to under US $1,000. There was even a US-made M240 machine gun offered for sale at US $8,000 and a Soviet-type AGS-17 automatic grenade launcher at US $6,000 – pretty much bargain basement prices."

"Jesus," Rego breathed.

"There's growing evidence that the arms-trafficking market is becoming more organised, with even larger stockpiles being assembled. Last September, a bust in Kyiv netted 132 rounds of ammunition for grenade launchers.

These OCGs, their zone of operation is expanding closer and closer to the EU border."

Automatic and semi-automatic weapons in large numbers getting into the hands of one of the most violent OCGs out there? Grenade launchers? Rego's muffin threatened to re-visit the scene of the crime.

"That's scary as hell, Vik, but there's nothing specific to connect arms sales to what's going on down here."

"No, that's true," Vikram said slowly. "I'm only passing on what I've heard about Black Axe. We'd assumed that they'd be paying for weapons with Bitcoin, because that's what they've done in the past, but maybe trading conflict diamonds is another route for them."

"Expanding their range of services," Rego said bitterly.

They were both silent for a moment, thinking about the complex, multinational operations of major OCGs.

"This has got me wondering," Vik continued as his mind cycled in top gear. "Were the diamonds supposed to be in payment for something specific, something major, or just an alternative way of accessing foreign currency?"

"Something major? Christ, I hope not!" said Rego.

He hoped like hell that his friend was wrong about this. Unfortunately, Vikram was rarely wrong.

"You've got to pass this up the line, Rob," said Vikram, his voice serious. "But make sure you've got all your ducks in a row first – you don't want some pen-pusher shutting this down before it's even started."

"I can't go in, guns blazing – no pun intended – and scare the shit out of everyone with talk of an arms deal, but I'll pass on everything you've said about the Hawks, Black Axe, Alf Worth's mystery buyers, and the Kloppers-Viljoen connection."

Vikram's voice was worried.

"Just don't leave it too long."

"I'm heading back to the office now, Vik. Thank you for everything, brother."

Rego's legs had cramped up while he'd been sitting on the giant pebble, and his backside was numb. He hobbled a few paces, walking like an 80-year-old, before getting into his stride.

He was just heading into the station's car park when his phone rang with a call from HQ.

"Good afternoon, DI Rego. This is Maggie Tyacke from Chief Constable Evans' office."

She always spoke so formally, as if they'd never met before.

"Yes, Maggie, what can I do for you?"

"Chief Constable Evans asks if you're free at 3pm today. He'd like to see you urgently."

"Are you able to tell me the reason?"

Maggie paused.

"Well," she said at last, "if I can put your mind at rest, you're not in trouble," and she gave a small, embarrassed laugh. "The Chief anticipated your question and just wanted me to say, you're being asked to take over an enquiry."

"The Viljoen enquiry?"

"That information has not been shared with me," she said primly.

Rego would have bet a month's salary that she knew exactly why he was being called in.

"Thank you, Maggie. I'll leave now and see you at 3pm."

A grim smile came over Rego's face. He was certain it must be the Viljoen case, it must be. But that meant that his time was almost up on trying to put all the pieces together.

Rego had only a two-hour drive to work out what he was going to say to the Chief to persuade him that the case was about to explode.

What if Viljoen's glittering surfboards weren't a gimmick, but a signal – an identifier – passed through encrypted messages between ghosts in a criminal machine that spanned continents? Diamonds. Surfboards. Foreign networks. If even half of what Vikram had hinted at was true, Rego wasn't just picking up a dropped investigation, he was walking blind into something tangled and deadly dangerous. Something old-school, but digital. Something the Chief wouldn't want spiralling out of control.

Rego had seen operations collapse under the weight of politics, but this, this had the fingerprints of something bigger and much darker.

And now, for better or worse, it had his name on it.

What he really needed was to establish the exact cause of Viljoen's death. There was so much circumstantial evidence that pointed away from suicide or accidental drowning. Viljoen was up to her neck in international criminal activity: running diamonds for Black Axe or a Confidential Informant for the Hawks? But which side of the fence was she sitting on?

If he knew that, he'd have a bloody good idea of who had killed her – or had her killed.

Rego wasn't familiar with how the Hawks ran their informants, what levels of protection they put in place, how they were briefed, or what control they had over their engagement with the crime they were reporting on. In the UK, CIs were tightly controlled, and they pretty much had a contract. Their police handlers would brief and debrief them on a regular basis, and if a CI stepped outside that contract or undertook any actions that hadn't been authorised, they'd be dropped like a hot brick and even took the chance of being prosecuted.

So, which side of the fence had Viljoen been sitting on when she died?

CHAPTER 14

Rego was halfway to the Chief's office in Exeter when his sergeant called.

"DI Lloyd is off the case, boss," he said, his voice excited.

"Have you been told why?" Rego asked.

"Not officially, but between you and me and the gatepost, I've heard that the coroner has been on to the Chief, complaining that Lloyd has been trying to influence his decision. And you know how well something like that will go down."

His voice became muffled as if he'd put his hand over the phone, then moved to a quieter area.

"He's been so busy kissing the mayor's arse that he's hasn't come up for daylight. This investigation has been shit – nothing's being followed up properly and since Mimi got back..."

"When did she get back? I thought she was away till Monday?"

"Eh, her trip went a bit sideways and she ended up flying back. Jen twisted her arm to come back to work early, and she's been running herself ragged since yesterday trying to plug all the leaks. We need an SIO who knows what the hell he's doing."

"It sounds like Lloyd has been pushed to follow an agenda, not the evidence," said Rego, feeling a smidgeon of pity for Lloyd who wasn't necessarily a bad copper, just one who was letting politics and maybe ambition colour his decisions.

Stevens suddenly realised that Rego was talking from his car phone.

"Where are you, boss?"

"I've been summoned to Middlemoor by the Chief."

"Yeah? Do you think they'll put you back on the Viljoen case?" Stevens asked hopefully.

"I don't know, but I'll get back to you in an hour or so, Tom. Thanks for keeping me updated."

"One other thing before you go, boss," said Stevens urgently. "The Fords checked out of Watergate Bay Hotel this morning."

"What the hell? When exactly? Does Lloyd know? Did he say they could go?"

"I believe he did, boss," said Stevens, suddenly sounding diplomatic several minutes too late.

"What time did they leave?" Rego snapped.

"Before breakfast. I only just heard the news myself."

"Jesus! That was, what, four hours ago? I want to know where they are, Tom. Urgently! Whether or not I'll be put back on the case, we need to know where they are."

"Are they suspects?" Stevens asked, sounding really worried.

Rego wanted to yell, *Yes, they fucking are!* but there was still no evidence to back that up.

"It just seems off to me, Tom. Two days ago, Phil Ford made the formal ID of the body and told me how much his wife wanted to 'take Erin home', all after telling me that they thought of her as a daughter. Jesus, he was even asking me about her will and I told him how to apply for Letters of Administration to get the legal authority to handle Viljoen's estate. If we don't manage to locate any relatives, they could even be her next of kin. Phil Ford told me that they planned to repatriate the body – they even started a crowdfunding page for it! So, even if DI Lloyd gave them permission to leave, they've pissed off without saying a word about having her cremated or buried or anything else. It's a bloody shambles and..."

He left the sentence unfinished.

"Call them now, Tom. If they answer, ask them what their intentions are and why they've left the area when two days ago they were desperate to repatriate Viljoen's body. If they don't answer, leave a message to that effect and get some cell site analysis done on their phones."

If the phones were no longer in service, that would tell its own story.

Rego was mentally ticking off his list of immediate actions.

"Got it, boss," said Tom.

"And find out if there's a tracker on their hire car. Most rental companies have them these days – get them to activate it asap. I want to know where the Fords are going. And while you're at it, put an ANPR check on their rental vehicle and hot-list the car."

The Automatic Numberplate Recognition database allowed officers to upload a car's registration number, and as soon as the car went through an ANPR camera on the road or at a traffic light, it would send an alert to the person asking for the car to be hot-listed. Additionally, Traffic Officers had vehicles with ANPR cameras and received alerts when a hot-listed car passed them.

"But, Tom, put a warning on the system that the vehicle should *not* be stopped, but to notify me on my mobile. We don't know for sure if they're involved in anything or not. If they are, I don't want officers confronting people who may be violent or carrying firearms."

The officers would need to know exactly what they are dealing with, and right now, Rego couldn't give them that information. But if Vikram was right about arms dealing – and he prayed his friend was wrong – there was no knowing what sort of situation an officer could be walking into.

"When we know where they are, we'll put a plan in place to talk to them or to pick them up, if necessary."

"We could lose them, boss," Stevens said honestly. "If they're involved, they could swap cars, then we'll be up shit creek without a paddle."

"I know, Tom, but there isn't enough evidence to arrest them on anything at this point. Not a single thing, although..." Rego paused. "Find out how much money is on their crowdfunding page for taking Viljoen's body back to South Africa."

"You think it could be an attempt to defraud members of the public?" Tom asked.

"If they keep the money without doing what they said they were going to do, then yes."

There was a short pause before Stevens replied.

"I'm on their GoFundMe now – it's up to nearly £7,000 – that's got to be more than enough."

"I'm assuming that they paid their hotel bill and didn't abscond, seeing as DI Lloyd let them leave?"

"They paid, boss."

Rego was filled with frustration and had no energy left to feel any sympathy at all for Lloyd.

"Okay, get details of their credit card, and contact the manager to stop them cleaning the room, if they haven't already. I want a room search immediately. And has the analysis of their key card usage been analysed while they've been in Newquay?"

"Not yet, boss."

"Then get someone onto that. Find out when their room key card was used over the whole time they were in Newquay. I also want to know if they used the room phone to make or receive any calls. Get a techie in there to see if they can learn anything from the router: is there an individual router per room? If so, we'll be able to see what websites they've looked or any WiFi-calling they've done."

"On it, boss."

Rego didn't care whether or not he was the SIO of this case or not – these needed to be actioned urgently.

When Rego arrived at HQ, he headed straight for the Chief's office – where he then had to cool his heels for another ten minutes.

Maggie Tyacke offered him coffee, but any more caffeine and they'd be peeling him off the ceiling. He was already too restless to sit, so he leaned against the wall, scrolling through the remainder of reports from the Viljoen case that he hadn't yet read, trying to put all of the jigsaw pieces together.

Every now and then, raised voices penetrated through the door. Maggie studiously avoided catching his eye, but Rego was shamelessly listening in.

"I was assured that this was a suicide, Stephen! Inspector Lloyd specifically told me that the whole situation was under control. But I've had the bloody coroner on the phone telling me that he's not ruling it a suicide until he gets answers to his questions. What the hell is he talking about? What questions? I've just done an interview with *BBC Spotlight* – they've got me on camera saying the damn woman killed herself."

Rego recognised the voice of Newquay's mayor, who sounded like he was tearing a strip off the Chief Constable.

"What the hell are you people playing at, Stephen? You've made me look like a complete fucking fool on national television."

Rego couldn't hear exactly what the Chief had said to the mayor to try and calm him down, but his words were clipped, his tone crisp.

Whatever was said, it didn't work.

"I don't care about that!" yelled the mayor. "I've got two major sponsors threatening to pull out of Boardmasters! I've got the press hounding my staff and phoning constantly! Speculation is rife and it's making a farce out of everything. Do you know how much Boardmasters is worth to Newquay? Not just a few million but *forty million pounds!* At least! I want answers, Stephen, and I want them *now*. I want this matter resolved *now*; I want this investigation sewn up *now*; and I want a competent fucking officer on the job. We need to move on and have a successful last two days of the festival. I want this all cleared up before the men's finals and the bloody trophy ceremony tomorrow. What I *don't* want is the press saying that this woman was murdered and Cornwall's police are bloody well covering it up because they're institutionally transphobic ... or just bloody incompetent!"

The Chief's voice was louder but still deliberately calm.

"That's all very interesting, Andrew, but I suggest you go out of my office, take a breath, and come back in when you're more reasonable and we can have a proper chat."

There were more heated words, then the voices dropped so Rego couldn't hear them anymore.

The argument left Rego feeling depressed and suddenly weary.

It was all about the way things looked; it was all about the way the case was being perceived by the public. Neither the mayor nor the Chief seemed to care about the body lying unburied in Treliske Hospital's morgue.

It was all about the politics.

Rego slumped into a chair. He wasn't naïve – he knew politics mattered and he knew that budgets were created by politicians, but the thought left him feeling utterly demoralised. It should be about truth; it should be about the voices of the dead crying out for justice because they couldn't speak for themselves.

It should be, but it wasn't.

The door opened suddenly and Rego saw the Chief's staff officer, Inspector John Casey, beckoning him into the office.

Rego had a feeling that he was rubbernecking a car crash as he walked into the room. Everyone looked tense and the mayor's hands were clenched into fists as if he was tempted to take a swing at someone: probably the next SIO on the case.

"Good afternoon, sir," Rego said to the Chief, then glanced at ACC Gray who was sitting next to the mayor, along with Isla Forrester and DCS Richards.

Forrester gave him a tight-lipped smile and raised her eyebrows. Rego didn't know if that was a comment on the meeting so far, or a warning.

Richards looked furious but nodded at Rego, and Casey was clearly feeling the strain as he made the introductions.

"Rob, this is Mr Andrew Bissoe, Mayor of Newquay; Mayor Bissoe, this is Detective Inspector Robert Rego."

"Sir," said Rego, holding out his hand to the mayor.

"DI Rego is one of our best investigators," the Chief

added smoothly, "and our new Senior Investigating Officer on the case."

Although being SIO on this case was a bit like playing musical chairs.

The mayor looked at Rego suspiciously.

"One of the best or *the* best?"

"I have a very good team," Rego replied.

There was a short silence, then the Chief stepped in.

"Rob," he said, "we need a fresh pair of eyes on the Viljoen case, taking into account all the evidence I have before me ... and some very interesting material that I've just received."

He gave Rego a meaningful look.

"So, Inspector Rego," the mayor said in a challenging tone. "Can you tell me what the bloody hell is going on? Did Erin Viljoen commit suicide or not?"

Rego glanced at DCS Richards and then at the Chief who nodded for him to continue.

"The evidence is still being gathered," said Rego. "But I promise you we'll leave no stone unturned until we get to the truth."

"For God's sake," the mayor yelled. "Can't anyone give me a straight answer?"

"I can tell you where the investigation is at, or I can make an assumption that might prove to be wrong," Rego replied. "Your choice, Mr Bissoe."

The mayor looked surprised then gave the ghost of a smile.

"Alright, inspector. Where is the investigation at?"

"I'm keeping an open mind and following several lines of enquiry. There are a number of forensic opportunities where we're waiting on results; there are technical enquiries to be done, and witnesses that need to be seen. Then I'll review everything to date."

It was a non-answer at best, but all Rego could give in the circumstances.

The room was silent.

Thankfully, DCS Richards was quicker on the uptake than the others and raised his eyebrows at the Chief who finally cottoned on that this meeting needed to be over.

"Right, I'm going to have to ask you to leave this with us now, Andrew," he said to the mayor, his tone conciliatory. "There are clearly things that need to be discussed in private and we're short of time. I'm sure you can appreciate that."

The mayor looked dubious and as if he was about to argue, but then he gave a curt nod and stood up to leave the office.

"I'll wait to hear from you, Stephen," he said to the Chief. "I want to know everything ... and for once I'd like to know it before the bloody press get hold of it!"

Which was a bit rich coming from a man who'd been seduced by the promise of a two-minute slot on a BBC news programme.

Bissoe ignored everyone else, but jerked his head in Rego's direction.

"I hope you can live up to your billing, Inspector Rego," he said tersely as he strode out of the office.

Rego was hoping the same thing.

As soon as the door had closed, the Chief glanced at the press officer.

"Thank you, Isla. If you could draft something appropriately vague in the next half-an-hour, I'll review it personally. Thank you."

Dismissed, Isla Forrester glanced at Rego with a faint smile, then hurried out of the door.

A full minute passed before the Chief spoke. Instead, he opened the file in front of him, underlined a couple of passages, then looked up, fixing his gaze on Rego.

"South African crime gangs? Is this really what you think is happening here, Rob?"

"It's looking more and more like that, sir," Rego replied.

"How the hell did Lloyd miss this?" asked the Chief, his voice rising with concern.

"The intel is new, sir. I only had it myself minutes before I left Penzance."

"Yes, but *why* did you have it?" ACC Gray snapped. "You weren't even on the case."

"Does it matter?" the Chief asked incredulously. "We've got a major problem here, Ian."

"My concern is that Rego has been running a parallel investigation and not disclosing information in a timely manner," Gray shot back.

Rego's own anger began to simmer.

"No one had told the IT techs that I was no longer SIO, so the information on Viljoen's phone came through to me in the usual way. The information on Alf Worth came from one of the PCs at Penzance station," he said, hoping to keep Tamsyn's name out of it. "That was a result of good policing."

"Ah yes, your little protégé PC Poldhu," Gray said nastily. "What a coincidence."

Rego didn't rise to the bait; he simply stared coolly at Gray.

"Actually, sir, PC Poldhu came across the intel at the Mousehole versus Evesham football match. I believe you personally requested that Inspector Walters send an officer as part of a neighbourhood initiative. So, thank you for that, sir."

Richards smiled but ACC Gray flushed a dark red, his eyes narrowing.

The Chief was getting impatient.

"That's enough point-scoring, gentlemen," he said acidly. "We have more important things to discuss. Now, tell me where this Alf Worth character comes into the picture."

"He doesn't," said Rego, "not really. He's just an old bloke who thought he could make a couple of quid off the books by selling his boat cash-in-hand for way more than it was worth and buying a fancy Ford Ranger pickup that was more than he could otherwise have afforded. I was interested in who would pay over the odds for an old fishing boat."

He paused but no one asked a question, so he explained the rest.

"And that's where things get interesting. This boat was seen in the vicinity the night of Viljoen's death – it's even in the background of the footage where PC Poldhu is attempting CPR. I passed the phone number that the men used in the boat's purchase to a friend and it came up as a number of interest at the Directorate for Priority Crime Investigation in South Africa. They've been trying to infiltrate an OCG, Black Axe, and Viljoen was one of their assets. Or rather, Ryan Kloppers was."

"Who the hell is Ryan Kloppers?" Gray fumed.

"It's Erin Viljoen's cisgender name," said Rego, but saw only blank incomprehension on Gray's face. "Viljoen's name before she transitioned."

Gray looked irritated but kept his mouth shut.

"Good God," said the Chief. "Are we looking at a gang-related murder here?"

"I don't know," Rego said honestly. "Not yet. Like I told the mayor, there's a lot of evidence to sift through first."

ACC Gray made a *tsking* noise in the back of his throat and folded his arms across his chest. Rego ignored him.

"I can tell you that the Fords have left Watergate Bay

Hotel. I've got my DS trying to find out why they left so suddenly."

"You're not the SIO!" Gray shouted. "Your DS should have reported the Fords' leaving to DI Lloyd."

Rego didn't have a chance to say that Lloyd was fully aware of the Fords' departure.

"Haven't you been listening, Ian?" the Chief said coldly to his ACC. "I reinstated Rego as SIO five minutes ago." He turned to Rego. "Continue."

By now, ACC Gray was almost purple with anger and gripping the arms of his chair so tightly, his knuckles were shiny and white. There were a lot of colours going on in that office.

"As I said," Rego continued, "my DS is looking into this and getting techs to check on the room, especially anything we can glean from their internet usage and WiFi-calling. The Fords' rental car is being hot-listed on ANPR. If they're still driving it, we'll know where they are."

"Is it about drugs?" Richards asked.

"It's possible," Rego admitted. "But based on the fact that Viljoen visited the Hockley area of Birmingham, I m thinking it could be about trading conflict diamonds."

"Diamonds! Now there's diamond smuggling involved!" the Chief barked.

"Potentially, sir."

"Good God! What next?"

"I still need the police up there to check any CCTV in the Hockley area, but if it's an under-the-counter transaction, I'm not sure how much CCTV will help. We know Viljoen was there, but at the moment, we can only guess why."

Rego didn't want to mention anything about arms dealing until Vikram came back with something solid.

"And the forensic opportunities you mentioned to the

mayor? The technical investigations, what of those? What the hell has Lloyd been playing at?"

"Managing the budget," Rego offered, even though it had been a rhetorical question. "Forensic tests are expensive, especially if it had turned out to be suicide."

The Chief eyed him thoughtfully but didn't comment further.

Rego's phone vibrated silently.

"That's probably my DS. Would you mind if I take this, sir?" he asked politely as he slid the phone from his pocket.

The Chief nodded impatiently.

"Tom, what have you got?" Rego asked as soon as he confirmed his sergeant's name on the screen.

"Sorry to bother you, boss," said Tom. "I know you're with the Chief, but I thought you'd want to know asap. The Fords paid their hotel bill in cash, which seems fishy. I mean, it was more than four-thousand quid! They're not answering their phones and they're not pinging any cell towers – I'd say they've turned them off or ditched them. But," he continued, his voice excited, "I found a Sainsbury's receipt for a new phone in their wastepaper bin – thank God the cleaners didn't get to the hotel room first. I've sent an officer down to the supermarket now to check the CCTV and obtain their new mobile number. We'll be able to track that as soon as they turn it on."

"Good work, Tom. Anything else?"

"The hotel manager, Martin Caterham, he's being a bit arsey about giving us the WiFi-calling and internet usage from the suites' two routers."

"For what reason?" Rego asked.

"Says he's busy."

"I don't care how busy he is. Go and sit on him till he gives us what we need, and if he still doesn't cooperate, inform

Mr Caterham that obstructing a police officer in the execution of their duty is a criminal offence."

"On it, boss."

Rego looked up at the Chief.

"Potential new leads, sir."

The Chief nodded.

"Keep me informed, Rego. We need a quick result on this – do what it takes."

In Rego's opinion, wanting a quick result was what had got them into this situation in the first place.

"I don't like cases being played out in front of the press," the Chief continued. "It's looking very messy and I don't want any more mistakes that make the force look bad."

You don't want to look bad.

It was all spin, and by pushing Rego to the front with Newquay's mayor, the Chief had carefully distanced himself if it all went sideways.

Rego's thoughts were grim as he left police headquarters.

But at least there was one piece of good news: DC Mimi Eagling, his number-one data analyst was on the case and waiting for him at Newquay police station.

When Rego arrived, Mimi was sitting with her back to the door, chatting to her friends on the detective team and showing off her engagement ring over a glass of bubbles. Rego was pleased to see that they were drinking elderflower pressé and not champagne in the middle of the day but frustrated that she wasn't working the software, which is what he'd assumed she'd be doing.

As soon as Rego had the thought, he knew it was unfair. Mimi had cut short her leave to come and help them out, and he knew that the rest of his team had been pulling 14-hour days: he could give them ten minutes to enjoy a quick break before he filled them in on the latest developments.

"Boss! You nearly missed out," said Mimi, smiling at Rego. "I brought a box of Polish gingerbread biscuits from Luka's grandmother, but these gannets have nearly eaten the lot."

"Thanks, Mimi, and welcome back," said Rego, taking the second to last biscuit and remembering that he hadn't had time for lunch today.

"It sounds like I should say that to you too, boss," she said slyly, nicking the last biscuit as she gave him a broad smile. "So, it sounds like it's all been kicking off here while I've been away. How's it going?"

"It's an odd one," said Jen. "There are a lot of loose ends."

Rego thought that was putting it mildly, but he was interested to hear that his team were also identifying holes and finding things that weren't adding up.

"How come you ended up doing the data analysis?" Mimi asked Jen.

"I must have volunteered," Jen laughed. "I just don't remember doing it," and she smirked at Rego.

"No way!" Mimi laughed. "I guess you can teach an old dog new tricks."

Rego was glad that Mimi had been the one to say that and not him.

"Are you calling me an old bitch?" Jen laughed, elbowing Mimi in the ribs.

"If the dog collar fits..."

"Oh, I'll get you back for that, Mimi! But I'm still glad you're here," Jen admitted. "I won't be sorry to hand over the data analysis – it's driven me nuts."

"I'm sure that you've done a good job," Rego said, half-sincere, half-hopeful. "And you're no more nuts than usual."

"Thanks, boss, for that faint praise."

She turned to Mimi.

"Tell him about Ukraine!"

"It was a loooong drive, that's for sure," said Mimi. "But it was amazing, too. There were three other ambulances from other parts of the country, and we travelled in convoy. Luka has done the journey a few times now – his garage has been stuffed with donations from members of the public. It's been really fantastic how many people wanted to help. I really wanted to go on the other trips too, but what with work..."

They shared commiserating looks – every police officer knew how far ahead holidays had to be planned to fit in with their shift work, and they'd all missed birthdays, weddings and even funerals when leave was suddenly cancelled because of a major incident.

"Anyway, Luka said I'd be able to talk him out of trouble if he got caught speeding," and she laughed. "It was so cool that every time we stopped, people were coming up to us and saying we were doing a great job and giving us donations, buying us cups of coffee and lunches. We see a lot of shit in this job," she said thoughtfully, "so it was pretty special to have people supporting us and really caring about what we were doing."

"Even with a sticker on the van that said *Aid for Ukraine donated by Devon & Cornwall Police*?" DC John Frith asked, his tone cynical.

"Even then," said Mimi. "And loads of police on the journey stopped to say hi or give us a quick flash of the blue lights. At the Harwich ferry, we practically got VIP treatment, and were upgraded to a room for free! That was great because it meant we slept pretty well, and it was a helluva lot of driving: the journey from Amsterdam to Warsaw took twelve hours. We stayed with Luka's *babcia* in Pruszków, just outside the city, then pushed on for the border the next day. Luka had arranged with some aid organisation over there to take all the donated items. But then our luck ran out and the bastard ambulance broke down. It's always breaking down, but he won't get rid of it because he says the ambulance is symbolic," and she smiled with annoyed affection.

"What a pain!" Jen sympathised.

"Yeah, and Luka's gran had packed all these amazing cakes and biscuits, like fifty pounds of food," she laughed. "But I had to leave them with Luka so I know for sure that he'll have scoffed everything by the time he gets back." She sighed. "He didn't know how long he'd have to wait to get the ambulance fixed and I had to be at work on Monday, so I got a ride to the airport, flew into Gatwick and picked up the morning flight into Newquay. Then Jen blackmailed me to coming straight into work."

Jen held up her hands. "All true! I couldn't do without you. When do you think Luka will be back?"

"I'm not sure – he's driving by himself, so he'll need to take more breaks. Maybe in a couple of days? I can't even call him till he's back in the UK because he forgot to put roaming on his phone, so I've no idea where he is." She frowned. "I hope he's okay."

Before Mimi could say anything else, Rego stood up.

"Sorry to break up the party, Mimi, and I'm glad you're back in one piece, but we need to crack on with the case."

He proceeded to give them a rundown of everything that he'd discussed with the Chief, and some of what he'd found out from Vikram, whilst not revealing his sources.

"So, these are our priority actions: 1) locate the Fords, 2) track down the *Penrose Pride*, and 3) Tom, your message said that you finally got the hotel manager to cough up all the data on Viljoen's and the Fords' room keys. What was the problem with that?"

DS Stevens shook his head.

"I don't think he was deliberately impeding the investigation, but he's had a few staff leave suddenly without giving notice; some of the hotel guests have been complaining to him about police on the premises; and I gather the owners have been giving him a hard time about that, too." He shrugged. "I've got all the data on a flash drive now, so some lucky person gets to analyse it all." He waved it in the air. "Who wants it?"

"I'll take it," said Mimi.

"No, I want Jen to take you through the data analysis," said Rego. "I know she's dying to hand it over."

DC Jack Forshaw raised a hand.

"I'll take it, boss."

Stevens tossed him the flash drive with a relieved smile.

"Cheers, Jack."

Rego's own workload included questions that hadn't yet been adequately answered: how did the sleeping pills get into Viljoen's stomach? People taking pills didn't usually grind them up, and not in such quantity, so if Viljoen hadn't knowingly ingested them, who had administered them and why?

And no one had been able to explain the injuries to Viljoen's head. Tamsyn had confirmed that there were no buoys in that part of the bay and no other surfers or boats had been seen nearby – just the *Penrose Pride*. So, what had struck Viljoen?

There were too many questions and not enough answers.

Rego rolled up his sleeves.

CHAPTER 15

The sun was hot on Tamsyn's bare shoulders as she wound her way through the crowds on Fistral Beach.

The tide was a long way out and the competition surfers were no more than tiny black dots in the distance. The waves were mediocre at best and with no offshore wind to hold them up, they crumbled quickly, giving short, choppy rides in the whitewater – hardly enough to surf on at all. But a low pressure was rolling in from the southwest, and the swell was predicted to be 6 foot and clean by the finals the following day.

The panel of judges sat on a raised platform, their long telescopes bristling like cannons aimed out to sea.

An air horn sounded loudly, ending the current heat, and the judges all relaxed as the competitors picked their final waves to ride back in.

Tamsyn wasn't at Boardmasters in any official capacity. She'd come to watch the surfers, maybe take her own board out and generally soak up the festival vibes. But she'd found it impossible to shut off the police side of her, and everywhere she looked, she saw petty violations, from underage drinkers, to public intoxication, which led to public urination, as well as littering on an epic scale.

She saw several colleagues sweating in their uniforms, their duty belts, helmets, and tactical vests weighing them down. She didn't envy them the heat, the blistering hot pavements, or the dickish behaviour of a few members of the public. She also didn't talk to them, feeling that she needed to maintain her TPO persona to protect the rest of the team still up at the campsite. It probably wasn't necessary, but she didn't want to take any chances. And yes, maybe she was still bitter about having been yanked from the assignment in the first place.

Even though the majority of tourists and locals were enjoying the sunshine and the spectacle, Tamsyn knew that her festival vibes had gone on strike. She wondered half-heartedly whether she'd ever be able to enjoy it again in the years to come.

Maybe it would have been different if Jess was with her, but she was working today. Summer was always the busiest time for local estate agents: tourists were seduced by the beaches and laidback lifestyle, dreaming of owning their own little slice of paradise. Jess and other estate agents were happy to help them achieve that dream, even though the subject of second homes was a touchy one.

She felt her phone vibrate and lifted her sunglasses to squint in the bright sunshine while she read the text message. It was from her grandmother, but the content of the message was not what she might have expected.

> Jonas Jedna asked Grandad to pass on a message to you. He says Penrose Pride berthed at Portreath last night.

Tamsyn read the message twice. She wondered if the

whereabouts of Alf Worth's old punt was still important, but then again, she knew from experience that lowly PCs weren't kept informed of how important cases were going. She also knew that it was unfair of her to be annoyed about that fact, because intel in big cases was kept on a strict need-to-know basis. She'd learned the hard way not to make assumptions about what Inspector Rego did with the information she gave him.

She dialled his number and he answered immediately.

"Rego."

"Sir, it's Tamsyn. I don't know if you're still interested, but Jonas Jedna left a message with Grandad saying that Alf Worth's punt was berthed at Portreath Harbour last night."

"Portreath?"

"Yes, sir. It's only twenty miles southwest of Newquay, and it's a non-statutory harbour with no Harbour Orders – fewer rules, more under the radar. I don't know if it's important..."

She wasn't sure, but she hoped he'd say that the information was important.

"Thank you, Tamsyn," he replied. "Good work – and please thank your grandfather for me."

Then he ended the call.

Disappointed, she put her phone away and slid her sunglasses back over her face again.

She wandered down to the shoreline, letting the water lap around her ankles as she took a closer look at the next heat of competition surfers. Two women carried their boards to the water's edge, their gazes intense, their bodies loose as they rolled their shoulders and jogged on the spot.

Tamsyn recognised Alana Bright, the top European female competitor, and the local favourite. She was wearing a wetsuit with an aquamarine Lycra vest over the top to identify her to the judges, and she'd chosen a 5'10 twin fin from her quiver today. Tamsyn used a similar surfboard herself – although hers was a lot older and more battered – but it was a small-wave destroyer.

The other quarter-finalist was a 14-year-old French girl who'd taken the surf world by storm. Tya Zabrowski was tiny, not even five feet tall, but built like a gymnast – all muscle and flexibility.

Bright was heavier, taller, and well-muscled. On these small waves, Zabrowski should have the advantage, but on the other hand, it was Bright's home break.

Zabrowski didn't look the least bit intimidated; instead, she was utterly focused, her eyes scanning the small Atlantic swell, looking for the best place to paddle out and assessing which section provided the best breaks. She wore a hot pink Lycra vest over a full-length black wetsuit, and her light brown hair tied in a high ponytail. She was young to be so highly ranked, but her parents had both been pro snowboarders, and the girl had been raised partly at Hossegor, one of the gnarliest breaks on France's Atlantic coast, and had spent her summer months on the mountainous waves of Tahiti.

Tamsyn knew that the British surfer was going to have a fight on her hands. Zabrowski had won the Women's Division at Boardmasters the previous year when Bright had been injured, and this year, there was only a point between them. When Viljoen had been in the running, the pollsters had ruled out both of them. But now, well, it was anyone's guess, and both women had a lot to prove.

It was a shame that the waves were so rubbish

In a rare moment of envy, Tamsyn wondered what her life would have been like if she'd had two parents, both professional athletes – would she have still become a police officer? No, almost definitely not.

The death of her father when she was just ten years old had been the most profound moment of her whole life. Her mother had left years before and she barely remembered her, rarely thought of her. But the day her father had died, she'd watched as his cold, dead body had been brought into Newlyn Harbour. She'd watched as it was lifted onto the jetty wrapped in a tarpaulin, and she'd stared, stunned and scared, until a police officer had led her away and taken care of her.

The officer had been so kind. He'd talked to her, comforted her, and wiped her tears. She'd never forgotten him, ever, even though she never knew his name.

That was the moment her life changed forever.

Tamsyn watched the two women paddle out with a critical eye. Bright was strong, but Zabrowski was quick and light. Although, to Tamsyn's mind, Bright had chosen the better position on the line-up.

She watched with interest as Bright was poised to catch her first wave when she felt someone coming up to her and standing way too close, invading her personal space.

"Hey, aren't you that chick from the video?"

A short, stocky man at least a decade older than Tamsyn was staring at her with unblinking eyes. He looked like a surfer with his long, blond dreads and green boardshorts but he had an intensity about him that was off-putting.

As he moved in even closer, she could smell the beer on his breath and she took half a step back.

"Yeah, yeah, that was you! Hey, Brodie, look! It's that chick from the video."

He laughed, but it sounded humourless and there was no warmth in his eyes, instead she felt repelled by him.

Tamsyn was about to walk away when awareness hit her. Oh yeah, she was definitely staying to talk to this man who had a strong South African accent.

The friend 'Brodie' sauntered over, smiling widely as he ran hungry eyes over her bikini top and cut-off denim shorts.

"Yeah, bruh! Saw you on TikTok," he said. "But you look hotter in real life."

Tamsyn wanted to gag but forced a smile.

"Howzit! I'm Brodie and this ape is Pongo. You wanna hang?"

Tamsyn gave a bright smile.

The nickname 'Pongo' took her straight back to one of those boozy nights when Joe and Jess's boyfriend Jason, both ex-bootnecks a.k.a. Royal Marines, were swapping stories. They kept going on about 'pongos', and falling about laughing, until Jess has lost her patience and asked what was so funny.

"Pongos are squaddies – you know, wherever the Army goes, the pong goes, too!"

Which was hilarious, if you had the maturity of a five-year-old.

Was Pongo ex-army? There was a certain watchfulness about him that she recognised in Joe and Jason at times. Maybe she found him repellent because he didn't seem to care that the video showed her doing CPR on a woman who hadn't survived.

Tamsyn concentrated on the seedy-looking pair in front of her, the reek of weed clinging to their hair and clothes.

"Hey, guys! I'm Tammy. Wow, I love your accent," she said to Brodie, doing her best to sound like the stereotype of a dumb blonde. "Are you, like, Australian?"

"Fuck no! I'm from Cape Town," he said, sounding insulted. "Pongo's from Durbs."

"Oh, wow! I've always wanted to go to South Africa," she giggled. "I hear the waves there are epic. Did you know Erin Viljoen?"

His smile dropped and his expression became closed off.

"Not really."

Tamsyn heard the coolness, maybe even annoyance in his voice, and changed the topic quickly, not wanting to lose his interest just yet.

"Hey, are you one of the pro surfers here?"

Brodie puffed out his chest and nodded.

"You shoulda seen me yesterday. I was going *off!*"

"Yeah, he was cranking, it was epic," said Pongo automatically, as if his job was to stroke his friend's ego.

"That sounds so cool!"

"I'm the king of cool, pretty lady," said Brodie, slinging his arm around her and winking at his friend.

"Oh, wow," Tamsyn said again, gently slipping out from under his heavy arm. "I'd totally love to hang out but I have to meet a friend."

"Blow 'em off, *bokkie*. Hanging with the big dog is way more fun."

"I bet you are," she said with a flirty smile.

"Or tell your friend to join us," Pongo added with a leer.

"We know how to party," said Brodie.

The two men exchanged grins.

"Maybe I could meet you guys later?" Tamsyn said suggestively. "I bet there are some bitchin' parties in town. I could maybe bring some friends then?"

"Sounds good," Brodie nodded, his attention already wandering now he knew that nothing was happening right away.

"Yeah, I got a line on some blow, or maybe crank's more

your speed," said Pongo, cracking up at his own joke. "And we're going to have a *braai*, maybe even a spit-roast, if you're lucky."

Tamsyn knew that was a nickname for a sexual act involving two men and one woman – an act which she never wanted to hear of again, but she laughed as if it was the funniest thing she'd ever heard, and had to endure more of Pongo's vile remarks until he had given her the address of a local surf hostel where they'd be partying later.

Still maintaining her TPO persona, she walked away quickly, glancing over her shoulder once to see if they were watching her, but they were already hitting on some other women.

She wasn't entirely sure what she was doing, but they were from South Africa and one of them was a pro surfer. She pulled out her phone and looked up the listing of pro surfers at Boardmasters and recognised Brodie's name. According to the website, he'd been eliminated from the competition in the first round. Even so, the men might have known Erin Viljoen better than they'd been prepared to admit. Brodie hadn't been happy when Viljoen's name had been mentioned, and she couldn't help wondering why.

Besides, Tamsyn wasn't about to forget that when she'd still been a TPO, Inspector Rego had specifically tasked her to find out if Viljoen had any friends, who she talked to and who she hung out with. Surely, other South African surfers would have met her and know something?

But she also knew it would be foolish to go to the party without informing anyone. She'd made a mistake like that once before – and it had been a very dangerous error.

She typed out a long text to Inspector Rego, re-read it quickly then sent it.

His reply was swift and unnerving.

Less than an hour later, Tamsyn was back at the campsite sitting in the stuffy tent where she'd started her week. It smelled even worse than she remembered, and was littered with discarded pizza boxes and empty beer cans. No one looking at it would think that it was an intelligence hot spot for Devon & Cornwall Police.

DI Rego wasn't there and it was DS Tom Stevens who was leading the meeting. Tamsyn knew Tom Stevens but hadn't had much to do with him. Currently, he was rocking a pair of bright orange boardshorts with a t-shirt from a death-metal band called *Simbulis*, which he swore he'd borrowed from his son.

"I know you've had a long week on this," said Stevens, glancing around him at Andy, Jamie and Sully, "but you've gathered some solid leads which means a lot of scrotes are going to be off the streets a few weeks down the line. But this briefing is linked to some information that Tamsyn has come across which needs to take precedence."

Tamsyn felt her cheeks heating as she met the curious gazes of her colleagues when they all turned to stare at her.

"As you've probably heard," Stevens continued, "the death of Erin Viljoen is still being investigated and we're interested in talking to anyone in the surfing community who knew her, particularly any other South African fans, surfers, sponsors or pro surfers."

The three men nodded, still casting curious glances at Tamsyn, wondering where she came into this, especially as she'd been removed as TPO several days before.

"Earlier this afternoon, Tamsyn was approached at Fistral by two South African males. One of them was this man, Brodie Bekker, a pro surfer from Cape Town who was eliminated in the first round of the competition," and he turned his laptop screen towards them, showing a photograph from Bekker's social media page. "Interestingly, Bekker shares two of the same sponsors as Viljoen, Komsurf and Mami Wata, both South African surf apparel brands. Despite a request from the public for information on Viljoen, this man has not come forward." Stevens looked around the tent. "We want to know how well he knew Viljoen."

"Is he a suspect?" Sully asked, looking excited.

"At this point, he's just someone we want to talk to," Stevens clarified. "This is the second man," and he clicked a new screen to bring up a passport photo. "Wilhelm Dale Kaap, a.k.a. 'Pongo'."

"Is that because he stinks?" Sully chuckled.

No one else laughed and Stevens shot him a look that said he wasn't even slightly amused.

Sully's shoulders tightened in annoyance but he kept his mouth shut.

"Kaap is not a professional surfer but he does have a record: he was arrested in possession of cannabis and was in the process of being prosecuted when the law in South African changed in 2024, removing cannabis from the country's list of outlawed narcotics. People who'd broken that law previously had their records wiped clean."

Tamsyn frowned, wondering how DS Stevens had come across this information if Kaap's record had been wiped.

It was Andy who asked the question.

"So, how do we know about his non-record, sarge?"

Stevens gave a faint grin.

"Just because his record was wiped doesn't mean that the authorities took their eyes off him. He's also ex-military, enlisting in the South African National Defence Force – their army – but he's been out for a few years now."

They all nodded, looking like a row of puppets pulled by a single string.

"Kaap told Tamsyn that they'd be at a party later tonight at a surf hostel near Towan Beach where blow and crank will be available. As I'm sure you're aware, these are street names for crack cocaine and methamphetamine."

"Count me in, sarge!" said Sully.

Stevens gave him an appraising glance.

"Do we need a DSA, sarge?" asked Andy.

"We have to be lawful, Andy," Stevens replied. "We're targeting two individuals. It's not speculative, it's a crime hot spot where we think a crime could happen; we're looking to gather evidence against these two."

His gaze was assessing as he looked at each of them to make sure they understood.

"In essence, we're breaching their human rights for privacy: that's Article 8 of the European Convention on Human Rights. But – and this is the important part – we can lawfully breach that by demonstrating the intelligence we have, the intelligence we hope to get, *and* that our activity is proportionate, i.e. the balance that protects their human rights is significantly outweighed by the intelligence of evidence we believe we can obtain about the serious crime we're investigating, and that the surveillance is necessary."

He glanced around the tent again.

"Detective Chief Inspector Finch has signed off on a Directed Surveillance Authority, so it'll be legal to video and record within the surf hostel. I've got the authorisation here, which I'll pass around for you all to read. And there's also a copy of the risk assessment, so make sure you've read that, too."

Once he'd shared the paperwork, Stevens got down to the nitty gritty.

"Right, Andy, you're team-leader; Sully and Tamsyn, you're with him; Jamie, I want you to stay here and continue your TPO duties. There are still a few faces that we'd like to catch on this operation."

Jamie scowled, unhappy to be left out from the party group.

"Do you have a problem with that?" Stevens asked, glancing up.

Jamie shook his head.

"No, sarge."

"Good."

"Just the A-team at the party," Sully laughed, not noticing that DS Stevens was looking at him with irritation.

He paused just long enough for Sully to finally notice the weight of his stare.

Tamsyn wished that Jamie was going to the party instead of Sully. Every word that came out of Sully's mouth annoyed her.

"The three of you will be wearing buttonhole video cameras."

He handed Tamsyn a tiny spy camera concealed in a necklace, and the two men were given pin badges which also held hidden cameras.

"You're there to look and listen. Find out what you can about these two characters, specifically how well they knew Viljoen. Because you're already known as being on the shady side from your work at the campsite, this will be a good chance for you to pick up some extra intel, so keep your ears to the ground."

Stevens glanced around the tent as the men nodded.

"DI Rego, myself, and someone from tech support will be in the van, and there'll be an additional unmarked van with uniformed officers and a dog handler. We'll also have a drone up in case people try to exit the building across neighbours' walls, or if they attempt to dispose of any drug paraphernalia over the cliff. Everyone clear so far?"

There was a quiet chorus of, "Yes, sarge."

"Okay, that's the big picture. Now, I know that you've done TPO work this week, but this is different. Remember, it's a party, so try and be yourselves. Clear your head: you're not a police officer tonight. Think about what you did before you joined the police. Avoid using any police jargon, and don't ask too many questions – let people talk to you."

They were all listening intently, so Stevens continued.

"Check your pockets: if you usually keep a handcuff key on your key ring, take it off. You'll need your Warrant Card with you, but make sure it's well concealed and isn't going to fall out of a pocket. Right, the rules. These are crucial and you don't break them, *ever*: don't go into a separate room or a corner, stay where people can see you; don't go into anyone's car; don't keep touching your camera – we can see and hear everything you'll see."

"Will we able to hear you, sarge?" Andy asked. "It's probably going to be pretty noisy in there."

"That's a good point, Andy, and the answer is no, you won't be able to hear us. Wearing an earpiece would be a dead giveaway, but we'll be able to hear you at all times. If you see something that you think is important, I want you to drop your sunglasses on the floor. If you're in trouble or there's an imminent threat of danger, the call sign is, *Bingo! Bingo! Bingo!* Then we'll all pile in and get you."

They laughed nervously.

"Watch your backs and watch each other. Any more questions?"

"No, sarge."

"Okay, one last thing, although I shouldn't need to remind

you," said Stevens. "Do not take a drink from anyone else. If you're handed a drink that's been opened, *do not drink it*, you don't know if it's been spiked."

Tamsyn already knew that one – Jess had once been roofied at a club in Falmouth. It had been a terrifying experience for both of them.

CHAPTER 16

The woman standing in front of Rego was short, reaching somewhere in the vicinity of his chin, but exuding authority and composed assurance.

He recognised her type immediately.

"Inspector Rego," she said, offering her hand. "I am Major Beverly Nkosi from the Directorate for Priority Crime Investigation in Pretoria." She paused, taking him in from tip to toe. "Although you might know the DPCI by our nickname: the Hawks."

While he was driving back from Exeter, Rego had taken yet another call from the Chief's office alerting him to the fact that a delegate from the South African Police Service would be waiting for him in his makeshift office in Newquay, and Major Nkosi was very keen to discuss the Viljoen case.

The information that a delegate from DPCI had arrived in Cornwall was conveyed to Rego a cosy quarter of an hour before arriving back in Newquay.

During those precious minutes, he'd used every second to run through a list of questions for Major Nkosi in his head; he hadn't even had a chance to take a sip from the take-out coffee he'd bought at a drive-thru on the A30.

"Please, have a seat," he said, after shaking hands with his unexpected visitor. "I'm sorry you've been kept waiting – I didn't learn of your arrival until a few minutes ago."

Major Nkosi cocked her head on one side and gave him a clipped smile.

"I would have thought, Detective Inspector Rego, that you had been expecting a visit from the Directorate ever since you found out that Ryan Kloppers was a Hawks' asset embedded within the Black Axe criminal organisation."

"I'll rephrase," said Rego. "I had not been made aware that an in-person visit was on the cards."

Despite her diminutive height, Major Nkosi exuded confidence, her warm dark skin smooth and ageless, her hair pulled back in a tight bun.

"How can I help you?" Rego asked politely.

He wondered where this conversation was going and how much he was going to kick Vikram's arse for not giving him a heads-up.

"I believe we can help each other, Inspector," she replied.

Rego waited.

The major reached into a large briefcase and pulled out a thick file which she laid on the table between them.

"Five years ago, Ryan Kloppers was nothing more than another white boy who spent his days surfing, partying, and, we believe, selling cannabis to his friends to fund his lifestyle. Unlike many of his acquaintances, he actually showed some talent as a surfer and had a few minor successes at amateur local surfing events. Until he made the mistake of short-changing a drug dealer who worked for certain gang members in Durban."

"Black Axe."

"Indeed. It might have ended with Mr Kloppers losing no more than a few fingers to remind him not to be so careless in future, but because he was white and because he travelled legitimately across the country chasing his dream of becoming a professional surfer, he was deemed to be of use to certain criminal elements. He was given little choice in the matter."

"Selling drugs?"

She shook her head.

"No, as a courier. Kloppers was instructed to carry 'tokens', images on encrypted message platforms as a go-between for his masters, who were both buyers and sellers for a number of different commodities. Some of these commodities were drugs, some were women trafficked for the purpose of prostitution, but more recently the commodity was more likely to be guns."

Rego pressed his lips together. It was a scenario very similar to the one described by Vikram. He'd hoped – prayed – that such darkness would not be brought to this small county of beaches and blue skies.

"It's unclear whether or not Kloppers knew what commodities were being traded, but either way, he was very useful to Black Axe – a white boy, a half-vagrant surfer travelling around brought little attention."

"But somehow he came to *your* attention?"

She nodded and smiled.

"He did: through his cousin Wilhelm Dale Kaap, known as 'Pongo'."

"Wait, what? Kaap is Kloppers' cousin?"

"You know this man?" Nkosi asked, looking surprised.

"Yes, he's just come onto our radar. He invited one of our undercover officers to a party tonight where we believe drugs will be supplied or sold. But we didn't know he was related to Ryan Kloppers."

"A party tonight? Here, in Newquay?"

Rego nodded. "I've already arranged for three undercover officers to attend the party, with uniforms for back up."

"Kaap is a dangerous man, Inspector Rego," Nkosi said, her expression serious. "Especially when cornered. He served two years in the South African National Defence Force but was dishonourably discharged for beating a man half to death with his bare hands. Two months ago, he was drinking in Long Street in Cape Town when a man bumped into him and spilled his beer. Kaap nearly killed the man – he'll never piss straight again."

"He wasn't charged?"

"The victim was too scared to press charges and we couldn't find any witnesses, despite it being a crowded bar," Nkosi said bitterly.

It was not news that Rego wanted to hear but he nodded his thanks and glanced at his wristwatch. He had four hours before the undercover team would arrive at the party.

"I need to inform my officers about Kaap," he said, immediately picking up his phone.

"Wait, please," said Major Nkosi. "There is more to tell you. Quite a lot more."

Rego glanced at his wristwatch once more, but put his phone back on the table, making notes as Nkosi continued to talk.

"One of our officers made contact with Kloppers. It wasn't difficult for us to persuade him that his only way of getting *out*, was by getting further *in*. The more that senior members of Black Axe trusted him, the more intelligence we could gather to bring them down. But then Kloppers stopped checking in with his handler, and eventually, he disappeared."

"So, what went wrong?"

She shook her head.

"We don't know. At first, we thought that he'd been discovered, but in fact, that wasn't the case. It could have been any one of several possibilities. Perhaps he was simply too scared to continue. Perhaps Black Axe offered him more than we could. We didn't know that Kloppers wished to transition, and with a cost of more than R600,000 – approximately £30,000 – that could have been the key motivating factor. Whatever it was, Kloppers disappeared."

"And reappeared as Erin Viljoen."

"That is correct. Two years after Kloppers went missing, we received intelligence that he had in fact transitioned. We reached out to him ... to her, but she was not receptive to our approach. She said that she was no longer involved with Black Axe and that she simply wanted to be left alone." Major Nkosi gave an amused snort. "As if that was ever going to happen. However, we were prepared to watch and wait. We thought she would make contact with her cousin, Kaap, but that didn't happen either. In fact, it seemed as though she might be exactly what she said she was – a transgender professional athlete on an international surfing circuit."

"Then what happened?"

Nkosi turned several pages in the folder until she came to a photograph of Viljoen with Phil and Julie Ford.

"They happened: Michelle and Pieter Duprise, also known as Philip and Julie Ford, although they've used at least two other aliases that we know of. They approached Viljoen as potential sponsors for her surfing career, offering to support her on the World Surfing League circuit – paying her airfares, putting her up in five-star hotels, obtaining modelling contracts for her."

Rego sighed. "They groomed her."

"They did, and it worked. Kloppers/Viljoen, believed it all. But the Duprises were working with Black Axe to bring conflict diamonds out of Zimbabwe and selling them in Europe where they would command higher prices. We believe that the Duprises/Fords then transferred the money back to Black Axe via Bitcoin, taking their own commission."

Rego drummed his fingers on the table, his mind spinning with possibilities.

"So, where does Viljoen's death fit into this? Are you saying she was murdered?"

Nkosi gave him an appraising look.

"Your Chief Constable Evans tells me you're keeping an open mind about that."

Her smile was small and tight.

"Yes, but I didn't know what you've just told me. This information sheds a completely new light on the case."

"You knew that Kloppers was our asset, you could have drawn your own conclusions."

They stared at each other in accusation across the table.

"Yes," Rego said at last. "I believe that Erin Viljoen's death is suspicious, but I have no evidence which would stand up in court. The Fords have left Cornwall but I'm having their vehicle tracked as we speak. The rental company gave us access to their car's tracker – they're currently in a motorway service station on the M5." He paused. "So, you tell me: do you think Viljoen was murdered?"

Nkosi nodded once.

"It seems the most likely scenario, but I don't know why. It seemed like a very successful business arrangement. Somehow, she transported the diamonds – although we have not ascertained how she did that – and the Fords sold the diamonds across Europe."

"Well, I can help you with part of that," said Rego, feeling slightly smug. "Viljoen transported them in her surfboards – we believe that the foam interiors were impregnated with diamonds then covered with fibreglass. She was known for 'sparkly' boards," and he hooked his fingers in quote marks around the words.

Nkosi gave a startled look.

"Thank you, Inspector Rego," said Nkosi, a shred of respect creeping into her voice. "How ingenious."

"We're also liaising with colleagues in West Midlands Police and the National Crime Agency to ascertain who Viljoen's contact was in Birmingham's Jewellery Quarter where we believe the diamonds were traded," Rego added. "So, I'll ask you again: who had reason to kill Erin Viljoen?"

Nkosi sat silently for several seconds.

"I don't know, Inspector," she said thoughtfully. "But from intelligence received, we believe that the Duprises were skimming money from Black Axe – neither a safe nor intelligent thing to do. Perhaps Erin Viljoen was party to this and they silenced her, or she was also skimming and the Duprises silenced her, or perhaps Viljoen planned to tell Black Axe what they were doing to save herself..."

"...and the Fords silenced her. Yeah, I get it," said Rego, slapping his hands onto the table. "Right, with the information about the Fords that you've given me, that's more than enough to have them arrested," and he tapped the thick folder that Nkosi had laid on the table between them. "Plus, they're a clear flight risk."

Rego made the call then started to stand, but Nkosi leaned across the table.

"One moment, Inspector."

Rego frowned and sat down again.

"We have intelligence – unverified, I'm afraid – that suggests Erin Viljoen was not the only surfer involved with Black Axe," she said. "They never put all their eggs in one basket."

Rego leaned forward.

"Who?"

She raised her hands.

"We don't know."

Rego gave a slight smile.

"Maybe I do. Kaap has been travelling with another South African surfer by the name of Brodie Bekker. He's going to be at the party with my officers tonight, too."

Rego didn't know if things were coming together or splintering into a hundred different pieces.

He had three untrained officers going undercover at what had seemed to be just another drug-fuelled surfer party, but instead it could well be the tip of the spear for an OCG renowned for its violence.

Undercover operatives were usually exhaustively trained, with good reason: there were moral and legal dilemmas intrinsically involved, and the police didn't want another scandal like the Mark Stone case of 2010, where a Met officer who'd been undercover for seven years had formed sexual relations with a number of women; another officer had even fathered children with one of the political activists of a group which he'd been deployed to infiltrate.

The training and rules had been overhauled extensively since then, and even Test Purchase Officers were obliged to study for up to six different levels of technical and operational skills. Only one of three officers selected for tonight's party had reached even that level; Tamsyn and PC Freddie Sullivan had been chosen as TPOs for their youthful looks and ability to fit in with the Boardmasters festival crowd – but they'd had only limited training.

DCI Finch hadn't been happy about that when Rego had approached him for the Directed Surveillance Authority, but they both knew that older officers would be 'made' as police immediately. Rego believed that he had more than enough backup in place to keep them as safe as possible, but he also knew that the best laid plans could become fluid at any moment and to use a wonderful police euphemism, the situation could become 'dynamic'.

And it wasn't just the surf party that Rego had to plan for: he also had officers stationed at both Portreath and Newquay harbours in the event that *Penrose Pride* was spotted, and the Coastguard were patrolling in case they came across the mysterious owners of the fishing boat.

If that wasn't enough, Vikram was still hearing whispers about an arms deal that Black Axe were involved with: who, when, where and how, all remaining unknowns.

The fact that members of the press were breathing down Rego's neck now they'd been given his name as SIO on the Viljoen case was the least of his concerns.

Then Tom Stevens stuck his head around Rego's door.

"Boss, we've got another problem."

Rego ran a hand over his head.

"Jesus, Tom! What is it now?"

"The Fords' car hasn't moved for more than an hour-and-a-half. They wouldn't spend that long having a cup of coffee: my suspicion is that they've swapped vehicles."

Rego cursed himself for not having had them apprehended when he'd had the chance, although to be fair, there hadn't been enough evidence for an arrest warrant at that time.

"Tom, make contact with officers from Somerset & Avon Police. Fill them in and say that we're sending an officer up to Taunton Deane to check CCTV footage of the car parks and service areas to see if they can spot the Fords and identify their subsequent vehicle."

"I could send John."

DC Frith was one of the youngest members of Rego's team, good with IT and had an uncanny ability to spot people in a crowd who didn't want to be spotted.

"Good. And advise John that the Fords could well have disguised their appearances by now, but two people coming out of the service station who never went in – that's how he'll pick them up."

"I'll phone ahead so that the service station's head of security has the timeframe we're looking at downloaded onto a flash drive."

And on this occasion, they could narrow down the exact number of minutes of CCTV that DC Frith would need to scrutinise.

"At least we're not running up against the 30-day rule, boss," Stevens sighed.

Rego simply nodded.

ANPR footage could be retained for a year – usually more, in Rego's experience – but localised ANPR from car parks and so on, might only be kept for 90 days; as for CCTV footage, by law, that could only be kept for 30 days, then had to be written over.

Which fool had come up with that law?

Rego rubbed his eyes then moved on to the next issue to be dealt with.

CHAPTER 17

Joe called just as Tamsyn was waiting by the TPO van to head out to the party.

"How are you doing?" he asked.

"I'm so nervous that I've been to the toilet ten times already," she admitted.

He laughed quietly, his voice warm and reassuring as always.

"Nah, you'll be fine.

"Have you got any advice? Top ten tips for covert ops?" she asked, only half joking.

"Only one: try not to look too hot, because you'll get hit on. I know that'll be hard for you."

"Oh, yeah, sure," she laughed awkwardly.

"Do you remember your imminent danger call sign?"

"Of course, I do – I've been saying it every time I had to run to the toilet."

"I hope your video camera wasn't turned on."

For a moment, Tamsyn stopped breathing.

"Oh my God! For a second, there..."

"Keep your knickers on," Joe chuckled. "They won't have

started recording yet. Look, you'll be fine, Tam. Just call me when you're done."

"It might be late and I know you're on earlies tomorrow."

"Just call me," he said.

"Okay, I will." She paused, so many words unsaid. "I have to go now – they're loading up the van."

"Stay safe, Cornwall."

"I will."

The call ended and for a moment Tamsyn stood there staring at the blank screen, and she felt better, as if she could breathe again.

She didn't understand why he had so much faith in her; it just mattered that he did.

Within a few minutes, the TPO van was pulling up outside the surf hostel.

Tamsyn knew the place although she'd never stayed there. It was cleanish, smallish, and the website said that the rooms all had bunkbeds and there were two shared shower rooms at the end of the hall; but its amazing views overlooking Towan Beach were hard to beat, and there was a long, narrow garden down to the cliffs where you could smoke a doobie in peace.

The owners were tolerant, often absent, and the place had a laidback vibe. It was a great place to party.

The battered builder's van that they'd used at the Boardmasters campsite had been hastily kitted out with laptops and was bristling with antennas which boosted the signals for the miniature cameras each of the undercover team were wearing.

A second van crammed with uniformed police was parked a short distance away, a drone pilot was already in place down on the beach, and a third van contained the detective team with IT support.

For her first UC operation, Tamsyn had chosen to wear

cut-off jeans and a long-sleeved Roxy t-shirt paired with heavy black Doc Marten boots. They didn't look out of place but also gave her a slightly dangerous edge which she liked. More importantly, a kick from those could do someone an injury.

Cars with surfboards on roof-racks lined the street along with half-a-dozen classic VW kombi-vans. And as Tamsyn, Sully and Andy approached the open front door, the sweet smell of weed and vapes wafted out to greet them.

Sully was bouncing on the balls of his feet, nerves making him jittery. Tamsyn thought he looked like some tweaker who was craving meth, but that wasn't necessarily a bad look for a party like this.

The problem was, surprisingly, Andy.

"Shit, I stick out like a sore thumb," he muttered under his breath. "I'm twice the age of everyone here."

As if to reinforce the point, someone yelled out, "Woah! Who invited their dad?" and several people laughed, pointing at Andy.

He turned to give them the kind of hard stare that he'd been using as a TPO all week. It seemed to work, because the guy backed off and ambled into another room.

The main area was a kitchen-diner leading to the back garden. It would be really hard to spot their targets because the room was dark even though someone had strung a set of lights along one wall: *green, red, green, red.*

The lights flashed sequentially, making everyone look alternately either ill or sunburned.

Tamsyn glanced around the room casually but couldn't see either Brodie or Pongo.

"Let's check out the garden," said Andy, leaning in so that Tamsyn and Sully could hear him over the pounding techno beat.

"Nah, let's dance," said Sully. "We gotta blend in."

He grabbed Tamsyn, pulling her so close that her boobs skimmed his chest and his groin pressed into her. She stamped heavily on his foot.

He screeched and hopped away.

"Fuckin' hell!"

"Touch me again and I'll tear your knob off!" she seethed.

"For fuck's sake!" Andy snapped, stepping between them.

Sully scowled at her and Tamsyn stared back, unrepentant.

"I gotta hit the head," said Sully in a sulky voice.

"We're supposed to stay together!"

"I'm not going to stay and piss my pants," he snorted.

Andy shook his head in annoyance.

"Okay, find the bathrooms but be quick. If you see our targets, do not engage, okay?"

"Fine, *Dad*," Sully sneered, wandering off with an unopened six-pack in his hand.

Tamsyn watched him go, wondering if he was going to make trouble for her and considering whether or not she'd report him first.

Dickhead.

Andy jerked his head at her to follow him, then led the way through the smoke-filled kitchen-diner to the garden. The music was still loud enough to annoy the neighbours, but not quite as ear-splitting. Tamsyn sipped from a bottle of water that she'd brought with her, moving to the music and looking like any other surfer chick there to party.

Then she spotted their targets: Bekker had turned and looked like he was about to head off to another room, but Kaap was having an intense discussion with a dark-haired guy in his thirties, and it was clear that they were not in agreement. Unfortunately, there was no way of getting closer to them without being too obvious.

"I see Kaap," said Tamsyn. "He's arguing with someone. Oh, wait, the unknown just passed something over to Kaap but I couldn't see what it was."

"Did he receive anything in return?" Andy asked.

"Yes, an envelope, I think it's money ... yes, he's counting it and he doesn't look happy."

Andy glanced in the direction she'd indicated. His body stiffened, then he awkwardly fumbled with his sunglasses so they fell to the floor. He crouched down to pick them up.

Tamsyn's eyes widened, knowing that this was one of the prearranged signals.

"Shit," he muttered, pretending to scrabble on the floor for his sunglasses. "I know the other man and he knows me. He knows I'm a copper."

"Who is it?" Tamsyn asked.

"We've got to get out of here before he sees me," Andy said urgently, grabbing Tamsyn by the hand and pulling her back through the hostel.

Neither of them could see Sully.

"I'll check upstairs," Andy said, his voice tense. "Tamsyn, go! Walk towards our van. Go past it and if it's safe for you to enter, they'll open the door. Go!"

His urgency was contagious and she had to force herself not to run.

The crowd had thickened in the short time that they'd been there, and what had seemed like a fun crowd, now felt claustrophobic. Tamsyn hated the feeling of strangers surrounding her, their hot, sweaty bodies leaning into her.

The air was dense, scented with booze, drugs, and joss sticks; people who were drunk or high pressed around her, shoving her from side to side as she fought to reach the front door.

She put her head down and pushed her way through,

using her elbows and boots to make space. Someone yelled at her, but she surged on, looking neither left nor right.

She almost made it.

"Hey, *bokkie!*"

Brodie was standing between Tamsyn and the front door, completely wasted and barely able to stand. But he was tall, heavily-muscled, and much stronger than her.

He swayed on his feet, a bottle of whiskey in one hand and an unlit doobie behind his ear.

Tamsyn gave a weak smile.

"Oh, hey! Yeah, sorry, gotta go and meet my boyfriend."

"What boyfriend?" he slurred, reaching for her hand and missing as she yanked it away.

"I saw Pongo in the back garden," she said. "I think he was looking for you, dude."

He turned to gaze blearily in the direction of the kitchen-diner, so Tamsyn slipped around him and out into the fresh air.

Her heart was pounding as she headed for the police van, and she desperately wanted to look over her shoulder to see if Bekker was following. She didn't think he would, but she felt incredibly vulnerable during those 60 seconds. As she approached the van, the door slid open and two hands pulled her inside.

She collapsed onto a box seat, adrenaline making her shaky.

Rego crouched next to her, his expression full of concern. DS Stevens was beside him, hunched over a laptop with an IT tech.

They were all staring at her, and Tamsyn realised that she was breathing too fast, as if she'd just run a four-minute mile.

"Are you okay, Tamsyn?" Rego asked.

She blinked and took a deep breath to slow her breathing,

then wished she hadn't. The van was airless, the men hot and sweaty.

"Yes, sir. I'm fine," she lied, trying to calm her racing pulse.

"What happened?"

"Bekker and Kaap were there. Kaap looked like he was arguing with another guy. We couldn't get close enough to hear, but I saw the unknown male pass something to Kaap, and then Kaap handed him an envelope that looked like it had a large quantity of money in it." She took a deep breath, still feeling shaken by the encounter. "But then Andy said that he knew the unknown male so we had to leave. Well, he sent me outside but he had to go upstairs to find Sully."

"Why wasn't Sully with you?" Stevens asked. "You were supposed to stay together."

"Uh, he went to find a toilet," Tamsyn stammered, giving him a partial truth.

Rego was more interested in why the surveillance had gone sideways so quickly.

"Did Andy say who the man was or how he knew him?" he asked.

Tamsyn shook her head.

"There wasn't time – he just told me to go."

Rego shared a worried glance with his sergeant.

"If Andy and Sully aren't back here in the next two minutes, I want uniform in there."

But before the time was up, Andy was knocking quietly on the door, Sully at his side.

"What happened in there?" Rego asked urgently.

"It looked like Kaap was doing a deal," said Andy, pulling a face. "But I knew the other man he was talking to – it was Mimi's fiancé.

The stifling air seemed charged, and identical expressions of horror appeared on Stevens' and Rego's faces.

"The man doing a deal with Kaap is DC Eagling's fiancé?" Rego asked, hoping that he'd misunderstood. "Are you sure?"

Andy nodded miserably

"Yes, his name is Luka Mastemak. His family runs a business in Redruth importing food from eastern Europe. I've met Luka several times. I liked him – he and Mimi seemed good together. I don't know, maybe I was wrong..."

Rego turned to the techie.

"Check the video feed," he ordered.

It took the techie several minutes to line up the video from Tamsyn's spy necklace camera to the correct place. Then they all leaned in, peering at the laptop.

"You're saying that this man is Mimi's fiancé?" Rego pressed.

Andy sucked in a deep breath.

"That's definitely him."

"You're sure?"

Andy nodded again.

"One hundred per cent, boss."

Rego turned back to the screen, appalled by this new intel. He'd have to deal with what was sure to be a shitstorm later.

"We can clearly see that Luka passes something to Kaap," he said, squinting at the video, "but I'm not able to identify the item."

But there was no doubt that Kaap had subsequently passed Luka an envelope filled with banknotes, and that Luka hadn't been happy about the amount.

Rego and Stevens stared at each other – could there be a legitimate reason for the exchange?

It was possible, but given what they knew about Kaap, it didn't look good. Not to mention the fact that Mimi believed her fiancé was still in Poland and not expected back for several days. She'd even told them that he didn't have roaming on his phone so she wasn't able to be in touch with him.

It didn't look good for Luka Mastemak.

But was it enough to send in uniform?

Sully raised his hand as if he was still in school.

"Um, when I went to the bathroom, I saw what looked like someone buying drugs: a packet of pink powder was exchanged for cash. I think it might have been pink coke."

Rego raised his eyebrows. He hadn't been aware of any incidents of pink coke being seized in Cornwall. He'd heard that it was being found in Manchester where it was popular on the party scene, especially among the Latin American community.

Contrary to its name, it didn't usually contain cocaine and was actually a synthetic designer drug made from a mixture of MDMA, ketamine and amphetamines. It could even contain LSD, mescaline, and sometimes opioids like fentanyl.

But Sully's find certainly suggested that he'd seen drugs being sold.

"Okay, thanks, everyone. Good work, guys," Rego said, trying to sound upbeat even though he was worried about the connection to an officer from his own team. "We believe that there are drugs on the premises. I'm sending in uniform."

Then he turned to stare at Sully.

"But if you ever lay hands on another woman without her permission, let alone a fellow officer, I'll have no hesitation in reporting you."

The next few minutes were chaotic. Officers moved into the premises and the sniffer dog had a field day. Seventeen arrests were made, and a fleet of police vans was needed to transport those detained to custody suites across the two counties of Devon and Cornwall.

Newquay Police Station had been recently refurbished to provide 25 custody suites, but that wasn't nearly enough, so the rest of the detained persons were shared out to police stations at Camborne, Exeter, and St Austell.

Rego made sure that, Kaap, Bekker, and Luka Mastemak were sent to Newquay where he intended to work out a strategy for interviewing all three at the same time. Whatever their connection, he intended to find out what it was, but with three key players, time would be against them; Rego could hold them for a maximum of 24 hours before having to either charge them or release them.

He phoned both DCI Finch and DCS Richards to update them about the raid; he wouldn't bother ACC Nash or the Chief Constable until he had something more concrete to tell them.

The worst part had been when Rego informed Mimi Eagling that her fiancé was in custody. She hadn't believed him at first, then she'd been angry, and eventually tearful. She'd begged to be allowed to see him, but there was no way Rego could allow it, not after DCI Finch had expressly forbidden it.

"Get her back to Newquay nick now, Rob," Finch had ordered. "She needs to make herself available for questioning."

"She's already on her way now, boss."

"Keep me updated."

"Yes, sir," said Rego.

He hated this.

He hated having suspicions about an officer he'd trusted.

Rego knew that Mimi could no longer be part of the Viljoen investigation. He didn't want to dwell on the irony that he was still under investigation himself, but *his* integrity had been underwritten on the back of ACC Sue Nash's career.

And now DCI Boyd from Professional Standards was standing in front of him waiting to see Mimi, to serve her a Reg 9 notice.

"Evening, Rego," he said affably. "Late night or early start?"

Rego wanted to ignore the pleasantries, but DCI Boyd was still the ranking officer.

"Both, sir," he said. "I assume you're here to see DC Eagling?"

Boyd nodded and introduced his colleague from the Professional Standards team who'd be interviewing Mimi about her involvement with Luka.

They'd been to Newquay before so knew where to find a quiet space for a formal chat.

Minutes later, Mimi arrived accompanied by a Federation rep.

She'd always been a tiny, turbo-charged powerhouse, but now she looked utterly shellshocked, fragile and already beaten. And no wonder, when the man she wanted to marry was involved with a drug-dealing criminal like Kaap; no wonder her eyes were haunted and red-rimmed.

When she saw Rego, her lips trembled and she put her hand over her mouth, tears filling her eyes.

"Mimi..." Rego began.

She shook her head wordlessly and looked as though she wanted to get away from him as quickly as possible.

"Mimi!" he said more loudly.

She turned around but seemed to find his shoes fascinating.

"I'm sorry about all of this, Mimi," he said. "But I have to ask, do you recognise this set of keys?"

He held out an evidence bag with the set of keys that Mastemak had given to Kaap. The keyring was distinctive and in the shape of a Cornish pasty.

"Where did you get...?" She slapped her hand over mouth as if trying to push the words back in.

"Mimi?"

She swallowed and looked down.

"They're Luka's," she said, her voice tight. "I gave him that keyring. He has a lockup in Plymouth. It's for the business though. It's not ... it's not..."

She couldn't finish the sentence, but turned and hurried down the corridor away from him.

Rego ran a weary hand over his face. All it needed now was for Tom Stevens to get a Reg 9 notice, and half his team would be under some sort of investigation.

He shook his head. He couldn't think about this now; he had three interviews to prepare for and the custody clock was ticking – a solid strategy would be crucial.

CHAPTER 18

Rego was exhausted. He'd worked through the night to prepare for this morning's round of interviews.

Nkosi had refused to return to her hotel, choosing instead to share the load, working with him and Stevens to prep the interview packages for the following morning, going over and over the plans for questioning Kaap, Bekker and Luka Mastemak.

Nkosi had also contacted her office in Pretoria and was waiting for further intel from them.

All three of the suspects had requested solicitors and the briefs would be arriving shortly.

But there was one piece of good news – or bloody awful news, depending on your point of view – Luka Mastemak's lockup contained the battered old ambulance that he'd driven across Europe to the border with Ukraine. It still had a sticker on the side saying, *Aid for Ukraine donated by Devon & Cornwall Police.*

The ambulance had been lifted onto the back of a flatbed lorry and taken to a forensic garage. They'd brought in scanners which had detected the presence of a number of secret compartments, and when they'd pulled them apart, they'd found them to contain a large quantity of automatic weapons and ammunition. The team in Exeter had brought in specialists to 'make safe' the weapons before they could touch them, so the final quantity hadn't yet been ascertained.

But it looked very bad for Mimi's fiance – he was looking at a lot of years in prison.

Rego had no idea how she would cope with that ... when she was finally told.

And since Kaap had been the recipient of the keys, there was a clear link that he was involved in arms-trafficking. All they needed him to do was roll over on his association with Black Axe. But Rego knew the man would be a tough one to crack.

Yawning and stretching out his tortured muscles, Rego washed in the police station's toilets, splashing cold water on his face, but from long habit, he always kept a go-bag in the boot of his car containing clean clothes and a few toiletries. He was so tired, he'd nearly cut his throat shaving, and had stuck a piece of toilet paper over the nick on his chin.

Stevens looked like hell, which also made him look dangerous. By contrast, Major Beverly Nkosi looked as fresh as a daisy. Rego suspected that if he dropped her in the middle of the Amazon jungle, she'd still look smart and professional.

But all of them were sleep-deprived, having grabbed only an hour's rest before final preparations for the interviews.

During the night, Rego had come up with another really cunning plan. He was going to arrange for Nkosi to be in the custody block, then have Kaap and Bekker brought from their cells to wash or clean their teeth or whatever excuse worked best at the time. Nkosi would be chatting with the custody sergeant and they'd both hear her South African accent. Kaap would probably guess who she was, and Bekker might, as well. Rego hoped this could unnerve them or even perhaps get them wondering if the Hawks' officer would be unleashed on them using a different style of interview technique.

Any advantage would be beneficial even if it was purely psychological.

He tried to clear his mind and prioritise.

Items seized from the raid were still being processed, such was the quantity and variety of pharmaceuticals, including those found on Kaap and Bekker, and Rego was confident that they had Kaap for dealing, if nothing else. The ambulance's concealed weapons were more problematic because unless they found proof that Kaap had been inside the ambulance or the lockup – a fingerprint, a stray hair, *something* that would tie him to it – he could plausibly deny knowing what the keys were for when he'd been given them. And he could even say that the money he'd given to Mastemak was a loan or a gift, and nothing to do with the lockup.

Rego didn't know what reasons or excuses Kaap might give until he was questioned. But they'd found a large quantity of drugs on him that they suspected to be fentanyl.

That was something.

Not enough.

But something.

Rego yawned widely.

He needed coffee.

He needed a full Cornish breakfast.

He needed eight hours' sleep in his own bed.

He needed half-an-hour to nip into Sainsbury's café and get a hot breakfast.

When Rego had first joined the force, most police stations had their own canteens which were open 24 hours a day. You could get a '999 breakfast' served around the clock that fed hungry coppers doing shift work. The Met even had a mobile catering unit called TEAPOT 1, a meals-on-wheels vehicle that brought much needed cuppas and other refreshments to officers attending a prolonged incident.

Rego had got as far as reaching for his jacket when Tom and Jen knocked on the door of his borrowed office.

"Boss, can we have a word?"

Sighing, Rego collapsed back in his chair.

"What is it?"

"We got the CCTV from West Midlands Police yesterday," Tom began, looking worried. "There was a lot to look through."

Rego sensed an *oh, shit* moment coming his way.

He knew that viewing CCTV was everyone's least favourite task, although highly necessary. The officer viewing the footage had to keep a complete written record, the video viewing log or VVL, so you didn't have to keep looking at the video but could refer to the narrative. The schedule was written in columns with *date/time/video counter*, and a description of what was happening at that time.

The officer also had to check that the 'record time' and 'actual time' matched: older systems could have time slippage or sometimes hadn't been updated when daylight saving hours were changed at Easter and the end of October. Accuracy was vital.

It was boring, time-consuming and a complete ball ache.

"And...?" Rego prompted.

Jen cleared her throat.

"The CCTV clearly shows that Viljoen had two phones, boss. And, um, there's footage from the hotel bar that shows the same thing. It was missed at the time..."

She opened her laptop and pointed at a freeze-frame on the screen.

Rego felt the top of his head come off.

"For fuck's sake! Why are we only aware of this *now?*"

He was bubbling with anger, disappointed that someone hadn't raised this earlier – especially since he'd specifically told Jen to look out for 'mirror' numbers, phones that connected with others numbers that they were analysing. But it hadn't even been that hard – CCTV from the bloody hotel plainly showed Viljoen with two phones.

He took a breath, knowing that he needed to keep his professionalism.

"Jen, I'm not going to ask you who viewed these videos and failed to spot the second phone, I'm not going to put you in that position."

He paused, but she kept her eyes on his desk, knowing she'd screwed up. Rego looked at his sergeant.

"Tom, you'll have to sort this out. We have experienced detectives on this team, and it's just not good enough. Can you at least tell me that the Fords have used the burner phone they bought in the supermarket?"

Stevens grimaced and shook his head.

"It hasn't been turned on, boss?"

"And you're sure you've got the right number?" Rego asked bitterly.

"I'm sure," said Stevens, his voice neutral.

Rego rubbed his forehead. His last question had been uncalled for but he was royally pissed off.

"Right," he said tightly, "we'll put this behind us and treat it as a learning experience, but it's *not* going to happen again."

Jen and Tom exchanged quick glances. They rarely saw this side of Rego but knew the bollocking was well deserved.

He sent them off to get onto tech support about the recently discovered number belonging to Viljoen. The results wouldn't come through quickly enough to be useful for the interviews, but further down the line, there should be some good intel to follow.

Rego hated losing his temper. On another day, he might not have blown up at them but he'd just worked 24 hours without sleep, and today was shaping up to be just as long. He liked his team, trusted them, but being a manager, being a *good* manager meant that sometimes he had to 'manage' and not be everyone's friend. It was a balance.

Not many got it right all the time, and if he was honest with himself, he was still learning on the job.

Bloody hell!

Now he didn't have time to go out and hunt down a decent breakfast either.

Instead, he drank a cup of the filthy tar that Newquay nick called coffee. Honestly, it was so bad, he could have arrested the lot of them for false advertising under Consumer Rights Act 2015.

He glanced at his watch, aware of time ticking by too fast. He hoped that all three briefs would turn up soon – he didn't want to lose any more time.

Nkosi knocked on his office door and he waved her inside. Annoyingly, she looked wideawake and chipper.

"Good morning, Robert."

"Beverly, I saw you half-an-hour ago!"

"Yes, but that was 'last night'," she said with a smile. "Now it is 'tomorrow'."

He groaned.

Her smile slipped away.

"Brigadier Mphasha would like to know if you have been able to apprehend the people posing as Philip and Julie Ford."

She'd told Rego enough about her superior officer for him to know that Beverly was feeling the pressure even if she didn't show it.

Rego shook his head.

"We know that they changed cars at Taunton Deane services and from there they travelled to Cobham Services on the M25. That second car is still there with eyes on, but at this point, officers have not been able to spot them leaving." He saw her disappointed expression. "Officers from Surrey Police are scouring CCTV as we speak. Unfortunately, Cobham Services is the largest motorway service station in the UK – possibly in Europe – with nearly a thousand parking spots and up to 2,500 people each hour filling up with petrol alone. There are dozens of restaurants across two floors, as well as multiple entry and exit points." He paused. "There's a lot of CCTV to look at – the Fords chose their location well. Cobham Services is also equidistant between Heathrow and Gatwick airports."

"Then we've lost them."

"For now. But we'll pick up their trail again – as soon as they turn their new phone on. It's just a matter of time."

He just hoped that happened before they boarded their next flight.

"The Brigadier will be disappointed. I'm not going back empty-handed, Robert. I want Kaap."

"I can't just give him to you, Beverly, you know that."

"He will be prosecuted in South Africa," she said, her eyes narrowing. "This all originated in my country. There has only been a small amount of criminality on your little island – the core is back in Africa. We want Kaap."

Rego straightened in his chair.

"He's committed at least one serious offence on British soil and I suspect we'll uncover others. He paid for the keys to Mastemak's lockup – have you forgotten about all those AK-47s?"

She gave a quick, unimpressed snort.

"His attorney will argue that he has never been there and had no knowledge of what the ambulance contained."

"Kaap is involved in trafficking weapons."

"Which you will have trouble proving in court."

Damn it!

She was right.

"Whatever you say, Robert," Nkosi continued, "this negotiation is going on at a much higher level."

Rego nodded, certain she was right about that, as well. And he was too tired to argue with someone who'd been a pretty damn good colleague so far.

"I'm going to take you for a Cornish pasty when this is all finished," he said.

"I have seen them," she said. "Very dry-looking."

"Well, it's a good thing I don't work in Scotland, because then I'd be offering you haggis."

"I've heard of haggis – what is it?"

"The heart, liver, and lungs of a sheep, cooked with minced onion in the animal's stomach."

He thought she'd be revolted but instead she looked interested.

"Perhaps I will try that."

She smiled in amusement at the expression on his face, then shook her head.

"And now I'm feeling hungry. Well, breakfast will have to wait. What is your opinion of the Fords now, Robert?"

"I think they're involved in this up to their necks, but I'm hoping we'll know more after we've finished these interviews." He gave her a quick smile. "Ready to go?"

She gave a sharp nod.

"This woman was born ready."

Beverly Nkosi was slightly scary – she reminded Rego of his mother.

CHAPTER 19

Kaap, Bekker, and Luka Mastemak had been fingerprinted using LiveScan digital software. Rego had only seen ink pads on TV programmes – it looked messy.

The electronic method of capturing finger- and palm-prints was fast, and they'd used it to automatically check Kaap's and Bekker's prints against the national fingerprint database. This would show if a person was wanted and, importantly, whether they'd been fingerprinted in the UK on a previous occasion; if they had, the database showed the name associated with that fingerprint. Funnily enough, some persons in police custody had been known to provide false details.

The results were almost instantaneous, but unfortunately, none of the three key figures in custody were on the UK database, so Rego had sent the fingerprints to Interpol. He'd tried to speed the process by contacting his friend Rick O'Donnell at the National Crime Agency. They'd worked together on a case the previous year that had resulted in the arrest of a civilian investigator from Penzance police station – she'd got herself mixed up in an Albanian

OCG and had been sentenced to three years for leaking intelligence.

Rego had been impressed by the NCA team and occasionally shared a beer or three with O'Donnell.

Hopefully, Rick would get back to him quickly so they could sort this out on the back of a phone call, then follow up with the paperwork.

Next, the three men had been photographed and DNA samples had been taken from them. The photographs were automatically attached to the electronic custody record, but it would be weeks or even months before they received the DNA analysis – unless Rego could prove that the case should be a priority.

Nkosi was present for each of the procedures and Kaap was definitely aware of her.

Bekker was clearly worried but uncertain, casting surreptitious glances at the South African officer, and Mastemak looked like he might be sick, but that was nothing to do with Nkosi.

As for Kaap's emotional state, he was unreadable. He could have been queuing at a supermarket for all the interest he took.

Behind the scenes, Rego had been planning his interview strategy piece by piece. He knew that he was lucky to have held on as SIO for this case, because it was developing into a truly international investigation which could be handed back to the Major Crimes team at any moment, and he'd have sod all to say about it.

Rego was also very careful not to use the phrase 'terrorists' because then the investigation would definitely have to go to Counter Terrorism Policing South West.

This was *his* case and he wanted to see it through, but it seemed to be growing tentacles at every turn, becoming more and more complex and confusing. Vikram had told him to watch his back because if this turned out to be as significant as they both thought it could be, then other agencies who'd had an input on the case would be looking to claim it as being solved by them. Rego wanted some top cover to prevent that from happening, so for once in his life, he would be keeping the Chief Constable up to date with a blow-by-blow account of the progress of the interviews.

He'd decided that he was not going to conduct any of the interviews personally: instead, he would base himself in an office where he'd coordinate the interviews and update the ongoing strategy. He wanted oversight on everything that was happening in the interview rooms, and would be on hand to evaluate any further evidence coming to him from the ongoing searches and forensic testing.

It was imperative to maximise the time his team had to conduct the interviews, so he'd arranged that three interview rooms were for his team's sole use.

It could be incredibly frustrating when you had a suspect and you were ready to conduct an interview but there was no interview room free. This ate into the time a suspect could be held in police detention: 24 hours was the usual time a person could be held without charge, but this could be extended to 36 hours if the offence was very serious, but it had to be authorised by a Superintendent or above. After this, a suspect could be brought before a Magistrates' Court at which, dependent on the circumstances, a Magistrate could authorise detention at a police station without charge for a maximum of 96 hours.

The gloves were off with terrorism offences: questioning was permitted to take 14 days before charges had to be brought.

Rego had kept Vikram in the loop too, and on his friend's

suggestions, he'd contacted Border Force to see if they were aware of any ships out in the Channel who might be waiting to rendezvous with the missing fishermen from *Penrose Pride*. It was a longshot, but sometimes they proved useful.

Rego thought carefully about which of his officers to allocate to the interview teams. But with Mimi out of the picture and wanting to keep a step back himself, he needed to call in some favours.

He had DS Tom Stevens and DC Jack Forshaw down for the Kaap interview because he suspected that this man would be the hardest nut to crack. Stevens was Rego's most experienced officer and had more than a couple of tricks up his sleeve when it came to phased disclosure, giving him the maximum impact without revealing his hand in advance.

He was also very good at having casual chats with solicitors over a hot chocolate, and often was able to elicit information about their client's intentions.

Rego had asked DS Phil Brown from Exeter to link in with DC John Frith. John was well up to speed with the enquiry and needed to widen his interviewing experience: they would interview Brodie Bekker.

The problem would be finding someone to interview Luka Mastemak who wasn't readily associated with Mimi Eagling – that ruled out anyone from Penzance, Camborne or Newquay police stations. After considering his options, Rego phoned DI Frank Morton who was based at Exeter.

Morton had been surprised to hear from Rego but was happy to get involved and even offered to bring one of his own officers, DC Veronica Summers: very experienced and totally unflappable, he said.

Jen Bolitho would be in the viewing room with Rego. Despite dropping the ball on identifying that Viljoen had two phones, she'd been the data analyst on the Viljoen case and had the facts at her fingertips – not necessarily in the database where they belonged, but she was still the fount of all knowledge, and Rego needed her by his side.

Right now, she was hastily preparing interview packages. He watched as her fingers danced over her laptop's keyboard, occasionally scribbling into her official blue notebook. Her expression clearly said, *do not disturb – extreme risk of getting your head bitten off.*

Rego's next call was to ACC Sue Nash, and he explained his plan.

"No need to paint me a picture – get the fuck on with it and ring me if you need anything. By the way, Rob, the real music to my ears is that Gray sponsored the humanitarian runs where the guns have been found in the ambulances," and she cackled gleefully. "One for the back pocket!"

He could almost hear her stirring a cauldron in the background ready to roast ACC Gray. Funnily enough, Rego didn't feel the slightest bit sorry for the git.

He glanced up when Jen tapped on his door.

"The briefs are here, boss."

Two duty legal representatives had arrived, arranged by the custody officer; the third was a personal friend of Luka Mastemak.

All three solicitors were taken to their clients for an initial private consultation, and in a few minutes, the legal representatives would be asking for disclosure before the main interviews took place.

Showtime.

The custody suites at Newquay had recently been refurbished, so DS Tom Stevens and DC Jack Forshaw were squinting against the ultra-white walls and LED lights that were so bright, they should come with sunglasses as standard. The refurb was supposed to have improved things, but after just a couple of weeks' use, it was already smelling like damp dog, even with the air-conditioning working overtime.

Rego watched the opening manoeuvres with interest.

On the opposite side of the table from Stevens and Forshaw sat Wilhelm Kaap with his legal representative, who looked as though he might have hit puberty the previous week.

Dressed in the same clothes as the night before, Kaap wore a yellow-and-black lightweight summer rain jacket, its hood rolled up in the collar, with his blond rasta dreads hanging down his back.

Kaap sat in silence, his face blank, betraying no emotion, his eyes never seeming to blink. But as soon as Tom Stevens sat down and opened his folder, propping it up on his legs against the edge of the table, Kaap stood.

He unzipped his jacket, and Rego assumed that he was going to hang it on the back of his chair. He was wrong. Instead, Kaap unrolled the hood from the collar and put the jacket back on, stuffed his dreads inside, then lifted the hood over his head, zipping it up to its full extent, and pulling the drawstring tight, so only his eyes showed.

Stevens and Forshaw glanced at each other in amazement. They'd heard of this tactic during various courses on interviewing techniques. It had first been used in Northern Ireland during the Troubles of the 70s and 80s. Neither of them had ever seen it up close and personal before.

Legally, there was nothing they could do about it.

Stevens lifted an eyebrow, looking at Kaap's solicitor who seemed equally surprised, but the man simply shrugged his shoulders, before dipping his head to continue typing into his laptop.

So, that's how it's going to be.

Rego had a bet with himself that this would be a 'no comment' interview.

He would have won that bet – except for a single, chilling sentence.

Tom Stevens opened the interview in the usual way, including a description of how Kaap had half-hidden himself inside his jacket. Of course, in the fullness of time, how Kaap behaved would make little difference: it would be evidence that was going to send him to jail.

"The time is 9.35am on Sunday 10th August at Newquay Police Station, Detective Sergeant Tom Stevens and Detective Constable Jack Forshaw attending. Please identify yourself for the purpose of the tape, including your date of birth."

Kaap fixed his eyes on Stevens but didn't speak.

"Mr Kaap is refusing to speak. Is your name Wilhelm Dale Kaap, date of birth 3rd November 1989, of Durban, South Africa?"

Stevens paused then continued when no response was forthcoming, just that same implacable stare from Kaap.

Stevens glanced at the legal representative to introduce himself.

"Carl Neale, solicitor, DG Law."

Stevens nodded then asked him to confirm that his client was indeed Wilhelm Dale Kaap, which he did. At least one of them was talking.

Stevens then read the caution.

"You do not have to say anything, but it may harm your defence if you do not mention when questioned something which you later rely on in court. Anything you do say may be given in evidence." There was no response. "Do you understand the caution?"

The solicitor replied for Kaap.

"I've explained the meaning of the caution to my client and he understands."

Stevens nodded, then jumped in.

"We suspect that you may be dealing controlled drugs in the local area. Can you tell me about your involvement in your drug dealing activities?"

No response.

"You were found with a quantity of drugs on your person that we believe to be fentanyl. Can you tell me about your drug dealing?"

No response.

"I understand you have recently arrived in Cornwall," Stevens said pleasantly, continuing as if Kaap was answering his questions. "When did you come here?"

No response.

"Why did you come to Cornwall?"

Nothing.

Stevens worked his way through the list of questions they'd agreed, focusing on relevant evidence. In particular, the keys taken from him that led to the discovery of the lockup where the ambulance had been found.

"Mr Kaap, we have a video of you receiving a set of keys from a man we have identified as Luka Mastemak, and in exchange you gave him an envelope containing €15,000. The keys belonged to a lockup in Plymouth where we found a vehicle containing a number of firearms and quantities of ammunition: were you planning to sell these firearms?"

Nothing.

"Who were you going to sell these weapons to? How did you plan to contact them?"

No response.

"How did you know Mr Mastemak?"

There wasn't a single reply and, watching from the video room, Rego wasn't entirely sure that the man even blinked although he was fairly sure that Kaap was still breathing.

He watched as Stevens ploughed on, seemingly unfazed by Kaap's unnerving stare and refusal to utter a word.

After several more fruitless questions, Stevens looked up.

"Mr Kaap, in instances where a suspect doesn't answer a question, Section 36 of the Criminal Justice and Public Order Act 1994 becomes relevant. This is where a suspect fails or refuses to account for objects, substances, or marks found on his person, in his clothing or footwear, otherwise in his possession or in any place at the time of his arrest – in this case the keys, weapons, and what we believe are illegal substances found in your possession – if this goes to court, the court may draw an adverse inference about your possession of them."

Stevens then showed Kaap the video of the keys being handed to him by Luka Mastemak, and Mastemak receiving cash in return.

Still nothing, but this time the solicitor offered a short sentence.

"You keep asking Mr Kaap the same question just with different words."

"He's not saying anything anyway," Stevens said with more than a trace of sarcasm.

The solicitor's gaze went back to his laptop.

"Mr Kaap, a number of automatic weapons and ammunition have been found concealed in the ambulance, accessed by the keys in your possession. I am now showing Mr Kaap photographs of Russian-made AK-47 automatic weapons found in the vehicle, as described."

Stevens laid out a series of photographs in front of Kaap and his solicitor. Carl Neale raised his eyebrows and made a note on his laptop but once again, there was no sign of response from Kaap, his eyes still fixed unblinkingly on Stevens.

Rego glanced at the other monitors showing the interviews with Mastemak and Bekker – at least they were getting some responses. He turned back to Kaap, wondering if there was a way to get him to speak – so far, it wasn't looking good.

"We have established that this same vehicle made two identical trips in the last six months: how many weapons did you illegally import on those occasions?"

Stevens paused to allow a response even though by then Rego thought he'd have fallen off his chair if Kaap spoke.

Rego really wanted to know about those damn weapons! Were they for Black Axe? Were they a side gig that Kaap was working on for himself? Would they have been sold on in the UK or sent to Africa? How were they planning to get them out of the country?

So many questions and too few bloody answers.

Rego knew that the next question on the list was about pink cocaine. Only one of the Cornish officers had heard of it, so Rego showed them some information on the DEA's website – a U.S. federal law enforcement agency that worked to combat illegal drug trafficking and distribution.

Pink cocaine or 'tusi' to give it another of its street names, was described by the DEA as almost entirely absent of cocaine but included a mixture of substances: ketamine, MDMA, methamphetamine, fentanyl, xylazine, and dyed with pink food dye to differentiate it from cocaine. Typically, it produced mind-altering hallucinogenic effects, and because each batch was different from the one before, the user would never know the content of the powder or its concentration, making it extremely dangerous.

The previous October, it had been incorrectly reported that pink coke was the drug which had killed pop star Liam Payne in Argentina – and, *God help us* – that had made it even more popular. The same month as the singer's death, €91,000 worth of the pink powder had been seized by the *Garda* in Dublin.

Perhaps the pink colour made it more attractive to young people: there was always a lethal new toy coming onto the market.

Stevens continued:

"Did you import the drug?"

No response.

"Were you involved with others importing the drug into the UK?"

No response.

"Did you supply the drug at the party?"

No response.

"If you're not involved, this is your opportunity to tell me now." *Pause.* "Have you been coerced or threatened to supply the drug?"

Stevens glanced up to check that Kaap was still awake, but those cold eyes continued to bore into him.

Under normal circumstances, suspects would take a second or so to compose an answer, but this was never going to be the case here.

Stevens switched to general questions:

"How long have you been in the UK?"

No response.

"How did you get here? Who did you travel with?"

Then back again to direct, specific questions:

"Do you know Ryan Kloppers? Ryan Kloppers

transitioned to a female and changed her name to Erin Viljoen. Can you confirm that she was your cousin?"

No response.

"Was Erin involved in your drug dealing?"

Stevens flipped through the pages in his interview pack and without looking up, asked Jack Forshaw if he had anything to ask.

This was a pre-determined strategy, and Jack shook his head saying, "not at this time."

Stevens looked up from his folder. There was one final question to ask: it would be loaded, confrontational and strategically placed. He hoped for a dramatic effect. The pause was a bit longer, the only sound being the gentle hum of the air-conditioning unit, then,

"Are you a pivotal member of the International Criminal Organisation that call themselves 'Black Axe'? This violent group is involved in international criminal activity, drug smuggling, smuggling blood diamonds, cyber-crime and human trafficking."

Kaap's eyes visibly narrowed, sharp, cold and surgical, like they were meant to cut out Stevens' heart without ever touching him.

But that was the full extent of his response.

Disappointed, Stevens concluded the interview with a recap of the questions, again asking for an explanation, but Kaap gave them nothing.

Finally, Stevens nodded at Forshaw who stopped the recording.

At this, Kaap stood up, untied the draw string from around his hood, unzipped the jacket, rolled up the hood back inside the collar, shook out his dreads, then pulled the jacket on again and sat down.

Kaap's gaze flicked between Stevens and Forshaw, then he leaned across the table and spoke.

"If I get out of here and I see either of you, I don't care if you're with your families, I'll kill you."

Kaap's solicitor was visibly shocked, stuttering, "I don't think those comments are appropriate and I'm distancing myself from them."

Kaap turned his head slowly, staring at the young solicitor who swallowed audibly.

"Don't bother coming back then."

Forshaw made a note of both comments, and then escorted Kaap to the custody officer.

"We concluded the interview at 09.57 hours. Mr Kaap didn't say one word, not even 'no comment'. PACE and the Codes of Practice have been complied with. I want it noted on his custody record that when the interview had been concluded and not recording Mr Kaap said, and I quote," Forshaw looked at his notes although the words would be imprinted on his brain forever: "'*If I get out of here and I see either of you, I don't care if you are with your families, I will kill you*'."

The custody officer glanced at Forshaw and raised his eyebrows, then finished inputting the information onto Kaap's electronic custody record.

Kaap was taken back to his cell and locked inside.

Forshaw walked into the viewing room, his expression tense.

"Good job, Jack," said Rego. "He was trying to intimidate you, but you held your nerve."

"Bloody hell, boss!" said Jack, shaking his head. "I wouldn't want to meet him in a dark alley."

"Me neither," Rego admitted.

Forshaw threw him a grateful grin.

"Right?! Boss, I'd like to examine Kaap's detained personal property again. I just want to see if anything was missed at the time of detention, something that might have seemed unimportant."

Rego waved a hand.

"Go for it."

Rego drummed his fingers on his desk, then checked the other monitors.

A few minutes later, Forshaw returned with an exultant look on his face. In his hands, he held an evidence bag that contained a business card showing manacled fists with a black axe chopping the chain between the wrist restraints.

"Look what I found, boss! This is evidence that Kaap has an association with Black Axe."

Rego gave a hard smile.

"Yes, it certainly does. Well done."

CHAPTER 20

Rego turned his attention back to where DS Phil Brown and DC John Frith were getting ready to interview Brodie Bekker; DI Frank Morton and DC Veronica Summers were interviewing Luka Mastemak in the room next door.

Bekker had taken a considerable amount of time with his legal representative, leaving Phil Brown and John Frith pacing in the corridor outside the consultation room.

As soon as Bekker had been signed over to Brown and Frith for interview, they became responsible for him, primarily to make sure he didn't escape or harm himself or others, but also to look after his overall welfare.

Frith had entered the consultation room on several occasions to replenish Bekker with water. With any luck, Bekker would drink too much and have an uncomfortably full bladder during the interview.

Rego stared ruefully at his own coffee. The only beverages worth having in a custody block were water or vending machine hot chocolate.

The tea tasted like piss, and the coffee like hot cat litter – the coffee grains never fully dissolved, despite frantic stirring.

Frith looked a bit sick – maybe because Rego had seen the young DC consume three hot chocolates before the legal rep declared that they were ready for interview, but it was DI Morton and DC Summers who were first to kick-off.

Luka Mastemak was a broken man.

Rego could see that the moment Mastemak walked into the custody suite. He sat with his head in his hands, his face ashen, his eyes sunken, the stifling room suffused with an air of desperation mingled with body odour.

His solicitor, Owen Barrowman, didn't look much happier. He'd arrived in a three-piece suit, but abandoned his tie and jacket as the heat in the police station crept higher.

Although this room was supposed to have air conditioning, and the dusty piece of metal bolted to the wall certainly looked like an air conditioning unit, the fan made an odd humming and began to pump out even hotter air.

DC Summers swore under her breath and quickly switched it off.

Barrowman was already sweating. He admitted that he didn't usually deal with criminal law – his speciality was property law – and he was visibly nervous. Mastemak had chosen him because the two were friends and had been to school together.

It was more than apparent to Rego that Barrowman was completely out of his depth.

"Detective Inspector Morton," Barrowman began. "My client wishes to make a statement."

He cleared his throat and began to read.

"I am Luka Mastemak. This is a statement of truth. I do not know Erin Viljoen nor have I ever met her. I was not

involved in any conspiracy which may have led to her death. With regard to my trip to Poland, it was with the sole aim of distributing aid to help families in Ukraine. I have made two previous trips to Poland with aid and this was my third trip. I drove to Warsaw with my fiancée Detective Constable Marie Eagling, known as 'Mimi'. The ambulance broke down at the border with Ukraine and two men who'd helped me connect with the local aid charity said they knew a garage where it could be fixed. It was with them for two days. Mimi had to fly back so she was not late for work as a data analyst with Devon & Cornwall Police. When the ambulance was mended, I drove home via Calais and got the ferry. I am not a criminal. I am a local businessman, a local Councillor in Redruth, and am of good standing in the community."

Barrowman laid the piece of paper down on the table and pushed it towards Morton with an air of finality, as if that was the case done and dusted.

Morton didn't even look at it.

"Mr Mastemak, you were found with €15,000 in small denomination used notes in your possession which we believe were given to you in payment for trafficking automatic weapons to the UK."

Barrowman looked shocked, his eyes darting to Mastemak who hadn't moved.

"We have identified you," Morton continued, "as the person who gave this set of keys to Wilhelm Kaap, a South African national who goes by the name of 'Pongo'. Those keys belong to your lockup in Plymouth. A warrant was issued to search the property and officers recovered the ambulance registered to you. The ambulance has been given a full forensic lift and taken to a secure garage where it is currently being pulled apart. I can tell you that at this time twenty

Russian AK-47s have been recovered, including magazines and ammunition."

Barrowman licked his lips nervously, clearly unused to the level of criminality he was obviously hearing about for the first time.

"We believe that you intended to supply these weapons to an organised crime gang in South Africa. The importation of firearms can lead to a sentence of up to fourteen years." Morton paused. "Is there anything you would like to add to your statement, Mr Mastemak?"

The man looked up slowly, as if waking from a bad dream, and shook his head wordlessly.

"For the tape please, Mr Mastemak."

"No comment," he croaked, his voice hoarse.

"Was DC Eagling involved in the illegal importation of weapons?" Morton asked.

"No … no comment."

"Was DC Eagling aware that there were illegal weapons in the ambulance?"

"No comment."

Morton paused.

"Mimi is in the building now," said Morton, and Mastemak's head jerked up. "She's being questioned by a DCI from Professional Standards. She could be suspended, lose her job, or even be arrested, and if found guilty, sentenced to up to fourteen years. I don't know if you know much about the prison system, Mr Mastemak, but former police officers don't do well there, so I'll ask you again: was she aware of what you were doing?"

Tears came to Mastemak's eyes but Morton had zero sympathy for him.

Morton knew that this line of questioning was pushing the boundaries of what was legally acceptable in an interview.

It was luck – or the brief's lack of criminal law experience – that hadn't forced Morton to move on already.

Morton hadn't said anything that wasn't a fact, but he didn't want it to be construed by any third party, such as Mastemak's defence barrister when the case came to trial, that Mastemak had been put under any undue pressure. Morton's little prod about Mimi, was meant to pull at her fiancé's conscience, but Morton wanted it to come across as a verbal slap to bring the man to his senses.

"Mimi didn't know," Mastemak said, then began to weep quietly.

The floodgates opened and Luka couldn't talk fast enough.

Through sobs and loud sniffing, he began his story.

He'd come to England as a two-year-old and had no memory of his homeland in central Poland. The family had settled in Redruth and set up a shop that sold Eastern European food and other products to a wide range of Poles, Russians, Latvians, Romanians and more recently, Ukrainians.

Rego was watching from the viewing room. If Mastemak was genuine – and Rego believed that he was – he'd simply wanted to help people in Ukraine by accepting donations of clothing, tinned goods, and money for baby food. Mastemak explained that his first trip had taken him to his maternal grandmother's home in Pruszków, a suburb of Warsaw. There, he'd been introduced to two uncles whom he'd never met before.

What he didn't know was that they were both former members of Pruszków Mafia, an organised crime gang which the Polish Police had busted apart in 2017. The uncles were working to resurrect it, and gun-running was their crime of choice.

Mastemak had been naively pleased to accept their offer of help because it had made it easier for him to make contact with aid organisations in Ukraine. He just hadn't known that his uncles had been helping themselves, too.

The ambulance broke down. Whether that was genuine or not, Rego didn't know. But the uncles had it 'fixed' at their friend's garage – and that was when the secret compartments were added. The next part was hazy and Rego couldn't tell whether or not Mastemak had known about the weapons.

"You know what, Luka," said Morton, leaning forwards, invading the man's space and forcing him to look up. "I don't believe a word you're saying. You were planning on using Mimi's police officer status to get you back to the UK with minimal checks."

"No, no, that's not..."

Morton talked over him.

"Maybe you lost your nerve, maybe the timing didn't work, but you still used her. She could lose her job over this and her reputation is already in shreds."

"I wouldn't do that! I love her!"

Mastemak stared desperately at DC Summers, as if a woman officer would understand, but she returned his stare unmoved.

Mastemak bowed his head forward, his eyes tightly closed. His hands were on the table in front of him, clenched into fists.

"I want to speak to Owen in private," he whispered without looking up.

Frank Morton and Veronica Summers gathered their papers together, but before turning off the digital recorder, they invited Mastemak to sign the prepared statement which was still on the table.

He scrawled his signature and pushed the statement back

to them. Only then was the recording halted, and the two detectives left the room.

Rego knew that legal consultations were sacrosanct, and under no circumstances could they be listened to or recorded, unless there was a very compelling reason to believe that the conversation was criminal: suspicion alone was not good enough.

Rego met Morton and Summers in the corridor outside the interview room. Morton spoke first.

"That was interesting. I thought we were going to be in there for the long haul when he started off with the 'no comments', but the mention of your officer Marie Eagling seems to have triggered his honesty button." He scratched his beard thoughtfully. "He looks fucked, so I'm not sure what this consultation is about."

"The brief is clearly out of his depth here," Summers added, "but we gave him quite a bit of disclosure before we started our interview, so they've already had a chance to discuss the matters we want to question Mastemak about."

Morton nodded in agreement.

"It'll be interesting to see if he closes up shop or wants to tell us everything."

"Are you feeling lucky, boss?" Summers grinned.

Five minutes later, the interview room door opened and Barrowman peered out, propping the door ajar with his foot.

His face looked even more flushed and he'd rolled up his sleeves.

"We're ready to continue, officers."

The opening procedure started in the usual manner, but Morton didn't glance at the folder of interview materials, he simply looked at Mastemak.

"Is there anything you want to change or add from the previous interview?" he asked.

"I want to make a deal," Mastemak blurted out, running a tongue over his dry lips.

Morton was an experienced investigator and had thought this was a possible outcome, even a likely one.

He replied in a soft tone.

"Luka, we don't make deals. But what will happen is that if you tell us the truth about your involvement in this matter, how the others fit into this or not, and, importantly, that what you do tell us is a full and honest account and we don't subsequently find evidence which undermines your account, there are methods of bringing this to the attention of the court which may influence any subsequent sentence. But I think you know yourself that if you *are* involved in importing firearms into the UK, it's highly likely that this will ultimately involve a prison sentence. Your total honesty will no doubt affect how long that sentence might be."

"You'll want to make this deal," Mastemak said more confidently.

He glanced at his solicitor who nodded.

"I know where the other two ambulances are," he said.

CHAPTER 21

As soon as Rego got the addresses, he was on the phone to Chief Constable Evans who immediately alerted his counterpart in London's Metropolitan Police.

Mastemak had identified two locations in Essex: MO19 firearms officers and Counter Terrorism Policing were already mobilising.

The Chief was delighted.

ACC Gray was not.

Mastemak's involvement and the fact that the ambulance and aid had been funded through Gray's support and initiative, these facts had not gone unremarked.

Rego was also keen to update Vikram with the new intelligence.

"I've been trying to make a mind-map of how the diamonds and weapons and drugs trafficking all interlink," he said to Vikram, "but my brain feels like it's been microwaved."

"Talk it through, Rob," Vikram advised. "You might not have all the pieces, but I think you've got a pretty good picture of the set-up by now."

Rego took a calming breath.

"Okay: so, diamonds come out of Zimbabwe via Black Axe in South Africa, are put into surfboards and brought into Europe. The diamonds are sold in Birmingham by Viljoen – presumably with the Fords' say-so, and the money is transferred back ... by Bitcoin? Or was the money taken by Mastemak to Poland to pay for the guns? He says not but he could be lying. Then he brings weapons back – we believe for Black Axe – but we don't know if they planned to sell them in Europe or transport them to South Africa. We've got Polish Mafia wannabes, a suspicious death, a possible murderer or murderers on the run, and Black Axe sitting in the middle like a big old spider. I'm knackered just thinking about it all."

"Yeah, that's a lot of stress on your poor, lonely brain cell," Vikram laughed.

Rego was too tired to even try to protest.

"Mate, I get it," said Vikram. "But it's complicated because that's the whole point: the crims make it as difficult as possible to track across multiple borders. OGCs build networks over long periods: crime has time, right? With arms-trafficking, weapons smuggled overseas will usually take several, shorter trips with multiple companies to mask the country of origin and their sellers. We're also seeing a new type of broker, often ex-military personnel or even current military personnel who have connections – politicians, in some cases." He paused. "In Europe, the criminals have traditionally preferred handguns and explosives, with heavier weaponry such as assault rifles, machine guns and RPGs, heading to other markets. Turkey seems to be developing as a key market place, probably because it's central to the bad actors in the Middle East, Africa and Central Asia. And because of the situation in Ukraine, arms-trafficking is on the increase in Europe, and it's well situated to supply that market."

Rego sighed.

"Well, we've taken down one potential route, Vik, and maybe whatever the Met find in Essex will have ongoing results, but it feels like we're sticking our finger in a dyke that's been built with wet toilet rolls."

"It's a result, Rob," said Vikram. "And if your surfer, Brodie Bekker, gives up Kaap, the Hawks will be well on their way to making a serious dent in Black Axe. Take the win, Rob. Take the win."

"Yeah, you're right, Vik."

"Music to my ears. But I do have one more piece of information for you: we're looking into how Viljoen got a Dutch passport. We think we know the *why* of it: to give her easier access to Antwerp and Amsterdam to bring rough-cut diamonds through two of the major diamond markets in the world. But we're looking into who facilitated that. But for now, buddy, watch this space."

Rego felt better after speaking to Vikram and he turned his concentration to the slow-moving Bekker interview.

When Bekker was first brought in the previous night, he'd looked scared stiff. Rego didn't know whether it was the fact of being arrested or if he was more worried about saying something that would infuriate Kaap. Bekker had undoubtedly seen examples of unprovoked violence of which Kaap was clearly capable. Perhaps Bekker had enjoyed that up until this point, feeling like he had his own personal bodyguard, but now any slip on his part and he might just find himself on the receiving end of Kaap's savagery.

Kaap reminded Rego of Begbie, the unpredictably violent character in *Trainspotting*: same build, same hair-trigger temper, same utter lack of empathy, morality or conscience.

But eight hours later, Bekker now appeared supremely

confident – perhaps it was the kind of invincibility that came with being a pro-athlete.

The custody sergeant told Rego that Bekker had spent the first hour pacing the cell, but then he'd started talking to himself. The custody sergeant was an old sweat who'd begun to wonder what Bekker was up to, but after listening in, he realised that Bekker was rehearsing what he'd say during his interview.

Perhaps he'd convinced himself that by spinning the right words and sounding a bit dumb, he could twist the truth and fool the detectives interviewing him that he knew nothing about Black Axe and his involvement; after all, a bit of personal cocaine, with no previous convictions ... well, that would likely result in a slap on the wrist, and even more importantly, if his interview were to be made public, Kaap would see that Bekker had kept his mouth shut.

What he didn't know, and hadn't yet been disclosed to his brief, was that Rego had taken Beverly Nkosi's advice to heart. She'd said, *Black Axe don't put all their eggs in one basket.*

So, Rego had sent a CSI team to Kaap's B&B, and his property was being searched minutely. He was quietly confident that PC June Aspen would find something they could use.

Phil Brown opened the interview in the usual way. He went on at length about the caution, breaking it down into its component parts.

"*You do not have to say anything*, do you understand what that means?"

"Yes, I do," said Bekker, rolling his eyes.

DS Brown didn't react to the childish behaviour, merely saying, "Tell me what you understand by that."

Bekker raised his eyebrows. "Well, that I don't have to say

anything!" He turned to his solicitor. "Hey, in Afrikaans, the word '*domkop*' means stupid. *Dumb cop!* Geddit? Do you think that's a coincidence?"

The solicitor gave him a warning glance, but Bekker just smirked and leaned back in his seat, arms folded over his chest, legs stretched out, utterly relaxed.

DS Brown didn't even blink but continued with the same style of questioning.

"*But it may harm your defence if you do not mention when questioned something which you later rely on in court.* Tell me in your own words what you think that means?"

Bekker sighed. "I must tell the truth and tell you everything because if I change my story later, it may harm my defence. Right?"

Brown didn't even look up.

"*Anything you do say may be given in evidence.*"

Bekker closed his eyes as if he was bored.

"What I say will be used in evidence," he yawned.

Rego smiled grimly. Phil Brown was following the interview strategy that they'd worked on during the night, and it had already led Bekker into a false sense of security. His body language spoke volumes about his attitude.

But DS Phil Brown had been playing this game a lot longer than Brodie Bekker.

Brown looked up for the first time and came straight to the point.

"Brodie, you were found with a white powdery substance in your pocket, what is it?"

Bekker was smart enough to know that there was no point arguing that one – he'd been caught with the product on him – but he also knew a small amount of coke for his personal consumption wasn't going to be a big problem.

Bekker gave a deprecating *just-between-us-guys* grin that he shared between Brown, John Frith, and the solicitor.

"It's coke – just a little something to get the party started, like the song says. You know? Pink? The chick with the pink hair? Come on, guys, that song's a classic! You must know it?" He sighed. "It was a really small amount for my own personal use. I bought it for 35 quid from a dude on the beach. He was English, mixed race, and he had a strange accent. He might have come from Birmingham."

Brown appeared mildly interested. "Birmingham? How do you know that?"

"When I was a kid, I came to the UK with the rents, hung out with this family from Birmingham. They had a daughter about the same age as me – great tits – so I picked up the ... accent, if you know what I mean!"

He winked and gave a lecherous smile.

Brown didn't smile and simply continued with the questions

"You've already been arrested for the offence of possession. Were you intending to supply it to anyone else?"

Bekker shook his head.

"No way, bruh. I don't deal drugs. I'm a pro athlete! Getting busted for that would kill my career and they would never let me into the US."

Rego noted that as a potential weakness – Bekker had a career that he cared about. That knowledge might come in handy later.

"Tell me in your own words how you came to be in the UK," said Brown. "Travel arrangements, who you travelled with, the purpose of the visit and how you financed it."

"Sure, bruh, sure. So, I traveled with Pongo and he made all the arrangements. He likes to think he's my manager, but he's kind of a dick – you've met him, right? Ha ha! He hangs around the surf scene 'cause I'm the big dog and I get the cream of the crop, women, if you know what I'm saying."

"How long have you known Wilhelm Kaap, a.k.a. 'Pongo'?"

"Man, a while, I don't know exactly. I think I met him at a bar in Durbs – Durban. Anyway, I'd got a chance to do Boardmasters and Pongo said he could score some cheap tickets. A return flight into Heathrow was just 15,800 Rand. Sweet!"

Bekker was on a run, speaking with confidence, convinced he was spinning a yarn that was plausible, even brilliant; thinking he was the boss with his rehearsed lies rolling off his tongue.

"Did you know Erin Viljoen?" Brown asked.

Bekker's lip curled with distaste.

"Yeah, I knew her ... him. I met Ryan through Pongo – they're second or third cousins or something. You know how interbred all those Boers are, ha ha!" He laughed, but no one joined in. "I competed against Ryan, but he just wasn't in my class, you know? Can you believe the *dorp idioot* accused me of dropping in on his wave during a competition? Bruh, please!"

Bekker took a drink of water. He almost looked like he was enjoying himself, talking fast and telling jokes, when Rego knew for a fact that his solicitor had advised him to answer 'no comment' to everything.

"Did you know Erin Viljoen after she'd transitioned?"

Again, Bekker's lip curled.

"Ryan dropped off the scene for a while, but I didn't take much notice because he was never a serious threat in competitions. He was a middle of the road surfer at best. Then one day Pongo tells me that Ryan had come back as a *meisie*. I mean, what the fuck?!"

Brown and Frith looked at each other, then at Bekker.

"Ah, sorry, I mean she was a girl; a six-foot *meisie* with tits and long dark hair, and calling himself 'Erin'. I thought I was tripping!" He shook his head. "Anyway, *she* was amped, ripping up the girls' pro circuit; she made loads of enemies, pro surfer women, who couldn't win a fucking thing now."

Bekker rolled his head back laughing.

"Shit, bruh, it didn't affect me, but the girls were fucking wild. That's when that leech, Ford, took an interest. Erin was all over the surfer sites and magazines. I bet Ford's eyes were rolling round with Rand signs. I was pissing myself laughing."

"Tell me what you know about Phil and Julie Ford," said Brown.

"Ford was a chaser," and he pulled a face filled with disgust.

Brown glanced at Frith for a translation, but he was just as puzzled and gave a small shake of his head.

Bekker realised that they didn't know what he was talking about and gave a cynical laugh.

"A chaser, bruh: a guy who's attracted to trans women. Erin turned him down but he kept hanging around her even though she wouldn't give him the time of day." Bekker slouched further down in his chair. "Until he promised her sponsorship deals and a promo tour – gave her the big talk, you know? Convinced her that he was hot shit and what she needed for her to have a career. Even got her a few local sponsors, surf apparel and that; got her some interviews in *ZigZag* and even in *Surfer*. Ford had it bad for her. Man, he was stupid, *dom nool*. And Julie, she *hated* Erin, like really despised her." Bekker gave a mean smile. "Yeah, that's right. I bet she was the one who killed Erin – Phil humiliated her by drooling all over Erin all the time. Pretty sick, right?"

It certainly threw a different light on the crocodile tears shed by the woman when Rego had interviewed her.

Brown made a sudden switch of topics to stop Bekker from getting too comfortable.

"Tell me about last night's party. Who did you meet?"

"Some *bokkies*, surfers, people who wanted to party." Bekker shrugged. "I'm the big dog, bruh! People want to hang with me. I don't know who they all are."

Something at the back of Rego's mind woke up, but he couldn't grasp what it was. What had triggered that psychic itch?

"Who was the man that Kaap handed something to?"

Bekker shifted in his chair, this time feigning nonchalance.

"I dunno, man. We hugged a few, but I didn't see anything."

Brown powered up his laptop, clicking on a file, then angled the screen towards Bekker.

Rego knew exactly what Brown was showing him. During the long, busy night, they'd isolated several short video clips of Luka Mastemak at the party. In the first, he was just one of several people in the background, standing by himself and looking around.

"Do you know this person?"

Bekker glanced at the video as if he really didn't give a shit, but wanted to continue the facade of being helpful and cooperative.

"Nah, bruh. No clue," he yawned.

Brown showed a second video clip, showing the exchange between Kaap and Mastemak. In this clip Bekker was standing immediately next to Kaap, watching the whole thing.

Bekker leaned forward, moving his head closer to the laptop, adjusting the screen, appearing to study the video.

"Can you identify the people in this video clip?"

Brown could read the concern in Bekker's eyes, seeing the moment when he realised that the police knew a lot more than they'd let on. This was the strategy of 'phased disclosure' which was designed to catch out people who were lying.

Brown sat back and waited.

Bekker cleared his throat.

'You'll have to ask Pongo. I've told you, I don't know the other dude. What Pongo does is up to him. He's his own man."

Brown closed the lid of the laptop.

"When Kaap was arrested, he was found in possession of some keys; those keys fitted the lock of a garage; in that garage was an old ambulance; concealed within that ambulance was a considerable number of automatic weapons and substantial amounts of ammunition." Brown looked directly at Bekker. "Do you know anything about that?"

Bekker swallowed, a small, involuntary lift of his Adam's apple, and a sign of his crumbling composure.

DS Phil Brown was a very savvy investigator. His training and years of experience had taught him that if a suspect wanted to talk, then you just ask them loads of open-ended questions; let them talk, let them think that their version of events was believable *and* that he was believing their account.

When the interview switched to closed questions, Brown knew that the body language was different: the fight or flight part of the brain kicked in, and there was very little anyone could do about it, revealing their natural reactions whether they wanted to or not: eyes flicking from side to side, fidgeting, scratching their head, scraping their beard, tapping their fingers, feet bobbing – all were signs of stress.

Brown had seen the involuntary swallow and the change of colour in Bekker's face, his tanned complexion appearing to pale, and there was also a change in the fluidity of his answers. The responses were slower now, with minuscule breaks where Bekker had to think.

Rego leaned forwards, almost able to read the ticker-tape running through Bekker's mind.

"Sorry," said Bekker with a weak smile. "I haven't got a clue what was happening there. Not my bag, bruh."

Brown pressed Bekker, but they both knew that these were 'fishing' questions. If there had been more evidence of Bekker's involvement, Brown would have put it to him – or so Bekker thought.

Brown summarised the interview, before finally asking Bekker for the PIN code to his phone, which he gave immediately.

Brown shuffled his papers into a neat pile, and Bekker visibly relaxed in his seat.

Without looking up Brown said, "Are you a member of Black Axe, the international crime gang responsible for drug trafficking, blood diamond smuggling, sex trafficking, cyber-crime and gun running?"

Brown looked up at Bekker and met his eyes, a big grin crossing his face that had been absent during the whole interview. It caught Bekker completely off guard.

"Uh, uh, no, not me. I mean, I've heard of them. Why are you asking me?"

Brown remained seated, saying nothing. Bekker stumbled his way through further denials, but Brown knew he had properly pushed Bekker's buttons, and there was something there.

The solicitor tapped his pen and asked Bekker if he wanted a break which he eagerly took.

Brown clicked his biro before putting it into the left inside pocket of his suit jacket.

The itch in Rego's brain intensified and he cycled back through his conversations with Vikram. What had triggered that reaction?

He flicked back through his notes: what had he said about the NCA's phone intercepts?

Then it came to him: Globetrotter, Sparkles and Groot Hond. They'd worked out that 'Sparkles' had been Viljoen, and 'Globetrotter' could be Kaap or Ford, but what about the third name? He googled it quickly – and then he knew the answer.

CHAPTER 22

While Brown and Frith were updating the custody officer about the interview so far, Rego glanced at his watch and made another call to the CSI team at Kaap's B&B.

"June, I need you to switch priority to Bekker's room," and he told her what she should be looking for.

He heard the surprise in her voice.

"That's a new one on me, boss. I'll call you back."

Rego decided to take a quick break. He left his suit jacket on the back of his chair so anyone who came looking for him would know that he wasn't far away.

The kitchen/breakroom was unusually busy for that time of the day, so Rego grabbed the only free table in the far corner and staked his claim by putting the biscuit tin on it.

He was starving and badly needed more caffeine and a sugar rush. He'd filled up the biscuit tin the day before as a gesture of good will to the staff at Newquay, but when he opened it, the tin was almost empty.

Rego grabbed the last two digestives and crammed them in his mouth, then, against his better judgement, made himself another cup of coffee.

He saw Nkosi coming up the stairs and guessed that she was looking for him.

"I'd offer to make you coffee," he mumbled, choking down a mouthful of crumbs as he waved her over, "but I generally don't do that to people I like."

Nkosi smiled and pulled a box of coffee bags out of her briefcase.

"Taylors of Harrogate," she said. "They're very good."

"They must pay the police in South Africa better than here," said Rego, raising his eyebrows.

"I doubt it," she laughed. "But I cannot take any more of the Wildebeest droppings and hot water that you make here." She handed the box to Rego. "To remind you of what good coffee tastes like since you have clearly forgotten ... if you ever knew."

"I'm afraid I can't even offer you a biscuit," he said, mildly embarrassed by the empty tin.

She shook her head and sighed. "There is already more than enough of me."

Rego knew from long experience that when a woman talked about her weight, the safest thing to do was look puzzled, as if you didn't know how they could possibly consider themselves overweight, then ignore it.

With his first decent coffee in days, Rego filled her in on what stage the interviews were at. She wasn't surprised that Kaap hadn't talked.

"He will be looked after by Black Axe if he remains silent," she said unhappily. "Their people are very loyal ... and very scared."

But before they could discuss Bekker, Rego saw Phil Brown and John Frith appear, looking knackered.

"Phil, John, good work," said Rego. "I think I've got something for you that's going to help get Bekker to open up."

The two men exchanged delighted glances.

"But get yourselves a coffee first."

Nkosi gestured to her stash of coffee bags and Rego wondered if they'd fall on their knees at her feet.

There was a spare chair at Rego's table which Brown and Frith fought for. The promise of good coffee had perked them up and they acted like a pair of children playing musical chairs, both shoving each other to get the seat.

The chair scraped across the floor, which got the attention of most of the room, bashing the table and causing coffee to slop over the top.

Frith got the upper hand, so Brown had to drag a spare chair over from another table, squashing himself into the corner. But when Frith got up to get some paper towels to mop up the spilt coffee, Brown moved into Frith's seat.

Rego shook his head smiling to himself, but while they were blowing off some steam, he got a text message that made him smile and eager to continue the interviews.

Even so, it was several minutes before Brown and Frith were ready to get serious and begin the debrief.

"What do you think, Phil?" Rego asked.

Brown pushed up his glasses so that they balanced on his forehead and rubbed his eyes.

"I honestly think Bekker is there for the taking. The man's a chancer and he can't half bloody talk. He thinks he's only going to get charged with a bit of coke, but I have a feeling that if something tipped the balance, he'd sell his granny for a quick snort."

Nkosi smiled.

"I think I can help you with that, gentlemen. The South African authorities are very keen to talk to both Mr Kaap and Mr Bekker about a serious sexual assault that took place in

Cape Town last year. There is good evidence that could send them to jail for a very long time." She raised her eyebrows. "Once they're into our system, we have some very skilled interrogators. Brigadier Mphasha is sending an extradition request through the proper channels to the UK." She leaned forward. "South African jails are not as pleasant as in your country," and she smiled knowingly.

Brown stood up.

"I think I'm going to pop my head around the cell door and ask Bekker if he wants anything to drink," he grinned. "Then I might just drop a subtle hint about Major Nkosi's interest in him. Then we'll leave him to stew on it for an hour or so before we have another chat with him."

"Before you go," said Rego. "I've got something for you, as well."

"It must be my birthday." Brown grinned.

Rego told them about the connection he'd made with the NCA's phone intercepts.

"So, 'Sparkles' was probably Erin Viljoen, and 'Globetrotter' could be either Kaap or the Fords, but the third name is 'Groot Hond'."

He glanced at Nkosi.

"It means 'big dog'," she said. "You think that is Bekker?"

"Yes, I do. He even refers to himself that way," and Rego read his notes back to them. "In this section, he's talking about Kaap: 'he hangs around the surf scene because *I'm the big dog* and I get the cream of the crop'. The idiot comes right out and says it!"

Nkosi, Brown and Frith all stared at him, grins creeping over their faces, then Brown and Frith high-fived each other.

Then just when they thought that they'd got enough to make Bekker crack, Rego dropped his bombshell.

"Oh, I've just had a text from PC Aspen, the CSI at Kaap and Bekker's B&B," he said. "She found something interesting." He paused, enjoying the moment of triumph, the culmination of a challenging and complex case. "PC Aspen reports that she's recovered a large number of uncut diamonds hidden inside three of Brodie Bekker's surfboards: about 50 carats worth more than £100,000 ... which has been verified by a local jeweller. And she still has three more surfboards to check."

John Frith let out a yell and punched the air, and everyone in the canteen turned to stare at them.

"Got 'em," said Brown.

"*Sikwenzile!*" Nkosi whispered, her expression fierce as she nodded her agreement.

As they headed back towards the cell block, carrying their precious coffees, Nkosi looked at Rego seriously.

"You treat your prisoners so well, Robert, but these are very, very bad people. There was a time when we would probably have used a more, how shall I say, coercive interrogation method. It's banned now, but Bekker probably doesn't know that."

Rego understood what Nkosi was saying – but he thought that the threat of being returned for trial in South Africa would be enough of a weapon in taking Bekker down.

Thirty minutes later, as Brown launched into phase three of the interview, Rego leaned forward listening intently.

Brown started with a belter.

"Right, you're still under caution, Brodie ... or do you prefer to be called 'Big Dog'?"

Bekker's smile dimmed for a second but he waved it off.

"Sure, bruh! That's what all the *bokkies* call me."

"A warrant was issued to search the property where you

and Mr Kaap were staying. Officers recovered a number of surfboards with the name 'Big Dog' on them, which we believe are yours."

Bekker's eyes widened and he licked his lips but forced a smile.

"In Afrikaans, that translates to '*Groot Hond*' – a name that has come up during our inquiries from a colleague in the South African Police Service. Perhaps you saw her when you came in? Major Beverly Nkosi from the Directorate for Priority Crime Investigation: their speciality is organised crime – maybe you've heard of that department as the Hawks."

Bekker was silent, but he couldn't contain his stress and his body was showing it: his eyes widened then narrowed as he frowned, his fingers drummed on the table, and his left leg bounced up and down.

John Frith took over, talking casually.

"I used to surf," he said. "I wasn't that good, not in your league, Brodie, but I was okay. I even shaped my own boards for a while. You start with a foam blank, add the stringer for strength, then shape the blank, add your artwork, fin box, top off with fibreglass. But the skill is all in the shaping."

Brown looked at Frith as if he was genuinely interested. "Is that right, John? I wonder if Brodie makes his surfboards the same way."

Bekker took a sip from his beaker of water.

"Only one way to find out," said Frith. "We should tear one apart."

"I wonder what we'll find," Brown mused.

Bekker's solicitor was looking annoyed and puzzled, but Bekker knew exactly what was happening.

Brown turned to Bekker.

"Brodie, are we going to find conflict diamonds smuggled inside your surfboards?"

Bekker knew the game was up, and there was a gut-clenching moment when they wondered if he'd go the 'no comment' way.

Finally, the truth came out, or some of it, and Bekker was looking desperate. He began to speak faster and faster.

"Once Ryan transitioned to Erin, she wanted nothing to do with either me or Pongo. She blocked him, ghosted me, and refused to even talk to us at any of the surfing events. Pongo was pissed and gave her a few slaps but then he seemed to leave her alone. He didn't say why and I wasn't going to ask him. I found out later that he was blackmailing her – she paid him to leave her alone and it cost her R15,000 each month – about £600."

"That doesn't sound much to a man like Kaap."

Bekker rubbed a finger over his lip.

"Pongo thought that he could parlay up the amount – we could both see she was going to be big. International surf magazines were interested and sponsors were sniffing around." Bekker swallowed. "It suited Pongo to keep Erin in his back pocket. I was just happy doing whatever he told me, surfing and partying."

"Did you kill Erin Viljoen?"

"No, bruh! I swear it! Why would I?"

"Because you could make more money by selling her out to Black Axe," Brown stated.

Bekker shook his head emphatically.

"Nah, bruh! No way. They'd have killed us if they'd known Pongo was keeping that from them. Pongo was the man – I didn't ask how he was connected: I didn't ask who, I didn't ask why, and he didn't tell me any more than I needed to know. I didn't want to know."

Rego began to suspect that Kaap had kept Bekker in the dark when it came to the bigger picture – perhaps he hadn't fully trusted him; perhaps he knew the man would talk if caught.

"But you knew that Kaap was working for Black Axe?"

Bekker shook his head.

"Not at first. Man, when I found out, I puked my guts up. I thought I was going to wake up dead. I was so fuckin' scared. But Pongo said it was just business as usual. I just did what he told me. He's *befok* – a crazy mofo."

"Did Erin know that Kaap was working for Black Axe when she was Ryan?"

He shrugged. "I don't know. You don't ask Pongo questions if you want to stay alive."

"Who did Kaap deal with?"

Bekker lowered his eyes and shook his head.

"I don't know."

"We can keep you safe, Brodie," said Brown.

Bekker coughed out a laugh but didn't reply.

"Brodie?"

"Pongo never told me, but even if I knew, I wouldn't tell you. I'd be looking over my shoulder for the rest of my short life."

Brown nodded.

"Okay, tell me about Luka Mastemak's involvement."

"Who?"

"The man Kaap met at the party."

Bekker sighed and rolled his eyes.

"I don't know. I don't know anything about him. He came in, gave Pongo some keys and he got some notes – maybe Euros – in an envelope. That's all I know. Pongo didn't tell me anything and I don't know anything!" He swallowed nervously. "Look, bruh, I live to surf and doss, pull some *lekker* chicks. I'm a pretty good surfer, good enough to make the tour but only because Pongo was managing me in more ways than one. I was in deep and I couldn't get out. He said he'd slit my throat, bruh! He would have done it without blinking and tried not to get my blood on his shoes. Man, I wish I'd never met him. If it weren't for him, I'd still be on Ansteys Beach, smoking *dagga* till I pass out. And I'm telling you, I wish I was still there and I'd never fucking left."

"How were you planning to deliver the diamonds in your board?"

"You tell the judge I'm cooperating fully?"

"Yes."

"Okay then," he sighed. "I was supposed to paddle out to them the same night Erin died but there were police everywhere so I couldn't do it. I tried again the next morning but someone had sent a drone up and we couldn't risk it. Man, you police were everywhere up and down the coast. Pongo said to sit tight and wait for things to calm down. He said he'd arranged for me to paddle out at 9am this morning because eyes would be on the competition, not on me." He gave a resigned smile. "Guess I won't be making that appointment."

"Where was the meet supposed to take place?"

"One of the beaches in Newquay, but I don't know which – only Pongo knows."

"If I find out later that you knew all along, the judge will be told that you deliberately withheld information."

"I don't know! I just did what he told me. I don't know anything!"

Brown nodded at Frith to stop the recording.

"Wait!" said Bekker. "I know I'm gonna go to the mung, but it will be in this country, yeah? You send me back to SA and I'm a dead man walking."

Back in the viewing room, Rego slapped the desk with his

hand. *An hour ago!* They'd missed the chance to pick up the men on the other end of the deal by an hour. The meeting place must be close by, it must be!

Maybe the Coastguard could still find them.

Rego picked up the phone.

CHAPTER 23

It had been a tense morning, draining, but completely worth it. Bekker had rolled over on Kaap, spouting information almost faster than Brown and Frith could keep up with; Mastemak had given up his Polish uncles, and that information had been passed to Vikram's contacts at Poland's *Biuro Operacji Antyterrorystycznych*, the state anti-terrorist investigators. Mastemak's uncles would be in handcuffs by the end of the day. And they were waiting to hear if the raids in Essex had been successful.

Kaap had continued to refuse to speak, and as Major Nkosi had pointed out to Rego, it would be up to people several rungs higher up the political ladder whether or not Kaap would be tried in the UK or extradited back to South Africa. Rego thought probably the latter as the evidence against Kaap's criminal activities in the UK was more limited. It was clear to all of them that Kaap could argue in court that he was just looking after the keys for Mastemak and didn't know about the weapons. Equally, none of the rough-cut diamonds had been found in his luggage – just in Bekker's: Kaap had been too wily for that.

But none of this would be Rego's problem for much longer – nor the UK's, because it was almost certain that Kaap would be extradited back to South Africa. Bekker's future was less clear-cut, but Rego's money was on Nkosi's boss getting his way.

Even so, the case was coming to a conclusion and there was no need to keep his team up in Newquay, although the incident room would remain in place until any charges had been authorised by the Crown Prosecution Service.

Rego and the rest of his team were finishing off their reports and getting ready to pack up and go back to their own station in Penzance.

Although, there were still several loose ends, which was frustrating.

Rego massaged his temples, wishing the insistent headache would take it back a notch.

He still didn't know how Viljoen had died. Perhaps it had been Julie Ford who had ground up the sleeping pills and put them in Viljoen's food, either with or without her husband's knowledge, but they only had Bekker's word that Julie Ford had hated Viljoen. Moreover, the injuries on Erin's head remained unexplained, and without further information, the coroner would have no choice but to record an open verdict.

The Fords were still missing and it was assumed they'd left the country on fraudulently obtained passports. At least their fingerprints and DNA were on file, and Rego suspected that as habitual criminals, they'd be picked up again someday. It annoyed the hell out of him that they'd slipped through his fingers, even though he hadn't been the SIO at the time they'd fled Cornwall.

And then there were the mysterious purchasers of *Penrose Pride*: where were they? The Coastguard were searching for them but Rego thought they'd be long gone by now – the moment Bekker had missed the handover slot, they'd have been suspicious. Although, with a hell of a lot of money at stake in the form of diamonds, maybe they'd hang around trying to get to Kaap.

The B&B where Kaap and Bekker had been staying was under surveillance, so if someone came asking for them, they'd be picked up. But as CSI had been all over it, it was probably a case of locking the stable door after the horse had bolted. Still, there was a team in place keeping eyes on, just in case.

But if the men had already left Cornwall, they could have ditched the boat somewhere along the coast and picked up a car; or they could have rendezvoused with a yacht or larger boat out in the Atlantic and sent *Penrose Pride* to the bottom of the sea where it would never be found, so that meant...

There was a knock on Rego's door, interrupting his train of thought.

DI Lance Lloyd was the last person Rego had expected to see when he glanced up.

"Hello, Rob."

"Lance."

Lloyd didn't try to play it cool, and his usual arrogance was absent.

"Congratulations on the Viljoen case – that was a big one."

"Thanks. A few loose ends but ... thanks."

Lloyd cleared his throat.

"I fucked up. I shouldn't have assumed that Viljoen killed herself. But I had the mayor, several major sponsors and ACC Gray breathing down my neck, and ... and I let their eagerness to get a result make me jump the gun and ... well, the mistakes were mine."

He thrust his hands in his pockets.

"Okay?" said Rego, wondering why the man had driven from Camborne to tell him what he already knew.

"The thing is, I heard what you said to the Chief about me – when I dropped the ball on the forensic opportunities that I hadn't followed up, you could have thrown me under the bus. You didn't. I heard that you told him I was 'managing the budget'."

Rego nodded. "Forensic tests are expensive, especially if it *had* turned out to be suicide."

Lloyd gave a small smile.

"Yeah, they are."

And he held out his hand to Rego.

The two men shook hands, an understanding passing between them.

Lloyd nodded once, then left the office.

They both knew that this would leave a stain on Lloyd's career and ambitions, but at least the man had owned it, and for that alone, he was due some respect.

It was like happy hour at an all-you-can-eat buffet in Rego's office that lunchtime.

Before he could get his mind back on finishing up the case files, ACC Nash walked in and plonked herself in a chair across the desk from him.

"You're a lucky bastard, Rob," she began.

"I've often thought so, ma'am."

"Don't be smug, it doesn't suit you," she said briskly. "De Jeles is dead."

Rego's smile vanished.

"I thought he was in a secure wing?"

"He was. Turned out it wasn't secure enough," she said bluntly.

"Jesus."

"It's not on you, Rob. I interviewed de Jeles about the

complaint, pointing out certain benefits if ... when ... he retracted. Coincidentally, Complaints and Discipline and the IOPC are both in agreement that there is no case to answer against you. The theory is that Domi assumed de Jeles had talked and had him silenced ... or punished, which is the same thing for a piece of scum like Dritan Domi."

Rego shook his head.

"And Domi gets away with it again."

"Yes and no. He's been moved to a Cat A prison, so he'll find it a lot harder to run the Hellbanianz drug empire from there. Word is that his second in command has already taken over. Either way, Domi's finished. He's got another 18 years to serve. It's extremely unlikely that he'll make it back to anything like the level of control he has now."

"But he won't serve time for de Jeles' murder."

"It's being investigated. Someone will squeal for a deal – they always do. Eventually."

She paused.

"I was sorry to hear about DC Eagling. I know she was a valued member of your team."

"She still is."

"Indeed."

ACC Nash stood up to leave.

"By the way, I hear that the crime plan you gave to the Chief on car thefts resulted in Traffic finding a chop shop on the Lizard this morning – full of bits and pieces from loads of stolen cars. Good work, Rob."

And she swept from the room, leaving Rego feeling as if a tornado had just ripped through his office. Or maybe a colonic irrigation. Rego had never had one, but he imagined the relief that it was over would be similarly bracing.

But thank God the complaint against him had been withdrawn and Domi's long reach had been curbed. Even

Lloyd had apologised to him – although, thinking about it, the man had managed to avoid using the word 'sorry'.

Still, Rego ruminated, *you can't have everything.*

And he picked up his phone to tell his wife the good news – then remembered that he hadn't told her the bad news of being removed as SIO in the first place.

She answered on the second ring.

"I was just thinking about you!"

Hearing her voice made him smile.

"Are you driving?"

"Of course I am! I'm on speakerphone: the kids and Patricia can hear you, too," and he heard their voices in the background. "You do remember that we said we'd all go to the Boardmasters Caribbean beach party this afternoon?"

Shit! Shit! Shit!

"Nah, I hadn't forgotten," he lied. "I had to work all night and I'm just a bit sleep-deprived."

"Are you okay?" she asked at the same time his mother shouted in the background, "Sleep is important, Robert!"

"Hi, Mum," he said. "Don't worry, I'm fine. I'll see you ... where are we meeting?"

"Fistral Beach, outside Rick Stein's at 3pm."

Rego glanced at his watch – he had just under 90 minutes to get himself sorted out. It should be enough.

"If you're going to be late," Cassie said sharply, "you will let me know, won't you?"

"When am I ever late?" he asked, pretending to be hurt.

Cassie laughed.

"Oh, you definitely don't want me to answer that! See you at three."

Rego had a broad smile on his face as the call ended, a smile that fell away completely when he saw Mimi Eagling enter the incident room escorted by two officers from Complaints and Discipline.

Her face was drawn as if she'd lost weight that she couldn't afford to lose.

The whole team was watching, embarrassed and awkward. Jen Bolitho was the first to react, standing up and wrapping her arms around Mimi, whispering something which made the younger woman's eyes fill with tears as they hugged tightly.

John Frith and Jack Forshaw had both worked closely with Mimi but clearly didn't know what to say. They stood with their hands in their pockets, self-conscious and uncomfortable.

"It'll be okay," Jack mumbled, patting her on the shoulder.

"Yeah, you'll be fine," John added lamely.

It was clear that neither of them believed what they were saying.

Tom Stevens stepped forward and gave Mimi another hug.

"Chin up, Mimi. We're all on your side."

She nodded quickly but couldn't quite meet his eyes.

Rego went to the door of his office, waving her inside and shutting the door.

"Come in, Mimi. Have a seat."

She trudged inside, her footsteps slow and reluctant.

"How are you?" Rego asked with genuine concern.

"Shit," she said, her voice shaking. "I couldn't sleep last night; I feel sick all the time."

Her chin wobbled.

"How could he do this to me, to us?" she asked, her voice filled with pain. "How could he do it? I've known him my whole life. We had our first date when we were 15. I can't believe it ... I just can't." Her words trailed off and her gaze fell to the folder on her lap. "But this was his third trip – his third! The ambulance broke down like that on the first trip – we joked about it happening again, and then it did."

Rego wondered if she realised that this contradicted Luka's statement and further implicated him. He'd have to report what she said, and in all probability, Mimi would have to give evidence against her fiancé ... her former fiancé. He noticed that she was no longer wearing her diamond engagement ring.

Mimi's distress was genuine, but she was still a cop.

"He knew! He must have known. How could he do that to me?" she asked again.

Rego had no answer that she'd want to hear.

"His family are blaming me, saying that I drove him to it because we were buying a house together and he needed the money. But how is it my fault? He has a job, I have a job." Her eyes squeezed tightly shut. "None of them are speaking to me, as if I was the one who did something wrong!"

"You trusted the man you were going to marry," said Rego.

"I've been such a fool!" She wiped her nose with a damp tissue. "Anyway, I'm suspended with pay while the case is investigated. They've already taken my Warrant Card, phone and laptop; now they're going to escort me from the building."

Rego nodded because he'd already been informed.

"God, it's awful. I feel so ... so humiliated." She bit her lip. "I'm going to try and get my head together and decide if ... well, if I'm allowed back ... I don't know ... if I did come back, would anyone even trust me?"

She shook her head.

"I know you can't discuss this, boss, but ... maybe I could have a non-operational role? I'm sorry, I shouldn't ask..."

She stood up to leave, then sat down again, sliding the manilla folder that she'd been holding across his desk.

"I nearly forgot. These are my notes from the Viljoen case before ... before..." she sighed. "Jen had been following the money and I tracked one source to an offshore account – you'll need a forensic accountant to unpick that mess." She paused. "Viljoen's missing key card for her room was found with the ones the Fords left behind. They made a mistake by using it to try and open the door to their own suite *after* we know Viljoen was dead. At that point, they must have realised that we'd have found out about that eventually, so they made plans to run. I also heard back from IT and found out who sent the nastiest messages to her on social media – it was the Fords again, well, at least 90% of them were from the Fords. IT managed to track down the servers they used and ... all that IT stuff linked them to several email addresses that they'd created. Techs are going through the rest now. I think they'd been setting her up for months, so that when she 'killed' herself, everyone would assume it was because of all the trolling; then the Black Axe OCG would assume the diamonds vanished when she drowned. Or something like that."

She shoved the folder across the desk with finality, then stood up again.

"Thanks for everything, boss. I've really enjoyed working with you."

"Mimi," said Rego as she turned to leave. "Luka told you that the ambulance broke down again on this third trip and he suggested you fly home so that you wouldn't miss work. Maybe he just didn't want you there ... in case anything happened and he was caught. Maybe, in his own way, he was trying to protect you."

Her eyes filled with tears but she couldn't speak. Her face spasmed as she tried to smile at him. Instead, she simply nodded and closed the door behind her.

Rego watched her go, swiftly escorted from the building.

CHAPTER 24

It was the final day of Boardmasters.

Tamsyn had been too drained to drive home the night before and had gratefully accepted a lift with PC Jason Johnson, Jess's boyfriend. He'd been on the raid at the party and it had been good to know that the former Marine would be there to help if things kicked off.

Usually after a successful op, they'd have been buoyed up with high spirits, but both had been subdued, wondering about the involvement of DC Eagling's fiancé.

They hoped for the best, but each, in solitude, was preparing for the worst.

She'd been subdued when she'd called Joe, but he hadn't been able to reassure her.

Jason broke the long silence just as Tamsyn was nodding off.

"Is Joe coming down for the house-warming party? It's going to be epic."

Tamsyn jerked upright.

"Yeah, he's swapped shifts with someone on his team, so he'll be down for at least one night, maybe two."

Jason nodded.

"Tell him to get a bottle of whiskey. None of that cheap blended crap – a decent single malt."

"I'll tell him."

"Make it something expensive: Macallan or Bowmore. If he turns up with Teacher's, tell him he's not getting through the front door."

Tamsyn laughed.

"Yeah, I think I'll remember that – just the good stuff, right?"

"Quinn's a cheap bastard," Jason grinned, winking at Tamsyn.

"Funny – he said the same thing about you," she replied.

He hadn't, but she wasn't going to let Jason get away with dissing Joe like that.

In any case, she'd already chosen an air-fryer for a housewarming gift, and she was happy to say it came from both her and Joe. Not only that, Tamsyn's grandmother had promised to make two-dozen Cornish pasties for the party.

Jason dropped her off outside the cottage, then hesitated, as if wondering what to say to her. But in the end, words failed him.

"Well ... I'd better get home and catch some zeds. You too, Tam."

"Will do. Thanks, Jason."

"'Kay. Let me know if you need a lift to Newquay tomorrow to pick up your car. I'm on lates, so I won't be going first thing."

"That would be great, thanks. I'll walk over for about eleven. Night, Jason."

He nodded and drove into the night.

Bone weary and a little depressed, Tamsyn climbed the

steep stairs to her single bed, smiling to see that she wouldn't be sleeping alone.

Morwenna opened one eye and gave a wide yawn. Tamsyn had to shift the small dog to the side so there was room for both of them.

But she didn't sleep well.

Her mind would not let her rest, going over and over the moment when Andy had identified DC Eagling's fiancé. It was one of the things that her police tutors at Middlemoor had warned her about: the possibility of having to arrest a friend, someone you knew, or someone you'd gone to school with, and how to prepare for that mentally. But how could you prepare for finding out that the person you were going to marry had betrayed you so profoundly?

There was no doubt in Tamsyn's mind that if Luka Mastemak was dealing with a scary piece of shit like Pongo, he wasn't a decent guy, and he definitely wasn't someone a police officer should be marrying.

But how would DC Eagling feel about coming to terms with that knowledge? After all, her career was on the line now. There were whispers going around that Mimi Eagling would be suspended ... or maybe she had been already. The details were sketchy, but no doubt by morning, the gossip mill would be up to date.

Tamsyn knew how she'd felt when a so-called friend had betrayed her whole family: sickened, gutted, furious, cheated. And she'd felt a fool for not realising what had been happening.

She wondered if she should say something to DC Eagling. But then again, she didn't know her well, and after all, what would she say? *People are shit. Sorry your fiancé is a criminal. Sucks to be you.*

The next morning, Tamsyn woke alone, blinking in the bright light that filtered through her thin curtains.

Little Mo had long gone and was probably mooching around the back garden or dozing in the sunshine after a long night of even more sleeping. It was a dog's life.

Tamsyn stretched in the narrow bed, wondering if she could be bothered to go and watch the Boardmasters finals, but her car was still in Newquay and the only other thing she had to do was crack out her policing degree textbooks.

One sour look at the foot-high pile of reading and study folders, and Tamsyn decided that surfing won hands down.

Morwenna appeared as soon as Tamsyn reached the kitchen, watched her carefully as they shared a slice of toast, then shadowed her every move as Tamsyn got ready to go out, the little dog clearly wondering if she was being left again or going to spend the day with her favourite human being in all the world.

Tamsyn was in two minds, as well, but in the end, she decided that Morwenna wouldn't enjoy the crowds.

"Sorry, Mo, it's going to be really busy there, too many people – you wouldn't like it."

Morwenna's tail drooped with disappointment, and she stared at Tamsyn with wounded eyes, as if she'd just been orphaned.

"And the Oscar for best actor goes to ... drum-roll ... Morwenna Poldhu."

Tamsyn scooped her up, kissed her on the nose, then put her down on her grandfather's chair.

"Be good," she told the little dog.

Morwenna curled into a ball with her back to Tamsyn, making it patently obvious what she thought about that.

The cottage was already silent and empty. Tamsyn knew that her grandfather would be down at the harbour chewing the fat with the other fishermen, then eating a Sunday roast at the Mack Shack.

Her grandmother had also left early to clean the church before service on a Sunday morning although she didn't attend, following quite a different religion. But after, she'd go for a coffee with a couple of her friends before meeting Ozzie for lunch. With only one cleaning job on Sundays, her grandmother counted it as a day of rest.

Tamsyn texted her grandmother to ask her if she could pick up Morwenna on the way to lunch. Little Mo loved a roast dinner, too.

As forecast, the weather had changed overnight, with a low pressure building out in the Atlantic. The heat had been whisked away with a fresher easterly, which would make it offshore at Fistral. The sky was pale blue, and clouds were building in the distance. The surf forecast promised a 6-8 foot swell – near on perfect conditions for the Boardmasters finals.

Tamsyn walked along the promenade lost in thought.

She loved living in Penzance, and she couldn't imagine not living in Cornwall, but the world was a big place, and Joe had made her think about broadening her horizons. Certainly, working in a busy city like Plymouth would give her more experience, but was she ready to leave everything she'd known behind?

She thought about how Jess and Jason were moving on with their lives: moving in together first, maybe buying a house together next, maybe getting married some day. Who knew what the future held?

Tamsyn walked up one of the steep narrow roads that spread up the hill from Penzance's Market Jew Street, stopping outside Jason's Victorian terraced house.

For just one more week, he'd be sharing this house with a couple of older men. It was a real bachelor pad and the spartan living conditions reflected that. Jess's occasional presence had added a few brighter colours and scented candles, but it was lived in by single men and the neglected square of grass in front of the granite-walled building showed it.

Tamsyn went to knock on the front door but Jason was already jogging down the steps.

"Hey, Tam! All good?" he asked. "Sleep okay?"

"Yeah, fine," she lied. "I bet you're looking forward to moving."

Jason's face lit up. "Yeah, I can't wait." He shot her a side-look. "My lucky day when you couldn't move in with Jess."

Tamsyn grimaced. "Yeah, lucky for you."

"You're welcome to come over anytime," he offered generously.

"Really?" she said, raising an eyebrow. "Shall I sit in the middle on the couch when you're watching Netflix on a Friday night?"

"You can have Jess's beanbag," he snorted.

"Thought so."

"Quinn definitely coming to the party next week?"

"Yep, as long as they don't cancel his leave at the last moment."

"Yeah, that never happens." Jason smiled, rolling his eyes.

It happened more than a few times over the course of a copper's life: a big case, a sudden incident, and leave was cancelled without notice. Didn't matter if it was your mother's birthday, your son's graduation, or if your wife was in hospital having a baby – leave got cancelled. Tough shit.

That was the great thing about Joe, about having a boyfriend in the job: they both understood that these things could happen. It was harder dating a civilian, but Jess understood that she had to go with the flow – so far.

It took twice as long as usual to get into Newquay because of the crowds in town, but finally, Jason parked at Newquay police station, gave Tamsyn a quick smile and darted inside. For a moment, Tamsyn felt a wave of loneliness wash over her and considered collecting her car and simply driving home, but she hadn't been in the water since she'd found Viljoen's body four days earlier. Had it only been four days? It felt longer.

A shudder ran through her as she remembered the jarring thud when she'd run into Viljoen's body, then being tossed into the black water, the surge of adrenaline as she'd dragged the woman back to the beach, her futile attempts at CPR.

She tried to shake off the shadow of fear she'd felt.

Yes, it was definitely time to get back in the water because the longer she left it, the more the darkness would try to pull her down.

She recognised Inspector Rego's car in the car park and wondered what was happening with the case. He'd probably been there all night, prepping the interview packages. She wondered what DC Eagling's fiancé would say, what excuses he would make.

She snorted with disgust. The man deserved what was coming to him – DC Eagling didn't.

For just a moment, she wondered if Mimi Eagling could be involved, then she dismissed the thought – it was too horrible to think about.

Tamsyn's surfboard was strapped to the roof of her ancient Fiat, zipped into a battered boardbag; her wetsuit and towel in the boot of her car.

She packed what she needed for the day, threw in a bottle of water, then tucked her board under her arm and headed for Fistral.

Tamsyn took the backstreets toward the beach which was

nearly a mile away. It wasn't worth moving her car nearer – any beach parking would be long gone and traffic had congealed along Fore Street.

Once she reached Headland Road, the crowds grew thicker despite the grey skies. People with pasties, families with windbreaks and beach wagons, kids with ice creams, and seagulls scouting easy targets from the sky. A few surfers with fibreglass boards dotted the lineup, and dozens of beginners with the heavy spongie surfboards flailed in the white water.

The competition zone hadn't been set out yet, but when the finals started, they'd use a combination of flags and coloured buoys as markers. There'd also be a Beach Marshal with a megaphone ready to yell at anyone who strayed into the competition zone.

Tamsyn decided to head for an emptier part of the water at Little Fistral. It was more of a locals' spot, small and tucked away, a finger of sedimentary rock separating it from the wide sands of its much bigger cousin.

Tamsyn liked it for its right-hander with a useful rip to aid a dry-hair paddle-out, but because the water broke onto rocks, it wasn't a beginner's wave, and on a low tide, the swell could be bigger than anywhere else in Newquay.

Like now: the peaks were coming in smooth sets of 7-foot plus, but if it reached 9-10 feet, even Tamsyn would consider bowing out. That was a powerful lot of water breaking over the reef-like edges of the wave-cut platform. One mistake, and you'd be peeling yourself off the rocks.

From Fistral, she could hear the occasional riffs of a steel band and knew that the party was getting underway. She wished Joe was with her – not that he could surf, although he wanted her to teach him – but he would have enjoyed this. He worked hard, partied hard, and lived life to the fullest. He knew that life could be short – they both knew that all too well.

Turning her face to the sea, she picked her paddle-out spot, pulling through the cool water with long, easy strokes, the rip working like a conveyer-belt which deposited her beyond the breakers.

She bobbed on the water, the breeze lifting her hair as she scanned the waves. In the distance, a set started to build and she spun her board around, feeling the mass of moving water rising up beneath her. Then she was careening down the face of the wave, spray hitting her cheeks as she leapt to her feet, her weight shifting easily, leaning into the wall of water, her fingers trailing, and she'd never felt more alive.

Then she spotted something strange.

CHAPTER 25

Rego was waiting for his family outside Rick Stein's fish and chip restaurant on Fistral Beach.

He'd seen DCS Richards from a distance but Rego intended to keep a low profile so he wasn't dragged into anything work-related.

It had been a relief to leave his suit in the car and change into boardshorts, slides, and his favourite Jimi Hendrix t-shirt. He was spending the rest of Sunday with his family and he couldn't wait to see them.

He wasn't early, but neither were they – although he hadn't had to battle to find a parking spot either, so it was ten minutes before he saw Cassie walking towards him with Bill tugging at his lead, his ungainly paws scrabbling in the sand. Cassie's other hand held tightly to their daughter as Maisie skipped between her mother and her grandmother, swinging her arms happily.

Max slouched behind them all, his shoulders sloped and his face sullen in the way that only teenagers knew.

His son's gangly arms and legs were out of proportion with his thin body, and with a pang, Rego realised that Max was now as tall as Cassie. His son was growing up, and it wouldn't be long before the 14-year-old became a man. By taking a job in Cornwall, Rego had missed a whole 18 months of his son's life, months neither of them would ever get back.

He wondered again if he'd made the right decision by splitting up his family just so he could take a promotion.

When Maisie saw him, she ran forwards launching herself into his arms.

"Dad!" she yelled, clinging to him and screeching with delight.

At ten years old, his daughter was still a child. Thank God.

"Hello, May Day," he said, giving her a squeaky kiss that made her squirm out of his arms as she giggled.

Bill's bark was excited and high-pitched. Cassie had given up trying to hold him, so Bill was going wild with joy and trying to climb Rego's leg or hump it or look for a treat or a pat – it was hard to know with overgrown puppies.

Rego kept one arm around Maisie then bent down to give Bill a fuss with his other hand. Then he managed to untangle himself so he could kiss his wife on the lips and his mother on the cheek.

"Hello, Max," he said, at last.

Max lifted his chin.

"'Sup?"

Rego nodded, "I's cool, man," then grabbed his son in a very uncool hug that made the women laugh and his son cringe.

"Gerroff, Dad! You're embarrassing yourself."

Rego let his son go and winked at him. Max had to work hard not to smile.

The smell of Caribbean food wafted across the beach and Bill didn't know which way to turn as delicious scents assailed him from all sides. The kids hungrily scoured the stands selling Jamaican Jerk Chicken, Trinidadian Roti, Guyanese Pepperpot, Caribbean dumplings, curries, stews, and seafood dishes.

"Huh," said Rego's mother, putting her hands on her ample hips. "Nothing from Bermuda."

Cassie cast a look at her husband but otherwise ignored the comment.

"Maybe that's because Bermuda isn't part of the Caribbean, Mum."

"I knows that, clever clogs! But would it hurt them to have some proper food like..."

"...fish chowder with sherry peppers, Hoppin' John, and cassava pie?" Rego teased, naming some Bermudian favourites.

"Don't get smart with me, Robert! I am still your mother!"

Maisie giggled and Rego grinned, giving her a conspiratorial wink.

They bought enough supplies for a small army and plonked themselves down on a large beach towel, enjoying the music, the food, the holiday vibe. Bill was a rubbish bin on legs, eating everything they couldn't finish, then flopping down on the blanket and snoring contentedly.

The surfing finals hadn't started yet but quite a few of the finalists were heading to the shoreline with their boards, either to get in some last-minute practice, or just because they loved surfing more than anything else.

Rego recognised the teenage women's favourite, Tya Zabrowski, as she signed some autographs for her young fans.

He also saw the way his son's eyes widened as Tya walked past him, and he sat up straighter.

Rego smiled. Yep, the boy was definitely growing up.

Cassie had seen the look too, but it was Rego that she

hauled to his feet, and they danced together to Bob Marley, making Rego wonder why it had been so long since he'd danced with his wife. They used to go clubbing all the time before children and work and responsibilities crowded the calendar.

Maisie joined in and Rego twirled her round a few times, making her giggle hysterically, but they were all astonished when Patricia climbed to her feet with creaking knees then shook her hips and shimmied like she was 25 not 65. The woman had plenty of luggage in her trunk, but grandmother or not, she knew how to shake her bootie.

Whoops and cheers came from all sides, and soon Patricia was surrounded by a group of twenty-something guys who couldn't take their eyes off her. The crowd went wild as Patricia showed that a new hip didn't stop you from twerking.

"You think your generation invented this?" she crowed. "I been getting my groove on since before you were a twinkle in your daddies' eyes!"

And she romped through her repertoire of the mashed potato, boogaloo, and soul train, but at the funky chicken, she reached her limit and had to sit down with Bill.

Max couldn't look, embarrassed beyond words by his whole family, but Rego pulled him to his feet.

"Come on, Max! Let's show 'em how the Rego men can move!"

After a moment's hesitation, Max began to throw some shapes, and Rego was delighted that his son was joining in; impressed, too.

"You get that from your grandmother," he said.

Maisie stood on tiptoe and whispered in his ear.

"He's been practising in his bedroom, Dad!"

After a few more songs, hot and sweaty, they collapsed

onto their beach towels and Rego bought everyone an ice cream.

It wasn't a particularly warm day, but Rego's stomach was full, the tiredness of the long days and longer nights catching up with him, the satisfaction of a job well done, the warmth of hearing his family's voices around him, and he found himself drifting off.

Cassie eased his head onto her lap and stroked his hair, bringing a dopey smile to his face.

"You owe me a date, Ace Boy," she whispered.

"Can't wait," he mumbled.

Bill was asleep behind them, chasing something in his dreams, belly full, happy and relaxed.

This is the life, thought Rego.

Sometime later, the sound of an air horn jerked him awake, and Rego realised that the women's final had started.

He sat up yawning as two women in neon-coloured competition vests charged towards the sea, long hair flying behind them as they powered through the surf.

The announcer identified them as Tya Zabrowski, the 14-year-old from France, and Yolanda Sequeira, a 27-year-old Portuguese national. He was glad that the youngest competitor had made the final, but wondered what had happened to Alana Bright and how far she'd gone in the competition before being knocked out.

"I can't believe she's only 14!" said Maisie in awe. "Can I learn to surf, Dad?"

"Yeah, let's all learn," Rego said eagerly. "Right, Maximilian?"

Max shrugged, but Rego could see that his interest was piqued by a competitor the same age as him.

They all stood up to watch as the two women powered through the waves to the lineup.

"How do they judge it?" asked Maisie, clearly intrigued. "It's not like they can surf on the same wave."

"No, but they've got 25 minutes and they can catch as many waves as they like. The judges give them a score out of ten for each wave, then they work out an average score from the five judges. The two highest-scoring waves say whether or not they've won. A perfect ride is ten points, so a perfect heat is 20 points."

Maisie looked at him in awe.

"How do you know that?"

"I'm your father – I know everything," he replied.

"You just *think* you know everything," said Patricia firmly, and Maisie giggled.

Cassie looked as though she was biting her tongue, and she smiled at her mother-in-law, for once in agreement and harmony.

The waves seemed massive to Rego, easily dwarfing the two surfers. But Tya Zabrowski was a tiny dynamo, easily diving through the green walls of water, then tearing down the other sides, as each surfer performed rail-grabs, three-sixties and seemed to fly out of the water as they caught air.

"Dad! I want to learn!" Maisie yelled, and even Max nodded.

"We'll all learn," said Rego, suddenly feeling optimistic about the last three weeks of the school summer holidays.

Suddenly, the Beach Marshal blasted out a message through the PA system.

"WOULD THE FISHING BOAT BY LITTLE FISTRAL PLEASE LEAVE THE COMPETITON ZONE! YOU ARE INTERFERING WITH OUR COMPETITORS!"

He repeated the message two more times and Rego

peered out across the shoreline to see what everyone was looking at.

On the far right-hand of the beach, Rego could vaguely see a small boat just beyond the massive breakers. It was drifting perilously close to the rocks.

Rego squinted into the distance, noting that the size and shape was very much like the missing *Penrose Pride.* An uneasy feeling made his skin prickle.

"Just wait here a moment, Cass," he said to his wife. "I'll be back in a minute."

"What's wrong?"

"Probably nothing. I'll be right back."

He hurried toward the judge's table, flashing his Warrant Card to get past security, then asking permission to use their powerful binoculars.

It was hard to make out the boat's name at that distance.

"Shoulda gone to Specsavers," Rego muttered to himself.

He peered again, but there was no doubt it was drifting closer to the rocks.

"What are they playing at?" asked one of the judges. "Those idiots are way too close to the reef."

"Can you read the name on the side of the boat?" Rego asked.

The judge gave him an odd look but leaned into the large binoculars.

"It looks like ... *Ben* something. Hold on. *Benbo... Penrose...*"

"Is it *Penrose Pride?*" Rego asked urgently.

"Could be, man. Whoever they are, they're in trouble." And he turned to one of the stewards. "Get the lifeguards with jet skis out there – it looks like that boat has lost its engine."

"No!" Rego said. "They could be dangerous. I need to call an Armed Response Vehicle."

DCS Richards was suddenly standing beside him.

"What the hell's going on, Rob?"

"I believe those men could be involved with the wrongful death of Erin Viljoen!" he said, his voice stressing urgency. "And they could be armed, so we have to..."

"Dude, there's no time!" the judge shouted. "They're nearly on the rocks!"

CHAPTER 26

Tamsyn had been having such a good time that she hadn't realised that the women's final was about to start.

She heard the sound of the air horn in the distance but didn't feel like cutting short her own surf.

"Just one more wave," she said to herself, then laughed out loud, a happy, carefree sound.

It was the surfer's mantra and the excuse for everything from missed dinners and delayed dates to being late for work: *I just had to catch one more wave.*

She'd even heard that one guy had missed his own wedding, but that could have been an urban myth. Although, it could be true – it wasn't that far fetched...

She'd been looking towards the main beach so it was only at the last second that Tamsyn realised a huge swell was lifting her up, up, up, and she had to scramble, paddling hard to be in the right place to catch it, and not get completely slammed by a 9-foot monster.

She leapt to her feet, crouching low as the wave hollowed,

whooping with delight as she got tubed. When the wave's energy began to dissipate, she spun her board around and surfed over the back of it, ready to paddle out again.

That's when she saw that there was a boat in trouble.

It was a small fishing boat, not unlike her grandfather's punt, and far too close to shore to cope with the huge breakers. It would be slammed to matchwood on Little Fistral's reef if it didn't get the hell out of there.

With mounting horror, she realised that the boat was drifting beam-side on. Two figures were scrabbling at the stern and she guessed they were trying to re-start the engine – and failing.

They should be pulling out the oars and rowing like hell to get out of imminent danger, but the fools were shouting at each other instead.

And they weren't even wearing lifejackets.

"Hey!" she yelled. "Hey! Use your oars!"

But either they couldn't hear her over the roaring surf or they were too panicked to try.

Tamsyn had left her phone in her car's glove box, but even if she hadn't, there were thousands of people on Fistral – she couldn't be the only one who'd seen the fishing boat in trouble. Where the hell were the lifeguards? The Coastguard? The RNLI?

She saw the boat slammed by a large wave and for a moment, she thought they'd been beam-ended, but they popped back up like a cork. And she gasped: *Penrose Pride*. She could see the name clearly as the little boat was picked up and slammed down again.

The smaller of the two men was tipped into the sea and Tamsyn saw him go under. His friend didn't even try to reach for him but was hanging onto the side of the boat, still trying to start the engine which would almost certainly have been flooded by seawater several minutes earlier.

Tamsyn paddled hard, straining every muscle to reach the man in the water, but *Penrose Pride* was drifting too close and she was in danger of being smeared against its wooden sides.

The man still onboard had finally seen her and was gesticulating wildly, beckoning to her. But Tamsyn was searching for the man who'd fallen overboard – he was the one in the most danger.

"Help!" the man aboard screamed at her. "Help me!"

Penrose Pride was lower in the water now, either flooded or leaking or both.

She glimpsed a man in the churning foam just before he was swallowed up by another wave. She made her decision – he needed her the most and she started paddling towards him

The man in the boat screeched, then did the most insane thing she'd ever seen: he jumped into the water and started swimming towards her.

She had no choice but to paddle towards him.

His hands tried to grab the fibreglass board but it slipped from beneath his grasp and made her wobble dangerously.

Then his fingers scrabbled at her leash and he yanked her off the board.

Tamsyn was shocked but recovered quickly. She was still attached to her board, so it couldn't go far without her, but then the man began tugging at the leash, deliberately trying to pull it off her ankle: he wasn't trying to help her – he wanted the board all for himself.

He was bigger than her, heavier than her, and very, very scared.

His fist swung wildly, catching Tamsyn on the side of the head and momentarily stunning her. But there was little force behind the blow because the man was struggling too hard to stay on the surfboard.

Even as he hit her, her brain was already organising what she needed to do.

She slipped beneath the water, swam under the board and tipped him off.

He fell with a loud splash, his mouth open and filling with seawater, making him cough and inhale even more water.

He thrashed violently, trying to grab the board, but he was disorientated and weakening fast.

Tamsyn saw the next wave coming and duck-dived under it, her surfboard tugging at her ankle as it bobbed and danced on the surface of the water.

The man was further away now, his struggles weaker.

Tamsyn slid back onto her board and paddled towards him; again, he tried to pull her from it, but without hesitating, she drew her fist back and punched him in the face, his nose gushing with blood and seawater.

Adrenaline surged through her, and she grabbed a fistful of his hair, yanking his head out of the water. Then she wrapped her hand in the collar of his jacket and held on tight, fighting to hold on so she wouldn't lose him as the waves broke over them.

Tamsyn had just seconds before the next wave slammed them again. She spun her board around to face the beach, flipped it upside down and lined up the nose with the man as best she could. She grabbed his arm and jumped onto the board with both knees, using her weight to flip the board with his arm draped over it. She spread his legs, grabbed one thigh, then the other, and heaved him onto the board.

With only a second left, she pulled herself on top of him, the man's legs beneath her, and paddled like hell as the wave rose up, a roaring monster of white foam behind them, unforgiving rocks far too close.

Paddle.

Survive.

Paddle.

Survive.

Paddle! Paddle! Paddle!

And then she saw the wonderful, beautiful, amazing sight of the lifeguards' RIB zipping towards her.

Strong arms steadied her board and pulled them both into the boat, then floored it as they missed the rocks of Little Fistral by inches.

"There's another man in the water," Tamsyn gasped. "I couldn't get to him."

"I saw him go in," one of the lifeguards yelled over the noise of the engine and the howling waves. "Colin and Dave are looking for him now."

Tamsyn glimpsed two jet skiers circling the area near *Penrose Pride* where it was pinned against the rocks. But there was no sign of the first man, nothing but waves and rocks and the little fishing boat, broken and sinking fast. There was nothing to see and Tamsyn suspected that the lifeguards' search was hopeless.

"By the way," she coughed, pointing at the man she'd saved as his eyes flickered open. "He's under arrest."

Rego was standing at the water's edge when the lifeboat brought Tamsyn in.

DCS Richards was directing uniformed officers, keeping the crowds back, and two lifeguards were assisting as an ambulance reversed down to the edge of the slipway.

"Tamsyn! Are you alright?"

She nodded tiredly.

"I'm fine," and she jerked her head in the direction of the man who was being helped ashore. "He's one of the guys from *Penrose Pride.*"

"I gathered," Rego said dryly.

"I had to punch him in the face. I think I broke his nose," she admitted.

Rego's eyes widened.

"Any particular reason?"

"He was panicking and he grabbed my board. He was trying to get my leash off. I had to stop him or he could have drowned us both."

Sudden rage bubbled through Rego's veins. Tamsyn had put her life on the line to save this scum, and he'd tried to take her surfboard.

"You should have hit him harder," he said. "But you didn't hear me say that." He paused. "Did you see what happened to the second man?"

"The other one ... he fell overboard before I could get to him. I don't think he made it," she said, her mouth twisting into a grimace.

"If you hadn't reacted so quickly, neither of them would have made it."

She lifted one shoulder in a shrug, neither agreeing nor disagreeing.

"I wonder why they stayed around here – apart from the fact their engine wouldn't start. I would've thought they'd be long gone by now."

"We have an idea about that," said Rego. "I'll fill you in later."

Tamsyn could only nod wearily.

"You did well today, Tamsyn," Rego said seriously. "You keep on coming through, don't you?"

She cocked her head on one side.

"That's just the job, isn't it?"

"Still, you were pretty amazing. Unfortunately, now both my kids want to learn to surf. I thought I'd give it a go, too."

She laughed out loud.

"You get seasick just looking at the water!"

"I don't." *He did.* "Well, I *can* swim, you know.. "

"Good luck with that, sir."

Rego chuckled.

"Get checked out by the paramedics and I'll have an officer drive you home."

"My car's at the station; I can drive myself."

"Not after what you've been through. I'll get someone to take you to the nick, then they can drive you home. Deal?"

She nodded, too tired to argue, even though she didn't need to be driven and definitely didn't want to put out another officer just to chauffeur her around.

But as she walked towards the ambulances, she kept that thought to herself.

Rego directed his attention to the man she'd rescued. The paramedics were concerned about the risk of secondary drowning so after a brief discussion, they'd decided to transfer him to the main hospital at Truro. Rego knew that delayed respiratory distress could be possible for up to 72 hours after the initial exposure to water.

The man would need to be interviewed under caution, but treating any potential medical condition came first. And he looked like he had a broken nose as well – Tamsyn really packed a punch.

Rego couldn't help smiling to himself as he ticked off a list of tasks in his head: get the Coastguard to what was left of *Penrose Pride* and have it towed to a boatyard where a forensic analysis could be done. He wasn't hopeful, but if Erin Viljoen had been on that boat, there could still be evidence – it hadn't completely sunk, even though it had foundered off Little Fistral.

Another 20 carats of rough-cut diamonds had been found in Brodie Bekker's surfboards – a staggering quantity. But the Chief Constable had chosen to use the word 'terrorist' when referring to the cache of automatic weapons, so Counter Terrorism Policing South West had taken over that part of the case.

The two locations in Essex that Luka Mastemak had given up had led to the retrieval of significant weapons' caches less than 30 miles from the capital. So far, seven men had been detained.

And yet...

And yet Rego still didn't know how Erin Viljoen had died, although the Fords were chief suspects, and Bekker's testimony that Julie Ford had hated her definitely backed up that theory.

But, for now, the pair had disappeared.

He also wasn't sure how much Viljoen had been involved with Black Axe, whether blackmailed, coerced, or acting of her own free will.

On the other hand, his team had pieced together one helluva case and been responsible for removing more than a hundred automatic weapons from the illegal arms trade. How many lives had that act saved?

They'd also successfully shut down a route for Black Axe to sell conflict diamonds into the UK, and Rego knew that West Midlands Police had viewed hundreds of hours of CCTV footage and were close to making an arrest in Birmingham.

And, at the end of the day, Rego was a glass-half-full man, so he'd take it as a win, and there was always a chance that the lowlife bastard Tamsyn had saved would sing like a canary.

He doubted it, but a man could hope.

For now, he had to go and find his family and explain to his mother, wife and kids why he would be late home.

Again.

CHAPTER 27

Music spilled from the flat's windows, and laughter filled the summer evening as Jess and Jason welcomed friends to their new home.

The music was loud, but not so loud that it drowned out conversations, and groups of people were chatting in the kitchen and loading their plates with pasties made by Tamsyn's grandmother.

A strong pair of arms wrapped around Tamsyn's waist and she smiled over her shoulder as Joe kissed her neck.

"Do you think the happy couple liked their house-warming present?" he asked.

Tamsyn laughed out loud.

"They liked the air-fryer I gave them," she smiled. "I'm not so sure about yours."

"What's wrong with my present?"

"A frickin' six-foot rubber plant – sorry, a six-foot rubber *tree*. I'm sure they're thrilled. I don't even know how you got it in your car!"

"I had to open the sunroof," he admitted. "It wasn't raining, so it was okay."

The rubber plant took up half the tiny living room and Tamsyn wondered how long it would be before Jess practised some serious topiary on it. The top two feet of the poor tree were already looking rather battered, and Tamsyn suspected that's what happened when you were going at 90mph down the M5 sticking out of a sunroof.

Tamsyn could tell that Jess didn't think much of the rubber plant, but it was clear that Jason didn't care one way or another about anything. Tamsyn didn't think he'd stopped smiling since they'd arrived. He'd been drinking beer for hours and was at the happy, sloppy stage of being drunk.

"Good result in Essex last week," he said, clinking his bottle of beer against Joe's and spilling half of it on the new laminated wood flooring. "More scum off the streets."

Joe nodded. "Yep, put a lot of weapons and ammo out of circulation, too."

"AKs?"

"Twenty-three AK-47s, twelve Glocks, and seven Taurus TX22s. The other team recovered even more than us."

"Nice! Cal with you on that one?"

Joe nodded.

"Pity he couldn't come this weekend." Jason sighed. "Think he'll ever come back to Cornwall?"

Joe grimaced. "I dunno, mate. It was hard for him, just getting serious with Rosie then next thing he's going to her funeral. Still, maybe one day. Anyway," he said, making a clear effort to lift the mood again, "Congrats on moving in with your very own ball and chain."

"You won't be saying that when it's your turn, mate," Jason laughed, raising his beer to Joe and Tamsyn.

Tamsyn felt uncomfortable with Jason's comment but Joe just smiled and squeezed her fingers.

"I'll drink to that."

"Yeah, and congratulations on a good result for the Met. Cheers!"

Joe's whole team had been involved in the raid on two warehouses where the ambulances and weapons had been stored.

Tamsyn was glad she'd only found out afterwards, and she knew for a fact that Joe felt the same way. He'd gone white as a sheet when he'd heard about her battle to save the man from *Penrose Pride*, and how close they'd both come to drowning. Which was why she might have forgotten to tell him that they'd later found out that both of the men on the little fishing boat had been armed, too.

As if reading her mind, Joe asked, "Any word on the scrote you saved at Fistral?"

Tamsyn shook her head.

"Counter Terrorism Policing South West are questioning him – I'm not in the loop."

Joe gave her a commiserating smile. Junior officers weren't always kept informed of how a case was developing while it was in progress.

"But I did hear that they found evidence of Erin Viljoen having been in *Penrose Pride* at some point," Tamsyn added.

"They were lucky the seawater didn't wash it away," said Joe, thoughtfully.

"Very lucky, but the *Pride* hadn't completely sunk. They managed to pull her off the rocks and tow her to a forensic boat yard. They found Viljoen's hair and traces of blood on the oars and boat hook."

"She was killed with a boat hook?" Joe asked, and she knew that he was picturing the wicked-looking metal hook shaped like a harpoon that was used by sailors for docking and undocking.

"The pathologist said that one of the oars was a match

for the wounds on her head but it doesn't prove she was struck with it deliberately. I mean, she would already be woozy from sleeping pills and the guy could argue that he was using the boat hook to try and get her out of the water but missed."

"Is that what you think happened?" Joe asked sceptically.

"No, I think he or his dead friend used it to render Viljoen unconscious then kept pushing her under the water until she drowned." Tamsyn shrugged. "The coroner will have to record an open verdict."

Joe held her more tightly but didn't say what they were both surely thinking.

"What about your DC and her Polish fiancé?" Joe asked quietly.

"Oh, God! Poor Mimi – it's been awful. Her fiancé had tried to say that he'd no choice, that he'd been blackmailed to bring in the guns, but they've proved that's a lie, too. He went to Newlyn Harbour more than two months ago to source a fishing boat for his cronies. They wanted something local and something old, because they thought they could sail around and no one would notice them. Huh, shows that they don't know the first thing about fishing around here – everyone knows everyone and they gossip like crazy. They were all talking about who'd bought Alf Worth's old punt and wondering why."

Her voice had started to get louder so she tried to speak more softly.

"Grandad identified Mastemak as the man who'd come to the harbour two months before the final Ukraine trip. Two months!" She shook her head. "He's lied so many times it's going to be a hard job for the investigators to discover the truth."

Joe nodded in understanding.

"Did they find the other guy from the fishing boat, the one who went overboard?"

"His body washed up at Polly Joke a couple of days ago. Two dog-walkers found it."

Joe's eyebrows shot up.

"Are you serious, or is that a wind-up so you can tell the locals from the in-comers?"

Tamsyn smiled.

"No, it's a real place, honestly! It's the name of a beach about five miles southwest of Newquay. It's *Pol-Lejouack* in Cornish, which means 'jackdaws pool'."

Joe looked slightly mollified but also as if he still suspected that he was the butt of a joke.

Tamsyn lowered her voice and whispered in his ear, hamming up her Cornish accent which was naturally only slight.

"We allus knows emmets when we sees 'em, me 'ansum."

His eyes closed and his lips curved upwards as she nipped the lobe of his ear.

And despite the fact that at least half of the house-warming guests were serving police officers, for the rest of the evening they didn't talk about bodies, or guns, or the grim side of life that too often constituted their work.

Later, when the party had died down and the final stragglers had found their way home, Tamsyn and Joe made love athletically and passionately, then gently and more languidly, and Tamsyn had stroked the puckered white scars on his skin that told the many stories of his life.

She finally drifted asleep with Joe's arms around her, her usual anxieties soothed by the soft laughter of Jess' and Jason's voices in the next room, the warmth of Joe's body against hers, and maybe soothed by the beers that she'd drunk, as well.

The following morning, she was still in that happy half-sleep with consciousness only just out of reach, when someone knocked loudly on their door.

Joe jerked awake and Tamsyn shot upright, clutching the sheet to her chest.

"Wake up, guys!" Jason yelled. "You've got to see this."

"What?" Joe shouted.

"Just hurry up!" Jason yelled again.

Joe slid on his jeans, hopping on one leg as he tried to hurry, and Tamsyn pulled on his t-shirt and a pair of knickers, then walked into the living room, slightly self-conscious at her state of undress in front of Jason, who was, after all, a colleague.

But his eyes were fixed on the TV as he watched a BBC news report.

"Police recovered the remains of two bodies at Heathrow Airport earlier this morning when workers reported an unpleasant smell coming from the unclaimed luggage area. Sniffer dogs were brought in and police located two dismembered bodies hidden inside suitcases.

The bodies are believed to be those of South African nationals Philip and Julie Ford who were wanted for questioning in connection with the death ten days ago of transgender surfer, Erin Viljoen, in Cornwall. Police ask that anyone with any information call the hotline number on..."

Jason muted the sound as they all continued to stare at the screen.

"That's so horrible," Jess said. "I can't believe anyone would..."

Her words trailed away.

The problem was that they could all believe it only too well.

"So, that's it," Tamsyn said flatly, glancing at Joe and her friends. "The people responsible for Erin Viljoen's death are dead."

"Black Axe?" Jason asked quietly.

Tamsyn shrugged. "Maybe, probably."

"It's over then," said Jess softly.

Tamsyn shook her head.

"It's never over. It'll never be over – not while people like that think they can do what they did and get away with it. Then they're murdered and stuffed into suitcases, and there's no justice, no way of knowing the whole truth. It's all about money and greed and more money. It'll never be over."

"No," Joe said firmly, wrapping his arms around her and holding her tightly. "Take it as a win, Tam. The Fords won't be able to do it to anyone else – they're finished. And as for the people who killed them, we'll get them. It won't be today or tomorrow, but eventually we'll get them."

"You really believe that?" she asked.

"I do," he said. "I have to believe that or I couldn't do my job."

She stared up at him. He sounded so sure of himself.

Yes, they both had shadows at the edges of their lives, dark shadows, deep shadows. But it seemed to Tamsyn that Joe had found a way to live with them and not to fight them all the time; she hoped that she could learn from him, and learn to live like that one day.

"Okay," she said. "Okay."

She'd try to believe that their work made a difference, too.

EPILOGUE

F*ive months later...*

The wind came from the north-east, bitter, filled with salt and the certainty that none of the small fishing boats would put out from Newlyn Harbour today or for many days to come.

It didn't matter, not for the Poldhus, because Tamsyn's grandfather had not gone to the harbour, had not seen fit to mend his pots, fiddle with his punt's sparkplugs, or sit in the Mack Shack and tell tall tales with the other fishermen.

Today, he had put on his fusty old suit, black, the only one he had which was usually reserved for weddings and funerals, then he'd driven his ancient Rover, coughing chip fat fumes to Exeter in Devon, a place he pretended to hold in contempt simply because it wasn't in Cornwall.

Tamsyn's grandmother sat beside him, uncomfortable in a floral dress instead of her usual dungarees but beaming with pride.

Tamsyn had travelled up with Jess and Jason, Jess talking

a mile a minute the whole way, hopped up on excitement and strong emotions. And Joe. Joe, who'd taken time off work to be there because he loved her.

As if he'd sensed her thoughts, he held her hand, gently squeezing her fingers and smiling at her.

"It's a medal, not surgery, Cornwall," he said. "You're supposed to smile."

So she did, and it felt real.

Tamsyn greeted her grandparents at the entrance to Middlemoor, Devon & Cornwall Police HQ. Her grandfather scowled at Joe, but shook his hand any way. He'd scowl at any man who'd won his granddaughter's heart and hand.

Andrea Poldhu hugged Tamsyn, then hugged Joe, so handsome in his best uniform of tunic and pressed trousers, his many medals and ribbons bright against the dark material.

This time last year, I killed a man, thought Tamsyn, *A bad man. I wrapped an anchor rope around his neck and pushed him overboard. I watched as he sank to the bottom of the sea, the waves closing over his head.*

And now she'd saved a life. He'd been a bad man, as well, and perhaps by saving him she'd condemned him to life in a concrete box, living many, many years in a British prison. *But maybe*, she thought, *where there's life, there's hope, because otherwise, there'd be no point to any of it.*

She stood proudly in her best uniform, freshly dry-cleaned, receiving the Chief Constable's Commendation, an award 'for exceptional service, bravery, or professionalism that goes above and beyond normal expectations': for saving a criminal from a watery grave at Fistral.

Erin Viljoen's body had been quietly repatriated to South Africa and buried in a small township on the coast near Durban. The South African authorities hadn't been able to locate any next of kin.

The Metropolitan Police were working on the Fords' murder and had arrested several members of Black Axe. Against his will, Brodie Bekker had been extradited back to South Africa and was currently being held in solitary confinement for his own safety.

Luka Mastemak was also awaiting trial and was being held at Exeter prison. Tamsyn had heard that Mimi had been to visit him, but she hadn't returned to work and no one seemed to know if she would.

But Tamsyn wasn't going to think about that today. Everyone had told her it was a day of celebration. She wasn't sure about that.

She knew that Inspector Rego had put her name forward for the award and that he was sitting somewhere in the audience. Her eyes searched for him, and when she finally found him, he smiled and nodded, and her heart swelled with gratitude. Nearly two years ago, he'd told her that she'd make a good officer – she was starting to believe him.

And she allowed herself to feel the quiet warmth of pride as her grandparents watched with tears in their eyes, Joe standing tall and unassailable beside them, Jess waving too wildly, her colleagues applauding.

There was only one person missing – little Mo had not been permitted to attend the ceremony. But Tamsyn had promised the little dog that she'd stop at the farm-shop on the way home and buy Morwenna the biggest steak she could find.

She smiled as she shook hands with the Chief Constable, accepting her award.

And maybe, she thought, *maybe everything is going to be okay.*

WHAT TO READ NEXT...

DEAD AND BURIED book #5

Lithium: the new gold.

With the government's move for greener energy and the rapid growth of EV car sales, mining lithium could transform sleepy Cornwall into a new industrial power.

But when a body is found deep underground at the county's first lithium mine, there's a lot at stake.

DI Robert Rego is trying to work the case but is being frustrated at every turn. When it seems as though the answer is buried deep in the past, he turns to local officer PC Tamsyn Poldhu whose family roots go back across the centuries.

Out on 31st March 2026
available for pre-order

Turn the page to read the first chapter...

DEAD AND BURIED, BOOK #5

CHAPTER 1

Wheal Noweth stood on the site of a tin mine that had workings going back to medieval times, but instead of granite chimneys, steam engines and iron gearheads, Tamsyn could see miles of gleaming stainless-steel pipes with bright red metal chimneys, clouds of evaporated water curling from the tops like mist.

She could also see protesters at the mine's entrance, separated by a cordon of only three police officers and a piece of police tape that fluttered in the breeze, while the opposing sides hurled abuse at each other.

"Murders! Rapists! You're violating the Earth!" screeched a woman with a homemade placard.

"Go back to the dark ages and stay there!" mocked a protester from opposite camp.

"You'd think they'd all be for a new lithium mine," said PC Jamie Smith out of the corner of his mouth. "All those expensive electric cars the Greens are driving."

Tamsyn nodded, only half listening to her colleague. Jamie spent most of his life and all of his working hours at Penzance police station moaning about something or other.

She was used to it, and at this point, it was almost a sort of white noise.

Besides, she wasn't supposed to be here. She should have been spending some rare quality time with her boyfriend, Joe. He was in the job too, and it was hard for them to coordinate their days off. They'd even booked an Air BnB to give them some privacy away from the tiny cottage that Tamsyn shared with her grandparents. But Tamsyn's leave had been cancelled and she'd been given a Movement Order to work out of Camborne where they were short staffed. She did *not* want to work there and she did *not* want to be here.

Jamie nudged her, sensing that he'd lost her attention.

"Look! There's a BBC news van. Do you think we'll be on TV? My mum would like that."

A security officer for the mine raised the barrier and allowed the news van inside, parking just behind Tamsyn and her colleagues.

She glanced in the van's direction as the camera crew clambered out, her gut twisting when she recognised the reporter who was with them: Jules Carter. She'd last seen him at her friend's funeral nearly a year ago. He'd been working for a small, local paper then – it seemed he'd gone up in the world.

Carter shook hands with a group of men and one woman waiting to meet him, then smiled at a nervous-looking man who was standing by himself with a sign that proclaimed, *Not in Mine Name!*

The arrival of the news van had encouraged the small crowd to inch forwards, but still not close enough to be of concern.

The officer standing on Tamsyn's left seemed to think otherwise and broke in on her thoughts.

"It looks like it's all going to kick off," PC Ben Gundry

announced as he straightened his spine and thrust his chin forwards.

"Our job is to keep the peace," Tamsyn reminded him, her patience strained after double-crewing with him for the last two weeks.

Gundry was a probationer at Penzance, but already a man who thought he knew it all and was certain that every situation called for a show of testosterone.

Tamsyn thought differently. During her 23 months as a police officer, she'd learned that words de-escalated situations much more effectively, and that being young, blonde and female could often work in her favour because the local hardcases saw that there was no rep to protect or face to be saved by beating up a woman.

Gundry tensed at her side, staring a challenge at every male near the front of the cordon, and Tamsyn muttered under her breath.

She hoped this would be over soon and was glad when she saw the journalist nod to the cameraman, ready for his piece to camera.

"I'm here today at Wheal Noweth in West Cornwall at the UK's first commercial lithium mine – a key component of electric batteries. When South Crofty tin mine closed its doors for the last time in 1998, it was mourned as the end of Cornwall's proud industrial heritage. But with the growth of green-energy projects and the government's £650 million grant to support sales of electric vehicles in the UK, many here believe that mining lithium will reverse the downward spiral in the county's economy, and could be the golden ticket the area has long been waiting for. But concerns have been raised about the environmental impact of lithium mining."

He turned to his first interviewee.

"Keith Henry, electric vehicles are seen by many as being less harmful to the environment, so why is the *Keep Britain Green* campaign opposed to the opening of Wheal Noweth?"

"This isn't about green energy – that's a smokescreen," the nervous-looking man answered, without any apparent sense of irony. "Anyone exploiting the resources in Cornwall isn't thinking about the impact on the environment, no matter what they say; they're just trying to feather their own nests." His face reddened. "It's just another example of big business taking what they want from Cornwall – the money goes out and locals never see the benefit."

Carter nodded seriously, then turned to his second interviewee, a middle-aged woman in a smart winter coat who'd been shaking her head vigorously.

"Councillor Rowena Jones, you'd disagree with that?" the reporter said, inviting a response from the woman.

"One hundred per cent," she said firmly. "West Cornwall needs this sort of investment in the future – our young people deserve better than seasonal, low-paid jobs in tourism. As Councillor for this ward, I see the poverty hidden behind our beautiful scenery. Investing in Wheal Noweth is investing in the future for our whole community."

Again, Carter nodded, then turned to his third interviewee, a ruddy-faced man wearing a mayoral chain of office.

"John Penhaligan, you're the Mayor of Pool, and you're very supportive of this project."

"I am indeed," he said. "I'm proud to be standing here today at the Wheal Noweth lithium mine welcoming a new era of hard rock mining to West Cornwall. My father was a hard rock miner, my grandfather before him, and my great grandfather before that. They used to say that if you dig a hole in the ground anywhere in the world, you'll find a Cornish

Jack staring up at you, boy!" He turned to the small crowd as he began to rev up his speech. "Like many of you here today, I'm proud to be part of a tradition that fuelled the first industrial age. And here we are now, at the brink of a new, greener industrial age: lithium is our new tin – or maybe our new gold. We've relied on our looks for too long – and I'm not just talking about my 'ansum boyish looks, mind! I'm talking about our tourist trade. We need proper industry. We need to provide a future for our young people beyond serving pasties and clotted cream teas."

There were some cheers and a few laughs, and Carter gave an appropriate smile as he turned to his fourth and final interviewee.

"Edward Eddy, as CEO of Wheal Noweth, would you agree with that?"

Eddy was a large man with hands like shovels who looked as though he could have dug the mine by himself.

"When South Crofty closed in '98, that was the end of an era. They said mining was finished in Cornwall. D'you know what they wrote on Crofty's gates that last day?

Cornish lads are fishermen and Cornish lads are miners too.

But when the fish and tin are gone, what are the Cornish boys to do?

That's what we asked and there was no-one left to answer, so we've had to do for ourselves, and that's the truth of it."

Tamsyn wondered if Cornish women were included in that.

"I've worn out more pairs o' shoes than I've 'ad hot dinners going to meet the men with the money," said Eddy, "talking to them, telling them that investing in lithium mining in Cornwall is an investment in the future. They said it would never work, but I'm here today to tell you, all of you, that those men in suits were wrong! Wheal Noweth is proud to be part of a mining tradition that's centuries old. But the way we do things today is different now, and we chose the name 'Noweth' because it means 'new' in Cornish. Our mining practices are sustainable with minimal environmental impact, and we're committed to fostering long-term partnerships with the local community because it's *our* community, it's our home! Technology has moved on, and the techniques we'll be using are cutting edge. We'll be pumping up hot brine from deep underground and removing the lithium – you could just say it's a giant version of a Brita water filter."

There was a faint rumble of amusement as he grinned at the crowd, ignoring the minority who shouted, "Rubbish!" or "Traitor!"

"You're all here today," Eddy bellowed, "at the dawn of a new industrial revolution – a green revolution that starts in Cornwall! We'll lead the way in mining lithium for all o' them electric cars and those smartphones we can't get our kids off! And in years to come, you'll be able to say you were here, day one, the day we rebuilt Cornwall!"

He turned to the mayor.

"You do the honours, John," and he handed over a giant pair of scissors so the mayor could cut the black and gold ribbons, the colours of Cornwall's coat of arms, which were tied across the mine's entrance.

"I hereby pronounce Wheal Noweth mine open!" Penhaligon shouted enthusiastically.

The mayor cut the ribbons and the reporter turned to face the camera again.

"This is Julian Carter from *BBC Spotlight*, reporting from Wheal Noweth, Cornwall's newest mining success story."

Tamsyn smiled to herself. It seemed that now *Julian*

Carter worked for the BBC, *Jules* had been relegated to the history books.

Carter held his smile for another second then nodded at the cameraman.

"That's a wrap."

Suddenly, a woman wearing an orange boilersuit and hard hat came sprinting out of the mine's office.

Her face was pale and her breath came in short gasps.

She whispered something in Eddy's ear and Tamsyn saw the man's expression darken. He shook his head several times and seemed to be trying to shoo the woman away, but she was insistent, her hands clenched into fists.

"But there's a dead body down there!" she screamed. "I saw a dead body!"

Julian Carter had missed the scoop of a lifetime.

MORE IN THE CORNISH CRIME THRILLER SERIES

There are five books in this police procedural crime fiction series so far, with more planned. Each standalone story features Police Constable Tamsyn Poldhu and Detective Inspector Robert Rego, along with a cast of recurring characters, all set in the beautiful seaside county of Cornwall.

Read the blurbs and sample chapters from each book.

Book #1 DEAD WATER

Book #2 DEAD MAN'S DIVE

Book #3 DEAD RECKONING

Book #4 DEAD SHORE

Book #5 DEAD AND BURIED

www.berrickford.com

DEAD WATER, BOOK #1

It's Tamsyn Poldhu's first day as a police constable in her home town of Penzance in Cornwall. She already knows that life can be cruel, but she has no idea how tough it's going to be.

Detective Inspector Rob Rego has just transferred to the coastal southwest from Greater Manchester Police, and he gets seasick just looking at a boat.

When a body washes up on a remote Cornish beach, Tamsyn's involvement in the case goes deeper than she could ever have imagined.

You can also enjoy *Dead Water* as an audiobook, at all good retailers, including Audible, Spotify, and many others.

DEAD MAN'S DIVE, BOOK #2

It started as a date with a diving instructor, but when Tamsyn finds a body during a wreck dive off the Cornish coast, her work-life balance is in serious jeopardy.

Who is the mysterious diver with the Cyrillic tattoos, and why has nobody reported him missing? Is this an accident or evidence of organised crime, and why are fingers pointing towards the military naval air station of RNAS Culdrose a few miles away?

Tamsyn is just a student constable so DI Robert Rego is

brought down from Devon to take over the case. He's missing his family in Manchester and gets seasick just looking at a boat.

But this crime is bigger than both of them, and the pressure isn't just to solve the case ... but to forget about it completely.

DEAD RECKONING, BOOK #3

When Besnik Domi, the feared enforcer for organised crime gang the Hellbanianz, is extradited to the UK, Tamsyn has to face the man who tore her family apart. Detective Inspector Rego has to make sure that the case against the killer is watertight.

But the Domi brothers have a long reach, and when threats are made against Tamsyn's and Rego's families, they have to make a choice.

And it might not be justice.

ACKNOWLEDGMENTS

To PC Emily Humphreys for background info and hot chocolate.

To Sue Nash, a great boss who died too soon.

To Trevor Albutt, former Royal Marine and Detective Chief Superintendent, West Mercia Police.

To DS Dave Stamp (rtd) for his great stories and for always being supportive.

To PC Teresa Boulden (rtd) for proofing help, local sayings, West Cornwall surnames and background info.

To Andrea Rego for wonderful touches of local dialect, and of course, for loaning her and Ozzie's names.

To Phil and Julie Ford who are not diamond smugglers, nor have they been dismembered, but live very happily in Cornwall with their dog, Stan. They are, in fact, rather lovely neighbours who asked if they could be villains in a book.

To Karen, Tim and Buster for telling me what the call sign 'Cornwall' means to them.

To Alex and Kamla Millson, Mimi Eagling, Jack Forshaw, Nathan Richards from Broadoak Services, and Isla Forrester from Penguin Random House who are depicted as white hats; and to Dale from Vodafone who wanted to be a black hat. Thank you for letting me (mis)appropriate your names.

To Anne King, Lesley Exton, Peggy Moerman, Lesley Bown, and Kamla Millson for comments and proofreading.

To Taye for his description of the Boardmasters festival.

To Stone's Reef, a home from home.

To Sisu for the world's best chocolate brownies™.

To Sharkfin Media for the website and all things techy.

And last but never least, to Coby Llewelyn: reader, editor, friend – as always.

FORENSIC FILE

In each edition of my monthly newsletter, I'll cover a topic of interest from the forensic files.

Topics covered so far:

Fingerprints

More correctly called 'finger ridges', these are formed on a foetus by six months, due to the movement of amniotic fluid, and even the fingerprints of twins aren't identical.

Digi dogs

Search dogs have been trained to locate drugs or explosives, but they can also be trained specifically to sniff out technology such as laptops, mobile phones, USB sticks and even SIM cards. First trialled in the UK by Devon & Cornwall Police, with assistance from the FBI.

Drones

At the beginning of 2023, more than 400 drones were

used in police forces across the UK. Drones are being trialled in remote rural areas: 'Drone as First Responder'.

Police Divers

How do divers work in murky or pitch-black underwater conditions? What precautions do divers have to make when working with Explosive Ordnance?

Police Computers

From HORT1 self-carbonating pads to LED database, a cloud-based system which incorporates both the Police National Computer and the Police National Database.

DNA

From the first prosecution of a cold case in 1988 to the difficulties in testing substances for DNA.

Firearms in the UK

Contrary to popular belief, all officers in the UK are trained with firearms - did you know that incapacitant spray is classed as a firearm?

Learn more on my website and sign up for the monthly newsletter www.berrickford.com

Printed in Dunstable, United Kingdom

77052177R00211